Rosie
GOODWIN
Yesterday's
Shadows

HEADLINE

First published in Great Britain in 2008
by HEADLINE PUBLISHING GROUP

First published in paperback in 2009
by HEADLINE PUBLISHING GROUP

This edition first published in 2022
by HEADLINE PUBLISHING GROUP

1

Cataloguing in Publication Data is available from the British Library

ISBN 978 1 0354 0310 3

Typeset in Calisto MT by Palimpsest Book Production Limited, Falkirk, Stirlingshire

Printed and bound in Great Britain by Clays Ltd, Elcograf S.p.A.

Headline's policy is to use papers that are natural, renewable and recyclable
products and made from wood grown in well-managed forests and other
controlled sources. The logging and manufacturing processes are expected
to conform to the environmental regulations of the country of origin.

HEADLINE PUBLISHING GROUP
An Hachette UK Company
Carmelite House
50 Victoria Embankment
London EC4Y 0DZ

www.headline.co.uk
www.hachette.co.uk

Rosie Goodwin has written many hugely popular novels and her most recent books have been *Sunday Times* top ten bestsellers. She is the first author in the world to be allowed to follow three of Catherine Cookson's trilogies with her own sequels, *Tilly Trotter's Legacy*, *The Mallen Secret* and *The Sand Dancer*. Having worked in the social services sector for many years, then fostered a number of children, she is now a full-time novelist. Rosie lives in Nuneaton with her husband and their beloved dogs.

Keep up to date with Rosie's news at www.rosiegoodwin.co.uk, or follow her on Twitter @RosieGoodwin.

Praise for Rosie Goodwin's heartwarming novels:

'A touching and powerful novel from a wonderful writer' *Bookseller*

'The tear-jerker of the season . . . [a] heart-rending tale'
Western Mail

'A gifted writer . . . Not only is Goodwin's characterisation and dialogue compelling, but her descriptive writing is a joy'
Nottingham Evening Post

'Goodwin is a fabulous writer . . . and her style involves lots of twists and turns that are in no way predictable'
Worcester Evening News

'Goodwin is a born author'   *Lancashire Evening Telegraph*

'Rosie is the real thing – a writer who has something to say and knows how to say it'   Gilda O'Neill

'Rosie is a born storyteller – she'll make you cry, she'll make you laugh, but most of all you'll care for her characters and lose yourself in her story'   Jeannie Johnson

'Her stories are now eagerly awaited by readers the length and breadth of the country'   *Heartland Evening News*

'The new Catherine Cookson'   *Coventry Evening Telegraph*

'An incredibly consuming, uplifting read . . . splendid company for when you're feeling down in the dumps'   *Readers' Digest*

For my first born, Donna, my daughter and my friend.
I am very proud of you.
Love you millions,
RG xxxxx

Acknowledgements

I would like to say a huge thank you to the following people:

First of all to Wilf, a neighbour, who generously gave his time during the research for this novel talking to me about the area of Durham and grave digging as it was done back in the fifties. It was invaluable.

To Flora Rees, Kate Byrne, Maura Brickell, Jane Morpeth and all the staff at Headline, and my agent, Sonia Land, for their unfailing support, as always.

Joan Deitch, my copy editor. I SO look forward to your comments!

To Gail, Paul and the staff at Waterstones in Nuneaton for a great night in July to mark the publication of my tenth novel.

To Viv and Sarah at Astley Book Farm, always on the end of the phone to help with a book needed for research on any subject.

Mum, Dad and my family, for always being there for me.

To Aaron and Rachel. Welcome to the family Rachel, another daughter to love.

Christian and Aaron, congratulations on your new jobs. I'm really proud of you both.

Nikki, Daniel and Charlie Bear, the bright stars in my life.

Not forgetting, Steve, son-in-law extraordinaire, Sarah and Jason, of course.

And last but never least, to Trev . . . for everything.

Prologue

'Right then, Mam. I'll see you on Thursday.'

'Are yer quite sure as you'll be all right goin' down that lane all alone, our Diane?' her mother murmured, her voice husky with concern as she stood at the door.

'Oh Mam, stop worritin',' Diane Dorkin laughed. 'I've been down there so often I know it like the back o' me hand.'

The mist of early evening had thickened into a fog so dense that the older woman could barely see the end of the path that led from the front door of her tiny terraced house to the gate. She watched as her daughter switched on the light that perched precariously above the basket on the front of her bike before turning to peck her mother affectionately on the cheek.

'I really ain't so sure that yer should be venturin' back in this. It's a real peasouper,' she fussed, but Diane only laughed.

'You get yourself inside now, it's enough to cut you in two,' she urged. 'And don't get frettin' about me. I'll be back home with Colin and the kids before you've even had time to make your cocoa.'

Pushing the bike to the gate, Diane gave a final wave,

1

clambered on and set off. Within minutes she was sweating despite the harshness of the night as she pedalled up the hill. Soon the Lord Nelson public house came into sight and she grinned as the strains of Doris Day singing 'Secret Love' floated out into the night. Now the ground levelled out and she was cycling around the roundabout that led to Ansley Lane and home. She smiled to herself. No doubt Colin, her husband, would have a hot cup of tea all ready for her. Her two young daughters would be tucked up all warm and cosy in bed. Her legs pushed harder on the pedals in her haste to be home. The lights of Ansley village soon faded and she was in total darkness save for the dim glow of her bicycle light, which did little to penetrate the all-enveloping fog. The lane was deserted and when an owl suddenly hooted from a nearby tree, she jumped. Swerving, she cursed softly, but then quickly righted herself and concentrated her efforts on the road ahead.

For no reason that she could explain, a sense of foreboding settled over her. It was almost as if the fog had swallowed up every sound and the only thing she could hear was her laboured breath as her legs pumped the pedals. The mist from the ditches that ran either side of the lane swirled around her feet, making it impossible to see the road beneath her, and for the first time she wondered if she should have taken her mother's advice and stayed the night. It was then that the front wheel of the bicycle suddenly hit something and she tumbled across the handlebars to land in an undignified heap in the road.

'Ouch! Sod it,' she muttered aloud as she rubbed at her ankle. The bike light had gone out, but for now she was so winded that she could do nothing about it. After sitting there for some seconds she pulled herself together enough to drag herself across to her bicycle to inspect the damage. It was impossible to see, so tentatively she felt along the ground.

'Ugh!' When her hand sank into something soft and cold she recoiled, but as her eyes adjusted to the light she saw the cause of the accident. A dead rabbit lay beneath the bicycle wheels. She shook her head sadly. Dead rabbits were a common sight lately since the disease myxomatosis had swept the country. In fact, she vaguely recalled reading in the newspaper that almost ninety per cent of the burrows in Southern England alone were infected.

However, she didn't linger long on the fate of the dead rabbit as her thoughts turned to the predicament she herself was in. As she ran her hands along the bicycle she could tell that the front wheel was badly buckled. She wouldn't be riding that again tonight, that was for sure. The bicycle light was broken too, so what was she to do? Chewing on her lip, she looked ahead and behind her. It seemed that she was as bad burned as scalded as she estimated that she was somewhere about halfway between her mother's house and her own.

Hauling herself painfully to her feet, Diane winced as the pain in her ankle shot up her leg. She didn't think it was broken because she could still stand on it, just about, so she decided that she'd probably just sprained it. Looking down on the useless bicycle, she knew that she couldn't just leave it there in the road where it might cause yet another accident, so yanking it up she began to limp along, leaning heavily on the handlebars for support.

It was then that she heard the sound of a car coming behind her. Instantly she made a decision. It would take her hours to get home at this rate, by which time Colin would be frantic with worry, so she would throw the bicycle into the ditch until he could fetch it tomorrow, flag the car down and beg a lift.

She stopped and looked back, to be rewarded with the sight of headlights faintly slicing through the fog. The car was only a matter of a hundred yards away from her when suddenly it stopped. Waving frantically, she cried, 'Hello! Hello there! Can you hear me? I've had an accident and I wondered if you could—'

The throb of the engine suddenly cut out, and at the same moment the lights on the car were extinguished.

Again the sense of foreboding settled on her as she stared nervously into the darkness.

'Is . . . is anyone there?' There was no answer. As she stood indecisively, wondering what to do, she heard the car door open and shut.

'He . . . hello?' Again there was no answer and now panic gripped her. She started to wheel the bicycle away, trying to ignore the pain that was rampaging up her leg with each step she took. Her shoes were making a tap-tapping sound on the cold tarmac beneath her feet. It was then that she suddenly heard the sound of heavier footsteps behind her. Gulping, she stopped to stare back, but whoever was there was cloaked in fog. The footsteps stopped as abruptly as hers, and again she implored: 'If you're there, will you please help me?'

Nothing . . . save the freezing air that floated around her like a shroud. She began to half run and half hop in the direction of home, and once again the footsteps began

4

to follow her. Tears rolled unchecked down her cheeks as hysteria gripped her. She began to pray, 'Our Father, who art in heaven . . .'

The hairs on the back of her neck stood to attention as the footsteps grew nearer. Sobbing, she stumbled on. There was nowhere to run or hide now, the footsteps were right behind her. And then, someone suddenly grasped her shoulder and she was swung around to stare into dark smouldering eyes. The bicycle clattered to the ground as he dragged her across the ditch. Visions of her children's angelic faces floated before Diane Dorkin's eyes as the icy water penetrated her clothes, and she tried to focus on that, rather than what was happening to her. She didn't fight; she knew that her strength would be no match for his. Thankfully she had fainted into a welcoming darkness long before his cold fingers closed around her slender neck in the icy field behind the hedge.

Chapter One

Durham, June 1954

The sound of the woman's shoes echoed on the cobbled street between the rows of terraced pit cottages. Her lungs felt as if they might burst, but she didn't pause until the house she was making for came into view. At last she was standing on the polished red step, and without waiting to draw breath she began to hammer on the door. Almost immediately it was opened by a slender dark-haired young woman who raised her eyebrows questioningly when she saw who it was.

'Why, Mrs Wickes, whatever's the matter?' Her dark eyes were kindly and full of concern, but ignoring her question the much older woman flapped her hand at her as she tried to catch her breath.

'Kate – you have to come straight away, pet. It's yer da. There's been an accident down at the pit. I don't know how bad it is, but—' She had no time to say any more, for already Kate had turned to snatch a cardigan from the back of a chair.

'Nuala!' she called as she stepped out into the street, and the note of urgency in her voice made the young woman sitting inside at the table sigh. She had just been about to tuck into the large plateful of pease pudding

6

that Kate had put in front of her, and as it happened to be one of her particular favourites she was none too pleased at being disturbed.

'*What?*' she said resentfully after dragging her plump body to the door.

'Nuala, we have to get down to the pit. There's been an accident and—'

'It's Da, ain't it?' Nuala's voice was expressionless, but for once Kate had no time to pander to her as she normally did.

'Yes, it is,' she snapped. 'Now pull the door shut and come along.'

Without a word the three women began to hurry down the street. As they reached the end of it, an ambulance sped past them with its bells clanging. The sound lent speed to Kate's feet and soon she was way ahead of the other two, who were impeded by age and weight.

In the small village of Heseldon in Durham where she lived, numbers named the streets, and soon she had run along Third Street, Second Street and First Street. After turning a sharp corner, the pit where her father worked came into sight. A small crowd had collected at the gates but Kate elbowed through them and spoke to the gateman who was desperately trying to keep the crowd at bay.

'It's me da,' she gasped, and nodding sympathetically he let her pass without comment. Slowing now, she headed towards the ambulance that was parked at one of the entrances to the pit.

A sombre-faced man whose white teeth stood out in stark contrast to his soot-blackened skin was leading a huge pit gallower, as the pit ponies were called, from the shaft, and behind him she could vaguely see two ambulancemen carrying a stretcher, upon which lay the still figure of a man. Instinctively she knew that this figure was her father and she also somehow knew that he was dead. The snow-white sheet that covered his face confirmed her feelings as the men carried him out into the bright sunshine.

A short, bald-headed man who was standing wringing his cap in his two hands crossed to Kate and without thinking, slung his arm around her shoulders, covering her cardigan in coal dust.

'Eeh, Kate pet. I don't rightly know what to say to yer. It seems that one o' the pit props collapsed, an' yer da . . .'

'It's all right, Mr Wickes.' Kate felt numb as she smiled at him. This kindly man was married to the woman who had fetched her. He had worked as a putter at the pit for as long as Kate could remember and he was, or had been, one of her father's drinking chums.

His arm fell away and he looked at her helplessly. He had always had a soft spot for Kate and for more than one reason. Firstly because of the way she had cared for her younger sister, who was what you might call 'a bit slow', in the absence of a mother; secondly because of her gentle voice – so different from the broad dialect of the other girls in the village. Of course, there was no doubt that this was due to Miss Frost, the spinster teacher at the village school, who originated from London. She had taken Kate under her wing and given her elocution lessons from day one of Kate starting school, possibly because she knew the child was motherless. At one stage, Miss Frost had tried to do the same with Nuala, but she had soon given up and Mr Wickes could see why. Not even Miss Frost could make a silk purse out of a sow's ear. Not that Kate's soft-spoken voice would help her now; everyone knew what happened to families whose loved ones died down the pit. Sighing again at the injustice of it all, Mr Wickes turned to watch his drinking chum being loaded into an ambulance.

There was nothing to be done here now, and Kate felt the need to be alone. Dry-eyed, she pushed her way back through the crowd, ignoring the murmurs of sympathy. She could see Nuala and Mrs Wickes still labouring their way up the steep incline towards the pit gates, but turned the other way and headed for the sea.

Soon the pit was far behind her and she stood on the sand letting the sea breeze ruffle her hair and cool her hot face. Further along the beach, huge pipes spewed the pit waste into the ocean and she could see people with prams and bicycles picking through the waste in the shallows as they hunted for coal. Leaving them, she headed along the beach towards Black Hall Rocks. It had always been one of her favourite places; there the sea was clear and blue rather than soot-coloured as it was in her hometown. She stopped briefly to take off her shoes before walking on in a daze.

Eventually the black sand gave way to white and her footsteps slowed as she let the quiet beauty of the place wash over her. She made for the cliffs that rose majestically into the clear blue sky, and there she sank to the sand and hugged her knees as she watched the sunlight reflecting on the sparkling blue water.

He was dead. Her father was dead. The words throbbed in her head, yet strangely she couldn't take them in. At home his favourite meal was cooked and ready for him. The tea was stewing in the pot just as he liked it. But he would never eat or drink again. He would never shout at her because the tea was too weak or not sweet enough or not hot enough. She would never again have to get between him and Nuala when he came in drunk from the pub and took his belt to her younger sister. Nuala was what the kindly people in the village called 'slow'. Her father had other, less kindly expressions for her, such as gormless, backward and mad.

Kate started to laugh, a weird unearthly laugh that made two seagulls that were waddling along the beach not an arm's length from her take flight. Eventually the laughter turned to tears and then to harsh racking sobs that shook her slender frame. But they were not tears of regret. They were tears of relief. Her father had been a drunken bully, but now he could never scare or hurt her or Nuala ever again.

She sat there until the sun began to sink into the sea, then wearily rose and after brushing the sand from her crumpled clothes, slowly made her way home.

It was strange, she thought, as she walked along the familiar streets, that everything looked just the same. The children were still playing hopscotch and kicking footballs up and down the cobbled alleys. The rows of back-to-back, two-up two-down terraced houses remained as they had been; the women still standing on their doorsteps, their heads bent together as news spread of the tragic accident up at the pit. The men were returning from work, their snap boxes tucked under their sooty armpits. And yet – nothing was the same, nor would it ever be again. Now that she had got over the shock of her father's sudden death she would have to look after Nuala all on her own. But then, hadn't she always done that? Their mother had died when both girls were little more than babies and Nuala had relied on her for every little thing ever since. Before, Kate had looked after her father too. Realistically, now that there was just Nuala to care for, life should be easier.

Guilt washed over her. She knew that she shouldn't have run off and left Nuala as she had earlier on, but the need had been on her to get away, far away from everyone. Now she felt stronger and ready to cope with her sister's grief, so resolutely she pushed open the door to their little terraced house.

Nuala was sitting at the table that took up the whole of the middle of the kitchen, softly crying into a clean white handkerchief, and Mrs Wickes was just emptying the last of the untouched meal into the pigswill bin.

'Eeh, pet. We've been worried sick, what wi' you runnin' off as you did,' she scolded softly. 'But never mind. You're here now so sit yourself down an' I'll mek you a nice strong brew. There's nowt like hot sweet tea for shock, so they say.'

Before Kate could object, the kindly little woman had pottered away to fill the kettle at the deep stone sink, so she turned her attention to Nuala. 'Are you all right?' she asked.

Nuala broke into a fresh torrent of tears. 'Oh Kate, what are we goin' to do? The pit boss has already bin round an' said as he'll call tomorrer to discuss the funeral. But then we'll be given notice to quit the cottage. Where will we go, an' what will we do? An' me da . . .'

Kate was shocked to hear the genuine grief in Nuala's

11

voice. She had expected her to feel relief at his passing as she did, and yet Nuala was inconsolable, which was strange as the younger girl had always taken the brunt of their father's wrath. Kate had lost count of the number of times he had come in drunk and taken his belt to her for no reason at all. Not that she herself had escaped scot-free – until she had begun to stick up for herself, that was, and from then on things had been easier for her and he had directed his temper tantrums at Nuala.

Her sister's pale grey eyes were red-rimmed and swollen from crying which, added to her spotty face and plump body, did nothing to enhance her looks at all. Kate's heart went out to her. Poor Nuala. She was suffering from a severe case of puppy fat and an even more severe case of lack of confidence, but once again Kate blamed her father for that. How many times had she heard him scream at Nuala how she would die in Grange Gorman, the mental hospital that nestled in the mountains of Ireland, as their mother had?

As babies they had lived with their parents in Ireland in a small village called Glencree on the outskirts of Wicklow, but following their mother's untimely death, Liam Cleary had moved them all to Durham where they had lived ever since.

Kate had no recollection of her mother, and as her father had always refused to talk of her apart from to tell them that she had been a raving lunatic, it was unlikely now that she ever would. She didn't even know where her mother was buried, which saddened her every time she thought of it. But now was not the time for brooding on the past. Now, as Nuala had rightly pointed out, she would have to look to their future. Suddenly weary, she dropped into a chair.

'Don't get worrying, pet,' she comforted her sister. 'We'll be all right, you'll see.'

'Well, there's nowt so sure as that,' Mrs Wickes agreed. 'I'm a firm believer that when one door shuts another door opens, so let's just get these next few days over wi', eh? An' then we'll 'ave to see what's to be done.' She placed a steaming mug in front of Kate.

Mrs Wickes left as darkness was masking the sooty rooftops of the town, with promises that she would be back first thing.

Nuala had barely said a word following her outburst when Kate first came back, but now she gazed at her sister from frightened eyes.

'Where will we go, Kate? An' what will we do? The pit boss won't let us stay here now that Da's . . . gone.'

'There's plenty of time to worry about that,' Kate told her with a confidence she was far from feeling. 'But for now, I think we ought to get ourselves off to bed. There's nothing more we can do tonight, an' after a good night's sleep we'll see things differently.'

Nuala sniffed and dragged herself up from her chair. 'I'll go up then. Are you comin'?'

'Yes – yes, o' course I am. I'll just lock up an' I'll be right behind you.'

Nuala nodded as she headed for the stairs door and Kate was finally left alone to gaze around the kitchen in the only home she could remember.

For the first time in her life she realised how very little they had. The house, as Nuala had quite rightly pointed out, belonged to the pit and now that their father was dead it was highly unlikely that they would be allowed to stay there. Every stick of furniture inside it was second-hand, shabby if she were to be honest, although everything shone from the care with which she had polished it. The table was oak, almost white from the many times she had scrubbed it, and standing around it were odd chairs that her father had picked up from here and there. At the side of the fireplace was an old over-stuffed armchair. The headrest was stained from the Brylcreem that her father used to flatten his hair with, and which no amount of scrubbing would remove. He would stagger in from the pub each night and collapse into it; sometimes even stay there all night because he was too drunk to negotiate the narrow staircase that led to the two tiny bedrooms above.

Kate shuddered involuntarily, as if thinking about him might conjure him up from thin air, but then she pulled herself together with an effort. He would never stagger in again. Crossing to the back door, she quickly shot the bolt home, and then after switching off the light she took herself away to bed. Tomorrow would be soon enough to worry about what would become of them; she had had more than enough for one day.

After patting her dark shoulder-length curls into place and pulling on her cotton gloves, Kate smoothed her full flowered skirt into place. She should be wearing black as a mark of respect for her father, but as she hadn't had time to go shopping for anything of that colour for either herself or Nuala as yet, she supposed that this would have to do for now.

'Are you ready?' There was just the slightest hint of

impatience in her voice as she glanced across at her sister. Nuala scowled; Kate looked stunning as usual, which only made *her* feel plainer still. Her own dress, although a similar style to Kate's, was a dull drab brown colour and did nothing at all to compliment her; in fact, the cinched-in waist emphasised the roll of fat around her middle. Normally Kate would have been fussing around her, trying to tease her limp mousy hair into some sort of style and reassuring her that she looked fine, but today she was too preoccupied to bother about such things.

'Nuala, we *do* have to be at the solicitor's in less than an hour, you know? And if we miss the bus into Durham and have to wait for the next one, we shall be late.'

Sulkily lifting her handbag, Nuala followed Kate to the door. Many of the women from the neighbouring houses were standing outside on their doorsteps, talking in hushed voices. The girls had barely set foot out of the door when Mrs Gleeson, their next-door neighbour, pounced on them. Mrs Gleeson was heavily pregnant, not that this was any surprise; she had turned out a baby a year for the last nine years. Sometimes Kate was amazed at how the poor woman managed to cram so many bodies into a tiny two-up two-down house, not that she was a rarity: in the house that joined the other side of them, Mrs Thomas was already up to six, and she too had another on the way.

'Eeh, Kate pet!' Mrs Gleeson exclaimed. 'It's right sorry we all are to hear of your da's accident. I know he weren't always the best da in the world, but still, he were the only one you had an' if there's anythin' we can be doin' for you, you only need to ask.'

'Thanks, Mrs Gleeson.' Kate felt the colour rushing

to her cheeks as she found the women's eyes tight on her. 'I . . . er . . . Don't think I'm being rude but we have an appointment with me da's solicitor an' if we don't hurry we'll be late.'

'You get yerselves away then, pet,' Mrs Gleeson said kindly, patting her on the shoulder. 'I'll pop round when you get back an' see if there's anythin' I can be doin' to help wi' the funeral arrangements an' whatnot.'

Kate inclined her head and grasping Nuala's elbow propelled her down the street towards the bus stop at a pace that had the younger girl almost running to keep up with her.

They reached the solicitor's office in Durham with only minutes to spare and were promptly ushered into Mr Granger's office. Immediately, a grey-haired gentleman with a pair of gold-rimmed spectacles perched on the end of his bulbous nose rose to meet them. He shook their hands solemnly and once they were seated, he smiled at them sympathetically. Nuala was clinging tightly to Kate's hand, but Kate's chin jutted proudly as she held her head high and looked calmly back at him. It struck the solicitor how different the sisters were in all ways. Kate, at nineteen and only three years older than Nuala, was obviously the strong one, which was probably just as well; after what he was about to tell the girls he could only think that she would need to be.

'Before we begin,' he cleared his throat, 'I would just like to express my condolences. I cannot pretend to have known your father well. In fact, I only met him on a limited number of occasions, the first being when he moved to Durham. You were both little more than babies then. Your mother left a sizable inheritance. She came

16

from a good family and I advised your father on how the money should best be spent, as well as encouraging him to make a will. I believe that your home was tied to the pit whilst your father worked there. Would I be right in thinking that?'

When Kate nodded, he frowned. 'I see. Then I imagine that you will be asked to vacate the premises now. Do you have anyone you could go to? A relative, perhaps?'

'No, we don't,' Kate told him. 'But if my father has left us any money, we are intending to rent or perhaps even buy somewhere.'

Without another word he bent his head to the Last Will and Testament of Liam Cleary and as he read it aloud, Kate's eyes filled with despair and Nuala began to snivel.

'So, I'm afraid that's about it, my dears,' he told them gravely when the reading was finally done. 'I wish I had better news for you. Over the years your father dipped into the money at an alarming rate, so much so that I once visited him to suggest some investments, but he wouldn't hear of it.'

Again determination flared in Kate's eyes. 'We'll manage,' she declared. 'From what you've just told us, the small amount of money my father left will at least bury him. Later today, the manager from the pit is coming to see us. I believe that in cases of accidents such as this they give a small amount of compensation to the remaining family, and with that we'll be able to look around for somewhere for us to live.'

Mr Granger nodded. It troubled him to see the girls in such a dire situation. The first time he had met them, they had been little more than babies and had just arrived in Durham with their father. The second time, he had had cause to visit them at their home and it had been immediately apparent that Kate had taken on the role of their dead mother, although she had been little more than a child herself. This had saddened him to the core, but it explained the obvious bond between the sisters now. Silently he cursed the selfish man who had placed this heavy burden on such young shoulders whilst he drank his life away in the Hardwick public house. Still – there was nothing more that he could do for them now, so standing, he extended his hand.

'Goodbye, my dears. I wish you well for the future. If only I could have given you better news.'

Kate shook the proffered hand as she pulled Nuala to her feet with the other. 'Thank you, Mr Granger. Goodbye.'

He watched them walk to the door and after a few moments crossed to the window of his first-floor office and followed their progress along the busy street of Durham town. Noting that Kate had her arm protectively around her younger sister's waist, he cursed Liam Cleary.

'I *told* that idiot to put his house in order and make some sort of provision for his children,' he muttered to himself, but just then the bell on his desk tinkled, heralding the arrival of another client, and Kate and Nuala were pushed to the back of his mind. He wished with all his heart that he could help them, but there was client confidentiality to be considered – and although Liam Cleary had drawn his last breath, that must still be respected. How could he have told them that the money their mother had left had been intended for *them*?

* * *

The sunshine had disappeared behind a bank of grey clouds and as the two girls caught the bus that would take them home, a fine drizzle began to fall. When they arrived in the small pit village where they lived, they hurried through the streets past the rows of terraced cottages. Every one looked the same, with only the colours of the paintwork and the patterns of the curtains at the windows to distinguish one from another. The doorsteps and the small, shared backyards where the women usually stood to gossip as they strung their washing on the clothes-lines were deserted now; everyone was inside, out of the weather.

After fumbling with the key and unlocking the door, Kate pushed Nuala before her into the small kitchen-cum-sitting room. The rain had penetrated their clothes and they were shivering, so Kate struck a match and put the kettle on to boil before pressing Nuala into a seat.

'Come on,' she urged. 'Don't look so worried. We'll get by.'

'*How?*' Nuala asked bluntly. 'Mr Granger just told us that Da left barely enough for us to bury him. An' even if the pit bosses *do* give us a bit, how will we live when that's gone? We won't survive on the money you earn at the pickle factory an' the bit I earn deliverin' groceries, that's for sure.'

'Oh yes, we will,' Kate told her confidently. 'A full-time job will crop up for you in time an' then we'll be fine with two proper wages to live on.'

'Huh! There ain't much chance o' that,' Nuala commented. 'You know as well as I do that jobs are like gold dust round here. You only got *your* job 'cos old

19

Mrs Chitty got too old to carry on goin'. I *have* tried since I left school, you know I have.'

'Of course I know you've tried,' Kate assured her. 'But I think we ought to just take it one day at a time at the minute. Let's get the funeral over with and then we'll worry about what's to become of us.'

Nuala's face suddenly crumpled as fresh tears spurted from her eyes. 'You won't leave me, will you, Kate?'

'Of *course* I won't!' Kate had covered the distance between them in no time to snatch Nuala into her arms. 'You and me will always have each other. We're sisters and we'll stick together, no matter what.'

Staring off into space she cradled her heavy sister in her arms. She was just nineteen years old and yet she felt as if she had the weight of the whole world on her young shoulders.

Chapter Two

Hand-in-hand, Kate and Nuala walked away from the graveside in the tiny cemetery on the cliff top. Behind them, two of the men from the village were already beginning to shovel earth onto their father's coffin and the sound followed them, echoing hollowly on the still air. Now they must endure the funeral tea that Mrs Wickes had prepared for the mourners back in the cottage.

It was a beautiful day with not a cloud in the sky, and in the distance the surface of the sea was as still as a millpond, twinkling in the bright morning sunshine. Overhead, seagulls wheeled in the sky and the dark clothes of the mourners seemed strangely at variance with the colourful wildflowers that peeped from the hedgerows.

It was a solemn procession that wound its way back through the cobbled streets and Kate found herself wishing that this day could just be over. It was four days since their father's death and during all that time she had put on a brave face for Nuala, but now the strain was beginning to tell.

Immediately following the funeral tea the pit manager

would give them notice to quit their cottage. According to custom, he would also give them some money. But would it be enough to set them up somewhere? Kate doubted it, although she hadn't dared to say as much to Nuala.

The people of the village had been marvellous to them, popping in with kind words and posies of flowers. But flowers and kind words would not pay their rent. Her gloomy thoughts were interrupted when someone placed their hand on her arm. Looking up, she found herself staring into the eyes of Matthew Williams, a young man who lived in the next street to hers. Her heart flipped as he smiled at her sympathetically before asking, 'Do you mind if I walk along with you?' When Kate shook her head he fell into step beside her. 'I know at a time like this words mean nothing,' he said quietly. 'And I also know there's nothing I can say that will bring you any comfort, Kate. But what I will say is, if you need anything – *anything* at all – you only have to ask. I have a few pounds put by and if it will—'

'No, Matthew,' Kate interrupted proudly. 'Thanks all the same, but the money you've saved is going to take you to art school. You've worked so hard for it.'

Feeling strangely embarrassed, he shrugged. Kate always had that effect on him. There was something about her that set her apart from the other village girls. However, before he could say any more, Nuala sniffed loudly.

'We *are* going to need every penny we can get,' she argued as Kate glowered at her. 'Me da barely left us enough to bury him an'—'

'*Nuala!*' Kate's nerves were at breaking point, but her

pride was still intact. 'We are far from charity cases just yet, and as I said, Matthew has been working his fingers to the bone to get to art school for as long as I can remember. We'll get by just fine without handouts from anyone.'

She glanced at Matthew apologetically. 'She's upset,' she said, covering up for her sister. 'But I meant what I said. You *must* get to art school. I've never known anyone as gifted as you when it comes to painting.'

Colour began to climb her neck and seep into her cheeks as he smiled. Thankfully, by now the cottage was in sight and Kate was saved from having to say any more as Matthew shepherded them inside.

Mrs Wilkes had done them proud. In the centre of the room the table was laden with food, some made by her and the rest supplied by friends and neighbours as was the custom in the village, and Kate wondered how they had managed it with the food rationing. There was a great dish of pease pudding, one of her father's old favourites, a leek pudding in a tasty suet pastry supplied by Mrs Gleeson next door, split peas and ham, and copious amounts of lardy bread and a big dish of Oxo gravy for those that wanted it. Despite her grief, Nuala filled her plate in a jiffy and retreated to a corner where she could enjoy her feast. Kate felt that if she tried to eat anything it might choke her, so she hurried to the walk-in pantry to fetch the jugs of homemade ale from where it had been keeping cool on the thrall and began to fill the men's glasses. Many of them had taken a day off work from the pit to pay their respects. They were all dressed in dark suits and ties with dazzlingly bright starched shirt collars. Kate had no doubt that their women would have been up early, boiling water to fill the tin baths that hung on the outside wall of every cottage. Yet despite their Sunday best the coal dust was ingrained in the skin of their faces and hands, and no amount of washing could ever remove it. Only the manager of the pit, who remained quietly to one side, stood out from the rest, his soft white hands looking out of place amongst those of his workers.

As the jugs were emptied the hushed tones became louder and the atmosphere lightened.

'Ain't no doubt about it, the cricket team won't be the same wi'out Liam Cleary to bat for us.' Mr Wilkes shook his head sadly as his wife frowned at him. That was the third pint she had seen him down in almost as many minutes, and if the silly old sod kept it up she had no doubt that she would be putting him to bed before dinnertime.

The food kept appearing as quickly as the men ate it, supplied by red-faced women who had spent the entire morning and most of the day before, preparing it.

As morning gave way to afternoon, the day began to take on an air of unreality for Kate. She was more grateful to her neighbours for their support than she could say, but now the need was on her to be alone again.

Nuala, who had barely moved from the chair in the corner since they arrived home, was watching Matthew as he moved about the room, her eyes like those of an adoring puppy. Kate sighed.

Matthew had made it more than obvious for some time that he liked Kate, and she knew without a doubt that she could easily have returned his feelings. But there

24

had always been too many things standing between them, the first being the fact that her father had always been violently opposed to her courting anyone. Kate would have gone against his wishes, but it would have meant leaving Nuala alone with him while she was out with Matthew, and Liam would then have taken his displeasure out on her poor sister.

And now her father was dead and the obstacles that had been in their way had been removed. But had they? She doubted that Matthew would want her now. After all, what could she offer any man? She could never leave Nuala to fend for herself, and not many men would want to take on the responsibility of a wife with a younger, quite difficult sister in tow. Scolding herself, she guiltily pulled her thoughts back to the present. What was she doing, thinking of herself, today of all days?

The mixture of the warm weather, warm food and numerous bodies had made the room stiflingly hot. Many of the men had spewed out onto the pavement, their ties and even some of the stiff collars long since discarded, their shirt sleeves rolled up to display their white hairy arms. All the doors and windows had been flung open, and as Kate glanced around she caught the eye of the pit manager. She nodded towards the front parlour.

'Would you like to come through there?' she asked, sensing his impatience, and he nodded gratefully.

They weaved their way through the remaining mourners and the women who were distributing the last dregs of ale left in the jugs. Once inside Kate quietly closed the door behind them, studiously avoiding looking at the table where only a short time ago her father's coffin had lain.

'Shall we get this over with then?' she asked without preamble. She had no doubt that now the formalities were over with, he would want to get back to work.

Nodding solemnly, he handed her a brown paper envelope.

'May I say, Miss Cleary, how very sorry myself and the pit owners are about this unfortunate accident.'

As Kate took the proffered envelope he found himself admiring her courage, as she stood straight-backed, her head held high.

'Thank you. But I think everyone in Heseldon knows the risks of working down the pit. May I ask how long my sister and I may have before we have to vacate the cottage?'

Coughing uncomfortably, he shuffled from foot to foot. 'You . . . er . . . have a month from today. You will find your notice to quit in there along with a sum of money that we hope will tide you over for a short time. If, after a month, you and your sister have not found anywhere suitable to go, then of course we will—'

'A month will give us *more* than enough time to find alternative accommodation, thank you,' Kate told him, her dark eyes holding his. 'Now – if there's nothing else, I'm sure that you will be wanting to get back to work. Thank you for attending the funeral.'

Words momentarily failed the man and he found himself wondering how Liam Cleary could ever have managed to turn out a daughter like this. If he were to be honest, he personally had never been that keen on Cleary. From what he had seen of him, he had appeared to be a big man with an even bigger mouth. But then, he had also been a good worker, so the manager had turned a blind eye on more than one occasion when Liam had rolled up for work the worse for wear from drink the night before.

As he backed towards the door, Kate had to restrain herself from laughing aloud. He looked so awkward, but her good manners stopped her and instead she inclined her head politely as he shuffled away.

Alone with her thoughts, she stared down at the brown envelope in her hand. This was it then, a few measly pound notes and notice to quit the cottage. But then she had known it was coming. She thrust the envelope deep into the pocket of her dress. There would be time to open it later, but for now she had guests who needed attending to.

Thankfully, when she re-entered the kitchen, she saw that the mourners had considerably thinned out, probably due to the fact that the ale was running dry. No doubt they would continue their wake down at the Hardwick, as was the custom following a funeral in the village.

Mrs Wilkes was at the sink, scrubbing the dirty pots, and several other women were emptying the table and tidying away as best they could. Kate felt a lump form in her throat. They had always been so kind to both Nuala and herself, probably because they knew how aggressive their father could be. At least that's what she supposed it was, for how could they have failed to hear the rantings and ravings and Nuala screaming like a stuck pig when he had come home in a drunken stupor and clouted her?

27

As her eyes travelled around the room she saw that her sister was missing.

'Has anyone seen Nuala?' she asked anxiously.

Rubbing a soapy hand across her sweating face, Mrs Wilkes looked up from the sink full of pots and nodded. 'Ah, last I saw of her she were headin' for the outside lavvy wi' her hands clapped across her gob.'

'Oh no!' Kate's face puckered in a frown. 'Nuala always gets sick when she's anxious.'

Mrs Wilkes snorted with derision. 'Anxious? More like she's overeaten, if you ask me. Why, she's put enough food away this afternoon to feed a whole cricket team!'

Kate swallowed the hasty retort that sprang to her lips. After all, she didn't want to upset Mrs Wilkes after everything her neighbour had done to help them. She turned on her heel and was heading for the back door when Matthew took her elbow.

'Why don't you leave her to it, Kate? Come and sit down for a while. It's been a big day for you too and you look all in.'

Reluctantly she allowed herself to be led to a chair. She had just sat down when Nuala, who was the colour of uncooked pastry, entered the room wiping her mouth on the sleeve of her cardigan.

Instantly her eyes settled on Kate and Matthew and she pouted at them.

'Nuala, it's been a long day and you don't look at all well. Why don't you go and have a lie-down for half an hour, eh? I'll see to whatever else needs to be done,' Kate suggested kindly.

Frowning, Nuala swung about and marched from the

28

room, slamming the door that led to the stairs resoundingly behind her.

Matthew looked ruefully at Kate. 'Someone's in a bad mood. Right – I'd better be getting off now. That is . . . unless there's anything you want me to do before I go?'

'No, I'll be fine. But thanks for coming, Matthew.'

Their eyes briefly locked and for a moment they might have been the only two people in the room, but then Matthew turned abruptly on his heel and marched from the room into the sunlit street outside. Kate heaved herself wearily from the chair and set to, and within another half an hour the house was back to rights and the neighbouring women were ready to leave.

'Thank you all so much. I really couldn't have done it without you all,' Kate told them, and then they were gone and she was finally alone. Sinking onto a hard-backed chair she slowly withdrew the envelope from her pocket.

From her bedroom window, Nuala watched Matthew stride away down the cobbled street, his head bent and his hands thrust deep in his jacket pockets.

She scowled. It really wasn't fair. Why did Kate have to have all the looks while she was so plain? Everyone had always preferred Kate to her – even her father. He had never beaten Kate for the least little thing. He had never hurled as much abuse at Kate as he had at her. And yet, for all that, Nuala had still loved him – not that her love had ever been returned. She remembered back to when she was younger. She would wait for a sight of him returning from work from the small front window, and when he appeared she would rush to the door to meet him. She would help him drag the soot-blackened boots from his feet and run to fetch his slippers, and then she would plump up the cushion in his favourite chair at the side of the fireplace. But he had never, looking back, so much as acknowledged her efforts, let alone given a kind word.

And then she had started to grow and the abuse had started. Nothing she ever did was right for him. He would look at her with loathing and tell her that she was as useless as her mother before her had been, but he had never said that to Kate, not once in all the time she could remember. And now he was gone and there was only her and Kate left. Although at times she was envious of Kate, she was terrified of being without her. For as long as she could remember, Kate had been like a mother to her. It was Kate she had run to as a child if she tumbled and hurt herself. It was Kate who had tucked her into bed each night and told her a story, even though Kate had been barely more than a child herself. But Kate was so beautiful and so grown-up now. What if she and Matthew . . .

Nuala gulped as tears pricked at the back of her eyes. What were they going to do? She had seen Kate disappearing off into the front parlour with the pit manager and had guessed why. She had seen it happen to other families, following the death of someone who had worked at the pit. He would have given Kate notice to quit the cottage and a small sum of money to tide them over until . . . until what? Sighing, she dropped onto the bed she shared with her sister and after crossing her hands behind her head she stared up at the cracks in the ceiling. Her thoughts went back to what Mrs Wilkes had said: *when one door shuts, another door opens.* She could only hope that she was right, or what was to become of them?

Chapter Three

'Kate – I don't think I can do this.'

Kate sighed as she buttoned her coat and turned from the mirror above the mantelpiece to look at Nuala.

'I *have* to go to work,' she pointed out. 'At the moment we need every penny we can get our hands on, and I can't be there *and* here sorting Da's things at the same time, can I? If I don't get back soon they'll give me the sack, and then where will we be, with no money at all coming in?'

Nuala's lip quivered. 'Well, what am I supposed to do with his things then?'

Kate pointed to some bags she had put on the table. 'I've already told you. Empty his wardrobe, go through any pockets and put his clothes in those bags. He didn't have that many and they weren't up to much, but the Salvation Army might know someone who will be glad of them. It will give you something to do.'

When Nuala shuddered and pulled her cardigan more closely about her, Kate strode towards the door.

'Will you be home for dinner?' the younger girl asked hopefully.

Kate shook her head. 'No, I won't. In my dinner-hour

I'm going to scout round to see if there are any flats or anything that we can afford to rent. I know we've still got almost three weeks but it's no good leaving it until the last minute. Mrs Gleeson was saying that the flat above the corner shop might be coming up for rent soon, so I might go and try there.'

'But that flat ain't been lived in for years,' Nuala objected. 'It's been used as storage an' I've heard it's damp an' dirty.'

Kate shrugged. 'Beggars can't be choosers,' she replied. 'And at least it would beat being out on the street.' She smiled at her sister wearily before slipping away without another word.

By lunchtime a row of brown paper carrier bags with string handles was lined up along the tiny landing. Inside them was every item of clothing that Liam Cleary had possessed. Nuala had carried his work clothes out to the dustbin in the shared yard, all apart from his steel-toe-capped boots that was, and Mr Gleeson next door would probably be glad of those. She had folded the rest, which was pathetically little, into piles: shirts and starched white collars in one bag; his Sunday best suit in another; pyjamas and long johns in yet another and so on. Wiping the sweat from her brow she decided that it was time to take a break. Kate would be pleased with her efforts, she was sure of it, and after dinner she would start to empty the drawers.

As Kate left the gates of the pickle factory, she paused. She knew that she should get straight home to Nuala, but suddenly she felt the need to feel the wind on her face after being cooped up in the factory all day. Her job was monotonous at the best of times, filling endless glass jars with pickles and screwing the lids on, but today, with everything else she had on her mind it had been worse than normal.

'Night, Kate, see you tomorrer.'

Turning, Kate waved at the girl who sat next to her in the factory before setting off for the cliffs. Without really thinking about where she was going she found herself heading for Crimdon Dean. It was a good walk from Heseldon but the sandy white beach and the glorious views from there had always drawn her like a magnet. As a child she and Nuala had gone there often with other children from the village. One summer they had made a raft from pieces of driftwood that had been washed up on the beach and ever since, the place had held happy memories for her.

She strolled along the shore, enjoying the feel of the warm sand as it trickled through her toes, her sandals swinging from one hand. There was nothing to be heard save the sound of the seagulls wheeling overhead and the surf crashing on the beach, and slowly the tension that had built up in her like a festering boil drained away. She passed through Monk Heseldon where the cliffs surrounding the beach were dotted with caves. One of them was reputed to run right the way through the cliff to the church, and it was whispered that the monks had used to hide in it in days gone by, but try as she might as a child she had never managed to find it.

The sun was turning the froth on the waves to silver when she reached the beach at Crimdon Dean, and just as she had known he would be, there was Matthew. He had his back to her and was leaning across a canvas that was propped against a homemade easel as his brush flew furiously across the picture.

Silently she crept up behind him, her bare feet making no sound on the warm sand. The painting he was working on was breathtaking. It was almost as if he had taken the scene before him and magically transferred it onto the canvas. Sensing her presence he quickly turned and when he saw her, his face lit up.

'Kate.' He made to stand up but she pressed him back onto the tiny stool.

'No – don't stop, please. Just carry on as if I'm not here. I like to watch you work.'

Flushing, he turned back to the canvas but his concentration was broken and after a moment he shrugged and began to wipe his brush on an oily rag.

'It's almost finished anyway.'

On the horizon a fishing boat slumbered on the waves, its mast gleaming in the early evening sun, the sea around it glittering like a million shattered diamonds.

The scene was mirrored in his seascape and Kate sighed with admiration. 'It must be nice to be so talented,' she remarked softly.

Looking slightly embarrassed, Matthew began to stuff his paints and brushes into an old rucksack. 'What brings you here at this time then?' he asked.

Dragging her eyes away from the painting, Kate sank to the sand and hugged her knees. 'I came out of work and just felt the need for some fresh air.'

'Mm – first day back, was it?'

She nodded as he sat beside her.

'Have you had any luck finding somewhere for you and Nuala to live yet?'

Her head wagged from side to side. 'No, not yet. I went to look at the flat above the corner shop in my dinner-hour. It's in a pretty bad state, to be honest. But then I suppose if nothing else crops up it would do at a push. Not that Nuala is very pleased at the prospect.'

He chewed on his lip. He had loved Kate for as long as he could remember, and yet somehow they had never got beyond passing the time of day although he had often been tempted to tell her how he felt about her. The words were there, hovering on his tongue like a bird about to take flight, but they refused to pass his lips. The whole village knew how possessive Liam Cleary had been with his elder daughter. Added to that was the fact that Kate was fiercely independent, and Matthew had been afraid to speak in case she didn't feel the same way. And now Liam Cleary was gone and to all intents and purposes the road was clear and he could have risked telling her how he felt. God knew he wanted to, but some inner voice warned him that this would not be the right time. If he spoke up now, she might think that he was offering his heart out of pity because she had nowhere to go. He had to bide his time so that when he did tell her how he felt, she would know that it was because he loved her with all his heart.

Lapsing into a companionable silence they let the peace of the place deeply relax them until eventually Kate rose and brushed the sand from her skirt as she told him, 'I ought to be getting back or Nuala will be wondering where I've got to.'

Collecting his things together and holding the still-wet

canvas carefully, he fell into step beside her and the two of them made their way back to Heseldon. When they reached the village, Kate put her sandals back on and smiled at him. 'Right, I'll be off then and you should do the same,' she said. 'No doubt your ma will have your tea on the table and I don't want her blaming me for it spoiling.' Her eyes were twinkling and appeared almost black in the light of the sun. Matthew watched as she hurried away, then turning slowly he made his own way down the road that ran next to hers.

Beryl Williams, Matthew's mother, was a small plump woman with a ready smile and a big heart. Just as Kate had said, the instant her son set foot through the door she began to dish up his evening meal, glancing at his painting as she passed.

'Have a good session, did you?' she asked, smiling her approval at what she saw. She had been widowed some three years before, but fortunately because Matthew also worked at the pit as well as his father before him, she had been allowed to stay on in the cottage.

'Aye, I did.' Smacking his lips, he stared in anticipation at the laden plateful of shepherd's pie she placed before him.

'Wasn't that young Kate Cleary I saw you with a moment gone at the top o' the street? I was putting the milk bottles out an' I couldn't help but notice you talkin'.'

She saw the flush that spread up his neck and into his cheeks, and knew that what she had suspected for some time was true. 'A bad do that was,' she went on, and clicked her tongue. 'The poor lass – losin' her da like that. Not that he was the best da in the world, if rumour has it right. By all accounts she's had it rough. Brought that younger sister of hers up like a mother since she were knee high to a grasshopper. Still – I suppose she'll make someone a good wife wi' all the practice at house-keepin' she's had. An' she's a pretty lass and kind-hearted into the bargain, ain't she?'

When he didn't answer but kept his head bent over his plate, she frowned. Deciding that she needed to say more, she continued, 'Matthew, a blind man on a gallopin' horse could see that you're struck wi' the lass. Here's you an' me rattlin' round wi' this house all to ourselves. Me an' your da always planned to fill it to the rafters wi' children, but after you there were no more come along. Not that I'm complainin', o' course. You were a gift from God an' there ain't a day goes by as I don't thank Him for you. But her an' that sister o' hers will be chucked out on their ear now, an' where will they go? If you *do* think anythin' of her, ain't it time you told her so? I'd have 'em here like a shot, so if it's me you're worryin' about – don't! *Tell* the lass if you have feelings for her, for Christ's sake.'

'It ain't as simple as that, Mam,' he muttered miserably.

'Why ain't it?' she demanded.

'Well, what if I were to tell her how I feel an' she don't feel the same way? An' also – wouldn't she think I was tellin' her now 'cos I feel sorry for her?'

'Huh! You men! Sometimes I wonder if any of you have a brain. The lass is rock bottom at present. She'll be out on her arse wi' nowhere to go soon – an' then how will you feel? What's up wi' you? Scared of havin' your pride hurt, are you? Well, think on. What if she can't find anywhere to rent round here an' she moves away? You'll have missed your chance altogether then, won't you? If it's two women sharin' one kitchen you're worryin' about, then don't! Your Aunt Aggie in Bournemouth has been on at me for ages to go an' live with her, an' if I could see you settled I'd be gone like a shot. But that's enough said on my part. It has to be what *you* want. All I'm doin' is tellin' you that if you want the lass, then you have my blessin'. Now you make up your own mind, but think on. You don't want to miss your chance, do you?'

So saying, she shuffled away, leaving Matthew to think on her words as he stared off into space.

'Where have you been, Kate? I've been worried sick!' Nuala's tear-filled voice sent guilt raging through Kate the second that she set foot through the door. Glancing at the clock, she was shocked to see that it was almost seven o'clock. No wonder Nuala had been fretting.

'Sorry, pet.' Dropping her bag onto the nearest chair, she smiled at her sister apologetically. 'When I came out of work I felt the urge for a walk and a bit of fresh air and I lost track of time.'

'With Matthew, were you?' Nuala asked accusingly, but pointedly ignoring the question, Kate glanced at the rows of bags that had been carried downstairs and stacked neatly at the side of the door. Her annoyance forgotten for now, Nuala flapped her hand at her sister.

'Come an' look at what I found in one o' Da's drawers. They were tucked right under his socks an' I don't know quite what to make of 'em.'

Grabbing Kate's arm, Nuala dragged her to the table and pointed at a pile of envelopes.

39

'What are they?' Kate frowned as Nuala snatched up the card on top of the pile and waved it in her face.

'They're letters an' birthday cards – an' they're all addressed to you!' she informed her.

'All addressed to me? Who are they from?' Kate was bewildered and beginning to think that her sister had taken leave of her senses.

'They're all from someone who calls herself Aunt Beth. Apparently she lives in a place called Nuneaton. Look – this one says *Happy First Birthday*. There are letters too, though I ain't read them 'cos they're sealed. Some of 'em are addressed to Mammy an' some of 'em are addressed to you. There's a birthday card fer every year until you were three, but then they stop. Ain't that when we moved from Ireland to here?'

'Yes, it is.' Kate was totally bemused. Sinking onto the nearest chair, she took the card from Nuala and turned it over in her hand.

'There are none addressed to me,' Nuala said petulantly. 'An' it seems that they stopped when Da brought us to Durham.'

'That's strange. Da never mentioned that we had an aunt. And why aren't there any cards or letters for you? Perhaps this aunt didn't know about you.'

Nuala shrugged. 'That's the way it seems. But anyway, I'll make you a brew while you start to go through 'em.'

When Nuala hurried away to put the kettle on, Kate stared at the card in her hand. *To Kathleen with lots of love from Auntie Beth*, it said. But who the hell was Auntie Beth, and why had their da never mentioned her?

Lifting one of the sealed letters, she opened it and began to read. She then opened one that had been

40

addressed to their mother and after reading that too, she looked across at Nuala, who was watching her expectantly.

'It appears that this lady was our mother's sister,' she told her incredulously.

Nuala's eyes stretched wide. 'So why didn't Da ever tell us about her then?'

'At the moment I haven't the foggiest idea,' Kate admitted. 'But perhaps after I've worked my way through this lot we'll be a little wiser.'

'Is there an address on any of 'em?' Lifting the letter that Kate had just read, Nuala pointed exultantly to an address. 'Yes, there is. Look, here it is – Home Park Road, Nuneaton, Warwickshire.'

Kate chewed on her lip thoughtfully for a second before remarking, 'I believe that's where the novelist George Eliot came from. I learned all about her at school.'

'Well, now we know we've got an auntie, what are we going to do about it?'

Kate shrugged her slight shoulders. 'I'll tell you that tomorrow when I've had time to read through all these, but for now my stomach thinks my throat's cut, so let's have some dinner, eh?'

Long after Nuala had gone to bed and deep into the night, Kate sat at the kitchen table reading through the letters and cards that Nuala had stumbled across. They didn't paint a nice picture of the life that their mother, Jenny, had lived with their father, and Kate was deeply troubled. From what she could judge, their mother had written regularly to their aunt, but the replies that lay before her unopened must have led her to believe

41

that Aunt Beth had never replied, for they had obviously been intercepted by Liam.

Pushing them into a neat pile, Kate banked down the fire and locked the door, then crept upstairs to the small bedroom that she shared with Nuala. Her sister was curled into a ball beneath the blankets, smelling faintly of vomit. Kate sighed. Ever since Nuala had been a little girl the least stress had had her rushing to the toilet to be sick, and this week she had been worse than ever, not that it was surprising after the shock of losing her father.

Dragging her eyes away from her sister's slumbering form, Kate's thoughts returned to the letters. There was no mention of Nuala in any of them, which led her to believe that Aunt Beth possibly didn't even know of her existence. She slithered carefully into bed beside her sister and turning on her side, stared at the pool of silver moonlight that was reflecting on the bare wooden floorboards through a chink in the curtains. What was she going to do? They had less than three weeks left to vacate the cottage now, and apart from the small flat above the corner shop, which was hardly fit for human habitation, she had nowhere for them to go. Perhaps it would be worth writing to this Aunt Beth. She might be able to help them. But would she still live at the address on the letters – or even still be alive, if it came to that? Kate tossed and turned until eventually she fell into an uneasy doze.

Lifting the letter from the doormat some days later, Elizabeth Summers frowned. The handwriting was neat but unfamiliar, and the envelope bore a Durham postmark. She racked her brains trying to think of anyone she might know in Durham, then carrying it into the sitting room of her neat semi-detached house she poured out a cup of tea from a bone china teapot and slit it open. As she began to read, her face paled and her hand flew to her throat.

So Liam Cleary was dead. Good riddance to bad rubbish, as far as she was concerned. As thoughts of her sister flooded into her mind, tears pricked the back of her eyes. Liam Cleary had been a bad man, a cruel man. She had never liked him, but her sister had been besotted with him and would not have a bad word said against him. In the beginning, that was . . .

Her thoughts drifted back over the years. Liam had been a good-looking devil in those days, before drink got the better of him. Jenny had met him when he had come to work for a time in Nuneaton and he had swept her off her feet. Their mother had been alive then, and she, like Elizabeth, had had grave misgivings about him, but Jenny was adamant. He was the one she wanted and he was the one she would have.

Their wedding at the register office had been a quiet affair before he whisked her away back to Ireland, and for a time the letters she wrote home had been ecstatic. But then she became pregnant with Kathleen and Liam had begun to show his true colours. Their mother had visited her unexpectedly and had been appalled at what she saw. Jenny was a mere shadow of her former self, although she insisted that the bruises and the black eye had been caused by a fall. Their mother was no fool and had begged Jenny to come home, but she was loyal and certain that this was only a bad patch they were going through. Liam would soon revert to the charming man she had married, Jenny had assured her, but he never did, and the poor young woman's life had become hell on earth.

And now, out of the blue, here was a letter from Kathleen after all these years. She mentioned Nuala in her letter, the sister Beth had never met. Beth chewed on her lip. It sounded as if the poor girls were desperate. She had lost her own sister long ago, but perhaps she could help her nieces? Her tea was left to go cold as she hurried away to fetch a pen and paper.

As Matthew spread a liberal amount of Marmite across a slice of bread his mother peeped at him from the corner of her eye. He was sitting at the table, his shirtsleeves rolled up to his elbows following a shift down the pit. Beryl was filling the tin bath in front of the fire with hot water for him.

'So what do you think o' young Kate's news then?' she asked innocently.

Raising an eyebrow, he peered at her. 'What news would that be?' He had seen little of Kate since the night she had joined him on the beach some two weeks ago.

'Word has it that an aunt she didn't know about has offered to let her and Nuala go and live with her.'

She watched as the slice of bread stopped halfway to his lips and the colour drained from his face. 'What? Who . . . ?'

'Seems this woman was the sister of the girl's mother, but Liam never told them about her, that's what's being whispered anyway.' Carrying yet another large saucepan full of water to the bath, Beryl tipped it in before straightening to wipe the sweat from her brow. Her sister Aggie

44

in Bournemouth had just had an inside bathroom with
hot and cold running water installed, she had informed
her in her last letter. But now was not the time to think
of that, for Matthew was staring at her open-mouthed.

'So where does this aunt live?'

She pursed her lips. 'Somewhere in the Midlands, by
all accounts. Warwickshire, I think it is.'

'But . . . that's miles away!'

'Yes, well happen you should have thought o' that
when I spoke to you not long since. I told you to make
your intentions clear if that's what you were wantin',
but it looks now like you've missed your chance.'

Matthew's fingers strummed on the tabletop as he
stared off into space. Kate couldn't just go off like that.
He might never see her again. Suddenly standing, he
began to peel his shirt off.

'You're in a rush all of a sudden, ain't you?' his mother
remarked, a little smile playing about her lips as she got
up to leave the room and allow him to have his bath.

Without a word Matthew discarded the rest of his
clothes and clambered into the tin tub.

'Matthew? Er . . . come in.' Concealing her surprise as
best she could, Kate held the door wide as he strode past
her into the room. Nuala, who was sitting in a chair at
the side of the empty grate, looked up and stared.

'I heard that you were moving away,' he said abruptly,
then cleared his throat.

He looked decidedly uncomfortable and Kate, aware
that Nuala was hanging on his every word, felt herself
flushing.

'Yes – we go the day after tomorrow. We shall be

staying with our aunt in the Midlands. There's more work there, apparently, and there's . . . Well, there's nothing to keep us here now, is there?'

He glanced at Nuala and then back at Kate. 'You could always come an' stay wi' me an' me mam,' he said softly.

'We're *goin*' to me auntie's,' Nuala said stubbornly before Kate had a chance to get a word in. 'Like Kate just said, there's nothin' to keep us here now that me da's gone.' Her stance dared him to defy her and for a moment he was at a loss for words.

'Look, why don't we go for a walk?' Kate suggested hastily.

Nuala looked as if she were about to burst. 'What do you want to go out at this time for?' she challenged. 'We've got all our last-minute packin' to do.' She shot Matthew a withering glance, but ignoring her, Kate snatched her cardigan from the back of the chair and ushered him towards the door.

'We won't be gone for long,' she told her sister and then hurried outside before Nuala could voice any more objections.

Once out on the cobbled street, Matthew began to lope along and Kate had to almost run to keep up with his long strides. His hands were pushed deep into his coat pockets and his chin was bent to his chest, but Kate said nothing, she simply followed him until they came to the cliffs that overlooked the sea. When at last he came to a halt she let her gaze follow his. The sun was just sinking into the ocean, which appeared almost black in the fading light, its surface freckled with frothy white foam that caught and reflected the light from the fading sun.

They stood in silence for some time until eventually he said, 'Kate, you don't *have* to go, you know. Me mam said as how she'd be more than happy to have you both with us. I know I should have said something sooner but . . . well, I suppose with you just losin' yer da an' all I—'

'Please, Matthew, don't say any more,' Kate interrupted. 'I've agreed to go to my aunt now. I do appreciate the offer, I really do, but you see it's not that simple. I have Nuala to worry about, I'll always have Nuala and—'

'That don't matter. You can both come.' His voice had taken on a note of desperation now and Kate felt tears trembling on her lashes. He looked so handsome standing there, so strong and reliable that she had the urge to throw herself into his arms. If only he had spoken before. She shook her head. It was too late for 'if only' now. The decision had been made. They were going to Nuneaton.

Turning suddenly, she began to hurry back the way she had come and now it was Matthew trying to keep up with her.

'Kate, *please* . . .' he choked.

Stopping abruptly, she looked up into his face, her eyes sad. 'Matthew, I want you to promise me something. I want you to promise me that you'll go to art school. You have a gift and you should use it. I also want you to find yourself a girl, a nice girl with no commitments who will love you.'

'But Kate, I love—'

'No, please – don't say it.' She was crying now and he thought his heart would break.

47

'I missed me chance, didn't I?' he whispered brokenly.

She shook her head, setting her dark hair dancing on her shoulders.

'Will you keep in touch?' he asked.

'Perhaps, but even if I don't . . . I'll never forget you, Matthew.'

Clasping her small hands in his large ones he stared deep into her eyes. 'You'll always be there in every yesterday, Kate.' Slowly he bent his head and for the briefest of seconds their lips touched. He savoured the moment, knowing that it would be all he would ever have of her. And then she was walking away and a little part of his heart went with her.

Chapter Four

Nuneaton, June 1954

The crowd of girls outside the pub began to disperse in different directions, their happy voices piercing the silence of the town centre.

'I'll see yer tomorrer then, don't be late at the church now.' With a cheery wave Peggy Aldridge lurched away from her friends. They had just spent an enjoyable evening in the Pen and Wig and she was feeling happy, no doubt due to the numerous Babychams and Cherry B's she had downed. Still, she grinned into the darkness, it is me hen night so I'm allowed to get tiddly. Adjusting the silly hat that her workmates had made her, she skipped happily past the library. This time tomorrow she would be Mrs Brian Robinson. A bubble of excitement formed in her stomach as she thought of her wedding dress hanging on the wardrobe door back at home. Tomorrow night, she and Brian would be on their way to Blackpool on the train.

The night had turned nippy and Peggy shuddered as she hurried past the parish church. It was a good walk to her home in Marston Lane but she decided that if she went along Attleborough Road and took the short-cut through the jitty in Hall End, she could cut quite a bit off her journey. Her mam would have had a fit if she knew which way she was going. Since that poor young woman in Ansley Lane had disappeared off the face of the earth last February, her mam had been paranoid about her being out at night on her own. It was as well she did have a good walk in front of her, Peggy thought. The fresh air might sober her up a bit and save her from a tongue-lashing when she got in.

The young woman grinned. Poor Mam. If anything, she was even more nervous than Peggy was about the wedding. Peg was the only girl amongst four brothers so she supposed it was only natural that her mother would want her special day to pass without a hitch.

After passing the old folk's home and the Bull Inn, the jitty was soon in sight. It was off the main road and pitch black at night, but it held no fear for Peggy; she had lived in the area all her life and as a child had spent many happy hours playing in the woods and paddling in the stream.

She set off along the path that led to the small bridge over the brook. The streetlights faded away and soon she was in darkness. Her heels clattered on the wooden bridge but once she had crossed it, all became quiet again save for the nightlife of the animals that lived in the woods. A million stars shone down on her and, at that moment, she had never felt so happy in her whole life. However, just then, a sound behind her brought her to an abrupt stop as she strained her ears into the darkness. She frowned; it sounded like footsteps on the bridge behind her. Still, she supposed she didn't have sole rights to take the short-cut so she moved on.

The moon suddenly disappeared behind a cloud and

she was momentarily in total darkness. Slowing her steps, she tried to peer down at the ground. She was so intent on looking where she was going that the footsteps were almost upon her before she became aware of them again.

''Ere,' she called cheerfully into the darkness. 'Come an' let me hang onto yer arm. I can't see a bloody thing.'

There was no answer. The footsteps had stopped and now a cold finger suddenly ran up her spine.

'Is anyone there?' Only silence answered her, and slightly unnerved she began to move along again, cursing the high heels she was wearing. Within seconds she heard the footsteps crunching on the ground behind her, but this time she didn't stop to look back. Instead she bent and, kicking off her shoes, she snatched them up and began to hurry barefoot across the stony ground. The hat flew off but she didn't stoop to retrieve it. All she wanted now was to see the streetlights. The footsteps behind her grew louder and now she was running, her breath coming in painful gasps. The trees were on both sides of her, and just as the moon sailed from behind the clouds she felt a hand clamp down on her shoulder. She tried to slap it away, with no success.

''Ere, what's yer game?' she cried as the hand swung her about. The smart pencil skirt she was wearing split as she stared up into a pair of dark eyes, and then a hand came across her mouth and she felt herself being lifted and carried towards the trees.

She tried to scream but the hand clamped across her mouth made the sound lodge in her throat. She kicked and lashed out with her hands but her strength was no match for the person who was holding her. She was in

51

the woods now and the person towering above her was nothing more than a dark shape. Tears spilled from her eyes and streamed down her cheeks but then suddenly the hand left her mouth and she opened it to let the scream that had been building in her escape. It never got the chance to, for almost immediately, cold hands closed around her throat. In that moment, she knew that she would never get to wear the beautiful wedding dress waiting back at home.

'Brian,' she managed to say, but then darkness far blacker than the night began to close in on her and she knew no more.

Chapter Five

'This is it then?' Placing her suitcase on the ground, Kate rubbed her sweaty hands down the front of her skirt and looked nervously across her shoulder at Nuala.

It was a bright summer day and they were both tired following the long train journey to their aunt's home in Nuneaton.

'Are you sure this is the right house?' Nuala asked hesitantly as she checked the address on the crumpled piece of paper in her hand.

Kate nodded before lifting her hand to knock on the door. She had no chance to do so, however, because it was suddenly flung open and she found herself confronted by a small grey-haired woman with a kindly, excited face.

'So you're here at last then! I've been hovering by the window all day,' the woman exclaimed.

They stared at each other for a second then suddenly Kate was in her aunt's arms and they were both laughing and crying all at the same time.

'Oh Kathleen, I never thought I'd see you again,' Beth cried with delight. 'Come on in. Don't stand on ceremony out here on the doorstep. This is your home now and you're most welcome . . . And you too, of course.' She smiled at Nuala before leading Kate into the house.

Second best as ever, Nuala thought resentfully, lifting her case and following them inside.

'How do you do.'

Kate shook the extended hand of her cousin politely. 'I'm very well, thank you.' She had been at her aunt's for two days now, but this was the first time she had met David, Aunt Beth's son. She noticed that his smile didn't quite reach his eyes although his manners were impeccable. She supposed she couldn't blame him. After all, it must have been quite a shock for him to discover that he had two cousins he had never known about, and even more of a shock to discover that they were moving in with his mother.

David was a nice-looking man in his late twenties with dark hair and blue eyes. He was married with two small girls who Aunt Beth talked about all the time. He lived in Hinckley, which Aunt Beth had told her was a small town on the outskirts of Nuneaton, with his wife Rebecca.

'I hope you had a pleasant journey,' he said politely.

Kate nodded. 'Yes, we did, thank you. And your mother has made us so welcome.'

David opened his mouth to say something but a warning glance from his mother made him clamp it shut again. Aunt Beth was hovering like a frightened butterfly, so wanting him to like his cousins yet sensing that he didn't.

'My mother tends to be a soft touch for waifs and strays,' he said somewhat unkindly. 'No disrespect to you, Kate, but she is riddled with arthritis and I'm concerned that two extra bodies in the house for her to look after might be too much for her.'

'We ain't no waifs and strays an' she won't need to look after us!' Nuala informed him tremulously before Kate had a chance to retort. 'If anythin', *we'll* look after *her*.' Up until now she hadn't said so much as a word, but like Kate, she sensed that he wasn't too pleased about them being there.

'There really won't be any need for that,' David's voice was as cold as ice. 'My mother is perfectly aware that when and *if* she needs looking after, she is very welcome to come and live with Rebecca and me. Our house would be more than adequate to accommodate her.'

Kate frowned. Aunt Beth had told her on numerous occasions already that David had a very good job at the Council Offices in Nuneaton and his own four-bedroomed detached house in Hinckley. From where she was standing she had already formed the opinion that David was a snob, but she wouldn't tell her Aunt Beth that, of course.

Now Aunt Beth was a different kettle of fish altogether and Kate had loved her from the moment she clapped eyes on her. Small and dainty, she had springy grey hair and deep blue eyes that twinkled when she smiled. She was what Kate would have termed 'a lady' in every sense of the word, from her gentle nature, to the pretty twin-sets and pearls that she was so fond of wearing. Kate could never imagine her Aunt Beth standing on the doorstep gossiping with her curlers in as the women in Durham had. In fact, Aunt Beth didn't consider herself properly dressed until she had applied her lipstick in the mornings. Until Kate and Nuala had arrived her only companion had been a small Yorkshire terrier dog called Sally. Aunt Beth obviously adored her and within just two days Kate was beginning to as well. The dog followed Kate about the house like a shadow, although she didn't seem to have taken to Nuala. Now that Kate came to think of it, Aunt Beth hadn't either, but then, Nuala could appear very standoffish and grumpy because she was so shy, and Kate could only hope that as they settled in, they would all grow closer.

The atmosphere had become somewhat strained and hoping to lighten it, Kate smiled disarmingly at her cousin. 'Should I put the kettle on and make you a cup of tea?'

'No, dear, I'll do that. You stay here and talk to David and get to know each other a little better.' Struggling out of the depths of her comfy armchair, Aunt Beth headed for the kitchen, leaving David and the two girls alone. Nuala sank onto the settee with a nervous scowl on her face and after snatching a magazine from the coffee-table she promptly buried her head in it.

An uncomfortable silence settled between them until David asked bluntly, 'How long were you planning on staying then?'

'Well, I . . . er . . .' Kate felt herself flushing. 'I hadn't really thought about it, to be honest. Nuala and I need to find ourselves a job first, and then I suppose we *could* look around for somewhere to rent.' As realisation suddenly dawned on her she leaned slightly towards him. 'Please don't think that we've come to scrounge from your mother, David. We shall pay our way, I assure you.

And this . . .' she spread her arms to encompass the pretty sitting room '. . . this is *your* inheritance. Nuala and I are just grateful to have somewhere to go at present; we haven't come here to claim what is rightfully yours.'

David had the good grace to flush, but was saved from having to say any more when Aunt Beth swept back into the room with a tray laden with pretty china cups and saucers and a large pot of tea.

'Now then,' she beamed at them as she placed it on the coffee-table. 'Who's going to be Mother?'

For the rest of David's visit he and Kate were studiously polite to each other, but Kate sensed that she would have to work very hard on him if they were ever to be friends. It saddened her because after the rapturous welcome they'd received from Aunt Beth, she had hoped that they could settle here. Now she felt that David would always see them as intruders and it changed everything. She had planned to give herself a few more days to settle in and get to know the area before starting to hunt for a job, but now she decided that she would start to look around for both herself and Nuala first thing tomorrow.

Much later that evening, long after David had left and Nuala had taken herself off to bed, Kate and her aunt sat admiring the sunset from the French windows in the sitting room that overlooked the lovely garden.

Nuala had retired early to her room every night since they'd arrived. Although it was a small room, it was very pretty. It was the first time in her life that she had never had to share a bed with Kate and so it was somewhat of a novelty to her, and she loved going to bed.

Now as the soft breeze caressed their skin, Beth asked,

'So what do you think of Nuneaton up to now then, Kathleen?'

Kate smiled at the use of her full name. She had asked her aunt to call her Kate, but was happy with Kathleen. 'Well, to be truthful, apart from the bit we saw of it on our way from Trent Valley railway station, I haven't really gone beyond the end of the road yet.'

'Of course you haven't. It was a silly question to ask really. But there are some lovely places to visit in and around Warwickshire, I promise you. If it weren't for this damn arthritis I'd offer to take you on a sightseeing tour, but as it is . . .'

Kate reached across to pat her hand and Sally, who was curled up in a ball on her mistress's lap, promptly licked it.

Beth laughed as she fondled her pet's silky ears. 'You've certainly got an admirer here in this one, though I couldn't help but notice that you and our David didn't get off on the best of footings.'

When Kate flushed, her aunt smiled kindly. 'Don't get fretting about it, dear. In fairness to him, it must have been a bit of a shock to discover that two cousins he had never met were coming to live with me. But he'll come round – you'll see. He isn't a bad lad – he's just a bit over-protective of me, that's all, especially since he lost his father. Between you and me, he'd have me to live with him and Rebecca like a shot if I'd go, but . . .'

'Don't you get on with Rebecca?' Kate asked quietly as her aunt's voice trailed away.

'Oh, I *do* get on with her but . . . Well, Rebecca is very houseproud. She keeps the house spick and span and their two little girls are always turned out as neat as two pins.

58

Nothing wrong in that, of course; as you can see, I like to be orderly myself, but she doesn't like dogs for a start and I couldn't leave this one here, could I?'

As Kate's gaze dropped to the little dog, she shook her head. 'No, I don't suppose you could. Have you had her for long?'

'Since the night I lost my husband, strangely enough.' The older woman's eyes grew misty as her mind wandered back to that fateful night. 'I was here all on my own, wondering what I was going to do with myself when I heard this scratching at the door, and there she was on the doorstep – almost as if she'd sensed that I needed the company. I kept her with me all that night and the next morning I told the police that I'd found her. They offered to put her in the dog pound in case her owners came forward, but I persuaded them to let me keep her with me. Nobody ever did come to claim her and she's been here ever since. But that's enough about me. How are you feeling, Kathleen?'

Kate shrugged. 'Everything's happened so fast I'm not sure, to be honest,' she replied cautiously. 'First thing tomorrow I'm going to go out and look around for some jobs for Nuala and I to do. We can pay you a proper board then and maybe even look around for somewhere to rent.'

'You'll do no such thing!' Beth's voice was sharp with indignation. 'What would be the point of renting somewhere here? If you were going to do that, you might just as well have stayed in Durham. I want you to think of this as your home from now on, and I don't want any more silly talk about you moving out. Do you hear me?'

When Kate's bent head bobbed, her aunt's voice softened. 'Do you know something, Kathleen? Sitting there, you look so like your mother that it's almost as if she's here with me again.'

'Were you very close?'

'Oh yes, we were. When we were younger we were inseparable. Your mother was always the best looking, and she had the heart of an angel into the bargain. Not that she couldn't be feisty when it suited her, and stubborn. She and our mother used to have some right old ding-dongs.' The older woman chuckled as she remembered.

Kate had been longing to ask her aunt about her mother. There was so much she wanted to know but hadn't dared to ask.

'You must miss her,' she said softly.

Her aunt's eyes grew moist as she stared off into the distance, remembering. 'Oh yes, I do. There's not a single day goes by when I don't think about her.'

'Did you go to her funeral?' Kate ventured to ask, and suddenly her aunt's face hardened and she began to struggle out of the chair. Sally leaped off her lap and scuttled away as her mistress crossed to the French windows and began to close them.

'I don't know about you, my dear, but my bed is calling me. It's been a long day, hasn't it?'

Kate stared at her in bewilderment. It was almost as if a shutter had come down between them and she wondered what she had said wrong.

'Yes, I am a little tired,' she confessed. 'Mind you, I might take a stroll before I go up to blow the cobwebs away.'

'Oh no, Kathleen. Don't get doing that.' Her aunt's voice was heavy with concern now. 'There's been two young women go missing without trace in Nuneaton over the last few months, and I'd never rest in my bed if I knew you were walking around in the dark. One of them was a young mother with two small children. The other disappeared on the night before her wedding, poor soul. She was a lovely girl, bless her, and the apple of her mother's eye. Word has it that it's almost destroyed her poor mother, not to mention her fiancé.' Beth shuddered as she thought of the reports she had read in the papers. 'Why don't you wait till morning and then you can have a good scout round to your heart's content.'

'How can you be so sure that the two missing women didn't just run away?' Kate asked. 'The first woman might have been unhappily married. And as for the second . . . Well, she might have got cold feet and decided that she couldn't go through with the wedding. Perhaps she's just gone off somewhere till she can face her family again.'

'Oh no, dear. Peggy would *never* have done that.' Beth shook her head. 'I've known her and her mother for years. All the family talked about for months before was the wedding, and the lass was full of it. So I ask again, will you *please* not go out tonight?'

When Kate nodded reluctantly her aunt bent and kissed her on the cheek. 'Sorry if I was a little brusque with you back there. It's just that . . . Well, your mother is gone and I can see no good in raking up painful memories. We'll talk some more another day, eh? When you've had more time to settle in.'

'All right.' There was little more Kate could say, but

as her aunt hobbled towards the door with Sally close on her heels, she remained confused by what had happened.

Nuala stared from the bedroom window across the freshly mown lawn. The window was open and the smell of the flowers in the garden wafted into her. Her aunt's house was a three-bedroom semi-detached with what amounted to little more than a neat pocket-handkerchief garden front and back; even so, after the rows of terraced cottages that she was used to, it seemed like a little palace. Her bedroom was small but comfortable. Behind her, against one wall, stood a highly polished oak wardrobe with a mirror on the front of one door. Next to that was a matching chest of drawers and on the other wall was a bed with a wonderfully soft mattress all covered in crisp white sheets, a warm woollen blanket and an embroidered patchwork quilt. Pretty flowered curtains framed the sash-cord window and the floor boasted a carpet that stretched from wall to wall. Nuala felt that she would never tire of climbing out of bed to feel her toes sink into it; she could remember only too well the cold wooden floorboards that she'd had in the small bedroom she'd shared with Kate back in Durham. And yet for all that she was still unhappy. It seemed that once again, Kate would be the favourite with their aunt just as she had been with their father. Just as she had always been with everyone, now that her sister came to think about it. But that was because Kate was pretty whilst she was plain, and Kate was clever whilst she was what her father had called 'thick'.

Unbidden, a picture of Matthew Williams floated in

front of her eyes and a lump formed in Nuala's throat. She had worshipped Matthew ever since she was a little girl, although he could have had no way of knowing it, of course. She had dreamed that once she was grown up he would suddenly notice her and fall helplessly in love with her, and then they would be married and live happily ever after just as they did in the fairy stories of princes and princesses that Kate had used to read to her when she was small. But instead, she had been forced to stand by and watch the attraction between him and Kate grow. She herself might have been invisible, for whenever Kate was there, Matthew had eyes for no one but her. She had no doubt at all that, had they stayed in Durham, Kate and Matthew would have become an item and she didn't know how she could have borne it. Now she wouldn't have to; they would probably never set eyes on him again.

Sighing, she turned and caught sight of herself in the mirror. It was no wonder that everyone preferred Kate to her; they were as different as chalk from cheese in all ways. It was almost as if Kate, being the firstborn, had got all the good looks, leaving nothing for her. Kate was kind but strong, while Nuala was timid. Kate was the one who organised everything and took any crisis in her stride, while Nuala went off into a panic. Kate could talk properly, while she seemed to put her foot in it every time she so much as opened her mouth. It had always been that way for as far back as the girl could remember. Kate had been the favourite with everyone, even Miss Frost at the village school. Nuala sometimes wished that she could hate her sister and break away from her to stand on her own two feet, but deep down she knew that she never would. Without Kate to lean on, she was nothing. Nuala had hoped that in Aunt Beth she would find the mother that she had never known and always yearned for, but somehow she knew that her aunt hadn't taken to her as she obviously had to Kate. Oh, Aunt Beth had been kind to her and made her welcome enough, but there was something . . . something that she couldn't quite put her finger on that told Nuala they would never be close. And then there was hostile David, although in fairness he had made it more than clear that his dislike stretched to Kate as well as herself.

Turning away from the spotty-faced image in the mirror she grimaced in disgust. In her mind's eye she could see Kate's skin, smooth and unblemished, Kate's eyes, dark and deep as midnight framed with long thick lashes, and her hair falling in gleaming curls to her slender shoulders. Nuala threw herself onto the bed, creasing the pretty patchwork quilt, her face twisted in an ugly frown as she wondered why God had been so unkind to her.

Just along the landing in her own bedroom, Beth was pacing the floor as tears streamed down her face. The conversation she'd had with Kathleen had unsettled her and brought back memories that she had tried to forget. Kathleen was *so* like her mother, and so like the daughter she herself had always longed for. Once, she and William had dreamed of having at least three children, but after giving birth to David she had suffered one miscarriage after another until eventually her dream of having a large family died with her unborn babies. Oh, she had always thanked God for her son, but now she had lost him too.

Rebecca had him exactly where she wanted him, eating out of the palm of her hand. Until his marriage, Beth had been close to her son, but now she only saw him when his wife allowed him to visit.

In her loneliness, Elizabeth Summers had seized the chance to get to know her niece Kathleen and now that she was here, Beth was not disappointed, not that she could pretend that she had taken to Nuala. She was so . . . Beth searched for the word to describe what she felt about her. It didn't matter that the girl was a bit slow, not clever like her sister, and Beth knew she should have made allowances for her, but there was something else about her – she was sly. Yes, sly. That was the word that sprang to mind but then, Nuala was Kathleen's flesh and blood so she determined to try harder.

Her thoughts moved back to Kathleen. There was so much she could have told the girl about her mother – but how could she? She had made a promise to her sister and it could do Kate no good at all to know the truth. She and Nuala were obviously as close as two peas in a pod, and for that reason alone she determined that nothing should come between them.

Staring into the starry night, she offered up a silent prayer. 'May God forgive me.'

Chapter Six

Elizabeth Summers sighed as she set the breakfast-table. Upstairs she could hear Kate and Nuala arguing over who would use the bathroom first. She paused to listen and then, just as she had predicted, she heard Kate hurry back to her room. As usual, she had given way to her sister. Kate *always* gave way to Nuala and fussed over her like a mother hen even though there was only a couple of years between them.

Beth was still trying to come to terms with the fact that Nuala was here. She had heard nothing from Liam since he had informed her of the child's birth. She stopped her thoughts from running on. Nuala *was* here so she would do her best to make her welcome for Kathleen's sake.

When she heard the bathroom door open she hurried away to start cooking breakfast. It was as all three were eating toast and marmalade that they heard the mail drop through the letterbox.

'I'll get it.' Aunt Beth shuffled away down the hall to return seconds later with a bundle of letters in her hand.

'Ah Kathleen, there's one for you.' She handed Kate an envelope that had been handwritten.

When Kate saw the Durham postmark she remarked, 'I bet it's from Mrs Gleeson, our old neighbour,' and placing her half-eaten toast back on the plate she slit it open and began to read.

Nuala watched her intently and when she saw Kate flush she bit her lip. It was from Matthew. Somehow she sensed it. Kate confirmed her premonition when she glanced up and smiled, blushing prettily.

'It's from Matthew. Apparently he's finally going to finish at the pit and go to art school.'

'Where will they live? That cottage is like ours, tied to the pit,' Nuala said peevishly.

'It seems that his mother is going to live with her sister in Bournemouth. Oh, I'm so pleased for him. Matthew was a friend of ours,' she explained to her aunt. 'He's so talented. You should have seen some of his paintings. He had this knack of bringing everything to life. I saw a picture of the sea he did once and you could almost imagine that the canvas was wet, it was so realistic.'

'Mm.' Beth's face split in a grin as she noted the colour that had crept into Kate's cheeks. 'And was this Matthew *just* a friend?'

'Of course he was,' Nuala chimed in. 'Me an' Kate didn't have no time for boyfriends. We was always too busy lookin' after me da.' The colour had risen in Nuala's face too, but whereas on Kate it looked becoming, on Nuala it only seemed to emphasise her spotty skin.

'Well, it's lovely to hear from him. But I think it's time you and I tidied these pots away and got ourselves out job-hunting, don't you?' Kate said as she pushed the letter into the pocket of her skirt.

Beth was well aware that as usual Kate was trying to

cover up for Nuala's bluntness but tactfully let the subject drop.

'There's no need for you to do that, dear,' she told her with a smile. 'You run up and get yourselves ready. I'll see to the pots. I haven't got much else to do, have I?'

Nuala suddenly scraped her chair back and ran from the room with her hand pressed against her mouth.

Kate shook her head. 'Oh dear. She's going to be poorly again. Nuala always does that when she gets nervous. It's this job-hunting that's done it. She's worried because . . . Well, she's fairly limited in what she can do. She's never been too good at reading and writing, and she's scared of mixing with people she doesn't know.'

Beth frowned as she saw Nuala's wobbling rear end disappear up the staircase. 'Mm . . . Well try not to worry, dear. I'm sure there will be something for her.' She could have said a lot more, but felt it was too early to voice her opinion just yet.

Kate meanwhile had begun to load the breakfast pots onto a tray.

'Leave it, Kathleen. I told you I'd do it,' her aunt told her indulgently.

'You'll do no such thing,' Kate argued. 'You've gone to all the trouble of cooking it, so the least I can do is clear away. Now you sit there. I reckon you might squeeze another cup out of the pot if you're lucky. I'll have this lot cleared in no time.' With a worried glance in the direction her sister had taken she lifted the tray and disappeared off into the kitchen leaving Beth to frown thoughtfully into her cup.

The girls had been with her for two weeks and up until now she had managed to persuade Kate to put off looking for a job until they had settled in. In the short time that she'd known her, Beth had come to realise that Kate was much like her mother in nature, and that once she had made her mind up to something, nothing would change it. Her eyes went to the ceiling where she could hear Nuala pottering about her bedroom. From the little she'd gleaned from them since their arrival it appeared that Nuala had borne the brunt of Liam's wrath. She could sympathise with her for that, but it seemed that Kate had taken on the role of being Nuala's protector.

Sadness tempered with guilt flooded through her. She had taken to Kate straight away; her smiling eyes and her gentle nature would have made it hard not to. But Nuala was a different kettle of fish entirely. Beth was trying to like her, but the girl didn't make it easy. In fact, there were times when her aunt felt like screaming at her for her selfishness. She had Kate running around after her, fetching and carrying like an idiot. But then, once they both got themselves a job no doubt things would change, and hopefully for the better.

Nuala might come out of her shell and be less reliant on Kate when she made some friends of her own – that was if, God forbid, what she suspected wasn't right. Pushing the disturbing suspicions she was having to the back of her mind, Beth Summers determined once again that she would make more of an effort with the girl. After all, the poor soul hadn't had much of a chance with that great bully of a father making her life a misery up to now. Perhaps she could take her shopping for some new clothes, or make an appointment for her at the hairdresser's. Yes. She would suggest it to Nuala at the first opportunity.

* * *

'So when do you start then?' Beth asked brightly.

'Next Monday,' Nuala replied, as her eye twitched nervously.

'And you, Kathleen?'

'I can start on Monday too, though we won't be in the same factory.'

Both girls had managed to secure themselves a job in the nearby town of Hinckley in the hosiery factories. Nuala was to start at Fludes and Kate would be just around the corner at Bennets. Beth actually thought it was a good thing that they wouldn't be working together, although she didn't say it, of course.

'We'll be able to travel on the same bus there and back though,' Kate told her as she poured tea into her aunt's pretty china cups through a strainer. 'The wages aren't brilliant for a start, particularly as neither of us has any experience, so I might look round for a little part-time evening job too.'

'I wouldn't be too happy about that, dear,' Beth said immediately. 'There's still no sign of those two poor young women who went missing earlier in the year, and I'd worry myself sick if you were wandering about at night all on your own. The whole town was *teeming* with Bobbies for weeks after they went missing, but it's just as if they'd dropped off the face of the earth.'

'Of course it's terrible,' Kate admitted, 'but you know – if I'm working somewhere local I'll only have to walk home. It's not as if I'll be wandering the streets.'

Kate was almost twenty, so if she had decided that was what she wanted to do, there wasn't much she could do about it, Beth thought.

'Try and find somewhere close then, so that you don't

have too far to come,' she urged. 'The nights will be starting to draw in soon and it'll be dark for four in the afternoon before you know it.'

Kate felt a surge of love rush through her as she looked into her aunt's troubled eyes. She was fidgeting with the string of pearls she was so fond of wearing, and it was more than obvious that her concern was genuine. Kate had never had anyone to worry about her before and found that she quite liked it.

On 3 July 1954, Beth sat with the girls as they watched the women on the black and white television set tearing up their ration books in Trafalgar Square in London.

'About time too,' Beth commented. 'It took the government long enough, didn't it? Fifteen years it is since the damn war started.'

The girls had not long been in from work and had just finished their tea. Kate had settled well into her new job. She was training to be an overlocker. Around the corner at Fludes, Nuala was training to be a packer and hating it, as she told them every single night. Rather than bring her out of her shell as her aunt had hoped it would, it seemed to have had the opposite effect; if anything, Nuala was even more withdrawn. She didn't find it easy to mix with the other girls, who teased her about her accent and her unfashionable clothes. Her aunt had offered to take her shopping on more than one occasion, but Nuala had steadfastly refused. She didn't seem to want to go anywhere unless Kate was with her, and had even had a tantrum one evening when Kate had suggested going out with some friends she'd made at work.

'But Nuala, we're only going to the Palace to see a film,' Kate had pointed out. 'You could come with us if you liked.'

'Why can't you and I go on our own?' Nuala pouted.

Kate looked torn as her aunt observed them silently, praying that Kate would stand her ground. In her opinion, it was high time Kate made friends and had some time for herself, but Nuala's tears worked, as usual.

'Oh, all right then. You and I will go on our own.'

Beth had sighed inwardly but said not a word. She already knew that once Kate had made her mind up, wild horses wouldn't change it.

'Anything for me?' Kate asked as she looked up from the newspaper she was reading.

Nuala shook her head, and after sifting through the mail, handed the letters to her aunt. She'd taken to collecting the mail from the doormat every morning now, and Kate wondered if she was perhaps waiting for a letter from someone? Kate stifled her disappointment. Matthew had been writing regularly until a couple of weeks ago, and then the letters had just stopped coming. Perhaps he didn't receive my last one, she thought to herself, and determined that she would write to him again just in case.

'Come on then, you two,' Aunt Beth said brightly. 'You'll miss your bus and be late for work if you mess about for much longer.'

Kate hastily drained the tea in her cup as her aunt sniffed her disapproval. 'I don't know how you're supposed to get through the day on just a slice of toast and a cup of tea,' she commented.

72

Laughing, Kate snatched up her new swing coat. It was bright red and set off her dark hair and eyes to perfection. The September mornings could be nippy now so she had treated herself the weekend before, which was a rare occurrence as she usually spent any spare money she had on her sister or little treats for her aunt.

'Come on, Nuala,' she urged. 'As Aunt Beth says, if we don't get a shifty on we'll be late.'

Nuala stirred lethargically in the chair she had dropped into after fetching the mail from the doormat. 'I don't think I'll turn in today, I feel a bit sick,' she muttered.

Nuala had never made a secret of the fact that she hated her job, but just lately she had lost so much time that Kate was worried she might get the sack.

'Why don't you take a couple of aspirins?' she suggested hopefully. 'By the time we get to work you might be feeling better.'

'No, I think I'll go back to bed till it's gone off.' Nuala moved towards the stairs as Kate and her aunt exchanged a worried glance.

'They'll be giving her the heave-ho if she doesn't pull her socks up soon,' Aunt Beth said drily. Kate was in full agreement but she had no time to comment now if she was to catch her bus, so instead she pecked her aunt on the cheek and headed for the door.

On the way to the bus stop she wondered what Nuala would do with herself all day. Probably just stay in bed as she had taken to doing of late, she supposed. She sighed; she'd hoped that once they had settled in at Aunt Beth's that Nuala would make an effort to get out and about and make a few friends, but as yet there was no sign of her even trying to. She could understand Nuala being withdrawn when they had lived in Durham with their father. He had made her life a misery, but Aunt Beth had gone out of her way to make them feel welcome and still Nuala kept herself to herself.

There was nothing she could do about it for now so shrugging she hurried on her way.

That evening she arrived home to the mouth-watering smell of a beef stew simmering on the stove.

'Something smells good. I'm so hungry I could eat a horse,' she called as she hung her coat over the bottom of the banister.

Aunt Beth's head popped around the kitchen door. 'I'm glad to hear it. I've got enough in this pan to feed a regiment, which is just as well as David's calling in on his way home from work and he could eat stew till it came out of his ears.'

Kate managed to keep her smile in place although she didn't relish David's visits at all. He still seemed to think that Kate and Nuala intended to cheat him out of his inheritance and whenever they were together, despite all Kate's attempts to befriend him, the atmosphere was strained to say the very least.

'How has Nuala been?' she enquired as she joined her aunt in the kitchen.

'Can't say as I've seen that much of her, to be honest,' Beth replied. 'She's kept to her room for most of the day. She must have played that damn Chuck Berry record a thousand times. I feel about ready to smash the thing in two. I did ask her if she fancied popping into town with me to do a bit of shopping but she didn't want to come.'

'Aunt Beth, I thought I told you that *I'd* do the

shopping. You know your arthritis has got worse now that the weather's turned colder,' Kate scolded.

Beth grinned good-naturedly. 'Oh, stop fretting. I only picked up a few bits and pieces. To be honest, I fancied some fresh air. I might even take myself off to church tonight. Why don't you come along? The only time you ever get out is to go to work or fetch shopping for me. It might do you good.'

'I may just do that,' Kate replied, and then hurried away to set the table as her aunt dished out the dinner.

As they came out of Shepperton Church later that evening, Kate shuddered and drew up her coat collar. A fine misty drizzle had set in and the wind had turned cold. She had accompanied her aunt to church on a number of occasions since she'd lived in Nuneaton and thought the church was wonderful from the very first time she had set foot through the door. On a Sunday morning she liked to sit and watch the way the light caught and reflected the beautiful colours in the stained-glass windows all around the walls. At night, the many candles scattered around cast their own spell. Her grand-parents were buried in the churchyard and the first time her aunt had taken her to place flowers on their graves, Kate had been overcome by sadness to think that she'd never had the chance to know them. Her Uncle William, Aunt Beth's late husband, was also buried there and so it was natural that Aunt Beth often took flowers to place on his grave following the service.

Tonight was no exception, despite the bitterly cold weather, and after the service was over they turned as one and picked their way through the gravestones. The ground underfoot was sodden, and Kate felt the dampness seep into her shoes and chill her feet to the bone. It was as her aunt was bending to place the flowers on her uncle's grave that a movement from the corner of her eye made her jump. Some yards away, a faint light was glowing in the darkness.

'What's that?' She shook her aunt's arm, her eyes wide, and as Beth followed Kate's frightened gaze and peered into the darkness, she grinned from ear to ear.

'It's all right, dear. You haven't seen a ghost. It's the gravedigger. He always works at night to get the grave ready for the next day.'

'Ugh! How awful,' Kate remarked.

'Yes, well, awful it might be but somebody's got to do it, haven't they? Pity the poor devil who he's digging it for though, that's what I say.' Taking Kate's arm she led her away through the churchyard to the comforting street-lights of Coventry Road.

Chapter Seven

Susan Wiltshire tied the knot of her brightly coloured headsquare more tightly beneath her chin. With her head bent against the driving rain she then turned from the streetlights of Heath End Road onto the unlit stretch of lane that led down to Bermuda village, shuddering as the rain found its way beneath her coat collar and trickled down her neck. When she'd set out earlier in the evening the rain had been no more than a drizzle, but now it was coming down in sheets. Still, she comforted herself, only a few more orders to collect now and then she could get home to her fireside.

She sighed; no doubt she would be going back to an empty house again. Her son Simon would probably be out with his mates somewhere. Simon was beginning to worry her lately. Ever since his father had left them for that little floozy of a secretary of his six months before, Simon seemed to have gone off the rails. He had taken to dressing in the Teddy Boy outfits that were becoming so popular amongst the young men. But then – he was only fifteen and she supposed it was normal for him to want to spread his wings a little. It was shortly after Barry had left them that she had taken this job, delivering Avon books and taking the orders for cosmetics and toiletries from housewives. Even now in the fifties, married women were still expected to stay at home and keep house, but with the war nearly a decade behind them they were beginning to become more fashion-conscious and take more care over their make-up. She herself had stayed at home and played the dutiful wife until Barry had left her, but now the little extra she earned was needed. She cursed as she stepped into a deep puddle in the darkness. In the distance she could see the lights of the cottages twinkling far beneath her in the valley. Bermuda village consisted mainly of pit cottages, although odd new houses were now beginning to spring up on the outskirts of the village.

The sound of a car behind her made her step up onto the grassy kerb and pause. That was all she needed now, for a car to spray her with muddy water; she was wet enough as it was. She watched the car headlights approaching but then suddenly they were switched off and she found herself in total darkness again. She decided it was probably some courting couple stopping in a lay-by for a bit of a kiss and a cuddle.

She splashed on, her wet shoes squelching as she went. A lock of dark hair escaped her scarf and she reached up a mittened hand to swipe it away. There was nothing to be heard but the sound of the rain bouncing off the road, so when someone suddenly placed their hand on her shoulder and swung her about, she screamed in shock.

'What the—' She had no time to say any more for strong hands were propelling her towards the hedge at the side of the road. The bag of Avon books she was carrying flew into the air and landed in the deep puddles.

And then suddenly, like an answer to a prayer, yet more car lights sliced through the darkness coming from the direction of the village. The rough grip on her arms immediately loosened and she slid to the ground as heavy footsteps pounded away from her. Crawling into the middle of the road she held her hand up and seconds later the approaching car slewed to a halt in front of her. A man and a woman spilled out of either side of it and helping hands reached out to the woman, who was obviously in deep shock.

'Eeh, me love. Whatever's happened to yer?' A woman's voice came to her but the scream that Susan had been trying to emit seemed to be stuck in her throat.

Gasping for breath, she pointed over her shoulder and as they all peered in that direction they heard the sound of a car engine start up and reverse erratically away up the lane.

'Perverted bugger. Lucky we come along when we did, love, eh?' The man seemed to realise what had happened. 'Now lean on me an' we'll get yer down to the Manor Hospital an' get yer checked over. Happen we should get 'em to call the coppers an' all. It comes to sommat when a woman can't walk home at night in safety.'

The rescuers helped Susan into the back of the car and the woman climbed in beside her and tried to rub some warmth into her frozen hands as her husband started the car engine.

'Here, our George. You don't think that weirdo were owt to do wi' them other poor girls that went missin', do yer?'

Shrugging, he steered the car into the middle of the

79

lane. 'No way o' tellin', our Flo. Let's just be thankful we come along when we did.'

Shivering uncontrollably, Susan offered up a silent prayer of thanks.

Chapter Eight

'Good God above! Look at this.' Beth shook the evening newspaper she was reading at Kate, who had just come in from work. 'It says that *another* woman was attacked last night. Up Bermuda way, this time. Ugh, and just to think we went to church last night. We might have passed whoever it was that did it. In fact, it could have been one of the congregation.'

'That's highly unlikely,' Kate objected. 'Whoever it is that's doing this seems to target women who are alone. And anyway, there's nothing to suggest that this has anything to do with the other two disappearances. This woman hasn't disappeared, has she?'

'No,' Beth admitted reluctantly, intent on believing the worst. 'But there's no saying she *wouldn't* have done, if a couple in a car hadn't come along when they did. According to this, that's what made the man run off. Apparently she was out delivering Avon books and they found those floating in puddles all across the road leading down to Bermuda village.'

'Well, at least all's well that ends well this time, so stop worrying about it, eh?' A cold shiver had run up

Kate's spine and hoping to change the subject, she asked, 'Where's Nuala?'

Her aunt thumbed towards the ceiling. 'Upstairs. A letter came for her just after you'd left for work and I've hardly seen her since, though I have heard her rush along the landing to the bathroom a few times.'

'Right, I'll put the kettle on and then I'll pop up and see that she's all right.' Kate hurried into the kitchen leaving her aunt with a deep frown on her face.

'Pop up and see that she's all right indeed,' she muttered to herself. 'From what I can see of it, she's work-shy. And I have a feeling that that isn't all that's wrong with the little madam!'

After listening to Kate clatter away up the stairs she pulled herself painfully from her chair and went into the kitchen to check on the pork chops that were cooking in the oven.

'Are you all right then, pet? Stomach-ache gone off, has it?' Kate asked as she stuck her head around Nuala's bedroom door. Nuala started guiltily before looking hastily away. Kate could see at a glance that her sister had been crying, so she went over and slung her arm protectively around the girl's plump shoulders.

'What's wrong?'

Nuala looked miserably up at Kate. 'I had a letter come this mornin'. It's over there. You'd best look at it.'

Kate rose from the bed and crossed to the dressing-table where she took up the letter and began to read. When she had done so she looked across at Nuala.

'So – you've got the sack then?'

Shame-faced, Nuala hung her head. 'Looks like it.'

'Well, I can't pretend to be surprised.' Kate wiped a weary hand across her brow. 'Your timekeeping has hardly been exemplary since you started there, has it?'

''Tain't my fault if I ain't been well,' Nuala whined.

'I didn't *say* it was your fault,' Kate retorted, trying hard to keep her patience. 'But the thing is, we need to pay our way. It looks like I'll *have* to get a part-time job now to keep us going until you can find something else.'

'Aunt Beth wouldn't mind if you gave her a bit less,' Nuala muttered sullenly.

'No, I dare say she wouldn't, *but I would*.' Kate was having to work very hard to keep her temper now, and before Nuala could utter so much as another word, she turned and left the room.

When Kate re-entered the lounge, Beth patted the seat at the side of her. Once her niece was seated, she tried to think of how best to broach the suspicion that was foremost in her mind.

'Trouble, is there?' she enquired.

'I'm afraid so. You may as well know – the letter that Nuala had today was one giving her the sack.'

'I see.' Beth struggled to find the right words. 'Kathleen . . . if what I suspect is true, then I'm afraid that will be the least of your troubles.'

'What do you mean?'

Her aunt gulped and took a deep breath before going on. 'Haven't you noticed how much weight Nuala is putting on, and how often she's being sick?'

Kate's eyebrows met as she thought on her aunt's comment. 'Nuala has always had a weight problem right since she was child. It's just puppy fat. I'm sure she'll start to lose it soon.'

'Oh no, she won't, not if my suspicions are correct. You see, dear, I hate to say this . . . but I think Nuala may be having a baby.'

'WHAT!' Kate stared at her aunt as if she had taken leave of her senses. 'How can you even *think* such a thing? Nuala never sets foot out of the house except to go to work – when she *does* bother to go to work, that is. And even when we lived in Durham she only ever went out to deliver groceries . . .' Her lips clamped together as a terrifying possibility occurred to her.

'You don't think someone took advantage of her, do you? What I mean is, she *did* go out each day delivering groceries when we lived with our dad, and with her being as vulnerable as she is . . . Well, someone could have forced her or—'

Her aunt's head wagged from side to side, setting her grey curls bobbing. 'I don't know, dear. But think about it – the sudden weight gain, being tired all the time, the constant vomiting, and . . . Well, I've seen enough pregnant women in my time to recognise the signs. Perhaps it's time you had a little talk to her?'

Kate nodded numbly and without another word rose from her aunt's side and with her heart pounding, went to confront her sister.

'There's absolutely no doubt about it,' the doctor told Kate gently the following day as he turned away from Nuala, who was lying on the examination couch. 'I would say that your sister is at least four months' pregnant.'

Shock rendered Kate temporarily speechless as Nuala clambered from the couch and hastily began to dress.

'I'll make an appointment for the midwife and she'll arrange for the ante-natal care. Everything seems to be in order and . . .' The doctor's voice droned on and on, but Kate didn't hear him. *A baby!* Nuala was going to have a baby! The words swam round and round in her head, shutting out everything else. How would they manage – what would Aunt Beth say? And who was the father?

For once, it was Nuala who took Kate's arm and led her outside. It was there on the pavement that Kate's shock gave way to anger.

'Who did this to you, Nuala?' she demanded.

Nuala looked down and began to cry as Kate's anger grew.

'I said – *who did this to you*?' She was shaking the girl's arm like a dog might shake a rabbit, and Nuala's tears turned to sobs.

'I . . . I don't know,' she sniffled.

'Of course you bloody well know! Now come on – *who was it*?'

Terror rushed through Nuala's veins. Never in her whole life had she known Kate to shout at her as she was doing now. Eventually she took a deep breath and muttered miserably, 'It was . . .'

'*Yes?*'

'It was . . . Matthew.'

Kate dropped her hand as if it had been stung. Matthew! Her heart was crying although her eyes were dry as she stared at her sister incredulously.

'Why are you looking at me like that?' Nuala sobbed. 'Don't you believe me? Well, it's the *truth*. Why do you think he stopped writing to you all of a sudden?'

Kate felt as if her whole world was falling apart. Matthew had told her he loved her when all the time he was . . . She started to walk away, leaving Nuala to hurry along behind her. Nuala was soon breathless as she tried to keep up with her.

'I . . . I'm sorry, Kate – but it will be all right, won't it?' Ever since she was a little girl, Kate had always made everything all right for her, but this time there was no reply and Kate stormed on.

'Kate, *please*.' Nuala was sobbing so loudly now that people were looking at them, but for once Kate didn't care. Her face looked like a thundercloud about to break as she tried to digest what the doctor and Nuala had told her. Just how the hell was she supposed to support a baby *and* Nuala? And how was Aunt Beth going to cope, with a baby in the house? As for Matthew . . . *Oh Matthew,* her heart wept. *How could you have done this to me?*

When Nuala tried to drag her to a halt the anger suddenly dispersed as quickly as it had come, to be replaced by utter despair. Kate paused to look at her sister and when she saw the tears spurting from her eyes she gently stroked her cheek.

'Come on.' Her voice was full of sorrow. 'We'd better go and tell Aunt Beth and get it over with. Then we have to decide what we're going to do.'

'Do you think she'll kick us out?' Terror made Nuala's voice quiver.

A vision of Aunt Beth's genteel face swam before Kate's eyes. 'No, I don't think she will, but there's only one way to find out, isn't there?' They continued on in silence.

* * *

'*What?*' David gripped the edge of the table so tightly that his knuckles showed white as he stared at Kate, appalled. 'Nuala is WHAT?'

Kate stood her ground and continued to look him in the eye, although inside she was shaking.

'I think you heard what I said, David.' Her voice was dignified. 'I'm sorry – we're both sorry – but there's nothing we can do about it now, is there?'

Flinging himself away from the table, he began to pace up and down the room, running his hand through his hair as Aunt Beth wrung her own hands in distress.

He looked accusingly at his mother. 'Why didn't you tell me this before? And what do you intend to do about it?'

'Well, as Kate said, there isn't much I *can* do about it now.'

'Oh yes, there bloody well *is*!' he spluttered. 'You can put her out on the street where she obviously belongs. She must have the morals of an alley cat. No ring on her finger and a baby in her belly. What do you think the neighbours are going to say?'

Beth suddenly drew herself up to her full height as anger overcame her distress.

'David, I will *not* have you using bad language in my house. Do you hear me? *This is my house.* Therefore it is up to me who does or doesn't live in it. And as for the neighbours, it's been a long time since I worried about what they may say. I know Nuala has been – shall we say, foolish? – but from past experience I also know that this will be a nine-day wonder. She isn't the first and she won't be the last to get herself into this position. In fact, if I remember rightly, your firstborn appeared seven and a half months after your wedding, didn't she?'

David looked as if he were about to explode. 'Lucy was premature,' he snapped.

Beth sniffed. 'Yes, well, that's a matter of opinion. If she was, then she's the only premature baby I know of that weighed almost eight pounds. But that's by the by. Kate and Nuala are living with me and I say they stay!'

David's fists clenched and unclenched as he faced his mother. His mouth worked as if he were about to say something, but then changing his mind he turned on his heel and slammed from the room.

Beth stood as if she were cast in stone until she heard his car start up and roar away down the cul-de-sac. Then her shoulders suddenly sagged and she sank down onto the settee.

'Oh, Aunt Beth, I'm so very sorry.' Kate was distraught that she and Nuala were the cause of coming between a mother and her son, but her aunt smiled at her kindly as she fidgeted nervously with her pearls.

'Don't be, dear. I'm afraid David has been asking to be put in his place for some time now. He's changed since he married Rebecca. Got ideas above his station. She came from a very good family, you see. Not that David ever went without. His father adored him and worked every hour God sent to give him a good education. William never admitted that he was sad that we couldn't have more children, but I know he was. That's why he spoiled David shamelessly. Don't get me wrong. Your cousin is not a bad man at heart. He just tries to live up to what Rebecca thinks he should be. I don't agree with it myself. I'm the old-fashioned sort and believe that the man should wear the trousers. Still, what he does in his own house is his concern. What I do in my house is mine.'

Nuala rose clumsily from her chair at the side of the fire and sloped away as Beth looked at Kate with open affection shining in her eyes.

'Please don't get worrying about it, dear. You have enough on your plate as it is. Just know that you're not alone. A baby costs money and there I *can* help out. I have a little put aside for a rainy day and what better way to spend it than on a new baby, eh? We'll get by, you'll see, and sod what the neighbours say.'

Kate smiled through her tears at her aunt's uncharacteristic use of bad language and in that moment she wondered how she had ever lived without her.

The September rains gave way to bitterly cold October winds. Nuala had made no move towards finding another job; as Kate had pointed out, it hardly seemed worth it now. Kate had been half hoping to find them a flat or a house to rent. Aunt Beth's arthritis had become worse as the weather deteriorated, and she worried that having them there was too much for her. Kate also worried about how she herself would cope when the baby was born; she had no choice but to work and didn't want her aunt to have to take on the responsibility of looking after a child. She hadn't said as much to her, of course, because she knew that if she had, Aunt Beth would have protested. As things were, it was taking her all her time to pay board for both herself and Nuala, so the twelve and sixpence rent that was being asked for an average house was way beyond her for now.

She peered at her aunt out of the corner of her eye.

They were watching the evening news on the BBC and her aunt was tutting at the dock strike that had cut sea trade by half. Nuala was upstairs in her room and Kate could faintly hear her Bill Haley and the Comets record through the ceiling.

After waiting until the news had finished she said tentatively, 'I've got the chance of a part-time evening job if I want it.'

Aunt Beth's knitting needles stopped clicking. 'Where's that then?' she asked.

'Just along Coton Road at the Rose and Crown.' Kate held her breath as she waited for her aunt to erupt. She didn't have to wait long.

'*In a pub?*'

'Yes, in a pub. What's wrong with that?'

'Well . . .' Aunt Beth racked her brain to come up with a suitable argument, but when she could think of none, she shrugged. 'I just don't see you as a barmaid, that's all. Have you ever had any experience?'

'No, I haven't,' Kate admitted with her head held high. 'But I'm not stupid and I'll soon pick it up. I can give you a bit more board then, and I'll be able to get together the things we'll need for when the baby comes.'

'Huh! If that's the reason you're going then you can forget it. You do more than enough for me as it is. Not like—' She had been about to say, 'not like that idle little madam upstairs', but managed to stop herself.

'Look, Aunt Beth, it's only along the road. It can't be more than a five-minute walk from here,' Kate pointed out. 'We could really do with the extra money with Christmas coming up and the baby. And besides, it will get me out a bit. You're always telling me I should go out more and meet people. And where better to do that than in a pub?'

When Beth looked at it that way she had to grudgingly agree, and if Kate had to do it, it *was* nice and close. 'I suppose there is that in it,' she admitted, and so it was decided.

The landlady at the Rose and Crown took to Kate immediately, as did the customers. Vera was a large woman with a brash manner and a quick tongue, but beneath it beat a heart of gold, as Kate was soon to discover. Bill, the landlord, was small in size compared to his wife and could drink the customers under the table if given half a chance. He did not suffer fools gladly, which was why there was rarely any trouble in the pub, although when there was, Bill would escort the guilty parties to the door with a strength that belied his small stature. And then of course, there was Ruby Bannister, the cleaning lady. She was usually just leaving as Kate arrived for her shift, but always took the trouble to stop and ask how she was. Ruby loved bright clothes and large dangly earrings, and Kate was completely intrigued by her. Kate found it impossible to judge how old Ruby might be; she had fair hair spattered with a sprinkling of white and her face was etched with lines. And yet, her eyes were still bright and sparkled when she smiled, which led Kate to believe that she wasn't perhaps as old as she appeared. Ruby was a small, frail-looking woman, yet as Vera was often heard to affectionately say, she had a mouth on her like a parish oven and the language that frequently spewed out of it was enough to turn the air blue.

Kate had been working at the pub for almost a month

now and the two women were easy with each other. They were preparing to open one evening when Kate remarked, 'Ruby's a bit of a character, isn't she?'

'You can say that again,' Vera chuckled. 'I must admit when she first came after the job I took one look at her an' thought she'd never manage it. She looks as if one good puff o' wind could blow her away like a feather. But I've been forced to eat me words. Keeps this place like a new pin, she does, though her language can turn the air blue, as you've probably noticed. She had a bit of a reputation for the men too at one time, so I admit I was a bit cautious about takin' her on. But then my motto is everyone deserves a chance an' she turned out to be a little gem.' Vera paused in the act of restocking the bottled beers to smile at Kate kindly. 'All in all, I'd have to say I'm quite lucky with me staff at present. Credit where it's due, you never pretended to have any experience when you applied for the job, but you've took to it like a duck to water. The customers love you, an' it's nice to have a smiley, pretty face behind the bar.'

Kate flushed with pleasure at the praise. She was enjoying working there immensely. It took less than ten minutes to walk home after closing time and with the extra money she had earned Kate had already made a good start on her Christmas shopping although it was only early in November. All in all, things were looking up. At least, most things were. As yet, Nuala had made no effort at all to get on better with Aunt Beth. In fact, sometimes she was downright rude to her, and the more the child inside her grew, the more she kept to her room. The woman who had been attacked in Bermuda Road had caused a stir in the town and had scared Nuala, who was of a nervous disposition anyway, to the point that she was almost afraid to walk beyond the end of the garden path without her big sister at her side.

For weeks the town had been teeming with policeman brought in from other areas to investigate the attack, but as yet they had come up with nothing despite all their efforts.

Kate and Vera returned to their task of restocking the shelves before the customers started to arrive, and very soon the doors were opened and they were both busy pulling pints. It was almost ten o'clock when a tall fair-haired man entered and approached the bar.

'A pint, is it?' Kate smiled, feeling colour flood into her cheeks for no reason that she could explain. He was a good-looking man, not quite handsome, but there was something about him that immediately appealed to her.

'Yes, please.'

Placing a brimming glass in front of him she smiled at him disarmingly. 'That'll be one and tuppence, please.'

He fumbled in his smart jacket pocket for some coins and as Kate stood at the shiny brass till getting his change, she could feel his eyes boring into her back. When she placed the change from a silver half a crown back into his hand he asked, 'New here, are you?'

She nodded. 'Fairly new. I've been here for about a month now, but I don't think I've seen you in here before, have I?'

He grinned, showing off a set of gleaming white teeth. 'I don't get out much,' he told her, but there was no time for him to say any more because at that moment a regular approached the bar with an empty glass, and after flashing the man an apologetic smile, Kate hurried away to serve him.

After the last of the customers had left, Vera and Kate were clearing the dirty glasses into the sink when Vera looked across at her and grinned.

'Met our local heart-throb then, have you?'

Kate raised her eyebrows in confusion as Vera giggled. 'Martin Denby. The tall fair-haired bloke that came in just before closin' time. He only stayed for the one. Nice-lookin' bit o' stuff though, ain't he?'

'Can't say as I really noticed,' Kate mumbled.

Vera looked over her shoulder to wink at Bill. 'Yer must be the only woman in the pub as didn't then. Got a bit of a followin', that bloke has. Not that he ever takes up any of the offers. I've seen women set their caps at him time an' time again, but he don't seem interested. Hardly surprisin', I suppose. He's a widower. Lost his wife a couple of years ago, by all accounts. I reckon I heard someone say that he had a son an' all, though I don't know if there's any truth in it.'

Kate's kind heart was instantly saddened. How awful it must have been for him, she thought, to lose his wife so young, and she must have been young because he didn't look much over thirty or so himself.

'Live round here, does he?' she asked, trying not to sound overly interested.

'I think he lives in Heath End Road,' Vera replied as her face creased into a smile. 'Bit of a Jekyll and Hyde though, if his jobs are anything to go by.'

When Kate looked bemused, Vera leaned closer. 'In the day he works in the offices at the Union Wool and Leather. Smart as a new pin he looks in his nice suit and collar and tie. But by night . . .' She put her hand across her mouth to stifle a giggle as Kate gazed at her curiously. 'By night he's a gravedigger up at Shepperton Churchyard.'

'You're joking!' Kate gasped in disbelief.

'No, I ain't. Cross me heart an' hope to die – pardon the pun. It's as true as I'm standin' here. The day before a funeral, the young curate at Shepperton rings him up an' gives him the measurements of the poor unfortunate sod that's to be buried, then along goes our man that night to dig the grave.' A shudder made her plump bosoms almost bounce out of her low-cut top. 'Still . . .' She sniffed. 'I suppose somebody's got to do it, an' I dare say the poor bloke needs the extra money if he has a youngster to support.'

Noting Kate's horrified expression she grinned and reached across to pat her hand. 'That's enough o' that talk for tonight, eh? You've gone as white as a sheet an' I don't want that aunt o' yours to accuse me of givin' yer nightmares. You get yourself off home now, I can finish up here.'

'Are you quite sure?'

'Of course I am. Now – would you like Bill to walk yer home? It ain't safe for a young girl like you to be wanderin' the streets on her own of a night with all these young women going missing an' bein' attacked.'

Kate looked across at Bill, who was slouched on a stool at the counter. He had spent most of the night laughing with the customers about the portrait that Graham Sutherland had painted of Sir Winston Churchill. Sir Winston was reported to be deeply unhappy about the painting. But then, as Bill had noisily pointed out, he *was* eighty years old, so how had he expected to look? He had consumed so much beer that night that Kate wondered if he would manage the stairs to bed, let alone walk her home.

'No, I'll be fine really,' she replied. 'It's only a stone's throw to my aunt's and Coton Road is well lit.'

'Mm, well don't get dawdlin' on the way then,' Vera advised.

Kate shrugged her arms into her smart new coat and within minutes was out on the pavement and she heard Vera locking the doors behind her. The cold November night air snatched at her lungs and she shivered. A thick frost had coated the pavements and as she picked her way carefully along she cursed herself for choosing to wear high heels. They made a tap-tap-tapping noise and she found herself looking nervously back across her shoulder. The man she had spoken to earlier in the night must have been the very same man who had been digging the grave on the night she had attended church with her aunt. She shuddered again, but this time it was nothing to do with the coldness of the night. A full moon sailed from behind the clouds, making the pavements appear as if they had been sprinkled with fairy dust. Kate hastened on, intent on getting home to the comfort of her bed, studiously ignoring the tombstones in Our Lady of the Angels Catholic churchyard as she passed.

From the front bedroom window, Beth watched as Kate turned into the road and hurried towards the house. She sighed with relief. Every night since Kate had started at the Rose and Crown she had kept the very same vigil until the girl returned safe and sound. The glow from the streetlamps was turning Kate's hair to deepest ebony, and as Beth looked down on her she looked so like her mother, Jenny, that Beth's heart ached. She still missed her sister, and cursed the day Jenny had met Liam Cleary. They had been a happy family unit until then, but he had swept Jenny off her feet and back to Ireland where he had made her life hell until . . . She pushed the memories away. Even now, after all this time, they were too painful to remember.

When Jenny had first married Liam she had been much the same nature as Kate was now – kindly but spirited – but Liam had soon knocked that out of her, until she became little more than a terrified wreck, too afraid to open her mouth. The sound of Kate pushing the front gate open brought Beth's thoughts sharply back to the present as she hastily stepped away from the window. Ah well, at least she had Kate now. Guilt stabbed at her. Perhaps she should feel the same way about Nuala, but somehow she couldn't.

The girl had had a bad time of it admittedly, but sometimes Beth had the urge to shake her and tell her to pull herself together. Since discovering she was pregnant, Nuala had become even more demanding, if that was possible, relying on Kate for everything. And Kate, being the kindly soul that she was, allowed it to continue. On a couple of occasions Beth had tactfully tried to broach the subject, but Nuala had rounded on her and told her to mind her own business in no uncertain terms, which only went to confirm what Beth had originally thought. Nuala wasn't quite the vulnerable little soul that Kate took her for; she could also be very manipulative and conniving.

Although Beth had been completely against Kate taking the job at the Rose and Crown at the start, she was glad now that she had. At least it gave her an excuse to get out without Nuala tagging along all the time, though whether or not it would continue once the baby arrived was another matter. She heard the key in the front door and then Kate's light footsteps on the stairs. Holding her breath, she waited and sure enough, seconds later Nuala's bedroom door creaked open and her voice carried along the landing. 'Will you come and talk to me for a while, Kate?'

'Ssh,' she heard Kate whisper. 'You'll wake Aunt Beth.'

Beth was aware that Kate had been up since six that morning and out of the house for seven. She had then rushed home from her factory job, had her meal and washed and changed before shooting off to the pub. Beth knew that she must be tired out, yet still she heard Nuala's bedroom door click shut as Kate followed her inside.

Crossing to the bed she lifted the blankets and slipped inside, shivering as the cold cotton sheets settled around her. One of these days that little madam will get her comeuppance, she thought, and turning on her side she tried to lose her thoughts in sleep.

'Why, Nuala, it looks absolutely lovely.' Kate stared in awe at the beautiful Christmas tree as Nuala flushed with pleasure at the praise.

'Credit where it's due, she's made a grand job of it, hasn't she?' Hands on hips, Aunt Beth smiled.

Kate nodded and after shrugging her arms out of her coat, she hurried to the fire and held her hands out to the comforting blaze. There was just two weeks to go until

Christmas now and the weather was bitterly cold with a hint of snow in the air. The sapphire ring her aunt had given her the week before, for her twentieth birthday, glistened in the light from the fire and she smiled as she admired it.

Beth, who had been unwell with a bad cold and bronchitis for the last few weeks, began to struggle out of her chair. 'Your dinner's in the oven keeping warm. I'll just go and fetch it in for you,' she said, but Kate gently pressed her back into her seat.

'You'll do no such thing. I'm quite capable of fetching it myself. And how have you been today?' She was unable to keep the concern from her voice.

'Oh, fair to middling,' Beth replied brightly. 'This weather doesn't help. But then things could be worse. It'll take more than a touch of arthritis and a bad chest to keep me down. I've still got Christmas shopping to do.'

'There's no need for you to worry about that. You just make me a list and I can do the shopping at the weekend,' Kate said firmly before hurrying away to fetch her meal.

An hour later she stood in front of the mirror above the mantelpiece and patted her hair into place before setting off to her night job.

'Are you sure there's nothing you need before I go?' she asked.

Beth smiled at her fondly. Standing there with her dark hair shining in the glow from the fire, Kate looked so like Jenny that it brought a lump to her throat.

'Not a thing,' she assured her. 'I'm snug as a bug in a rug, though I can't say as you will be by the time you get to the Rose and Crown. It's enough to freeze the hairs off a brass monkey out there so see as you wrap up warm else we'll have you poorly too.'

Kate bent and lightly brushed her aunt's cheek with her lips. 'I shan't be late,' she promised. 'If you do need anything, give Nuala a shout.'

Her aunt nodded, but Kate couldn't fail to see the wry smile that played around her lips.

When she stepped from the house, Kate was brooding. Her aunt was giving her serious cause for concern. She stubbornly refused to see a doctor, despite all Kate's attempts to persuade her to. Kate had begged Nuala to keep an eye on her while she was at work, but Nuala's relationship with her aunt seemed to be going from bad to worse and Kate couldn't help but notice that sometimes the girl was barely even civil to her. As Nuala's stomach had grown she had became almost like a recluse, venturing out of her room only to eat and drink.

Then there was Matthew. Now Kate understood why his letters had just suddenly stopped coming and it still hurt her more than she cared to admit. Her cheeks flamed as she remembered the feel of his lips on hers, but then she gritted her teeth and held her head high. He hadn't cared as much as he had professed to, and now it was obvious why. All the time he had been taking advantage of Nuala.

Immediately her thoughts turned to Martin Denby. He came into the pub twice a week now as regular as clockwork every Tuesday and Thursday, unless he had a grave to dig, that was. She shuddered as much at the thought of it as the cold, but then a smile hovered around her lips. He was a remarkably nice man; a gentleman, in fact. Probably the sort her aunt would approve of.

Not that he had ever asked her out or anything. She wondered what she would do if he did, but didn't have long to ponder on it because in no time at all she was approaching the pub with a hard night's work ahead of her.

It was almost ten o'clock when Kate stifled a yawn. Her eyes were growing heavy and her feet felt as if they were about to drop off. The pub had been unusually busy for a Wednesday night and she was longing for her shift to end as thoughts of the soft feather-bed back at her aunt's floated before her eyes.

Suddenly the door banged open and Nuala erupted into the room. Her mousy hair was dishevelled and her eyes were red-rimmed as they searched the room for her sister.

'Nuala!' Kate came from behind the bar as the pregnant girl clumsily flung herself towards her through the tables and a haze of cigarette smoke. 'Whatever's the matter?'

'It's . . .' Nuala struggled to get her breath as her audience looked on. 'It's Aunt Beth. She took poorly an' I had to go out to the callbox and ring for an ambulance. They've taken her to the Manor Hospital an' we're to go there straight away.'

A cold hand closed around Kate's heart. 'What's wrong with her?' she demanded, shaking Nuala's arm to try and calm her down.

'I don't know – she said earlier on that she had a pain in her chest an' then I heard this bang, bang, bang. I'd come down from my room to get a drink an' when I came out of the kitchen she . . . well, she was lyin' at the bottom of the stairs an' wouldn't say anything, so I rang

101

for an ambulance.' Tears were spurting from Nuala's eyes as Kate stared at her in horror.

Vera, who had heard all that had been said, dragged her eyes from Nuala's swollen stomach and hurried away to fetch Kate's coat without a word. When she returned, she told her, 'Here, love, here's your coat. Would you like me to ring for a taxi or get someone to drive you there?'

Kate had gone as white as a sheet and stood as if in shock as Vera helped her into her coat and pushed her gently towards the door. 'No thanks, Vera, but I'd like to get straight off if you don't mind. I could be there while I'm waiting about for someone to take me.'

'Then ring me as soon as you can, to let me know how she is – an' try not to worry. She'll be fine, you'll see,' Vera told her.

Staring at her blankly, Kate followed Nuala to the door and then they were out in the cold night air and hurrying towards the hospital as if their lives depended on it.

Nuala was soon out of breath and clutching her side. 'Slow down, Kate, I've got a stitch,' she implored, but for once Kate ignored her and hurried on.

Once they had arrived at the hospital and had informed the nurse on the reception desk who they were, they were shown into a small waiting room and told that the doctor, who was still in with their aunt, would join them as soon as possible. Kate began to pace up and down like a caged animal as Nuala slumped in a chair and looked fearfully on. After what seemed an eternity the door opened and a small grey-haired man in a white coat appeared.

'Are you Mrs Summers's next-of-kin?' he asked.

Kate shook her head as she thought of David. 'Well, we are her nieces, but she does have a son,' she told him tremulously.

'Is he on the telephone?' The doctor's voice was kindly as Kate nodded.

'Yes, yes he has a telephone,' she said, 'but I don't have the number with me. How is my aunt?'

The doctor sighed. 'I'm afraid your aunt has suffered a stroke.' He looked at them gravely as shock registered on their faces, wishing for all the world that this shift could be over. Nuala had come to stand behind Kate like a little girl standing behind her mother's skirts, her eyes wide and fearful.

'But she will be all right, won't she?' Kate had to force the words from her lips.

'We can't be sure if she slipped down the stairs and shock and her injuries caused the stroke, or whether she had the stroke and then fell down the stairs,' the man said. 'As regards to whether she will be all right, I'm afraid I can't say at this stage, my dear. The next few hours will be crucial. She broke her leg *and* her hip in the fall. They will be set, of course, and will mend in time but . . . I should warn you, it was quite a severe stroke and even if your aunt does survive, it is highly unlikely she will ever be as she was again.'

'In what way?' Tears were stinging the back of Kate's eyes as she struggled to hold her head high.

'At present she is completely paralysed all down one side of her body. Of course, sometimes stroke victims do regain some feeling, but in a stroke as severe as your aunt's . . .'

'I see.' Kate gulped as the full implications of his

words slowly sank in, then with her usual courage she asked, 'What can we do?'

The doctor looked at her admiringly. 'I should think the first thing you should do is go home and inform your cousin of your aunt's condition, and then I should try to get some sleep. I assure you we are doing all we can and—'

'I'm staying!'

Her stance prevented him from arguing as she turned to her sister. 'Nuala, I want you to take a taxi home and then go out to the callbox to ring David,' she told her. 'And then I want you to make sure that Sally is all right, and stay there till I get home.'

Panic replaced the fear in her sister's eyes. 'But Kate – I can't go home on my own without you.'

'You can and you will,' Kate told her firmly, giving her money for the fare and pennies for the callbox. 'You have to be brave now for me. Aunt Beth can't stay here all alone, can she? And David needs to know what's happened.' Slipping off her coat she draped it around Nuala's shoulders. 'Now don't let me down. You can do this. You'll have Sally there to keep you company and once you've rung David you can go and get yourself off to bed. *Please*, Nuala, do this for me. I'll be home as soon as I possibly can, I promise.'

Sniffing miserably, Nuala nodded and slipped away, leaving Kate alone with the doctor.

'I'd like to see my aunt now,' she informed him.

He spread his hands sadly. 'I'm afraid that won't be possible just yet, my dear, but if you are quite determined to stay I'll have a cup of tea sent in to you and I'll let you know when you can see her.'

'Thank you.' Kate watched as he strode from the room and only then did she give way to her emotions. The doctor had told her that Aunt Beth might die, or at least survive to be a mere shadow of her former self.

She shook her head as a picture of her Aunt Beth's smiling face floated before her eyes. '*No, no!*' she cried aloud at the injustice of it all. For the very first time in her life she had known what it was to have someone other than Nuala to care for her, and she had thrived on it. But now it might be snatched away from right under her nose, and she had known her aunt for such a short time. It was so unfair, but then life *was* unfair – as Kate knew better than most. As she slumped onto a chair, the tears that she had struggled to hold back gushed from her eyes. They came so thick and fast that for a time she couldn't breathe and she had the sensation of drowning, but then she slowly pulled herself together. Aunt Beth *would* survive; she had to, for Kate couldn't envisage life without her now. And once she was well enough, Kate would take her home and nurse her back to health. In a more positive frame of mind, she straightened her back, folded her hands in her lap and watched the minutes tick away on the waiting-room clock.

It was almost twelve-thirty when the door finally swung open again and the doctor she had spoken to earlier reappeared.

'You may see your aunt now,' he informed her kindly. 'She is resting, though I should warn you, she may not know that you're here as she has been very heavily sedated.'

Kate followed him into a corridor that smelled of stale disinfectant and sickness. They passed through swing doors that clanged shut behind them and echoed eerily through the deserted hospital. One corridor gave way to another until at last the man paused in front of the doors that led to the Intensive Care Unit.

'Please try not to be too dismayed at all the tubes and drips,' he told her. 'They are all there for a reason and they actually look far worse than they are.'

Kate gulped and seconds later found herself in a ward where a Sister in a starched white cap hurried forward to meet them.

'Follow me,' she said, and Kate moved forward on feet that suddenly felt as if they were made of lead. When the Sister stopped in front of a bed and bent to stroke an imaginary crease from the sheet that lay across the unfortunate figure lying there, Kate almost cried aloud. Her aunt seemed to have shrunk and looked tiny and insignificant, almost as if she had already passed away. There were tubes and drips hooked up to seemingly every inch of her, and an oxygen mask was fixed across her nose and mouth. Through the mask, Kate could see that her lips were blue, as were the shadows beneath her eyes, and in that moment she felt as if her heart would break. Aunt Beth had aged in just the few short hours since she had last seen her. The only thing recognisable about her was the grey curly hair that lay like a halo about her head on the starched white pillow.

Seeing her distress, the Sister reached across to pat her hand gently. 'Why don't you sit down and hold her hand, my dear? She's very heavily sedated but I'm sure she'll know that you're here.'

Too deep in shock to reply, Kate sank onto the chair that the sister pulled out for her at the side of the bed, and then the nurse and the doctor discreetly faded away, leaving her alone. Dragging her eyes away from her aunt's grey face, she stared fearfully at the monitor at the side of the bed that was recording her heartbeats. Silently she willed it to be stable, realising more than ever in that moment just how very much this dear woman had come to mean to her.

'Please fight, Aunt Beth,' she whispered, as she cradled the blue-veined hand in hers. 'I don't know what I'd do if I were to lose you now, so soon after finding you.'

The only answer was the slow beat of the monitor. Kate lost all sense of time as she sat there, her eyes fixed on her aunt's beloved face. As the sun slowly rose, turning the frosted pavements to glass, exhaustion finally claimed her, and she slept with her head on the side of the bed.

Chapter Nine

The sound of a tea trolley being trundled across the tiled floor made Kate start awake. Blinking in the harsh fluorescent light, she moaned softly as she raised her head from the bed. She had a crick in her neck and her mouth was dry. For a second she was disorientated, but then as she remembered the happenings of the night before, her eyes flew to her aunt's face. Beth was still sleeping, but her lips had lost the bluish tinge that had struck terror into Kate's heart and she looked more peaceful.

'She's had a good night.'

The voice made Kate jump and turning she found a smiling young nurse in a starched white apron standing at her elbow. Kate straightened painfully and returned the smile. 'Sorry, I must have dropped off,' she apologised, as the nurse took a thermometer and advanced on her aunt.

'I should think you did. You've been here all night. You looked so peaceful I didn't like to disturb you. If you'd like to freshen up a bit there's a bathroom just down there.' She pointed to the end of the ward. 'The doctors will be coming on their rounds soon and they'll be able to tell you a bit more about how your aunt is doing.'

Struggling to her feet, Kate was just about to head in the direction of the bathroom when the swing doors that led into the ward flew open and David appeared, looking like an avenging angel. At his side was a cool and elegant woman, and as her eyes settled on Kate she looked her up and down as if there was a bad smell under her nose.

'Just what is going on here?' David ranted. 'Why wasn't I informed of this before?'

'Ssh!' The nurse grasped his elbow and pulled him aside. 'Would you *kindly* keep your voice down, sir? There are a lot of very sick people in here.'

Instantly contrite, David calmed down. 'I'm sorry.' He turned back to Kate and although his eyes were blazing, he kept his voice lowered.

'Why didn't you phone me last night when this happened?' he hissed. 'I only got a call from Nuala about an hour ago. What if my mother had *died*?'

Kate wrung her hands together. 'I'm so sorry, David. I sent Nuala home with strict instructions to phone you last night, truly I did. I can't think why she didn't do it until this morning.'

Rebecca had come to stand at his side. She looked as if she had just stepped from the pages of a magazine; there was not a blond hair out of place and her face was immaculately made-up. Kate was suddenly aware of her own wrinkled clothes and her tousled hair, and the fact that she didn't smell particularly nice either.

'It really is *extremely* thoughtless,' Rebecca remarked in her perfectly modulated voice. 'I can't think *why* you couldn't have called us from here.'

Kate stifled the urge to reach across and smack Rebecca's face there and then. 'I didn't call you from here because I don't happen to carry a phone book around with me and I didn't know your number!'

As if sensing that Kate was almost at the end of her tether, Rebecca stepped back, putting David between them.

'Well, we *are* here now, and seeing as David is her son, you can go. I'm sure it will be *him* she wants to see when she opens her eyes, not you.'

Swallowing her hurt as she looked back at her aunt's sleeping figure, Kate turned without a word and walked away. It wasn't until she was outside on the pavement that the tears of pain and humiliation that were stinging the back of her eyes began to fall. Why hadn't Nuala phoned David the night before as she had asked her to? In fairness, she could understand David being angry, but then, Nuala *had* been frightened half to death and had probably forgotten all about it in her panic. The girl had always been timid with anyone she didn't know, terrified of being on her own, and by now she would probably be almost beside herself with fear. The thought propelled Kate along the icy pavement, her breath swirling out in front of her like silver lace. By the time she turned into Home Park Road she was breathless and frozen to the bone. The second she put her key in the door, Nuala rose from the bottom step of the stairs where she was huddled. Her eyes were red-rimmed from crying and she was still in the same clothes that she had been wearing the night before, which told Kate that she hadn't been to bed. The annoyance she had felt towards her sister fled like mist in the morning and when she held her arms open, Nuala flew into them.

'Oh Kate, I was so frightened here all alone,' she

sobbed pitiably. Sally, who had skidded down the hall with her tail wagging furiously, rubbed against Kate's legs as if welcoming her home.

'Why didn't you phone David last night like I asked you to?' Kate asked gently.

Sniffing, Nuala rubbed her runny nose along the sleeve of her crumpled cardigan. 'I was going to, but . . . Well, David doesn't like us and I were afraid he'd shout at me.'

Kate sighed as she held her sister's shaking body in her arms. 'Never mind. He's at the hospital now and when we've had a wash and something to eat we can go back there together and see what the doctors have to say about Aunt Beth today.'

'*What?* . . . You mean she's still *alive*?' Nuala gasped as if she had expected to hear news to the contrary.

'Of *course* she is,' Kate snapped. 'What did you expect, Nuala? And she's going to get better if I have a say in it, even if I have to nurse her twenty-four hours a day.'

Nuala turned about without a word and slouched away to get ready as Kate shook her head in annoyance.

An hour and a half later the sisters set off again. Fine snowflakes were just beginning to fall and settle on the pavements, making them as slippery as glass. Nuala clung to Kate's arm until at last they turned into the road that led to the Manor Hospital.

They found their aunt awake, looking frail but infinitely better than she had the night before. There was no sign of David or Rebecca and Kate sighed with relief as she hurried towards the bed.

'You gave us a right old scare last night,' she joked softly as she bent to kiss her aunt's cheek.

111

The older woman's mouth worked as if she were trying to reply but no sound came out and Kate was shocked to see that one side of her face was not moving at all.

'Don't try to say anything just yet,' she urged. 'Just lie there and rest while I go and find the Sister.' After squeezing her aunt's hand she hurried towards the desk at the top of the ward where a nurse was busily writing up notes.

Kate stared at the doctor in despair. He had just informed her that her aunt would survive but it was highly improbable that she would ever be the same again. She would need careful nursing, and the chances were that she might never regain the use of her left side, and even if she did, she would be very weak.

Kate's head was spinning. How was she going to be able to hold down two jobs, supply the level of care that her aunt would need, *and* look after the new baby when it came? It was no good expecting Nuala to nurse her aunt. Nuala needed someone to take care of *her*. And if Kate gave up her job, what would they all live on?

The answer to her question came later that day as she and Nuala were sitting down to a meal back at her aunt's home. They heard the front door open, without any knocking, and the next second David strode into the room. He glanced at the small case that Kate had packed for her aunt, which she intended to take back to the hospital after they had eaten.

Grim-faced, he took a seat opposite them at the table. 'I thought I ought to come and warn you that an estate agent will be calling round first thing in the morning to value the house.'

Kate's mouth gaped open. 'What do you mean . . . value the house?'

'Exactly what I say. From what they've told us at the hospital, my mother isn't going to be able to look after herself, so she won't be able to stay here, will she? Rebecca and I have been trying to encourage her to move in with us for some time, and now that this has happened . . . Well, it doesn't really leave her with much choice, does it?'

'*We* could take care of her,' Kate told him, her voice choked.

David shook his head. 'Thank you, but that won't be necessary. Soon you will have a baby to care for between you, and anyway she's *my* mother and therefore my responsibility. I shall be putting the house up for sale, and when Beth leaves the hospital she will be moving in with us.'

'But – what will happen to us? Where . . .'

A warning glance from Kate silenced Nuala. Kate felt as if her world was falling apart but would have died rather than show her distress to David. 'Has Aunt Beth agreed to this?' she asked, her head held high.

'Of course she hasn't,' David said impatiently. 'She's hardly in a position to agree to anything at the moment, is she? But in time she'll see that it's for the best all round. As for you two . . . All I can say is, you are quite welcome to stay in the house until it is sold, so that should give you time to look around for somewhere to rent.'

Kate had the distinct feeling that David was enjoying himself but looked him in the eye without a flicker of emotion.

113

'Very well. Thank you for letting us know of your intentions. I shall make sure that the house is ready for the estate agent tomorrow, and I shall start to look round for somewhere for Nuala and me to live right away. Just one question – will you be taking Sally?'

David's eyes dropped to the little dog curled up at Kate's feet. He shook his head. 'I'm afraid not. Rebecca isn't a great animal lover and besides – she might snap at the children.'

'Sally would *never* snap at anyone,' Kate retorted indignantly. 'You know your mother loves this little dog. What are you going to do with her if she can't come with you?'

He shrugged. 'I suppose we'll have to have her put to sleep,' he said indifferently.

Kate stared into eyes that were as cold as the frost on the pavements outside. 'That won't be necessary. Sally can come with Nuala and me.'

'Please yourself,' David said. 'Though I think you might find it hard to rent somewhere with a dog in tow *and* a baby on the way. Most landlords won't accept pets or children.'

'We'll manage.' Kate watched as he stood and crossed to the fine porcelain ornaments displayed on her aunt's mantelshelf. He lifted them one by one before telling her, 'Rebecca will be over in the next few days to see what she wants to take from the house. The rest of the stuff can be left for the new owners.'

Too angry to speak, Kate merely nodded as he turned and walked towards the door. Every single thing in the house was special to Aunt Beth and yet David only wanted the things of any worth. Once he'd gone she began to shake with rage as she paced up and down the living room. Nuala was crying softly, her unfinished meal forgotten. For the second time in only a matter of months Kate drew her into her arms and reassured her. 'Now, now. There's no need to cry. The main thing is that Aunt Beth gets better. We'll soon find somewhere to live, you'll see. It probably won't be as nice as here admittedly, but we'll soon make it our own.'

'I . . . I thought Aunt Beth would leave the house to us if anything happened to her,' Nuala snivelled.

'Whatever made you think that?' Kate was shocked. 'Of course it's only right that her son should have the house, though that leaves us in a bit of a predicament, to say the least.'

'Then I think we should just go back to Durham,' Nuala sputtered. 'If we can't live with Aunt Beth and she won't give us the house there won't be anything to keep us here, will there? At least in Durham we have people we know.'

Kate stared across Nuala's bent head as she thought on her words. The idea was tempting, she was forced to admit, but then what was there to gain? A picture of Matthew floated in front of her eyes. She didn't think that she would ever be able to face him again and anyway, by now he could be anywhere. Wherever he was, he certainly wasn't worrying about her – and what would he say if he found out that he was about to become a father? At least here she had work and would still be able to see her aunt from time to time. She sighed as if she had the weight of the world on her young shoulders.

'Come on,' she said wearily. 'Let's clear this table and get the house looking nice, ready for the estate agent to come tomorrow. It's what Aunt Beth would want. She'd die of shame if everything wasn't just so when he arrived.'

Sniffing loudly, Nuala mopped her tears with a clean white handkerchief that Kate produced from her cardigan sleeve and resentfully began to carry the dirty pots into the kitchen.

'So how is your aunt now?'

Kate looked up from the bar into the concerned eyes of Martin Denby. It was her first night back at work in the Rose and Crown since her aunt's stroke and almost everyone who had come in had asked after her. She felt the butterflies start in the pit of her stomach and the colour pour into her cheeks. Martin was such a nice-looking man; in fact, he seemed to grow more handsome every time she saw him. But he always looked so . . . She searched her mind for the word she was looking for. *Sad* – that was the word. There was something in his eyes that told of deep sorrow.

'She's much better, thank you,' she muttered as she wiped the bar with a clean cloth. 'Of course, she still isn't well and the stroke has affected her all down one side . . .' A vision of her aunt's poor twisted face swam before her eyes. 'She still has a long way to go,' she finished lamely.

As if sensing her pain he reached across the bar and gently squeezed her hand, and his touch sent fingers of fire shooting up her arm.

'If there's anything I can do, you only have to ask,' he said quietly.

'Thank you.' She shuffled away to serve another customer, glad of a chance to compose herself. What was it about Martin that made her react that way?

Vera, who was standing enjoying a Woodbine at the other end of the bar, grinned as she blew out a lungful of smoke. Sidling up to Kate she whispered, 'I reckon you could have that one if you played your cards right.'

Kate's hand shook as she tried to concentrate on the pint she was pulling. 'That will be one and tuppence, please.'

Ignoring Vera for the present she flashed her customer a bright smile and turned to get his change from the ornate brass till. Only then did she reply, 'I think you'll find you're very much mistaken. Martin is just being friendly, that's all.'

The landlady chuckled. 'Well, you have it your own way if that's what you want to think. But I'll tell yer now – from where I'm standing it looks as if he's a bit more interested than that, and yer could do a lot worse. I mean . . . well, the night your aunt took poorly I couldn't help but notice that your sister is pregnant. You're going to have a lot on your plate looking after her, a baby *and* having to work to keep you all.' She turned and resumed her stance in the corner of the bar as Kate's cheeks flamed.

Someone inserted a sixpence into the jukebox and the next moment the sound of Bing Crosby's voice singing 'White Christmas' echoed around the bar. Kate had to choke back a sob. Christmas! It was almost here and she had been so looking forward to it – but now . . . now instead of enjoying a cosy Christmas with her aunt she would be spending it looking for somewhere for her and Nuala to live. In her drawer at home was the lovely silk headscarf she had lovingly chosen for her aunt, but it was unlikely that Aunt Beth would ever be well enough to go out and wear it now.

Her mood didn't improve as the night progressed, and by the time Bill rang the bell for last orders all Kate could think of was getting home. It had been a long day. She had risen at five that morning, done a full day in the factory and then visited the hospital before coming to do her shift at the pub. Her feet felt as if they were on fire and her eyes were gritty from lack of sleep, so when Vera pushed her coat into her arms, insisting that she could clear up by herself, Kate flashed her a grateful smile and didn't argue.

When she stepped out onto the pavement she paused for a moment to breathe in the clear night air. Over the last few days the snow had continued to fall and now it lay like a crisp white blanket for as far as her eyes could see. Everywhere looked clean and bright, but Kate was in no mood to appreciate beauty in anything for now, so she set off, lifting her feet high as she trod through the deep snow. A black shadow suddenly fell into place at the side of her own and she started. Swiftly turning, she saw Martin hurrying to catch up with her.

'Sorry if I startled you. I thought I'd hang around and see you home. You can't be too careful at the minute.'

They fell into step and silently continued along the deserted road. It was as they were passing Our Lady of the Angels Catholic Church that Kate remarked, 'You really shouldn't have put yourself out. I only live in Home Park Road – well, for now at least.'

'Are you thinking of moving then?'

Kate nodded. 'I'm afraid I'm going to have to. My aunt is going to live with her son in Hinckley when she comes out of hospital and the house has been put up for sale.'

'I see. Where are you thinking of going?'

'I'm not sure yet. I've looked at a couple of flats over the last couple of days, but to be honest I wouldn't want to put my dog in them. If I told you they were seedy I'd be being kind.'

'Mm.' With his hands thrust in his coat pockets he stared down at his feet, obviously deep in thought. They had just come to the end of Home Park Road when he suddenly said, 'I could always let you have a room at my place. I live in Heath End Road in a three-bedroomed house, and to be honest, it's far too big for me.'

'That's very kind of you,' Kate told him, 'but there isn't just me. I have a younger sister and now a little dog to look after too.'

She omitted to tell him that soon there would be a baby as well. Smiling at him, she thought what a genuinely nice man he was before pointing up the road. 'Right, I'd better be getting in or my sister will have a search-party out looking for me. Thanks for walking me home.'

'You're welcome,' he replied courteously. 'What night will you be working next?'

'Thursday,' Kate told him shyly, suddenly glad of the darkness that would hide her blushes as she thought back to what Vera had said earlier. Very aware of the fact that he was standing watching her, she hurried away. At her aunt's front door she looked back and raised her hand and he waved before striding off into the bitterly cold night.

A little bubble of excitement was growing in her stomach. Just for a second a picture of Matthew's face flashed in front of her eyes but she angrily pushed it away. Why should she worry about him after what he had done? Matthew was the past. Perhaps Martin was her future?

Her excitement evaporated as quickly as it had come. What was the point in even thinking that there could ever be anything between her and Martin? As soon as he knew about Nuala's baby he would probably be gone like a shot, and who could blame him? Her eyes rested on the For Sale board that had been hammered into the front lawn. Inside this house was her sister who was totally reliant on her; if the house sold quickly they would be homeless. Perhaps for now she should channel her energies into finding them somewhere to live instead of letting her head fill with silly romantic notions? Sighing, she inserted the key in the lock and let herself into the warm hallway where Sally was waiting for her with her tail wagging furiously.

Chapter Ten

Maria Farn cursed as her feet almost slipped from beneath her. The snow was coming down in great white flakes that clung to her nurse's cape and chilled her to the bone. Shuddering, she hurried along Greenmoor Road.

After just finishing the four till ten shift at the George Eliot Hospital she was tired and more than a little disgruntled. Matron had been in a right old mood tonight when she did her rounds, and Sister must have got out of the wrong side of the bed too, because nothing Maria or any of the other nurses had done during the entire shift seemed to please her. Still, she was off till Friday now and tomorrow she would go to Bingo with her mum.

The thick black nurse's stockings she was wearing were sodden, and rather than keep her warm they clung damply to her legs, making her shiver. The streets were deserted, except for someone who she noticed was some way behind her on the other side of the pavement. I bet they'll be glad to get out of the cold too, she thought as she tried to fix her attention on the brightly coloured Christmas tree lights that were twinkling in the windows of many of the houses she passed. I'll pop into town tomorrow when I've had a lie-in and get the rest of the Christmas shopping done, she promised herself.

Stepping off the kerb at the entrance to Cox's Close, she cursed again as the snow rode even higher up her legs. Blast! Soon she was at the entrance to the path that led to the Cat Gallows Bridge and she paused. The path ran steeply downhill and she wondered if she would manage it without falling; it was hard enough to walk on the straight let alone downhill. The alternative was a very long walk, again downhill along Greenmoor Road and then she would be faced with the hill on the Cock and Bear Bridge, which would probably be more slippery than the one she was faced with, because it would have had more people trampling over it.

'Sod it,' she muttered to no one in particular. 'Better the devil you know.'

Setting off again, she had soon left the streetlights behind as she picked her way down the path that wound its way through the allotments on either side of it. The fast-falling snow was making it difficult to see more than a few yards in front of her, and she wondered if she shouldn't have taken the long way round after all, but at last she saw the vague shape of the Cat Gallows Bridge looming in front of her. There was not a sound to be heard. It was as if the snow had swallowed up every living thing. Even the canal that ran beneath the bridge was frozen over as she clutched the metal handrail and began to cross it.

'Nearly there now,' she said aloud, as visions of a hot cup of Horlicks floated in front of her eyes. It was then that she sensed rather than saw someone behind her. Stopping abruptly, she looked back across her shoulder as she leaned breathlessly on the handrail of the bridge, and sure enough there was a shape looming towards her out of the snow.

'Brass monkey weather this, ain't it?' she shouted cheerfully, but whoever was there said nothing as they continued to advance like a spectre in the night. A worm of unease began to wriggle its way around her stomach and she moved on, trying to lift her feet higher and hurry this time. She kept glancing nervously across her shoulder and had almost reached the other side of the bridge when suddenly the person came abreast of her and stopped.

She opened her mouth to speak, but two great hands snaked towards her and caught her around her neck, cutting off her breath.

The force of the attack was so unexpected that her feet went from beneath her and she tumbled into the snow as the person on top of her increased his grip on her throat. She soon realised that she was fighting for her life. And fight she did, with every ounce of strength she possessed, until inevitably, she began to tire. Strangely, the cold didn't seem quite so cold now. In fact, if she closed her eyes she could almost imagine that she was tucked up in bed with a hot-water bottle at her feet . . . It wasn't long before Maria Farn stopped fighting and gave herself up to the comforting warmth.

Chapter Eleven

'Ruby, what a surprise. What are you doing here? I didn't even know that you knew my aunt.' Kate stared in amazement at Ruby, who was sitting at the side of the hospital bed.

'Kate! Why . . . er . . . did I never mention it?' Ruby hastily stood up and hovered almost guiltily, looking for all the world like a brightly coloured humming bird about to take flight. 'Me an' Beth go back years – I thought yer knew.'

Kate swallowed her surprise; the two women were as different as chalk from cheese. There was her Aunt Beth, so very prim and proper with her pearls and her twin-sets, and Ruby all decked out like a Christmas tree.

'Well no, I had no idea,' she said. 'But it's a lovely surprise to see you here.' Her smile was like a ray of sunshine as she bent to place an affectionate kiss on her aunt's cheek.

Ruby sidled towards the end of the bed, clutching her enormous handbag to her stomach and looking decidedly uncomfortable. 'I'd best get off then. I'll probably see you next week, eh?'

'You don't have to rush off just because I've come,' Kate told her, but Ruby's head wagged from side to side.

'No, no, I don't want to overstay me bleedin' welcome. I just thought as I'd show me face.' All the time she was talking she was inching away from the bed.

Kate looked down at her aunt, whose eyes seemed to be almost popping out of her head. She looked back up to say something to Ruby and was surprised to see the back end of her disappearing through the swing doors that led into the ward.

'Ah well, looks like you're stuck with me now,' she grinned.

One side of her aunt's mouth was working as if she were trying to say something, and noting her distress, Kate lifted her limp hand and raised it to her lips. 'Don't try and talk,' she told her soothingly. 'You need to rest. I'll tell you all about what I've been doing today, eh?'

Her aunt's eyes filled with tears.

A passing nurse quickly approached the bed. 'It might be better if you leave now,' she told Kate tactfully. 'Your aunt has had quite a few visitors today and we don't want to overtire her, do we?'

'Of course not.' Kate reluctantly rose from her chair at the side of the bed, her face mirroring her concern. 'She *is* all right though, isn't she?'

The nurse bent to straighten the blanket across her aunt's knees. 'Oh yes, she's doing as well as can be expected, but I just don't want her to get overtired. We still have a long way to go yet, don't we, Mrs Summers?'

Aunt Beth began to flap her good hand at Kate. She was obviously highly agitated about something but the girl had no chance to find out what it was, for the nurse took her elbow and gently propelled her towards the door.

'Come back tomorrow when she's had a good night's sleep,' she told her, and before Kate knew it she found herself back in the long corridor outside the ward.

The atmosphere in the Rose and Crown was subdued that night as the customers talked in hushed whispers of the latest young woman who had gone missing in Nuneaton the night before.

'Eeh! It don't even bear thinking about, does it?' Vera shuddered as she looked at the headlines that were blazened across the front of the newspaper spread across the bar. 'An' so close to Christmas too. What must her poor family be goin' through? That's *three* young lasses in less than a year now, an' not so much as a clue as to what's happened to any of 'em!' Her head shook from side to side in dismay. 'That somehow makes it worse in my eyes. I mean, if the poor girls are dead an' their bodies could be found, then at least they could be laid to rest in peace. But to just vanish off the face o' the earth . . . ugh! An' what are the police doin' about it, eh? I mean, the town is crawlin' wi' bobbies yet they've come up wi' nothing!'

'Makes yer wonder what the world's comin' to, don't it?' chipped in old Stan, one of the regulars, as he tugged at his cap. 'Seems to me like the newspapers are full o' nothin' but doom an' gloom nowadays. Did yer read that they're on about introducin' parkin' meters in the towns now? Huh! Parkin' meters indeed! Fancy havin' to pay to park yer car up. If yer were to ask me, I'd have to say that Harold Macmillan has a lot to answer for, an' all in the name o' progress. Here he is, pattin' hisself on the back 'cos he's built a record number of houses this year, but at what a cost, eh? I reckon—'

'Stan, we were talkin' about the poor nurse that went missin' last night, not the state o' the bloody country,' Vera pointed out.

Stan looked suitably subdued and lifting his pint from the bar, shuffled away with his pipe hanging out of the corner of his mouth to join his friends in a game of dominoes.

'Oh dear, I think I might have been a bit hard on him there,' Vera muttered, and then she too hurried away to serve a customer who had approached the bar.

Some time later, Vera suddenly clapped her hand to her mouth. 'Lord love us! I almost forgot. Somethin' came fer you earlier in the day,' she informed Kate. 'Come out the back with me fer a minute. I put 'em in a bucket so as they wouldn't droop.'

Kate followed her through to the back room and flushed with pleasure as Vera pointed at a modest bouquet of chrysanthemums, sent via Interflora.

'They were delivered this mornin', an' it don't take much guessin' who they're off, does it?' She looked on smugly as Kate blushed to the roots of her hair. 'Didn't I tell you the bloke's smitten?' Vera grinned from ear to ear before hurrying away, leaving Kate to disentangle the little card that was tucked among the sweet-smelling blooms. She opened the tiny envelope with trembling fingers and gazed with delight at the words written on the small card inside.

Thought these might cheer you up a bit, much love,
Martin xxxxxxx

The night suddenly improved and Kate even forgot
how tired she was. It improved even more when
Martin himself suddenly appeared at almost nine-
thirty. His fair hair was slicked neatly down with
Brylcreem and his twinkling blue eyes immediately
sought her out.

'Oh Martin, thank you so much for the lovely flowers,'
she told him shyly, then gasped as she saw the deep
scratch on his face. 'Been in a fight, have you?'

His hand moved self-consciously to his cheek. 'No,
nothing quite as exciting as that, I'm afraid. I just got
the wrong end of the cat's temper when I tried to put
him out last night.'

'Oh, I see. Well, as I was saying, the flowers are lovely.'

He shrugged his broad shoulders. 'Think nothing of
it. I'm glad you liked them. But I need to have a word
with you after your shift,' he told her as she pulled him
his customary pint.

'Oh yes. What about?'

He glanced around to see if they could be overheard
before looking back at her. 'I'd rather wait and tell you
in private.'

'All right.' Kate took his money and for the rest of
the evening she was consumed with curiosity as she
wondered what it was that he was going to tell her.
Finally Bill called last orders and Martin waited patiently
for Kate as she helped Vera to clear away the dirty glasses
into the sink beneath the bar.

Once they were outside, he tucked her arm into his

and, heads bent against the snow, which was still coming down with a vengeance, they set off.

'I've been thinking about what you told me the other night – you know, about your sister and the dog. Well, the thing is, I do have *three* bedrooms so there's no reason why all of you couldn't move in with me. All strictly above board, of course. I have my own room and there's one for you and one for your sister.'

'But . . .' Kate hesitated, wondering whether she should confess about Nuala's condition. 'But I thought I heard Vera mention that you had a son. Where does he sleep?'

Martin's lips set in a grim line. 'Yes, I do have a son, but Adam has lived with his grandparents for some time now. After my wife died it was . . . Well, I couldn't go to work and offer him full-time care so they stepped in and had him to live with them. He still comes home to stay at weekends sometimes, but that wouldn't be a problem. I could always sleep on the settee if necessary.'

'How old is Adam?' Kate asked softly.

'He's ten next birthday.'

'You must miss having him with you?'

He nodded. 'I do, which is one of the reasons I'd like to have someone there to come home to again.' He flashed Kate a smile that melted her heart. 'It can get a bit lonely in that house all by myself, so I'd really love you to come, even if it was only until you could find somewhere more suitable. Will you give it some thought?'

'Of course,' she lied. Deep down, as tempting as his offer was, she knew that once he learned of the pregnancy he would retract it.

By now they were at the end of Home Park Road.

Kate released his arm and stared at him above the flowers that she was clutching. It was then that he bent his head quite unexpectedly and planted a kiss on her lips. A thousand fireworks exploded behind Kate's eyes and her heart began to race, and yet it felt like the most natural thing in the world.

Straightening, he smiled at her. 'Go on, get yourself in out of the cold. I don't want you catching your death.'

Kate set off on legs that suddenly felt as if they no longer belonged to her. She turned just once to raise her hands in a final salute but he had gone, swallowed up by the snow, and she felt a pang of regret.

Nuala was waiting for her in the entrance hall. 'Who was that you were with at the bottom of the road?' she demanded.

'Oh . . . it was just a friend,' Kate muttered as she thrust the flowers at Nuala and bent to take her boots off.

'Oh yes? An' *friends* buy you flowers an' kiss you good night, do they?' the girl said peevishly.

Kate was too tired to argue so instead she chose to ignore Nuala's waspish tone. 'Actually, Martin is a very nice man. He's offered to let us move in with him until we can find somewhere suitable to rent.' She headed for the kitchen to put the kettle on to boil with Nuala and Sally close at her heels.

'An' where does this Martin live?' Nuala was on her shoulder and suddenly Kate felt like smacking her. Here she was holding down two jobs, trying to find them somewhere to live and doing all the hospital visits into the bargain, whilst her sister sat at home on her fat backside. It was a bone of contention that the girl had not so much as set foot in the hospital to see Aunt Beth for days, but then, Kate supposed that it was understandable – up to a point. The two had never bonded as she and her aunt had, and she doubted whether Beth would have missed Nuala. She suddenly remembered Ruby leaning over the bed earlier in the evening and her brow creased. How strange that neither her aunt nor Ruby had ever mentioned that they knew each other.

'So – are we goin' to live wi' him or what then?'

Kate's thoughts were tugged back to the present as Nuala's voice sounded in her ear.

'What? Oh, I doubt it. He doesn't know about . . .'

As her eyes dropped to Nuala's stomach, the girl scowled.

'He don't know about this monster, is that what you're tryin' to say?'

'It's a baby, Nuala, not a *monster*.' Kate's voice was chilly.

'Huh! As far as I'm concerned, it *is* a monster. I never wanted it. I don't want it now. Can you even *begin* to think what it's like to have to lug this around all day?'

Kate stared at her in consternation. Nuala had never really told her how she felt about the pregnancy, but now her feelings were crystal clear. She didn't want the baby! This made the situation a million times worse. Damn and blast Matthew Williams to hell!

'Look,' Kate sighed, 'I know things look bleak now, but once the baby is born you'll feel differently.'

'Oh, quite *sure* of that, are you?' Nuala grumbled. 'It must be easy for you to stand there and say that. After all, it ain't *you* that everyone's gossipin' about, is it?'

131

'I don't think that's quite the case, Nuala. Aunt Beth didn't turn her back on you, nor did I.'

'You might have thought she didn't, but you weren't trapped in here with her all day,' Nuala complained. 'I got sick of her "holier than thou" looks and her tutt-tuttin'. That's why I took to stayin' in me room.'

Kate bit down on her lip. The situation was fast developing into an argument and at the moment she was just too tired for it. 'Let's talk about this tomorrow, eh?' she suggested wearily.

Folding her hands across her swollen stomach, Nuala glared at her. But then curiosity got the better of her and she asked, 'So, when will I get to meet him?'

Kate poured boiling water into the pretty china teapot. 'Soon, I dare say. Not that there's much point. Look, Nuala, I'm absolutely done in and my feet feel as if they're about to drop off.'

Sensing that Kate was not going to say any more about the subject for now, Nuala headed away to her room, leaving Kate alone with her thoughts. After putting her flowers into one of her aunt's precious cut-glass vases she sat and admired them as she sipped at her tea. It had been a funny old day, one way and another.

'So, the long and the short of it is, your aunt should be discharged by the weekend,' the doctor told Kate. 'There really isn't any reason for her to stay here any longer. Of course, we shall be arranging for lots of nursing care. Should you have any concerns, you can always talk to your health visitor about this.'

'I'm afraid she won't be coming home to me,' Kate

told the doctor miserably. 'She will be going to live with her son in Hinckley.'

'I see, well, that shouldn't be a problem. I'm sure that he will see to her needs. Now, I really must be getting along to my other patients. Good day, Miss Cleary.'

Kate watched as the doctor marched away before turning to look at her aunt who was propped up on pillows in the bed. Obviously she had heard every word that had been said and a tear was trickling down her cheek. She doesn't want to go and live with David, Kate thought, but unfortunately there was not a thing in the world she could do about it.

Hurrying across to her, Kate draped her arm across her frail shoulders. 'Don't cry, Aunt Beth,' she soothed, although she was close to tears herself. 'I'm sure that you'll be happy once you get used to living with David and Rebecca, and think how nice it will be to see the children every day. You've always complained that you didn't get to see enough of them.' Her aunt's head tossed restlessly on the pillow and she gripped Kate's hand with her good one as if she were trying to tell her something.

'What is it, Aunt Beth?'

'She's just being silly, that's all.' David's voice almost made Kate jump out of her skin. He had come to stand at the end of the bed with Rebecca close behind him. 'If you'd like to get home now, Kate, we'll stay for the rest of visiting time.' It was said like a command, and bristling, Kate stood up and took her coat from the back of the chair as she stared at him coldly.

'We'll be calling in on our way home,' Rebecca informed her. 'I thought we might as well load the car with some of the things that we'll want to keep from the house.'

'Very well.' Kate inclined her head and after planting a hasty kiss on her aunt's cheek she swept from the ward without so much as another word.

She fumed all the way home. It was the week after Christmas and what a miserable Christmas it had been. It was set to get worse because as she approached the house she saw the estate agent's car parked outside. What would he be doing here on a Saturday afternoon, she wondered. Deciding that there was only one way to find out, she hurried on.

'So, Miss Cleary, all in all I would say we've had a very satisfactory outcome for the house sale, wouldn't you?' The plump middle-aged estate agent smiled. 'Mr and Mrs Barrett were so enamoured of the house that they've offered to pay the full asking price.'

Kate nodded wearily. So that was it then. Her heart ached for her aunt, who she knew loved her home. She had lived here in this little house all her married life, but now it would soon belong to someone else. She wondered how Beth would cope with it, but shrugged the thought away. After all, what could she do about it? It was up to David as the son and heir to decide what happened to the place, and he had made his decision.

'Thank you,' she replied, as the man shook her hand up and down until she was sure that it would drop off. 'Shall I take it that you'll be in touch to tell us when to vacate?'

'Absolutely, my dear. Mr and Mrs Barrett are in a very

good financial position so I assume it will all go through very smoothly within a matter of a few weeks.'

She accompanied him to the door and once he had gone she took a deep breath. That part of the day had been bad enough, but worse was to come: she still had David and Rebecca's visit to look forward to. Sighing, she picked up a duster and began to polish her aunt's treasures.

David and Rebecca's shining car pulled up outside the house within minutes of the end of the hospital visiting hours.

Rebecca stood in the hall and brushed the snow from the fur collar of her coat before striding into the lounge. Immediately she crossed to the fine porcelain figures that adorned the mantelshelf. They were Aunt Beth's pride and joy and Kate felt her heart sink.

'Ah, these are Royal Doulton, darling,' she informed David, reminding Kate of a cat that had got the cream. 'I'm sure I could find room for these. Would you mind wrapping them up for me, Kate? And *do* make sure they're *well* packed. I shouldn't like them to get broken.'

Gritting her teeth, Kate took some newspapers from the paper rack and began to pad the beloved ornaments as Rebecca poked about the room for anything else of value. She's like a vulture, Kate thought, keeping her eyes diverted from Rebecca's greedy face. By the time Rebecca was done in the lounge it looked sadly bare; everything of any worth had been packed into boxes that David had carefully carried out to the car.

'Right, that should do for now,' Rebecca said with a satisfied look on her face, as her gloved hands flicked at an imaginary speck of dust on her skirt. 'Of course, I shall be back tomorrow afternoon to start on the other rooms. There's not a moment to lose now that the house is sold. Are you ready, darling?'

When David nodded subserviently she moved towards the door like a ship in full sail.

'I'll see you tomorrow then, Kate. Don't bother going to the hospital. David and I shall be taking the children to see their grandmother. Expect us shortly after visiting hours. Such *good* news about the house sale, isn't it? I do hope you find somewhere soon for you and Nuala to live. We wouldn't want to have to throw you out on the street now, would we?' Her tone suggested that she would like nothing more than to do just that, but Kate bit her tongue and wouldn't give her the satisfaction of an answer. When she disappeared through the door Kate's hands clamped into fists of rage. No wonder Aunt Beth wasn't too enamoured of her daughter-in-law! She was a snob through and through, not that it had stopped her taking her pickings of all Aunt Beth's precious china.

'Oh Kate. What are we going to do?' Nuala had held back her tears as she watched Rebecca strip the lounge of everything that had made it a home, but now she could hold them back no longer and they gushed from her eyes to mingle with the snot from her nose.

'We'll be fine,' Kate told her with a reassurance that she was far from feeling, as she rocked her in her arms.

'Can't we just go home to Durham?' Nuala pleaded.

Kate shook her head dully. 'No, we can't. Our home is here now, whether we like it or not. There's nothing in Durham for us any more.'

Chapter Twelve

As Kate's eyes scanned the bleak little room, depression settled around her like a cloak. Although it had been advertised as a flat it was in actual fact little more than a bedsit, which she was quick to point out to the landlord who was hovering at her side.

'You'll do no better for the price,' he told her huffily as he picked at his nose with tobacco-stained fingers.

Against one wall a table leaned drunkenly at an angle. Two mismatched chairs were propped at either side of it and a dirty faded curtain hid what the landlord had described as a kitchenette. Against another wall, a settee that turned into a double bed took pride of place and on the floor were mats so filthy that Kate couldn't even make out what colour they might have been.

Through the thin adjoining wall the strains of a Fats Domino record wafted to her, along with smells that made her wrinkle her nose in distaste.

'Thank you very much for allowing me to view it, but I don't think it's quite what we're looking for,' she said politely.

'Hmm, well, you'll not find better fer thirteen shillin's a

week,' the man told her grumpily. He scratched underneath his armpit with nails that looked as if they had never seen a nailbrush.

Kate turned on her heel and clattered down the uncarpeted stairs as the man lumbered clumsily down behind her, his unwashed body emitting the most odious smell of stale sweat that Kate had ever come across. When she stepped out of the front door, glad to draw clean air into her lungs, she turned to thank him once again, but he slammed the door in her face.

Sighing, she looked up and down the length of Riversley Road. This was the third flat she had looked at in as many hours and each had been as bad as the one before. There was just a week to go now until she and Nuala must vacate the house, and panic was beginning to set in. Perhaps she should take Martin up on his offer after all? Just tell him about Nuala and see what his reaction was? Their relationship was going from strength to strength and yet . . . perhaps it was the thought of what people might say that was troubling her. It certainly wouldn't look good for him, taking in two young unmarried women, one of them already pregnant.

She didn't feel ready to confide in him yet, but if she didn't find something soon she would have to swallow her pride and tell him, and damn what people would say. Either that, or she and Nuala would end up on the streets. She thought sadly of her aunt.

Aunt Beth was now settled in at David's. Kate had visited her as often as she could since she had been discharged from hospital, and the look on her aunt's face when she saw her always made the journey on the bus worth it. The same couldn't be said for Rebecca, who would look down her nose at Kate as if she was something that had crawled out of the woodwork.

Rebecca had systematically gone through every room in Aunt Beth's house until there was nothing left that was worth taking. Not that Kate would ever dream of taking anything off her aunt. She mourned the fact that they had had so little time together. Her aunt was still unable to speak and as yet had gained no use in the side that had been affected by her stroke, although Kate lived in hope that one day she would.

She trudged along, her footsteps slowed by weariness. The snow had finally thawed but as the middle of January approached it was replaced by bitterly cold winds and driving rain. Deciding to walk back through Riversley Park to try and cheer herself up, Kate was soon strolling along the banks of the River Anker, admiring the leafless weeping willows whose branches trailed into the slow-moving water. Her mind was in turmoil. Nuala was now the size of a house and had just one more month to go until the baby was born, but they still had nowhere to go. Kate paused briefly as despair washed over her, then with a heavy heart she made her way home.

She had been in for no more than an hour when there was a knock at the front door. After hurrying to open it she was confronted by Martin.

'Sorry to intrude,' he said sheepishly. 'I just wondered how you were.'

He looked so embarrassed standing there, like a little boy on his first date, that Kate's lips twitched into a smile.

'Well, now that you're here you may as well come in.'

She held the door wide, wishing that she had taken more trouble with her appearance, and thankful that Nuala was upstairs taking a nap. She had just finished packing up the rest of the things that were left in Aunt Beth's spare room and was covered in dust from head to toe. Martin stepped into the hall and bent to stroke Sally, who was sitting at his feet. Kate led him into the lounge.

'I'll put the kettle on, shall I?' she said to break the tense silence that had settled on the room, and turned and scuttled away again.

When he and Kate were finally sitting at the table with a tray of tea in front of them, Martin looked into her eyes. 'No need to ask how the flat-hunting went,' he commented. 'You look as if you've got the weight of the world on your shoulders.'

Kate poured the tea into the only cups that Rebecca had left in the house and shrugged. 'I looked at three today,' she admitted. 'And not one of them was suitable. In fact, I'd be surprised if even cockroaches would have agreed to live in them.' She shuddered as she remembered. Their home in Durham had been poor and sparsely furnished, but at least it had been clean, which was more than she could say for any of the flats that she had looked at today.

'Bad as that, were they?' he asked sympathetically, noting her tear-filled eyes.

'Worse!'

'Then why don't you consider my offer – about moving in with me?'

Kate avoided his eyes as realisation dawned on him.

'You're worried about what people will say about us living together, aren't you?'

'I suppose I am,' Kate admitted reluctantly. 'It's not that I want to seem old-fashioned or anything, but . . . Well, there's something else too.' She had been so close to telling him about Nuala's baby but at the last minute her courage failed her and her lips clamped shut.

To her amazement he suddenly threw back his head and laughed aloud. 'Do you know something, Kate? That's one of the things I love about you. You're so conventional. More than can be said about a lot of girls nowadays who'll go with any Tom, Dick or Harry.'

The flush that had spread to her cheeks deepened as she thought of her sister upstairs. 'I'm sorry.'

'Don't be,' he grinned. 'But if that's the case, then there's only one way out of our dilemma, the way I see it. You'll have to marry me and make it decent, won't you?'

Kate's eyes nearly started from her head as she stared back at him in shocked disbelief, but his expression was perfectly serious.

'You shouldn't joke about things like that,' she mumbled, afraid that he was making fun of her.

Reaching across the table, he took her hand in his. 'I'm not joking. In fact, I've never been more serious in my life. You must have realised how I feel about you? Oh, I know we haven't known each other for long, but the minute I set eyes on you I knew that you were the girl for me. Under other circumstances I would have liked to court you for longer, but the thing is, we don't have the time, do we? So I ask you – Kate, will you marry me?'

Kate's mouth dropped open and now it was her turn to be speechless.

Quickly skirting around the table, he drew her into his arms. 'I can see that you're shocked so I won't push you for an answer right now. But will you at least think about it? I could get a special licence and we could be married by the end of the week.' He planted his lips on hers and again Kate had the sensation of floating on air. By the time he drew away she was breathless. He had awakened feelings in her that she had never known she had. Lifting a dark curl from her shoulder he twirled it around his finger as he gazed lovingly into her eyes.

'Martin, I have Nuala and Sally to think of. I couldn't—'

'Ssh! I know that and it's fine. I wouldn't expect you to abandon them. I realise that you all come as a package.'

'But it's not as simple as that. You see—'

'Enough said for now, young lady. I'm going to make myself scarce. You have things to think about, but I shall be back in the next couple of days, if that's all right, and if you give me the answer I'm hoping for, I can only say you will make me the happiest man on earth. After my wife Anne died I thought I would never be happy again, but then I met you and . . . Well, enough said for now. Goodbye, Kate.'

Turning on his heel he strode away without so much as a backward glance. When Kate heard the door close behind him she sank back into her seat and stared off into space. She was still sitting there when Nuala almost exploded into the room some minutes later.

'Who was that I heard?' Catching sight of Kate's face she stopped and frowned. 'What's the matter?'

'It was Martin, but he . . . er . . . he had to go,' she said lamely.

'Go where? Why didn't you call me and introduce us? Is it because you're ashamed of me?'

'Of *course* I'm not ashamed of you. He only popped in. You can meet him next time he calls.'

'Oh, there's going to be a next time then, is there?' Nuala said sarcastically.

'Perhaps.' Kate's voice was flat.

Seeing that her sister was not going to say any more, Nuala smoothed the smock she was wearing across her swollen stomach and walked from the room. Crossing to the window, Kate stared out into the late afternoon. The fine drizzle had turned into a downpour and she watched in fascination as the rain gurgled along the drainpipes before falling in swirling torrents to disappear down the drains.

Will you marry me? Martin's words echoed round and round in her head. What was she to do? She wished with all her heart that Aunt Beth could have been there to advise her.

The sensible half of her told her that it was far too soon to consider marrying him. After all, they barely knew each other. The other side of her, the side that had always longed for someone of her own other than Nuala to love, told her to accept. But then, what did it really matter what she decided? Once Martin knew about Nuala's pregnancy he might not *want* to marry her and the decision would have been taken out of her hands. Eventually she gave up wrestling with her thoughts and, no nearer to reaching a decision, she climbed the stairs to have a bath.

The problem of where the sisters were going to live was solved in the most unlikely manner the very next day when she turned up for her shift at the Rose and Crown. Kate was slightly early and found Ruby just putting her coat on to leave as she arrived. She had formed the opinion that Ruby had been avoiding her ever since the day she had found her visiting her aunt in hospital. Now Ruby looked at her sheepishly as she entered the small cloakroom where the staff hung their coats.

'Sorry about that mix-up at the hospital, love,' Ruby muttered. 'I should have mentioned that I knew your aunt – can't think why I didn't now. It must have just slipped me mind.'

Kate stared at her curiously. 'How *do* you know my Aunt Beth, Ruby?'

'Well, to be honest, I was a great friend of your mam's before she married yer dad an' moved to Ireland. We went all through school together,' Ruby told her.

Kate's eyes almost popped out of her head. 'But why didn't you tell me this before?' she asked incredulously.

Ruby shrugged, setting her dangly earrings dancing. 'I always meant to, but somehow I never got round to it. How is Beth, anyway?'

'Not too grand, to be honest,' Kate told her. 'She's holding her own but I think she misses living in her own home. I always got the impression that she didn't much care for Rebecca, David's wife, and now she's living with her. Not that she could manage on her own. I did offer to care for her, but David wouldn't hear of it. The house is sold and now Nuala and I have to be out by . . .' Suddenly she couldn't go on and to Ruby's horror she burst into tears.

'Eeh, love. Don't cry. Nothin' can be that bleedin' bad. Come on, sit yerself down an' tell me all about it, eh?'

Ruby led her to a bench and as Kate sank down onto it she placed her arm comfortingly around the girl's shaking shoulders. 'Now come on,' she urged. 'Get it off yer chest. You know what they say – a trouble shared is a trouble halved.'

'Well, the thing is,' Kate took a great gulp of air before gabbling on, 'the thing is, Nuala and I have to be out of the house for next weekend and up to now I haven't managed to find us anywhere to go. Then along comes Martin and asks me to marry him and—

'Whoa, slow down.' Ruby held up her wrinkled hand and stopped her mid-flow. 'You mean Martin Denby?'

When Kate's head bobbed up and down, Ruby frowned. 'But you hardly know him, apart from the times you've seen him in here, do you?'

'He *has* walked me home a few times. But then he called round the house the other day and asked me to marry him,' Kate told her solemnly.

'I see. Well, if you're asking my advice you don't know him anywhere near well enough to be thinkin' of weddin' him just yet. You might be marrying him for all the wrong reasons. Perhaps you're just frettin' about where yer can go – and that's where *I* can help.' She grinned as Kate stared at her curiously.

'For a start-off I'd say a few stolen moments together ain't no basis to build a marriage on. You need to get to know one another a lot bleedin' better than that before you make a commitment. So – how about you and your sister move in with me for the time bein', eh?'

Kate's eyes stretched wide. 'But, Ruby . . . I couldn't expect you to take us in.'

'Why not? It ain't no palace, mind you, and you'd have

to take me as you find me, but if you can put up with that then you're more than welcome.'

'I'm very grateful for the offer, Ruby, but the thing is, it isn't as simple as that. You see, Nuala is going to have a baby and—'

Ruby chuckled. 'You hardly need to tell me that. Word has a way of gettin' around, yer know? I knew some months back that Nuala was in the puddin' club.'

Kate shook her head as if she could hardly believe what she had just heard. If Ruby was serious, which she obviously was, then it could be the solution to all her problems. Not that she was dismissing Martin's proposal, but it *would* give her time to get to know him better and see what his reaction to the baby would be.

Taking a scrap of paper from her handbag, Ruby scribbled down an address and with a broad grin on her face pressed it into Kate's hand. 'Slip round tomorrow and see me, eh? Just go under the Coton Arches and you'll find Shepperton Street on your right.'

'I'll do that, Ruby,' Kate told her gratefully as she mopped at her eyes with a handkerchief.

After she had composed herself she made her way into the bar, and there was Martin being served by Vera, who winked at Kate as she passed her on her way to the till.

He grinned. 'Seems like I can't keep away, doesn't it? I'll only be having the one, mind.' He nodded down at the rough work clothes he was in, so different to the collar and tie that she was used to seeing him wear. 'I'm needed at Shepperton churchyard tonight, but I thought I'd just pop in and see that you were all right before I got started.'

146

Kate couldn't suppress a shudder. 'You mean you have to dig a . . .'

He nodded solemnly. 'I'm afraid so, though it shouldn't take me too long. I'm doing a reopen and they are always quicker to do.'

'What's a reopen?' Kate asked, morbidly curious despite herself.

'A reopen is where the husband or wife has already been buried in that plot. You only have to dig down four foot for them and it's always easier because the ground has been dug before.'

Seeing her pale he shrugged his shoulders as if in apology. 'I know it seems a bit ghoulish, but someone has to do it, don't they? To be honest I sort of inherited the job and now I feel obliged to keep it on. My uncle was the gravedigger at Shepperton Church for years and when he passed away I took the job on to help the vicar out. I was glad of the job when Anne died; it gave me another reason to get out of the house. My day job more than pays for my needs but the extra money does come in handy. I get ten pounds for digging a full grave and eight pounds for a reopen, which is not to be sniffed at. The following day I come back to fill in the grave after the funeral but that doesn't usually take half so long as digging it does, and then I give the money I earn from this job to Adam's grandparents to help out with his clothes and whatever.'

Kate was instantly sympathetic as she thought how awful it must be for Martin not to be able to have his son living with him. It must have been terrible to lose his wife, and now in a way he had lost his son too.

She glanced at the window. The rain was driving

against it and she looked concerned. 'Just make sure that you're well wrapped up, that's all.'

His smile stretched from ear to ear. 'Do you know, Miss Cleary, that *almost* sounded like you cared.'

Kate went as red as a beetroot. 'I do actually,' she told him shyly.

'So you haven't dismissed what I asked you then?' His voice was so hopeful that she found herself smiling. She glanced around, conscious that they could be overheard, before whispering, 'No, I haven't dismissed it but . . . Well, I need to talk to you away from here. You see, the thing is, I think we should get to know each other a little better first. Ruby has offered to let Nuala and me stay with her for a while and perhaps . . .'

'Ruby Bannister? *The cleaner?*' he asked incredulously. He shook his head in disbelief. 'You do know that Ruby has a certain reputation, don't you?'

'I have heard that actually,' Kate said coldly, 'but I've always believed in taking people as you find them – and *I* happen to like her.'

'Right, the sooner I start the sooner I'll be finished,' Martin said. He was obviously keen to change the subject. 'What say you let me take you to the pictures tomorrow? It is your night off, isn't it?'

Kate knew she should really say no, as there were a million jobs waiting to be done at her aunt's before the weekend. But then she looked into his deep blue eyes and she was lost.

'All right then, it's a date.'

A date! The words rolled round in her head. She was actually going out on her very first proper date with Martin.

'Shall I pick up you up at . . . shall we say about seven-thirty?'

She nodded and watched him swallow his drink and stride away through a haze of tobacco smoke. Almost before he had closed the door behind him she was planning what she would wear.

The first thing she saw when she got home that evening and stepped into the hallway was a pot of hyacinths standing on the draining board through the open kitchen door. She was soaked to the skin and feeling like a drowned rat, but this was forgotten as the little butterflies in her stomach fluttered to life.

Nuala appeared as if out of nowhere at her elbow and stabbed a finger at the plant. 'No need to guess who that's from, is there?'

Ignoring her peeved tone Kate took the little card that was attached to the pot and tucked it into her pocket. She would read it later when she was alone. No sense in upsetting Nuala any more than she was already.

'Is there any supper ready?' she asked, flashing her sister an affectionate smile. 'I'm so hungry I could eat a scabby horse.'

'Suppose I could get you some soup,' Nuala said grumpily, and as she waddled towards the kitchen Kate was shocked to notice how much weight her sister had piled on. Instantly she felt guilty. No wonder the poor thing was eating non-stop. She had nothing better to do all day. But that could soon be remedied, Kate determined. From now on she would make more time for her. Take her for walks and things and perhaps start to look around for another little job that Nuala could do to give her an interest after the baby was born.

Some time later when Nuala had retired to her room, Kate opened the card that had arrived with the hyacinths and her face broke into a smile as she saw Martin's familiar handwriting. He really was a lovely thoughtful man. Tiredness forgotten, she hurried away to rummage in her wardrobe for something to wear the next night.

Chapter Thirteen

'So that's it then.' Kate handed David the keys to his mother's house. 'I think you'll find everything is ready. The Salvation Army will be calling to pick up the boxes by the front door within the hour. Everything is packed and the Barretts will be moving in tomorrow.'

For the first time since she had met him, Kate detected a softening in his attitude towards her.

'Thanks, Kate. You've been a great help.' He looked guiltily at the suitcases containing the sisters' clothes, which was all they were taking away with them.

He had suggested to Rebecca that Kate and Nuala could keep the odd bits of furniture and knick-knacks that she hadn't claimed, for when they got their own place, since the Barretts did not want them, but his wife had been insistent that they should be taken away. David had become so used to being under her thumb that he had put up no argument. Now he suddenly wished that he had.

'You know that you're welcome to come and see my mother whenever you please, don't you?' He wanted to say so much more but the words lodged in his throat.

'Thank you, I shall.' Kate lifted her suitcase and with

her head held high, ushered Nuala in front of her until they were standing in the hallway.

Looking back across her shoulder she stifled the urge to cry. The house where she had known happiness for such a short time looked empty now. But then if she were to be honest, it had seemed that way ever since her aunt had left it. It had been a home with her there, but now it was just a shell. Nuala's face was etched with sadness and Kate felt a sharp stab of guilt. Once again, she was being trundled off to yet another temporary home. But what was the alternative?

Sighing, she gripped the handle of her suitcase tightly and began to walk away.

'Kate, wait!'

She turned to see David haring down the road. When he came abreast of them he held something out to her. 'Here – please take this. It might help you both out a bit until you get settled, with the baby nearly here.'

As her gaze rested on the small bundle of notes in his hand, she bristled. 'No, thank you.' She shook her head, setting the dark curls that caressed her shoulders dancing. 'It was nice of you to offer, David, but as I told you when we first arrived here, we're not looking for handouts.'

As he stared into his cousin's indignant eyes, he knew in that moment that he had gravely misjudged her. Deeply embarrassed, he returned the money to his pocket. 'Well, if ever you do need anything, you only have to ask. I'll tell Mother you'll be coming to see her soon, shall I?'

Kate inclined her head and without another word continued on her way. It wasn't until they had turned out of Home Park Road into Coton Road that she let out her breath. Anger had stained her cheeks and she found that she was shaking.

'Would you believe it, eh? All those times I tried to befriend him and then on the very day when we're moving out he decides to be nice to us!'

'Well, I think you're daft,' Nuala muttered. 'That few quid would have helped us out. You should have taken it off him.'

Kate glared at her as she tried to untangle Sally's lead from around her legs. Thinking that Kate was playing with her, the little dog began to yap and run around in circles, getting them in even more of a tangle. 'Huh! It will be a cold day in hell before I'd take a handout from *him*,' she finally managed to say.

''Tain't his fault if he's under the thumb.'

'Then whose fault is it? Is he a man or a shirt button?' Kate stormed.

Nuala was so unused to seeing Kate angry that she lapsed into silence as they passed beneath the Coton Arches. In the Pingles Fields to the left of them a fairground was setting up and Nuala sighed longingly. She had never been to a fair before and decided that when Kate was in a happier frame of mind she would ask her if she would take her. Crossing the road, they passed the Fleur de Lys public house and in no time at all they were at the entrance to Shepperton Street.

'Now you'll find that Ruby's house isn't quite as grand as Aunt Beth's,' Kate told Nuala, preparing her. 'But it is clean and very comfortable, and Ruby is lovely, though . . . a little loud.'

Nuala followed her sister to a small terraced house without comment. They passed through a long whitewashed entry that led to the back of the houses. Nuala saw that there were small, shared yards, and tiny gardens behind each one. Some of the houses had tin baths hanging outside the back doors next to the outside lavatories and coalhouses, and she shuddered as she was reminded of their home in Durham.

When Kate stopped to knock on one particular door it was opened by a small fair-haired lady with startlingly bright eyes, dressed in the most garish outfit that Nuala had ever seen. The delicious smell of a stew simmering on the stove wafted out to meet them and Nuala's stomach rumbled in anticipation.

'Ah, here you are then, loves. Come on in. I've done us all a bite to eat an' then you can get unpacked an' make yourselves at home. Though you do know you'll have to share a bedroom, don't you? I only have the two, you see, but there is room in there for a cot when the little 'un puts in an appearance.'

'That will be fine, Ruby,' Kate reassured her. 'It won't be the first time we've shared, will it, Nuala?'

Nuala sulked. She had become used to having her very own room at Aunt Beth's, and the prospect of having to share again didn't appeal. Plonking her case down on the floor she peeled her coat off before sitting at the table. At least it smells as if this Ruby can cook, she consoled herself before looking curiously around the room.

A blazing fire was roaring up the chimney, surrounded by a brass fender that was so highly polished she could see her face in it, and there were so many cheap plaster ornaments spread across the mantelpiece that Nuala didn't know which one to look at first. A large threadbare rug took up most of the floorspace and around the edge of it was faded linoleum. The table she was sitting at was covered in a chenille tasselled tablecloth, and around it were four hard-backed chairs, none of which matched. A door at one side of the room led into what Nuala guessed was the parlour and another one led directly to what she was to discover was a very steep staircase. It seemed that the room she was sitting in was a kitchen-cum-sitting room. She was also soon to discover that it was the only room in the house that was heated. Just as Kate had told her, she saw that whilst it was basic it was spotlessly clean, so perhaps it wouldn't be so bad living there after all.

'Nuala – I said, this is Ruby.'

Nuala jumped as Kate's voice interrupted her inspection.

'Hello, love.' Ruby's voice was kindly. 'It's nice to meet yer. Kate talks about yer all the time. I hope you'll be happy here. The place is a bit rough an' ready, as yer can see but I pride meself on the fact that it's clean as a new pin.'

Nuala gulped before saying, 'Thanks,' as she played with the fringe on the tablecloth.

Ruby kept the smile fixed to her face, although Nuala was nothing at all like she had expected her to be; certainly nothing like Kate. In fact, she would never have taken them for sisters, not in a million bloody years. She flushed as a thought suddenly occurred to her and then, somewhat flustered, she bent to stroke the dog before hurrying away to dish out the stew.

Sometime later she showed them upstairs to a small bedroom that overlooked the narrow strips of gardens

155

at the back of the houses. 'It ain't very posh,' she apologised as she saw Nuala's eyes flicking about the room. 'But the bed is comfortable, so I'm told, and if you need any more blankets you only have to say.'

'It will be absolutely fine,' Kate assured her gratefully, and Ruby slipped away to leave them to unpack.

Nuala bounced on the side of the bed and wrinkled her nose in distaste. 'She weren't wrong when she said it weren't very posh, were she?' she grumbled. 'An' she's a bit strange an' all, ain't she?'

Kate tutted in annoyance. Nuala could be very ungrateful at times. 'Compared to some of the flats I've looked at lately, this is like a hotel – believe me. And it *is* only temporary. As for her being strange . . . all I can say is you can be very unkind.'

Hearing the annoyance in her voice, Nuala was contrite. 'Sorry, Kate. It's just . . . Well, we'd just got settled in at Aunt Beth's an' then . . .'

Immediately, Kate's annoyance was forgotten as she crossed to take her sister in her arms and rock her to and fro. 'I know, pet. I know. But things will get better, you'll see.'

Above Nuala's head her eyes travelled the room. The double bed in the middle of it took up most of the space with just enough room at the side of it to squeeze a cot in, as Ruby had said, and there was a wardrobe and a chest of drawers that looked as if they might have been antiques to put their clothes in. There was even a mirror hanging above a tiny fireplace that was packed with newspaper and a huge chamber pot beneath the bed.

'See?' Kate teased. 'We've got all the mod cons. Now come on, let's get unpacked, eh?'

When Nuala refused to move, Kate unlatched the suitcase and began to take out their clothes, keeping up a continuous stream of chatter all the while. She was used to Nuala's moods by now and always made excuses for them because she knew that being a little slow, Nuala didn't always get things right and her mouth had a tendency to run away with her. Sometimes the responsibility of caring for her sister weighed heavy on her, but if she didn't look after her, then who would – especially once the baby had arrived.

She supposed that she was lucky to have met a man who might be prepared to marry her with Nuala in tow – and yet . . . *Matthew*. She angrily pushed thoughts of him away.

When the unpacking was eventually done she turned to Nuala who was still sitting sulkily on the edge of the bed, her swollen abdomen making her look uncomfortable.

'Right, I'm going downstairs now,' she said. 'Are you coming? I thought we might take Sally for a walk.'

Nuala ignored her, so shrugging, Kate left her to it.

'So, how's the new job then, love?' Ruby was just brushing the hearth when Kate came into the room.

Kate grinned as she saw that Ruby's face was covered in soot.

'I quite like it, though it's hardly a new job, is it?' she replied. She had just started to work at the Rose and Crown fulltime as she had been finding the journey to Hinckley and back every day quite tiring. It meant a slight drop in wages, but Ruby had a little cleaning job at Shepperton rectory lined up for Nuala after she had given birth, so Kate felt that they would manage, plus the shorter hours would mean that she had more time to help with the baby. Martin wasn't too happy about it – in fact, he didn't like her working at the pub at all – but Kate had stood her ground. As she had pointed out, the hours she was working now gave her more time to see both him and her Aunt Beth.

Aunt Beth. The smile slipped from her face as she thought of her. Each time she visited, Kate felt as if her aunt were slipping farther and farther away from her. The visits were not easy, although David now went out of his way to make her feel welcome. The same couldn't be said for Rebecca, however. Whenever Kate arrived, she would usher her into Aunt Beth's room with her mouth screwed up so tight that she looked as if she was sucking on a lemon. The house was always spotless, the children always fresh-faced and ridiculously polite. Rebecca looked as if she had just stepped off a fashion page, and Aunt Beth . . . Aunt Beth was unhappy. Oh, she couldn't say it, of course, lying there in a bed that looked as if it were daring her to put a crease in it, but Kate could tell. Her lifeless eyes said it all, and it broke Kate's heart.

'Kate – can you hear me or have you gone bleedin' deaf? I said – are you seein' Martin tonight?' As Ruby's voice pulled her thoughts back to the present she started guiltily.

'Oh, sorry, Ruby. I was miles away.' Kate grinned. 'No, I'm not seeing him tonight. He has to . . . you know.'

'Ugh!' Ruby shuddered from head to toe. 'What, you mean he has to dig—'

Kate nodded before she could go any farther. 'I think

158

I might just stay in, wash my hair and have an early night.' She yawned as Ruby smiled at her fondly.

'How has Nuala been anyway?' Kate asked as she filled the kettle at the stone sink.

Ruby pursed her lips. 'I worry about that girl, I don't mind tellin' yer. She don't care what she looks like, an' she makes no effort at all to get out an' make any friends. I know she's pregnant but even so she could still get out if she'd a mind to.'

'Well, you have to remember, besides being pregnant, Nuala is . . .' Kate strove to find the right words. 'Nuala is shy and a little . . .'

'Backward?' Ruby prompted.

Kate flushed. 'Not at all,' she snapped defensively. 'She's just a little slow.'

Ruby sniffed. 'Have it yer own way then, but I reckon she'll never even try to stand on her own two feet while you keep running round after her like a blue-arsed fly. You do have a life of your own to live yer know, lovie.'

Kate knew that the words were meant kindly so she took them in the way they were intended. 'Of course I have my own life, and I do live it. In fact . . .' She hesitated, wondering how Ruby would take what she was about to tell her. 'The thing is, Martin asked me to marry him some time ago, as you know, and now . . .'

A frown creased Ruby's brow. 'You ain't thinkin' of sayin' yes, are yer? You've barely known him five minutes.'

Kate giggled at Ruby's outraged face. 'I wasn't going to say that. I was going to ask you if it would be all right if I brought him back here so that he could get to know Nuala. The thing is, I haven't told him yet that she's pregnant.'

Ruby's eyebrows almost disappeared into her hairline. 'Ain't no skin off my nose,' she commented. 'But I ain't too sure how Nuala will feel about it. The way I see it, you've got a double problem in the makin'. She makes no secret of the fact that she don't like you goin' out without her, an' if you shove him under her nose all hell might break loose, so it ain't just down to how he'll take the news, from where I'm standin'.'

'I can't do much about that, can I? If – and I say *if* – I do ever marry Martin, she'll have to get to know him then anyway. It would be much better if they got to know each other now.'

'Yer can bring who yer like back here, as far as I'm concerned,' Ruby told her. 'While you're here I want you to feel that this is your home, but just . . . Well, be careful, eh? Don't get leapin' into anythin' yer might live to regret.'

Kate leaned over to kiss her wrinkled cheek, bringing a flush to Ruby's face. It was nice to have someone to care.

Chapter Fourteen

'Why, you arrogant bugger!' Pam Elliot's enraged voice echoed around the small living room as she stood hands on hips, confronting her husband, who had just staggered in from the pub more than a little worse for wear. 'How dare you come home in this state? We've only been married fer just over a month, we're still on honeymoon, an' yet already yer off wi' yer mates as if yer still a single bloke. I should 'ave listened to me mam. She told me yer were a waster, but would I listen to 'er – would I 'ell!'

'Now, now sweetie,' her husband slurred. 'Yer know I love yer. Come 'ere an' let me prove it.'

She slapped his hands away as he lurched drunkenly towards her. 'Don't touch me! Do you 'ear? Why, I can 'ardly bear to look at yer. In fact, fer two pins I'd go back to me mam's.'

His lopsided grin incensed her all the more and she began to tremble with rage.

'That is it!' she stormed. 'I'm off.' Snatching up her coat, she began to struggle into it as her new husband's face fell a foot.

'But . . . Pammy. Yer can't just walk out on me. What

161

about me snap? I thought yer might make me a nice little bacon sarnie fer me supper.'

'Make yer own bloody sarnie,' she snarled as she headed for the door. 'An' if yer want me when yer sober up, yer know where I'll be.'

He covered the distance to the door and blocked her way as he held his arms out to her beseechingly. 'Yer can't walk out at this time o' night. The last bus went ages ago.'

'So what. I've got legs, ain't I?'

'Yer mean, yer goin' to walk all the way from Bedworth to Nuneaton at this 'our? Don't be so bloody daft, Pam. It's rainin' cats an' dogs out there.'

Flicking her long dark hair from her shoulders she glared at him. 'Then I'll get wet, won't I? Far as I'm concerned that's preferable to stayin' 'ere wi' you. Now get out o' me way before I do sommat as I might end up bein' sorry for!'

He meekly stood aside as she swept past him, slamming the door resoundingly behind her.

Just as he had told her, the rain was coming down in sharp needle-like drops that had her soaked to the skin in seconds. Just briefly she looked at the window of their little terraced house and hesitated but then she squared her shoulders and set off. She loved Dennis but intended to start as she meant to go on. Better to show him now that she meant business before any little ones came along. As she stroked her flat stomach lovingly a smile spread across her pretty face. That just might be sooner than they had expected.

She had seen the signs seven times before with her mother and although it was early days she was sure

162

that she was pregnant. It must have been a honeymoon baby.

When she approached Griff House, the former home of the novelist George Eliot, which was the town's claim to fame, she turned a sharp right towards Hill Top. The road was unlit here and she stumbled blindly through the deep puddles wondering if this had been such a good idea after all. Still, she was almost halfway to her mother's now and pride would not allow her to turn back.

As she approached the top of Griff Hollows and walked beneath the leafless trees, she shuddered. The wind sighed eerily through the branches, making her eyes dart nervously from side to side. All the stories she had ever heard of the Hollows being haunted suddenly sprang to mind and she quickened her step. It was then that she became aware of headlights behind her. The howling wind had drowned out the sound of the car engine.

Stepping as near to the side of the road as she could, she slowed her steps to allow the car to pass. She watched it descend the steep incline and start to purr its way up the other side of the hill, and then she lowered her head and hurried on. She was so lost in thought that when she began to ascend the hill at the other side of the dip she almost collided with the back of a stationary car. It was empty and there was no one in sight. It must have broken down, she thought to herself, and was just about to move on when a shape suddenly loomed out of the trees at the side of the road and began to move towards her. It was so dark that it was impossible to see if it was a man or a woman, so plucking up her courage she called, 'Hello, have you broken down? Do you need any help?'

The figure didn't answer; it just continued to move towards her, seeming to float in the darkness.

'I said – have you broken down? If you have, my mother lives not far away. One of her neighbours has a phone and you could perhaps . . .' Her voice trailed away as the figure stopped directly in front of her, blocking her path.

Panic began to rise in her as the figure stood motionless and stepping to the side, she tried to skirt round whoever it was. It was then that they suddenly reached out and grabbed her arm. Caught off-guard she stumbled and swore as her knee scraped painfully along the uneven road surface. ''Ere mate, what the bloody hell do yer think yer playin'—'

A hand clamped around her throat and she felt herself being lifted off her feet and dragged towards the trees. She began to fight. Not the silly sort of fight she and Dennis had had a million times before; now she was remembering all the newspaper reports she had read about the women who had gone missing, and knew instinctively that she might be the next on the list. Her hand, which was flailing about, settled momentarily on her stomach and she began to cry. Swear words that she had never used in her life before began to spew from her mouth at the pointlessness of it all. Why had she ever stormed out like that in the first place? Why had she been so angry? All Dennis had done, after all, was go out and have a few beers with his mates down the Rose and Crown. Was that really such a hanging offence? It all seemed so petty now and she wished with all her heart that she could turn the clock back, then she would be at home now in her lovely little kitchen making her husband his supper, instead of here in this awful place with a stranger who was about to kill her. And he was going to kill her; some inner voice had told her so.

As he dragged her further into the woods that ran alongside the road she stumbled again, her legs and her knees becoming skinned as he hauled her along. She didn't bother to scream; she knew that no one would hear her. At last he paused; she could hear his breath coming in harsh painful gasps from the effort and she managed to scramble to her feet and confront him.

As he again reached towards her she gathered every ounce of strength she had and brought her knee up between his legs. A howl of pain pierced the night and he doubled over in pain. With a speed that would have done justice to a sprinter, Pam took to her heels. Thankfully she knew every inch of the woods, since playing in them as a child, and she didn't pause in her flight. Every second she expected to hear the footsteps crashing behind her, but all she heard was the sound of the bushes snapping as she pushed through them. They tore at her face, her hands and her clothes, but she was oblivious to the pain as terror lent speed to her feet.

After what seemed an eternity, she emerged gasping from the woods back onto the road at the top of Griff Hollows. Ahead of her she could see the streetlights and she sobbed with relief. Every hair on her body was standing to attention as she looked fearfully back over her shoulder. There was not a soul in sight. It was as quiet as a graveyard. With the last of her strength she struggled on. Soon she would be safe back home with Dennis where she belonged, and it would be a very long time before she left him again.

Chapter Fifteen

'Right, that's it! From now on I shall have to collect you *every* evening from work. I will *not* have you walking home alone, do you hear me?'

Kate solemnly nodded her agreement at Martin. They had just spent a very pleasant day together and had visited many places of local interest, but his mood had changed abruptly when he stopped off at a newsagent's to buy an evening paper on their way home and she had read of the latest attack on yet another unfortunate woman.

Kate listened to what he was saying with half an ear. She had promised herself that today she would tell him about Nuala's condition, but the day was almost over and still she hadn't plucked up the courage to broach the subject.

'Look, it's plastered all across the front of the *Tribune*,' she said. 'Another poor devil has been attacked. It was Dennis Elliot's wife. You know, the chap that comes into the Rose and Crown with his mates.'

'What?' Martin flinched as he started up the engine and pulled away from the kerb. 'Oh yes, it's awful – but weren't you saying there was something you needed to talk to me about before you started reading the paper?'

'Never mind about that now,' Kate said gravely, her attention still firmly focused on the story she was reading. 'According to this, the poor woman was pregnant, but she miscarried this morning. How awful is that?'

As Martin turned off Coventry Road into Shepperton Street, Kate's mouth clamped shut when she saw Ruby pacing up and down the pavement in front of her house. She was obviously highly agitated and when she saw them she began to wave her arms in the air and hobble down the road towards them.

'Kate.' Ruby took a deep gulp of air as the car drew up beside her. 'It's Nuala. They've rushed 'er into hospital. I couldn't go with 'er or there would have been no one here to tell yer what had happened. She started bleedin' an' I didn't know what to do, so I got Mrs Crewe across the road to ring fer an ambulance. I reckon she's havin' the baby.'

Shock registered on Martin's face but Kate was too distraught to worry about that for now. Turning to him she looked at him imploringly. 'Please, Martin, would you run me up to the George Eliot Hospital?'

'Of course.' Ever the gentleman, he got out of the car and opened the rear passenger door for Ruby. 'You'd better hop in too. If this is going to be a long job then Kate will need someone to keep her company.'

Without a word of argument, Ruby scrambled in, still wearing her bright wraparound pinafore, and within minutes they were on their way. When the car drew to a halt outside the maternity unit Kate turned to look at Martin with tears in her eyes.

'I'm so sorry you had to find out about the baby like this,' she said in a choked voice. 'I was going to tell you today, but somehow I kept putting it off because I didn't know how you'd react.'

'Ssh, don't worry about that for now. You just get in there and be with your sister. I'll call round tomorrow to see how things are.'

Kate climbed from the car and joined Ruby, who was standing impatiently waiting for her.

Grim-faced, Martin leaned out of the car window and squeezed her hand. 'Good luck,' he said, and then he roared away. Kate turned and hurried inside.

'Fer God's sake! Will yer please sit down, love? Yer makin' me feel dizzy with all this pacin' up an' down!'

'Sorry, Ruby.' Kate glanced up yet again at the large clock that was ticking away on the waiting-room wall. They had been at the hospital for almost three hours now, but still they hadn't been allowed to see Nuala.

'She's in the delivery room,' a vinegar-faced nurse had told them, and then after leading them to the waiting room she had disappeared and not been seen since.

'Do you think I ought to go out to the desk and see if they know if anything's happened yet?' Kate asked Ruby yet again.

Ruby sighed and was just about to answer her when the door suddenly swung open and a midwife in a huge blood-spattered apron appeared.

'Are you Kate Cleary?' Her voice betrayed her weariness.

Kate nodded, her frightened eyes huge in her pale face.

'I'm afraid your sister is having rather a bad time of it and she's asking for you. It's totally against all the rules for anyone but staff to be present at a birth, but your sister has worked herself up into such a state that I think your presence might help to calm her. Do you think you can face being present?'

Without hesitation, Kate nodded.

'Well done. Follow me then, would you?'

Ruby flashed her a reassuring smile and within seconds Kate was following the midwife along a winding corridor. Screams were echoing from a room at the far end of it and Kate's stomach turned over as she recognised Nuala's voice.

'Here, put these on and wash your hands – and hurry, please.' The midwife almost threw a mask and a gown at Kate, which she hurriedly slipped into, then they were going through the door and there was Nuala lying on a bloodstained bed.

'Kate.' Nuala's pain-filled eyes almost broke Kate's heart. She looked so very young and vulnerable lying there that in that moment Kate hated Matthew more than she had ever hated anyone in her whole life.

Crossing swiftly to her, Kate took a flannel from a bowl at the side of the bed and began to wipe her sister's sweating forehead. 'There,' she crooned softly. 'Now you just do everything the nurse tells you and it will all be over in no time.'

Nuala clung to her hand as another contraction ripped through her and Kate bit down hard on her lip to stop the tears that were brimming behind her eyes from falling.

Minutes later a stern-faced doctor strode into the room and after a hushed conversation with the midwife he approached the bed. 'I'm afraid we're going to have to cut you,' he told Nuala quietly. 'It's because your baby is in distress and we need to deliver it as quickly as possible. Now listen carefully . . .' All the time he was talking soothingly to Nuala he was pulling on plastic gloves. Leaning over the young woman whose screams were echoing off the walls, he told her, 'It's imperative that you do what I say.' He lifted an evil-looking scalpel that glinted in the harsh fluorescent light from a bowl, and Kate shuddered as he leaned across her sister's heaving stomach.

'Now in a minute when I tell you to push, I want you to do so with all your might.'

She watched in horrified fascination and seconds later the bloodstain spread even further across the starched white sheet. He nodded in satisfaction.

'Right,' he said with authority as his hands rested on her stomach and he sensed another contraction coming. 'Now Nuala . . . *PUSH*!'

Her face beetroot red with strain, Nuala did as she was told as she hung on to Kate's hand for grim death.

'Good girl!' The doctor panted as he hung over her. 'Now – *again* – and this time push with all your might!'

As tears coursed down Nuala's cheeks, Kate hung over her, whispering words of encouragement.

'I can't do this, Kate,' she screamed through gritted teeth, but Kate shook her hand.

'Oh yes, you bloody well *can*, now come on. Do as the doctor says – *push*!'

Lifting her head from the sweat-soaked pillow with a last superhuman effort, Nuala bit down on her lip and pushed for all she was worth. They were rewarded when the doctor shouted, '*Yes*, here it is. I can see the head. Now come on, Nuala, one more time should do it.'

Beyond tears now, Nuala gave one last push and suddenly a mewling little cry echoed off the cold clinical walls.

'That's it. Well done. You have a little girl and she's—' The doctor's voice stopped abruptly as he stared down at the tiny infant on the bed and suddenly all hell seemed to break loose as he and the midwife exchanged a worried glance. Before Kate could even ask what was wrong, the woman snatched the baby up, wrapped it in a towel and ran from the room as Kate watched in horror.

'What's wrong? Where has she taken the baby?' Kate's voice was shaking as the doctor ran a weary hand across his brow.

'Let's just concentrate on getting your sister sorted out for now, shall we? The midwife has just taken the baby to bath her.'

'But . . . but Nuala didn't even get to see her,' Kate faltered. Something about the firm set of his jaw silenced her and she sat quietly as he did what needed to be done to Nuala.

Once Nuala had been stitched, washed and put into a clean gown and propped up in bed, a nurse bustled in with a tray of tea. Nuala had said not a word since the birth and stared at the nurse from dull eyes as she fussed over her. Kate quickly poured her a cup of tea and discreetly followed the nurse from the room. Once in the corridor she looked into the woman's troubled eyes.

'There is something wrong with the baby, isn't there?'

The nurse looked away. 'Look, the doctor will be down to see you both as soon as he's finished examining her. If there is anything wrong I'm sure he'll tell you.

Meantime, go back into your sister, eh? She needs you right now.'

'The baby's dead, ain't it?'

As Kate closed the door softly behind her, Nuala's weak voice met her.

'Of course she isn't dead,' she told her reassuringly.

Nuala shrugged, causing her to wince with pain. 'I don't care if it is. In fact, I hope it *is*! I never wanted the damn brat in the first place.'

Kate's breath caught in her throat as the room spun around her. 'Oh Nuala, how could you say such a thing? You know you don't mean it. You'll feel differently once you see her and hold her. She's your baby.'

'*I won't.*'

Completely at a loss as to what she should say, Kate suddenly remembered Ruby who was still waiting in the tiny room at the end of the corridor. 'Look, I'd better just go and tell Ruby to get herself off home. You drink your tea and relax and I'll be back before you know it.'

Nuala turned on her side as Kate left the room.

The next hour was the longest of Kate's life. She sat silently at the side of her sister, who had slipped into a drug-induced sleep, but at last the door swung open and a tall dark-haired doctor entered the room with a stiff-faced Sister at his side.

'You are?' He directed his question at Kate, and feeling as if she were back at school in front of the Headmaster, Kate stuttered, 'I – I'm Nuala's sister.'

'And where is the husband?'

When Kate hung her head he nodded knowingly and sniffed his disapproval. 'I see. Well, I'm afraid I have some very bad news for you, Miss Cleary. Your sister's baby is very ill indeed.'

'But . . .'

'There is no easy way to tell you this so I'll just come out and say it. There is something wrong with the baby's heart.'

When Kate stared at him uncomprehendingly his manner softened. 'We can't be sure, of course, until we have completed our tests.'

'But she will be all right, won't she?'

'I'm afraid I can't answer that question just yet, but you can rest assured we are doing all we can.'

'But . . . but she's just a baby.' Kate's voice cracked as she tried to digest what the doctor was telling her.

'Tomorrow when all the tests are completed I should be able to tell you more . . . Meanwhile, I have already informed the hospital chaplain of the child's condition and he will be coming to see you shortly in case the mother would like the baby to be christened.'

Kate felt as if she were caught up in a nightmare. She looked across at Nuala who was now sleeping peacefully, and as if reading her thoughts, the doctor asked, 'Would you like us to tell your sister or would you prefer to do it?'

Kate gulped deep in her throat. 'I . . . I'll do it . . . thank you.'

'Very well.' The doctor looked at her sympathetically before asking, 'Would you like to see the baby? Your sister could be asleep for some time. It's highly unorthodox and Matron will have my guts for garters if she finds out, but Sister will be happy to take you along to the Intensive Care Unit, won't you, Sister?'

Sister drew herself up to her full height and pursed her thin lips, but not daring to defy the doctor she nodded.

Dragging her eyes away from Nuala's face, Kate suddenly wished with all her heart that she hadn't sent Ruby home. But then she thought of the infant lying somewhere all alone and slowly nodded. Without another word she rose from her seat and followed the Sister from the room.

At the door she paused to look back at the doctor who was studying the chart at the end of Nuala's bed. 'May I ask you just one question?'

'Of course.'

'If the worst should happen, how long before . . .' The words stuck in her throat but the doctor knew exactly what she wanted to know; unfortunately this was a situation he had been faced with far too many times before.

'I'm afraid that's a question that I really can't answer at this stage.'

'Thank you.' With a quiet dignity that hid the heartache she was feeling, Kate inclined her head and followed the Sister down the corridor.

The hospital corridors were deserted save for the odd nurse here and there, who reverently stood aside to let the Sister sail past them.

She finally paused at some double doors and after ringing a bell at the side of them she turned to Kate who was surprised to see that she didn't look quite so fearsome now. 'This is the Intensive Baby Care Unit, my dear. I shall have to get back to my ward now, but you are quite welcome to come back once you have seen the baby.'

She walked away just as a young nurse opened the

doors and smiled kindly at Kate. 'You've come to see the Cleary baby, have you?'

Kate nodded, her eyes huge in her strained face.

'It's this way. You'll need to wash your hands first.' She pointed to a sink and after quickly doing as she was told, Kate followed her down a ward that was full of tiny incubators where even tinier babies were hooked up to all manner of terrifying-looking equipment.

The drab cream-coloured bare walls did nothing to lessen the feeling of dread that had settled on Kate. It was hard to believe this was a nursery; it was all so cold and clinical. Her heart began to thump painfully in her chest as she licked her dry lips.

When they were almost at the end of the ward the nurse stopped in front of an incubator. 'This is the Cleary baby. She's your niece, isn't she?'

Kate nodded numbly.

'Well, I'll leave you to get to know her a little then. There's a chair at the side of the cot – look – and a hole where you can put your hand through and touch her if you wish. Try not to be frightened by all the tubes and drips. She's quite comfortable. She's sleeping quite peacefully at the moment.'

'Th . . . thank you.' Kate's eyes followed the nurse as she walked away. She waited until she'd disappeared into a small office at the other end of the ward and then slowly forced herself to look down on her niece. The sight she saw almost tore her apart, for despite her condition, the child was truly beautiful. She had a mop of dark hair that stood on end and thick black eyelashes that curled on her porcelain cheeks.

Tears sprang to her eyes and at last all the grief she

was feeling bubbled out of her. Apart from the fact that her lips were blue, the child looked like any other newborn baby, and it was hard to believe that soon she could die without ever having known any life at all.

This little scrap of humanity was her niece, Nuala's child . . . and Matthew's. The tears ran faster. Matthew. *Oh, Matthew*. She had never once, since Nuala had told her who the father was, questioned her sister, but now she hated him with a vengeance. He had taken advantage of Nuala – he *must* have done, the way Kate saw it – and this was the result. This poor little innocent. Her hand snaked through the cut-out in the side of the incubator and she caressed the baby's satin soft skin, relishing the feel of her. As she blinked through her tears her thoughts turned for the first time to Martin. What must he be thinking? Oh, he had driven her there, but she'd seen the shock in his eyes when Ruby met them in the street to tell them what had happened. She wished now that she had told him earlier in the day of Nuala's condition, as she'd planned to. But it was too late for wishing now; the damage was done and he would probably never want to set eyes on her again.

Suddenly a wave of utter tiredness washed through her. All her young life she had had to worry about other people and now here was yet another little person to fret about. *But not for long*, a wicked voice inside her head whispered, and as the hopelessness of the situation closed in on her she lowered her head and wept.

Chapter Sixteen

On a bitterly cold, rainy day in February, Kate took Jennifer Cleary home. The doctor's fears had been confirmed. The valves in the child's heart were faulty, but she was a little fighter and clung on to life with a will that made Kate proud of her.

Since her birth, Kate had seen neither hide nor hair of Martin, but she had more worrying things to think of at present, like Nuala, who was sitting at home locked in a world of her own. She had never once so much as visited the hospital or set eyes on her daughter since the day Kate had brought her home, despite all Kate's attempts to persuade her to go and see the sweet-natured infant.

It was Kate who had spent every spare minute at the hospital in the previous weeks. It was Kate who had stood solemnly by in the Intensive Care Unit while the chaplain christened the child, and it was Kate who had chosen her name, Jennifer, after their mother. Somehow it seemed fitting now that it should be Kate who was taking her home but she was sure that once Nuala saw her, she would soon come to love the baby as she herself did.

Following her to the doors of the Intensive Care Unit, the nurse pressed a list of care instructions into Kate's sweating hand.

'Now try not to get worrying too much. Just treat her like you would any other baby. If you have any concerns at all you can bring her straight back to us. As the doctor explained, when she's a little older he'll be able to operate. She's doing remarkably well, all things considered.' As she spoke she stroked Jennifer's dark hair fondly. 'Now go on, be off with you,' she grinned. 'And be sure to bring her back to see us.'

Kate gulped, suddenly terrified of the responsibility being placed on her shoulders, but then she looked down on the baby's sleeping face and hitching her more comfortably into her arms, she carried her towards the exit to the hospital. A couple of weeks before, she had phoned David to ask him to pass on the news of the birth to Aunt Beth and surprisingly, ever since he had been a tower of strength. Her cousin had further surprised her the day before with an unexpected visit and by offering to fetch the baby home, and now there he was waiting for her in his shiny Ford Popular just as he had promised. Kate trotted towards the car keeping the shawl tucked tightly about Jennifer. The rain was coming down in torrents and David hurried around to open the rear door for her. Kate clambered in with the child clutched protectively against her chest.

He smiled as he moved the edge of the shawl to peep at her. 'She's a right little smasher, isn't she?'

Kate nodded proudly as emotion swept through her. There had been times during the last two weeks when she had been sure that she was going to lose her, but

179

now, here she was taking her home to her mother. Her mother . . . Thoughts of Nuala snatched the smile from her face.

What if Nuala didn't accept her? Kate pushed the thought away. Of course she would accept her. Who could fail to love little Jennifer, once they had held her in their arms?

'Come on,' she said with false cheerfulness. 'Let's get this little scrap home to her mum.'

David grinned and, starting the engine, he swung the car in the homeward direction. When they arrived at Ruby's house he helped Kate from the car, carrying her bag for her.

'Right then, Kate. If there's anything I can do, or anything you need – just ring me, eh?' he said awkwardly.

Kate had no chance to answer because just then Ruby exploded from the front door, her face wreathed in smiles.

'My, this is a red letter day an' make no mistake about it,' she beamed. 'A couple o' weeks ago I wouldn't have given a penny fer the little mite's chances, an' now here she is comin' home to us.'

Suddenly feeling in the way, David climbed back into his car and raised his hand in a final salute before driving off.

'Huh! He can't be short of a bob or two,' Ruby commented dryly as she watched him go. 'Posh car, posh house an' a phone to boot. There ain't many around here as have that at his age. An' what's caused his sudden change of heart towards yer, that's what I'd like to know. Perhaps it's his guilty conscience.'

'What?' Kate said vaguely.

Dragging her eyes back to the young woman at her

side, Ruby's face creased with concern. Kate looked absolutely washed out and it was hardly any wonder, what with all she'd had on her plate over the last few weeks. And then there was Nuala. Ruby had never really taken to the girl, but since the birth of the baby she'd retreated into a world where no one could reach her, and this incensed Ruby because it meant that everything was left to Kate yet again. The doctor said it was delayed shock, but Ruby had her own thoughts on it. As far as she was concerned, the girl was simply gut selfish. She hadn't even bothered to go and see her own baby, and with the poor little mite at death's door too.

Still, life could be cruel, as she had discovered long ago; her life had hardly gone the way she had planned it either. Glancing down the road at the stained-glass windows of the church, which were just visible through the trees that surrounded the churchyard, she suddenly saw herself in her mind's eye standing there at the door as a bride all those years ago on her father's arm. He had been so proud that day and she had been so very happy. She was marrying her Leonard, an older man, but still the man of her dreams, and they were going to have lots of babies and live happily ever after.

Huh! So much for dreams. Less than eighteen months after they were married Leonard had suffered a massive stroke, much the same as the one Kate's aunt had recently had, and he'd never been the same again. Ruby had nursed him lovingly through one stroke after another until eventually a heart-attack killed him, making her old before her time. She'd learned to make every penny count and all thoughts of having her own children soon flew out of the window as she struggled to make ends meet any way she could – yet strangely, if she could have her time all over again, she knew deep down that she wouldn't have changed a thing. Leonard had been the love of her life and no man before or since could ever measure up to him. Still, things were looking up. She had Kate and a beautiful baby to care for now.

Suddenly becoming aware of Kate, who was leaning heavily on her arm, she pulled her thoughts back to the present and gently taking the baby from her she nudged her towards the open front door. 'Come on, miss. I reckon a good strong cup o' tea might go down a treat, an' no doubt this little 'un will soon be ready fer a feed an' all.'

As she ushered Kate in front of her she noticed someone striding towards them through the rain, which was now bouncing off the road. The breath caught in her throat – it was Martin. She wondered how Kate would react to him as bitter resentment rose in her. Just who the bloody hell did he think he was anyway, turnin' up like this out o' the blue after ignoring them for the last two weeks? And just when Kate had needed someone to lean on as well.

Glancing across at Kate she tried to gauge her reaction but when he drew abreast of them and halted, Kate merely looked at him through dull eyes.

'Right, I'm goin' to get this one in out o' the rain before she catches her death o' cold,' Ruby said shortly, and hurrying away with her precious bundle she left them to it.

'Kate, I . . . er . . . I hope you don't mind me turning up like this.' Martin's concerned eyes were fixed on her face. 'I heard about the baby's illness shortly after the birth, which is why I kept away. I thought you might need time to spend with her and Nuala. But now . . . Well, is there anything I can do?'

Kate slowly shook her head as he shuffled from foot-to-foot, obviously deeply embarrassed.

'In that case then, I won't keep you. It's an awful day, isn't it?' His mouth clamped shut at his unfortunate use of words, but he needn't have worried. Kate had turned to walk away as if she wasn't even aware of his presence.

'Perhaps we could go out?' he gabbled, as he felt her slipping away from him – but the rest of his words were lost in the wind as Kate closed the door firmly between them.

'Come on, Nuala. You have to eat,' Kate implored. It was four days since Kate had brought Jennifer home and still Nuala sat in the chair staring into the fire, seemingly oblivious to everything that was going on around her. It was a worry. For almost a month now, Kate had barely worked at all. Vera had been marvellous, telling her to take as much time off as she needed to, but now Kate needed to start earning again; Ruby was certainly in no position to support them. She held the plate of cheese and onion sandwiches out to her sister, they were her favourite, but Nuala just continued to stare absently into the fire.

Deciding that drastic measures were called for, Kate suddenly reached out and shook Nuala's arm roughly. She had tried pleading to no avail, now it was time to try another tack. 'Will you *please* listen to me! How long is this going to go on for, Nuala? I don't mind telling you, I'm just about at the end of my tether and I don't know how much more I can take. If I don't get back to work soon we're going to be in serious trouble. We can't live on fresh air, you know? Vera has had to take a part-time barmaid on because of all the time I've had off. You're going to have to start caring for your baby soon. We can't just keep expecting Ruby to take care of her every single time I have to step out of the door.'

A knock at the back door interrupted her and sighing, she dumped the untouched food on the table and went to open it. She was confronted by Martin clutching a box of Cadbury's Milk Tray.

'I . . . er . . . I bought you these.' When he held them out to her she automatically took them and stood aside as he stepped into the room. He stood just inside the door with a self-conscious smile on his face as Kate carried the chocolates to the table and put them down. It was then that they heard Ruby's heels click-click-clicking up the entry and the next second she barged in laden down with brown-paper carrier bags.

'Cor, these bloody string handles don't half cut into yer hands,' she remarked, as if it were the most normal thing in the world to see Martin standing there.

As she glanced across at Nuala her expression changed when she saw that the girl was watching Martin intently. She winked at Kate and when her eyes followed Ruby's she blinked with surprise.

'Please, sit down.' Turning her attention back to Martin, Ruby forced a smile to her face as her eyes settled on the chocolates. 'Cor, me favourites,' she muttered. 'They won't last long wi' me about but I'll make us all a nice cup of tea, eh? Do yer fancy one, Nuala?'

Nuala nodded, her eyes never leaving Martin, and Kate *really* smiled for the first time in weeks. Whether it was Martin's visit, or whether it was of her own accord, Nuala seemed to be coming back to them and Kate thanked God for it. Looking decidedly uncomfortable, Martin perched on the edge of a chair, keeping his eyes averted from the infant who was sleeping in her crib at the side of the fireplace. When he finally left some time later, Kate followed him out to his car.

'Thanks for the chocolates,' she said shyly.

His mouth worked for a time as he tried to put into words what he wanted to say. 'Look, Kate, I know I must have seemed a bit heartless over the last weeks, keeping away as I did, but . . . to be honest, it was a bit of a shock to find out Nuala was pregnant as I did. Why didn't you tell me?'

Kate lowered her eyes. 'I was worried about what you would think,' she mumbled miserably. 'I know I *should* have told you, and I honestly *did* intend to, but . . .'

'It doesn't matter now,' he said softly, sensing her distress. 'I'm only sorry that things turned out as they did, but now – do you think we could perhaps pick up where we left off? I'm so *very* fond of you, Kate.'

'It isn't that simple, Martin. I . . . I have a sister and a baby to worry about now.'

'It doesn't matter.' He sounded so sincere that a warm glow started in her stomach and began to spread through her as a becoming blush lent colour to her cheeks.

'Then I suppose we could try.'

He leaned forward with a broad grin on his face and, very aware that they were in the middle of the street, he kissed her chastely on the cheek. Kate stifled a grin; that was one of the things she found endearing about Martin, he was such a gentleman, which was probably why he objected to Ruby so much.

'Shall I pick you up about seven o'clock tomorrow? We could go to the pictures or something. Everyone's raving about that new film that's out, *The Dam Busters* – I thought we might go and see that.'

'All right, then. If Ruby can stay in with Nuala I'll see you tomorrow at seven.'

'And what will happen if Ruby can't stay in with her?' Martin questioned.

'Then I'll ask Doris Wright, one of Ruby's neighbours, to help out and if she can't then Winnie Trotter, one of the other neighbours, will have her.' Kate stood back as he climbed into his car and waved as he drove away. She watched until his Zephyr disappeared around the bend in the road then turning, she hurried back into the house out of the bitingly cold wind.

'So how was she then?' Ruby asked amiably as Kate flung her coat over the back of the chair and held her hands out to the warmth of the fire. Kate had just got back from seeing her Aunt Beth and was frozen through.

'Still not too good,' Kate replied, unable to keep the concern from her voice as she peeped at Jennifer who was fast asleep in a Moses basket at the side of the fire.

Ruby sighed. 'And what sort o' reception did yer get from Her Ladyship?'

Kate found herself grinning with amusement at Ruby's term for Rebecca. 'About the same as usual, though I have to say David goes out of his way to make me feel welcome now. In fact, he practically ordered Rebecca to make a pot of tea when I got there.' She chuckled as she recalled it. 'Honestly, Ruby, I wish you could have seen her face. I thought she was going to bust a gut.'

Ruby giggled as she carried a heavy brown teapot dressed in a hand-knitted tea cosy to the table. Lifting a strainer she began to pour the tea into two heavy earthenware mugs.

'So what is it that's worrying you about your aunt? The doctors did warn yer not to expect too much.'

'I know that, Ruby. But there's something I can't quite put my finger on. It's almost as if every time she sees me, she's trying to tell me something. Do you think it's something about my mother?'

'Doubt it.' Ruby kept her head down so that Kate wouldn't see the flush that had stained her cheeks. 'She's probably just frustrated with having to lie in bed day in and day out.'

'I suppose you're right,' Kate agreed as she spooned sugar into her tea, but deep inside, the sense of unease refused to go. 'Where's Nuala?' she asked, keen to change the subject.

'Not back from work yet. Should be in any second now.' Ruby preened with satisfaction. 'Even though I do say so meself, getting her that little cleanin' job over at the vicarage were the best bloody thing I ever did, though she still ain't made no move towards the little 'un. Still, it don't do to sit mopin' about the place day after day. Speakin' of which, I'm off out meself tonight. Thought I might go down the Bingo Hall with Mrs Watts from up the road. She's been askin' me for long enough, so I thought, why not?'

Kate struggled to keep the surprise from showing on her face. Despite all the rumours she had heard about

Ruby being a one for the men, she'd never known her to go anywhere, apart from to work and shopping, and thought that a night out would do her good. Now that she came to think about it, Ruby had never told her anything about her past at all.

Sometimes Kate wondered what she would ever have done without her over the last few months. Ruby had somehow conjured up almost everything they would need for the baby before Kate brought her home. Her pram had come from a second-hand shop in Edward Street and Ruby had spent hours scrubbing the wheels and polishing the chrome on it till it shone. The cot and the basket she had borrowed from a neighbour, and she had come across the glass feeding bottles at a rummage sale. On top of all that she had crocheted some lovely cot and pram blankets as well as painstakingly stitching some tiny white flannelette nightdresses that she had lovingly smocked and embroidered. Kate watched her peep into the cot, all the love she felt for the child shining in her eyes before turning her attention back to Kate.

'Oh, an' by the way, some flowers come for you today. I've put 'em in a bucket over by the back door. They may have to stay in the bleedin' bucket an' all if you don't throw the last lot out. I've only got one vase. I reckon we must have more bloody flowers in here than they've got in the florist's shop.'

As Kate's eyes moved to the bucket she grinned. Ruby was exaggerating slightly. It was only one modest bunch and by now the last lot were dead.

Just then, Nuala appeared through the back door. Ignoring her daughter, who was snuggled in Kate's arms, she looked at the latest floral offering and her face creased in a frown. 'Don't need two guesses to know who they're off, do we?'

Ignoring the sarcasm in her sister's voice, Kate patted the seat beside her. 'Come and sit down and get thawed out. There's some tea left in the pot and this Victoria sponge Ruby has made just melts in your mouth.'

Nuala's coat joined Kate's over the back of the chair and after cutting herself a huge slice of cake she asked, 'Are you off out tonight again then?'

'No, as a matter of fact I'm not, but Ruby is, so what say we have a nice quiet night in with the telly, just the three of us, eh?'

Nuala shrugged although her face brightened as she helped herself to another slice of cake. That was one good thing about staying with Ruby. Although the cleaner found it hard to make ends meet, she rented a television from a shop in town, saying that everyone should have at least one luxury in their life. Nuala couldn't have agreed more.

Sometime later, Kate was watching the news on the BBC as she gave Jenny, as they had now taken to calling her, her bottle, when the stairs door opened and Ruby appeared. Kate's mouth gaped open in amazement at the sight that met her eyes. Ruby was dressed in a smart two-piece suit in a lovely shade of duck-egg blue that complimented her petite figure. Her hair, which was prone to curl, had been teased into waves that framed her face and on her feet she wore cream shoes with a matching handbag and gloves.

'*Wow!*'

Ruby flushed as she smoothed her straight skirt self-consciously. 'I ain't overdone me powder an' paint, have I?'

189

Kate laughed aloud. 'Why, Ruby, you look a million dollars. You look so . . .' Her voice tailed off as she tried to think of the word she was looking for.

'Young?' Ruby ventured as a mischievous grin played around her lips.

'Why . . . yes, you *do* look young.' Kate could have added that she looked completely different without the garish clothes she usually wore but was afraid of hurting the woman's feelings.

'Ah well, happen I ain't as old as you thought an' I can still scrub up when I've a mind to. Don't forget I went to school with your mam, God bless her soul. I'm only just turned fifty, believe it or not, but I ain't had the easiest of lives, not that I'm complaining.' She laughed at Kate's shocked expression. 'I were a bit of a looker in me day, so I were told. Not that I could ever hold a candle to your mam, o' course. Now *she* were *beautiful* – much like you to look at. I dare say we made an ill-matched pair, what wi' your mam being so well brought up an' me from a council house. But it didn't stop us from bein' the best o' friends. It nearly broke me heart when she met your dad and cleared off to Ireland – but that's enough o' that. If I don't get off, Mrs Watts will be thinking that I ain't coming. Jenny's next feed is due about eight. Yer will be all right on your own, you and Nuala, won't yer?'

'Of course we will,' Kate assured her. 'Now you get yourself away and have a good time.'

'Ta-ra then.' Ruby tripped to the door and disappeared into the windy March evening as Kate stared into the flames that were roaring up the chimney. Within minutes her expression darkened as her eyes rested on the baby.

It had been a difficult few weeks for all of them, but now that Nuala had started her little job and Ruby was venturing out, she hoped that things would start to improve. As her eyes moved to the window she shuddered. Directly opposite the end of Shepperton Street was Shepperton Church. Martin would be there now, digging a grave in the churchyard in readiness for a burial next day. Gently lifting the baby to her shoulder she began to wind her.

Much later that evening she curled into a tight little ball in the fireside chair and fell fast asleep. The sound of someone hammering on the front door brought her springing awake. She knuckled the sleep from her eyes and on legs that were cramped from being curled beneath her she staggered through to answer it. She was shocked to see David standing on the step in a state of great agitation.

'Why David – whatever's the matter?'

He ran his hand through his hair as he stared back at her from red-rimmed eyes.

'Kate, it's my mother. She's ill. I mean *very* ill. The doctor is with her now and he doesn't expect her to last the night. I thought you might like to see her before . . .'

'Of course. Come in while I just grab my coat and shoes.' Kate tore away as he stepped into the room and looked around curiously. Funny, he thought, it isn't half as grand as my house and yet it feels homely. He didn't have time to think any more because just then Kate hurried back into the room, buttoning her coat as she came. Nuala was close behind her, a frown creasing her face into a mask of irritation. It was more than obvious

191

that she didn't want to come with them and was only doing so because Kate had commanded her to, but there wasn't time to worry about that now, so after Kate had lifted Jenny from her crib he herded them outside to his car.

Kate kept her eyes shut for most of the journey and prayed that they wouldn't pass a police car as David took the corners on two wheels, but at last they pulled up outside his impressive detached house in Hinckley. Nuala had never been there before and gazed at it in awe. She had thought that her Aunt Beth's house was grand, but this was like something out of a magazine.

The girls followed David up the drive to be met at the door by a stiff-faced Rebecca. 'Would you mind taking your shoes off, please?' Her voice was as cold as the look in her eyes but Kate, Nuala and even David meekly did as they were told. They then followed her up a sweeping staircase to a small galleried landing where she paused.

'Mother-in-law is in that room there and you'll find the doctor is with her. I'll be downstairs but do please *try* to be quiet. The children are in bed and Belinda has to be up early in the morning for a ballet lesson.'

'Blast the bloody ballet lesson, woman. Don't you realise my mother is in that room there *dying*!' David snapped uncharacteristically.

Rebecca looked as if she had been slapped in the face as colour flamed in her carefully made-up cheeks. 'Perhaps you should have remembered *that* when you went haring off to fetch . . . these two!'

David's hands clenched into fists of rage and Kate was surprised when she found herself feeling sorry for him.

'Don't you think we ought to go into her?' she asked tactfully, hoping to diffuse the situation.

Pulling himself together with an effort, David nodded. 'Of course, I'm so sorry. After you.' Taking the baby from Kate's arms he gave her to Rebecca, whose mouth gaped, then pushing the door open he ushered Kate and Nuala before him into the room.

Her first sight of her aunt made the breath catch in Kate's throat. There was no sign of the dignified pearls and twin-sets any more, just a wizened-up sick woman lying on the bed. 'Oh, Aunt Beth.' Once again Kate felt as if her heart were breaking. After the strain of the last few weeks she had felt sure that there were no more tears left to cry, but now they gushed from her eyes.

The doctor discreetly stepped away from the bed. In truth, there was really no reason for him to be there any more; there was nothing he could do, it was just a matter of time now. But he stayed all the same for the sake of the family.

Nuala huddled against the wall at the side of the door like a frightened fawn about to make her escape while David stood back as Kate bent to kiss her aunt's wrinkled cheek.

Her blue-veined eyelids suddenly flickered open and a smile played around her mouth as she saw Kate leaning over her.

'K . . . Ka . . . ty!' Every breath was an effort as she struggled to speak.

Shocked to hear her aunt managing to speak again, Kate patted her hand. 'Ssh. Don't try to talk, Aunt Beth. I'm here.'

Her aunt's eyes softened as she looked up at the girl

she had come to love as her own, but when she saw Nuala she visibly stiffened.

'N . . . Nu . . .' Her hand flapped weakly on the bedspread as she tried to say something and her face became agitated.

'Aunt Beth – what is it? It's only Nuala. Look – she's come to see you.'

Her aunt's head wagged from side-to-side on the fine linen pillowcases and seeing her distress the doctor stepped forward.

'Perhaps you should all leave the room and give her time to calm down?' he suggested.

At his words Beth clung to Kate's hand. 'N . . . No. M . . . mu . . . must tell.'

'Tell me what?' Kate leaned closer as Nuala suddenly slipped through the door and disappeared.

Instantly, Beth settled back against the pillows and became calmer. Her one good hand came up to softly stroke Kate's smooth cheek.

'Jennifer,' she whispered the word with no difficulty at all. There was so much love in the look she gave Kate that the girl knew instinctively that in that moment, her aunt thought she was her long-lost sister.

'Is there nothing you can do?' she implored the doctor as she dragged her gaze momentarily away from her aunt to look at him beseechingly.

'I'm afraid not.'

In the few short seconds it took to ask the question, Kate felt her aunt relax and quickly turned her attention back to her. A look of peace had settled on her face, and Kate knew then that her aunt's suffering was finally over, whilst her own was yet again about to begin.

Stepping to the bed, the doctor quickly felt for a pulse. After a few seconds he shook his head. 'I'm afraid she's gone, my dear,' he told her gently.

Kate clung to the hand resting in her own. 'I know,' she whispered. 'And may she rest in peace. Heaven will be a better place tonight when she arrives there.'

Chapter Seventeen

'Come on – let's get away, shall we? David can give Ruby and Nuala a lift home when they're ready.'

Kate glanced at Martin gratefully before turning her attention to the black-clad mourners spread around Rebecca's immaculate lounge sipping sherry from crystal glasses. It was almost as if he had read her mind. She felt that if she didn't get out of there soon she would go mad. She looked around the room for her cousin. He was standing apart from the rest, twirling the drink in his hand aimlessly as he stared out over the beautifully kept lawns that surrounded the house.

Picking her way through the mourners who were nibbling on dainty cucumber sandwiches and talking in hushed whispers, she approached him.

'I'm going to leave now, David.'

Her voice made his head swivel to look at her and she was shocked to see the torment in his eyes.

'Would you mind giving Nuala and Ruby a lift home?' she asked.

He had no time to reply, for at that second Ruby appeared at her elbow.

'There'll be no need fer that, love. I'm ready to go now.

We shouldn't be leavin' Jenny wi' Doris fer much longer, an' I think Nuala is ready to go too. That is, if Martin is happy to take us home?'

'Of course I am,' Martin assured her, and was amused to see a look of relief wash across Ruby's face.

'Right then. I'll just go an' collect our coats while yer say yer goodbyes.' Ruby bustled away and Kate was left with David who was watching her intently.

'Aren't you going to stay for the reading of the will?' he asked.

Kate shook her head firmly. 'No, I'm not. As I told you when we moved in with your mother, I was never out for what she could give me. Although I have to say she gave me something far more precious than anything that she could have had written into her will – and that was her love.'

He lowered his head. 'Do you know something, Kate? I'm ashamed to say it, but I have to admit that in the beginning I totally misjudged you. I'm sorry. Can we still be friends? We are family after all, whether we like it or not.'

Never one to bear a grudge, Kate smiled at him kindly. 'Of course we can. That's if . . .' She glanced at Rebecca, who was wending her way towards them with a face like a thundercloud.

'Going now, are you?' she asked.

Kate flushed. 'Yes, I am. Thank you for having us. The funeral was very . . .' Lost for words, she floundered until David came to her rescue.

'Make sure you keep in touch now. We're always here if you need us. *Aren't we, Rebecca?*'

Thankfully the tense moment was broken when

Martin appeared at Kate's side. Inclining his head politely towards David he took Kate's elbow and propelled her towards the door. Once it had closed behind them, Kate breathed a sigh of relief.

Martin ushered them all into the car and as he steered it away from the kerb, Ruby chuckled, despite it being the solemnest of occasions. 'Do you know, I reckon the worm has finally turned. Did you hear the way David spoke to Rebecca back there? And not before time, if you ask me. He's been under that little madam's thumb for far too long. Happen she won't get everything all her own way from now on. If looks could have killed, the way he just glared at her, she'd have been joinin' her mother-in-law.'

Nuala and Martin both acknowledged her comment with a grin, but Kate sat straight-faced, her hands fidgeting nervously in her lap. There was something not right, something that her aunt had been struggling to tell her. But what could it have been? She would never know now.

Martin risked taking his eyes off the road to reach out and squeeze her hand, but she was too locked in misery to notice.

Once they'd passed the Longshoot Motel, Ruby sighed enviously as Martin's car drove past the big houses along Hinckley Road. It was hard not to compare them to her tiny terraced house, but she kept her thoughts to herself.

Once again, she'd managed to shock Kate with her appearance. The smart black hat and suit she was wearing accentuated her petite figure and there seemed to be a glow about her that hadn't been there before. In fact, now that Kate thought about it, she seemed to have been taking a lot more pride in her appearance lately and Kate wondered if there was perhaps an admirer who had caused this sudden transformation. She hadn't asked Ruby, of course, but she hoped that she was right. As far as Kate was concerned, if dear Ruby could find a little happiness now then good luck to her.

When Martin drew the car to a halt outside Ruby's home the two passengers in the back climbed out first.

'I'll just get in an' put the kettle on then while you an' Kate have a few minutes to yourselves, eh?' Ruby suggested tactfully.

Martin nodded as Ruby grabbed Nuala's elbow and shepherded her up the narrow entry that separated the rows of terraced houses.

After switching off the engine, Martin draped his arm across the back of Kate's seat and fiddled with the dark curls that lay upon her slender shoulders.

'How are you feeling, love?' His voice was full of concern.

Kate managed to raise a watery smile. In truth, she couldn't honestly have told him how she was feeling even if she had tried; the pain inside her went so deep that she wondered how she would bear it.

In less than a year, she had lost her father, two homes and now Aunt Beth. It felt as if each time something dreadful happened, something even *worse* came along to follow it and she was tired, so tired of having to worry all the time.

Sensing her deep distress, Martin kissed her gently on the cheek. 'You're just about at the end of your tether, aren't you, sweetheart?'

She nodded as the tears she had struggled to hold

back welled from her eyes and ran unchecked down her cheeks. 'I just feel so . . . Oh, I don't know. Empty, I suppose. I'm forever having to cope with some crisis or another. I'm not even twenty-one yet, Martin, but I feel like an old woman. I'm tired of having to worry and struggle all the time.'

'So marry me then and let me do the worrying for you.'

Her head snapped around to stare at him. He hadn't so much as mentioned marriage again for weeks, but now – well, the offer was tempting to say the least.

When she didn't immediately reject his offer he drew her closer to him.

'Think about it, Kate. If we were married, I'd be the one doing the worrying. You wouldn't even have to go out to work if you didn't want to. We could be a real family – you, me, Nuala and the baby. We might even be able to have Adam back home to live with us in time, and who's to say we couldn't have some babies of our own? Seems to me that for all of your life you've been looking after everyone else. Now I say again, please Kate, marry me and let *me* take care of you. With two jobs on the go I'm comfortably off and I promise you'd want for nothing and never regret it.'

With tears still trembling on her lashes she looked back at him. A picture of Matthew flashed briefly before her eyes, followed by a picture of Jenny's tiny face. She adored her niece but each time she looked at her she was reminded of how Matthew had betrayed her. Martin was solid and reliable. As he had pointed out, if she married him, she would never have to worry about making ends meet again. Nor would she have to worry about where she and Nuala and the baby were going to live, and the responsibility of caring for them would no longer rest solely on her shoulders.

'All right, Martin. Yes, I'll marry you.' Her voice was dull, but Martin was too ecstatic to notice as he covered her face in kisses.

'I promise, you won't regret this. Come on, let's go in and break the happy news to Ruby and Nuala.'

'*No!*' The sharp tone of her voice made the smile slip from his face.

Instantly contrite, she squeezed his hand apologetically. 'Could we just wait for a couple of days or so? It doesn't seem right somehow, to be talking of happy things when we've just come back from my aunt's funeral.'

She detected a hint of annoyance in his face, but when he spoke his voice was steady.

'Of course, how thoughtless of me. I'm sorry, Kate. It's just that I'm so thrilled that you've said yes. I'm going to make you *so* happy, you just wait and see. But first, as you quite rightly say, you must mourn your aunt, and then we'll tell everyone. You just give me the nod when you're ready, eh?'

She allowed him to kiss her, although inside she felt numb. Shouldn't she be feeling elated, she wondered. After all, she'd just become engaged to be married. She dismissed the thought as annoyance coursed through her. Of course she shouldn't, she had just buried her beloved aunt! There was too much going on all at once, that was the problem, but soon, she told herself, soon, I *will* be elated.

'Off out again are you, Ruby?' Kate's voice held a teasing note, which Ruby was quick to pick up on.

'Less of your lip, young lady!' she scolded as she teased her hair into place in the mirror above the mantelpiece. Blushing becomingly, she drew her gloves on then picked up her handbag. 'Ain't you off out yourself tonight?'

Nuala was curled up on the settee oblivious to the banter that was going on, engrossed in *I Love Lucy* on the black and white television set.

'Yes, I might be going out later actually,' Kate replied.

The blush was replaced with a frown as Ruby glanced at her. 'Seeing a lot of that Martin lately, ain't you? An' who's goin' to keep an eye out fer the baby?'

Kate bristled at her tone of voice. 'Nuala is, of course. Jenny will be fast asleep by the time I leave, so all she'll have to do is listen for her. We've got to trust her with her own baby eventually. And as for seeing a lot of Martin, what if I am? He's perfectly respectable.'

Ruby paused. 'Yes, I don't deny that, but . . .'

'But what?'

A shrug of Ruby's shoulders told of her concern. 'I don't know what it is, really. It's just . . . well, he's a bit old for yer for a start.'

'Rubbish.' The word shot from Kate's mouth like a bullet from a gun. 'Ten or eleven years is nothing. Martin is . . . kind. Yes, that's what he is, and dependable. Not like most blokes my age who walk around in their Teddy Boy outfits causing mayhem.'

'There is that in it,' Ruby conceded grudgingly, 'but all the same, take it easy, eh? For me.'

Kate turned her attention back to the newspaper, somewhat offended. Here was Ruby telling her what she should and shouldn't do when only last night Kate had

202

seen a man escort Ruby to the front door. Talk about the pot calling the kettle black!

Her annoyance fled as soon as it had come when Ruby planted a kiss on her cheek. 'Don't mind me, love. I dare say I'm just a silly old worriet. I care about yer, you see? Like I cared about your mam before you – and I'd hate to see you make a mistake like she did.'

'I know you do, Ruby.' All was forgiven as Kate returned the kiss. She had been about to tell Ruby that tonight she was going to visit Martin's house for the very first time, but she thought better of it. Ruby wasn't too enamoured of Martin and for now, what she didn't know wouldn't hurt her. She would learn of their engagement soon enough and by then she would have had time get to know him a little better.

'Go on then, get yourself away,' Kate said, then added teasingly, 'you don't want to keep him waiting, do you?'

Ruby blushed an even deeper shade of red as she hurried towards the door and disappeared through it as if she couldn't get away quickly enough.

Kate chuckled, then rising from the table she prepared enough bottles to see Jenny through the night before hurrying upstairs to get ready for Martin.

'This is it then. It's not a palace, I'll grant you, but it's home.' Martin held the door wide as Kate stepped past him. The door led directly from the pavement in Heath End Road into what Kate guessed was one of two sitting rooms. She was proved to be right when he ushered her in front of him through another room that opened into the kitchen.

The first thing that struck her was how clean and tidy

everywhere was. There was a fire roaring up the chimney with an easy chair at either side of it. A drop-leaf table was neatly folded away against one wall surrounded by four matching chairs. And on the other wall was a settee with floral cushions arranged along the length of it. Bright flowered curtains hung at the windows, and the floor was covered in a huge patterned rug that reached almost wall to wall. It was obvious that a lot of thought had gone into the colour scheme of the room and Kate was impressed, although it was a little fussy for her taste. All the same, she could recognise quality when she saw it. Turning to look at him, she smiled.

'Why, Martin, it's lovely!'

Looking ridiculously pleased he helped her to take her coat off before hanging it away in a cupboard under the stairs.

'I'm glad you like it. Anne was very keen on colour co-ordinating and—' He stopped mid-sentence, as if he wished he could have bitten his tongue off.

Kate patted his arm. 'Martin, *please* don't worry. Anne was your wife, you had a child together and you obviously loved her very much. Just because you and I are going to be married doesn't mean that you won't still think about her.'

He hung his head as she crossed to a picture of a small dark-haired child in a gilt frame on the mantelpiece and asked, 'Is this Adam?'

He nodded. 'Yes, it is. That was taken when he was about four or five. Obviously, he's changed a lot since then. He's almost as tall as me now.'

'He's a lovely-looking boy.'

Martin nodded in agreement. 'He is actually, although

people say he looks absolutely nothing like me. He took more after his . . .' Again he stopped and flushed guiltily as Kate raised her eyebrows and smiled.

Before she could say anything he too crossed to the mantelpiece and lifted a small box that was sitting next to the clock. Turning to Kate he self-consciously held it out to her. 'Look.' He was almost squirming with embarrassment. 'I know it's only just over a week since your aunt's funeral, and I know I said I'd wait until you gave me the word to go public, but . . . the thing is, Kate, I'm so lonely rattling around in this house all on my own. You and Nuala can't stay with Ruby for ever and so I thought . . . Well, I want you to have this.'

Kate took the box from his hand and when she opened it her eyes almost started from her head. A beautiful three-stone diamond ring winked up at her. For a moment she was speechless, but at last she gasped, 'I can't take this, Martin. Why, it must be worth a small fortune!'

'What if it is? I've got savings, you know. It's only money at the end of the day, and you are worth it.'

Taking the ring from the box he slipped it onto Kate's finger as she gazed at it with a look of wonder on her face. In actual fact it was his late wife's engagement ring that he had had cleaned and polished, but he had no intention of telling Kate that. He somehow knew that she wouldn't have liked it.

'There you are. It fits like a glove.' He grinned from ear to ear at Kate's reaction.

She meanwhile stared at the ring, waiting for the rush of elation that she felt must come with it. She'd read about moments like this in the romantic books she was so fond of reading, and the heroine of the story always felt indescribable joy. But there was nothing; nothing but the deep-rooted sadness that seemed to have settled around her like a fog since the death of her aunt.

Oblivious to how she was feeling, Martin swept her into his arms and kissed her soundly on the lips. 'There you are then; it's official now. We're engaged to be married as of this moment.'

Kate freed herself, saying, 'But Martin, are you quite sure about this? What I mean is – you're not just taking me. I come with Nuala and the baby *and* Sally – talking of which . . .' A thought occurred to her. 'What about your cat? How will we manage with a cat and a dog under one roof?'

'Cat?' He looked vaguely confused as Kate grinned at him.

'Yes, *your* cat. The one that scratched your face not so long ago.'

As he remembered, he suddenly looked slightly uncomfortable. 'Oh, *that* cat. I . . . er . . . well, you've no need to worry about him. I'm afraid he got run over on the road a couple of weeks back.'

'Oh, how awful.' Kate's kind heart was immediately saddened, but she had no chance to comment before Martin had pulled her back into his arms and begun to kiss her again. Kate returned his kiss and slowly something inside her began to come back to life. She had mourned enough to last a lifetime. Martin was a kind man, a lovely man, and she determined there and then that she would be the sort of wife he would be proud of, come what may. As she gave herself up to the pleasure of his kiss she suddenly felt that she had a future to look forward to once more.

* * *

206

'*You're what?*' Ruby's mouth gaped, giving her the appearance of a goldfish as she stared at the glittering ring on Kate's finger.

'I'm engaged to be married,' Kate repeated, swallowing her disappointment at Ruby's reaction.

'But . . . but ain't it a bit sudden like?' The little woman was trying hard to hide her distress.

'Not really. Martin asked me to marry him weeks ago, as you very well know, but what with one thing and another going on, I didn't feel the time was right.'

'And now yer do?'

'Yes, I do.' Kate was surprised to realise how much Ruby's blessing meant to her. Apart from Nuala and the baby, Ruby was the closest person she had to a mother now.

'Can't you try to be pleased for me?' she asked wistfully. 'Nuala and I can't stay here for ever, after all.'

'Says who?' Ruby's voice was indignant. 'Have I ever said that yer weren't welcome?'

'No, of course not. But the thing is . . .' Kate paused, choosing her words carefully. 'The thing is, you have someone else in your life now and I'd hate for Nuala and me to stand in your way.'

Ruby blushed as red as a beetroot. 'If it's Victor Skinner yer talkin' about, then yer talkin' rubbish. Me an' Victor are just good friends.'

Kate grinned. 'You might be just good friends for now, Ruby, but how do you know it will stay like that? Please don't get me wrong. I have no intention of interfering in your relationship. To be honest, nothing would please me more than to see you both become *more* than good friends. I'm not blind, you know? I've seen the way Victor looks at you when he walks you home at night. Anyone can see that he's taken with you, and from what I've heard you say of him, he seems like a very nice man.'

'Oh, he is.' Ruby's head wagged up and down in agreement. 'There's none better.'

'So why are you keeping him on a just friends basis then?'

Ruby wrung her hands nervously. Somehow the conversation had steered from Kate's relationship to hers and she wasn't sure that she was ready for it. Lifting Sally onto her lap she began to play with the little dog's ears as she avoided Kate's eyes.

'I suppose I'm frightened,' she admitted eventually. 'The thing is, I've been on me own for a long time. My Leonard . . . well, he meant the world to me an' it don't seem right to think o' some other bloke in his place somehow.'

Her words seemed strangely at variance with the reputation she had but Kate tactfully refrained from mentioning it. Whenever Ruby talked of her late husband it was more than obvious that she had adored the ground he walked on, so Kate wondered why she had chosen to have so many men friends.

'Oh, Ruby.' Her voice was heavy with sadness. 'You shouldn't think like that. I'm sure you were the best wife in the world to Leonard, but he's gone now and you have to accept it. I know he would want you to move on. Do you think you *could* be happy with Victor?'

'Oh, yes.' There was no hesitation in Ruby's voice whatsoever. 'Vic lost his wife just before I lost my Leonard, an' he's made it plain that he's mine fer the takin'. He's comfortably off, I don't mind tellin' yer. He made his money from a rag an' bone business he had fer years. His house is like somethin' you only ever dream of. An' on top o' that, he's one o' the kindest, handsomest men I've ever met, but—'

'There shouldn't be a but,' Kate interrupted. 'Which brings me back to what we were talking about. You should take happiness when it's handed to you on a plate. I think "Ruby Skinner" has a nice ring to it. I *know* I'll be happy with Martin, and if Nuala and I are gone and you don't have us and the baby to worry about, then you could spend a little more time with Victor to really get to know him. Please, Ruby. If I can be happy for you, can't you find it in your heart to be happy for me?'

Ruby nodded dutifully, though she still had grave reservations. There was something about Martin that she couldn't quite take to. Perhaps it was because he always came across as being too good to be true? The flowers and chocolates, the opening of car doors; the politeness and concern that seemed to drip out of his mouth. Would he still be like that once he and Kate were married? Ruby doubted it. She and Leonard had enjoyed the closest of relationships, but she'd be the first to admit that after the honeymoon they'd had rows that turned the air blue. But oh, the makin' up . . . She still blushed now as she remembered.

She sighed and then smiled grudgingly. 'Well, if you've made up yer mind I dare say there's nowt I can say that will change it. Yer take after yer mam fer bein' stubborn. So I wish yer well, love. God knows yer overdue fer a little happiness after all you've been through in yer short life. I will just say this though. If ever, fer any reason yer change yer mind an' feel you've made a mistake,

209

even after the ring is on yer finger, then rest assured there will always be a home wi' me, wherever I may be, waitin' fer yer.'

'Oh, Ruby.' Her voice choked with emotion, Kate flung herself into the older woman's arms. This kind soul had been her rock over the last few months, despite her sometimes colourful language and clothes. Now all she had to do was break the news to Nuala.

That proved to be easier said than done. Kate had no sooner uttered the word 'marriage' later that evening when Nuala flew into a tantrum that would have done justice to a four year old.

'But Kate, you *can't* marry him. We've only just got settled in here, and what will happen to me an' . . . an' *her*?' Stabbing a trembling finger towards the baby she went on, 'How could you be so selfish? You don't really care about me or her at all, do you? All you care about is yourself!'

Kate felt her own temper growing but struggled to keep it under control. 'Don't be so bloody daft,' she snapped. 'How can you call me selfish? Why, I've always looked out for you, haven't I? Do you *really* think I'm about to abandon you now? You'll both be coming to live with us, of course, and you won't have to worry about ever moving again. We'll have a home for life. We could be a *real* family, if you'll only give Martin a chance.'

Nuala looked at her guardedly. 'What . . . you mean Martin will let me come and live with you?'

Suddenly tired, Kate's shoulders sagged. 'Of course he will. You don't think we'd just turn you both out on the streets, do you? He's even talking about the possibility of

210

Adam, his little boy from his first marriage, coming to live with us too when we're all settled.'

Nuala narrowed her eyes suspiciously. 'Does Adam know about it yet?'

'Well no, not yet. Obviously it would have to be done when we all felt comfortable about it. He's lived with his grandparents for some time now and we'd want him to feel right with it.'

Kate sidled over to her sister, who now seemed to have calmed down. 'Let's look on this as a new start, eh? Martin is a lovely man and I know you'll like him if you'll just give him a chance.'

Nuala slowly nodded. Perhaps it wouldn't be so bad after all.

Chapter Eighteen

'You know, Kate, you have lovely hair, but I think it would suit you shorter.'

As Martin smiled down at her, Kate's face creased with surprise. It was a beautiful Sunday afternoon in May and they had walked for miles along the canal towpath before stopping to rest in a buttercup field. Kate was flat on her back gazing up at a cloudless blue sky as Martin rested on one elbow looking down at her.

Blinking up at him, she frowned. 'How do you mean – shorter?'

'Well, sort of . . .' his hands flailed in the air as he tried to explain. 'Sort of like that new poodle cut that's all the go. All sort of layered and framing your face . . . like Lucille Ball wears hers.'

'Mm.' Kate tried to imagine it as she fingered her long curls uncertainly. 'I suppose it would make a change.'

'That's agreed then.' Before she could argue, he pulled two pound notes from his trouser pocket and pressed them into her hand. 'You make the appointment and get it done. I believe there's a rather good hairdresser's on the Cock and Bear Bridge.'

'I'm quite able to pay for my own haircuts,' she pointed out indignantly.

'No,' Martin grinned, 'this is my treat. In fact, I insist, seeing as it was my idea. Now that you're not working full-time I don't want you to leave yourself short.'

Kate felt a little pang of resentment but quickly stifled it. Since their engagement she had only been working at the Rose and Crown during lunchtimes because Martin was unhappy about her walking home at nights. She supposed that she shouldn't complain. Martin had taken to paying both hers and Nuala's rent to Ruby each week, and it *did* give her a lot more time to spend with baby Jenny. He'd also made it clear that she only had to ask if there was anything she needed, but Kate found it hard. She'd always been fiercely independent and it went against the grain to have to ask anyone for anything.

All the same, it was a lovely afternoon and she didn't want to spoil it so she tucked the money into the pocket of her pretty flared skirt and smiled up at him sweetly. A big fat bumblebee buzzed by and as Kate followed his erratic progress her eyes were drawn to the primroses and wild flowers that were peeping from the hedgerows. It was as if everything was slowly coming back to life after a long hard winter, just as she was. Through the gap in the hedge she saw a brightly painted narrowboat pass by, and a feeling of contentment settled on her.

'Ah,' she sighed. 'Things don't get much better than this, do they?'

Martin chuckled. 'I have to disagree with you on that, young lady. If you think this is good, then just wait until we're married. I intend to spoil you absolutely rotten.'

213

Kate giggled as she offered her lips for his kiss. At last it seemed that her life was going in the right direction.

Hand-in-hand they finally made their way back to Ruby's as the sun was sinking in the sky.

Martin paused at the end of the entry to peck her chastely on the cheek, ever conscious that someone might be watching them. That was one of the things Kate had come to appreciate about Martin – even now that they were engaged to be married he was ever the gentleman. He had never so much as offered to touch her other than to kiss and cuddle her, and she found it endearing that he wanted to wait until their wedding night to make love. *Their wedding night.* A little thrill of anticipation swept through her as she thought about it. It was only six weeks away now. Soon she would have to be thinking about an outfit to wear, that is, if she got to have a say in it. Ruby had got bridal magazines spread all over the house and every day she would approach Kate to show her some dreamy Cinderella dress or another. And then there was the church. That was another thing they would have to be organising fairly soon. But not now. Martin had to work in the churchyard tonight so she decided to wait until the next day to broach the subject. She kissed him back and tripped merrily away up the entry to see what Ruby had cooked for their tea.

The following day she was clearing the tables at the Rose and Crown following her lunchtime shift when David appeared. Hiding her surprise, she smiled at him brightly. He slid onto a stool at the bar and watched her as she carried the empty glasses to the sink.

'So what brings you here at this time of day?' she asked

pleasantly. She'd warmed to her cousin since the day of Aunt Beth's funeral and had seen him on a number of occasions.

'I thought I'd take a late lunch-hour and give you a lift home. There are a couple of things I'd like to talk to you about,' he replied.

Containing her curiosity, she finished clearing the bar before collecting her coat and joining him. 'I'm off now then, Vera,' she called, and Vera's voice carried back to her from the lounge.

'All right, lovie. See yer tomorrer an' mind how yer go.'

David took her arm and together they walked out into the May sunshine.

She smiled at him. 'This is a nice surprise, but there was no need for you to do this really. I only live a stone's throw away.'

'I know you do,' he muttered, looking suddenly embarrassed. 'But there was something . . . Look, let's get into the car, eh?'

Intrigued, she followed him to his car, which was round in the small car park at the side of the pub.

'So what is it you wanted to see me about?' She had barely settled into the passenger seat when her curiosity got the better of her.

Leaning heavily on the steering wheel, he gazed at the traffic that was going by on Coton Road. 'What do you think of Winston Churchill resigning? I'm not so sure that Sir Anthony Eden is the right one to succeed him, are you?'

Kate frowned. 'David, I'm sure you didn't come here to talk to me about politics. Now what do you *really* want to see me about?'

Looking decidedly uncomfortable, he reached into his pocket and withdrew a small box. 'A couple of things really. Firstly, I felt bad about you and Nuala not getting anything in Mother's will, so I thought you might like to have this.'

Once again, Kate found herself looking down at a ring, but this one brought tears stinging to her eyes. It was a thin gold band. Her aunt's treasured wedding ring.

Seeing the look of shock on her face he flushed. 'I know it's not much but I think she would have wanted you to have it.'

'But . . . but doesn't Rebecca want it?' she stuttered.

He scowled. 'Rebecca wouldn't wear it. You know what she's like. Unless it's solid platinum or worth a king's ransom it isn't worth having.'

'Well, I shall treasure it,' Kate assured him and slipped it onto her finger next to the sapphire ring that her aunt had bought her for her birthday.

'The other thing I wanted to see you about . . . er . . . was the wedding. I was wondering . . . would you like me to give you away?'

Kate's mouth dropped open. '*You?* Give me away?'

He nodded. 'Why not? You haven't got anybody else to do it, have you? No offence intended. The thing is, Kate, I've been feeling so guilty about the way I treated you when you first came to live with my mother and I want to make amends, or at least try to. I would be very honoured if you'd allow it. So . . . what do you say?'

Deeply touched, Kate tore her eyes away from the ring to smile at him through her tears. 'I'd like that very much. Thank you,' she said simply.

Smiling with satisfaction, David started the engine and drove her home.

'Ooh! Just look at this one. I can really see you in that.' Ruby's eyes were dreamy as she stared at the froth of silk and lace from a bridal feature in *Woman's Own*.

Nuala glared at the bridesmaid's dress that was next to it. 'Just so long as I ain't expected to swan about in *that*,' she mumbled in disgust.

'Huh! Yer should just think yerself lucky as we don't still need coupons to buy 'em,' Ruby told her sharply. 'Though I reckon some o' these might still be well out of our price range. Still, not to worry. I've always been a dab hand wi' a needle an' thread even if I do say so meself, so we could perhaps choose one yer like an' get the material an' I could run it up fer yer. Can't do much about the flowers, though. Young Gilda up the road paid three pounds an' three shillin's fer her bridal bouquet at Christmas.'

Kate giggled. 'I'll tell you what – we'll get the bride-groom's opinion when he comes to pick me up in a minute, shall we?'

'Yes, an' we'll get on to him about bookin' the church an' all while we're at it,' Ruby grumbled. 'If he goes leavin' it fer much longer you'll stand no bloody chance. Summer weddin's are popular. The half-baked way he's leavin' things to the last minute, you'll be lucky to be wed fer Christmas. Seems to me the only thing that's sorted is the weddin' cake. I've had the mixture soakin' in me best brandy fer the past two days now. That will save us a good six shillin's at least. It's just a shame as the little 'un ain't big enough to be a bridesmaid an' all.'

She smiled fondly at Jenny who was propped up on pillows on the settee next to her.

As if on cue a knock at the door heralded Martin's arrival. 'That will be him now,' Kate said merrily. 'You can register your complaint with the groom himself.'

'Huh! I'll certainly do that,' Ruby declared as Kate rushed away to let him in. She then glanced towards Nuala and was shocked to see the way the girl was staring at him from big cow eyes. Oh no, she thought to herself, that's all we need now – for Nuala to go an' develop a crush on him an' all!

Seconds later Martin was standing at the side of the table eyeing the magazine with amusement. 'What's this then?' He smiled. 'Somebody getting married, are they?'

'Well, that all depends on whether a certain bridegroom decides to pull his socks up an' get the arrangements under way,' Ruby told him indignantly. 'Fer a start-off, as I was just sayin' to Kate – there's the church to book an' the reception, not to mention sortin' out the bride's dress an' the flowers. If yer don't get crackin' soon an' start the ball rollin', it'll be this time next year before yer wed.'

Martin's eyes hardened although the smile stayed fixed in place. 'I'm so sorry if you've been fretting about the arrangements, Ruby. But you really don't need to. You see – everything *is* booked. I took the liberty of booking the register office last week, and we won't be needing a reception as I plan to whisk Kate away on honeymoon immediately after the wedding. As for the dress – I intend to take Kate shopping for it on Saturday. I thought a nice suit might be more fitting. She can't really go catching a train in something like that, can she?' As he waved his hand at the bridal gown Ruby was drooling over, a look of shocked horror settled on her face.

'*What?* A bloody *register office* . . . an' a suit? Call that a weddin'? Why didn't yer tell me this, Kate?'

Before Kate could answer, Martin smiled apologetically. 'She didn't tell you because she didn't know. I'm sorry if I've done wrong, but I thought with all that Kate's been through recently, she'd be glad for me to organise everything. It *is* all right, isn't it, darling?'

Kate gulped as visions of floating down the aisle in a froth of satin and lace on David's arm faded away. She wanted to say, 'No, it isn't all right, this is supposed to be the best day of my life,' but something about his downcast face made her bite her tongue. After all, he had *thought* he was doing right and it *was* his second marriage. Perhaps he couldn't face all the fuss again?

Besides, what did it matter? The main thing was that they would be married and he *was* taking her on honeymoon, which was a pleasant surprise.

'I suppose a quiet wedding would be more fitting under the circumstances,' she acquiesced, much to Ruby's disgust.

Ruby slammed the magazine shut and stamped towards the stairs door. 'I may as well leave yer to it then. It's obvious my help ain't needed. Victor will be here to pick me up shortly, so if you'll excuse me I'll just go an' make meself fit to be seen.' So saying, she disappeared through the stairs door, closing it behind her.

The moment the door had shut behind her, tears sprang to Ruby's eyes. Martin might have missed the look of disappointment that had flitted across Kate's face when he told her about the wedding, but *she* hadn't. The poor girl. How must she be feeling? Ruby knew that she'd been looking forward to shopping for the material for her wedding dress, and then *he* just breezes in and tells her she won't be having one. And who had ever heard of the groom taking the bride to choose her outfit? Ruby had always thought it should be the bride's mother who went shopping with her on that special day, and seeing as Kate didn't have a mam, Ruby had hoped that she could take her place. Well, Martin had certainly squashed *that* idea, but more disturbing than that was the fact that Kate had simply agreed to it. Ruby was still fuming at the barefaced cheek of the man, organising everything like that behind Kate's back. Surely half the joy of getting married was making all the arrangements *together*? Poor Kate hadn't had a say in any of it. Still, at the end of the day he was Kate's choice and there wasn't a thing she could do about it.

Nuala, sensing the charged atmosphere in the small living room, stood up from her seat and followed Ruby without a word, flashing Martin a sickly-sweet smile as she went.

At last they were alone and Martin looked at Kate in concern. 'You aren't disappointed, are you, darling? It never occurred to me that you'd want a big wedding. I thought I was doing right, taking all the worry of the arrangements off you.'

Swallowing her disappointment, Kate smiled. 'Don't worry about Ruby. She just got a bit carried away with it all. I'm sure she'll calm down when she gets used to the idea. And as for me . . . I suppose it does make sense to have a quiet wedding. And we *are* going on honeymoon. Do I get to know where we're going?'

'No, you definitely do not. It's a surprise.' Martin drew her into his arms.

'But . . .'

'But what?'

'What about Jenny?'

Masking his irritation, Martin forced a smile. 'Kate, I'm sure that Ruby and Nuala will be able to manage her on their own for just *one* week, don't you? After all, she isn't your baby, though there are times when I'm sure you think she is.'

Kate stiffened in his arms as her eyes settled on the baby who was fast asleep in her crib. Jenny was almost four months old now and the apple of her eye. She had never left her for more than a few hours up to now, but then she supposed that Martin was right, they *were* entitled to a honeymoon. Stifling a sigh, she turned her attention back to her fiancé as she tried to push the worries to the back of her mind.

Just as he had promised, Martin turned up bright and early on Saturday morning. Ruby was still sulking and managed no more than a barely civil nod in his direction before he whisked Kate away.

The second the door had closed behind them, Ruby sniffed in disgust. 'Ain't never heard o' nothin' like it in me whole life,' she complained to Nuala as she jiggled Jenny on her knee. 'Just fancy the bridegroom goin' shoppin' wi' the bride fer her outfit. In *my* day he wouldn't have even been allowed to get a peep at it before the bride arrived at the church – it was a closely guarded secret. An' as fer gettin' married in a register office . . . all I can say is, her dear mam must be turnin' in her

221

grave, bless her. I don't mind tellin' yer, it leaves a bad taste in me mouth. If he's rulin' her like that now, what will he be like after they're wed?'

Nuala shrugged. If she were to be honest, she was relieved that there wasn't going to be a great fuss. For a start-off she'd cringed at the thought of wearing a soppy bridesmaid's dress. It was all right for Kate, with her figure and looks; she could have carried it off, while she would have been left looking like a fat frump as usual. No, as far as she was concerned, a register office wedding was fine. It was the honeymoon that was worrying her, or more to the point, what would happen to her while the happy couple were away. She dreaded being taken to Martin's house and being left there all alone. The thought of caring for the baby on her own terrified her. She wondered briefly if perhaps they might take her and the baby with them, but then dismissed the thought. Someone would have to stay behind to look after Sally, the damned mutt. Eyeing the object of her displeasure, curled up at Ruby's feet, she shuddered. She could never understand people who billed and cooed over babies and animals. She thought dispassionately of her baby daughter. Thankfully Kate had taken over the role of mother, which was just as well. Nuala knew that she could never feel anthing for the child. Sometimes it was hard to believe that she had actually carried her for nine long months and given birth to her. Still, Jenny was probably the reason why Kate had gone along with all of Martin's suggestions about the wedding without argument, so she had *something* to thank her for, at least.

Thinking of Kate made her frown. Her big sister had changed over the last few months. Some of the spirit had gone out of her and she didn't laugh as much as she used to.

She'd still come out on top though, hadn't she? Oh yes, Kate *always* came out on top, with some bloke or another flinging themselves at her feet. First it had been Matthew . . . the girl smiled as she thought of him. Kate certainly wouldn't be bothering with *him* any more. And now it was Martin. *Martin* . . . just the thought of him made her break out in goosebumps. He was just *so* handsome and *so* kind and *so* in love with her sister. Not for the first time, Nuala thought how unfair life was.

Chapter Nineteen

At the door of Husselby's in Primrose Hill Street in Coventry, Martin laid a gentle hand on Kate's arm.

'Now I don't want you worrying about the price of your wedding outfit,' he told her. 'We're only having a very modest wedding so I want you to have something you really like, although I think blue would suit you down to the ground.'

Kate grinned at his contradiction. Here he was telling her to choose something *she* really liked, and in the very same breath he was telling her what *he* would like her to have. Not that it really mattered. She would have been quite happy to shop for her outfit in Nuneaton and wasn't too set on anything. It was Martin who had insisted they come to this particular shop in Coventry.

The bell above the door tinkled merrily as they entered the shop and immediately a smart middle-aged shop assistant pounced on them.

When they had told her what they were looking for she tapped her lip with her forefinger as she eyed Kate thoughtfully up and down. 'Mm,' was all she said. Without adding any more, she disappeared, only to reappear a minute or so later with her arms full of clothes.

'Would Madam care to follow me?' she trilled, and casting a grin at Martin across her shoulder, Kate followed her to a fitting room while he took a seat outside.

'Oh, I like this one.' Kate ran her hands down a pretty flowing skirt with a matching short tailored jacket as the assistant held it up for her inspection. The background was a very pale pink and tiny flowers were dotted here and there all over it.

'A very wise choice,' the assistant simpered. 'Perfect for your hair and colouring. Would Madam care to try it?'

Kate nodded, and after slipping into the fitting room she quickly undressed and put the suit on. It fitted like a glove and Kate smiled at her reflection in the mirror as she twirled this way and that, admiring the layered net underskirts that gave it a floaty effect.

'What do you think?' she asked Martin as she emerged from the fitting room.

He frowned. 'A bit fussy, if you ask me,' he declared, and pointing to a tailored suit in a soft shade of blue he said, 'Now *that* looks more like it. Why don't you try that one?'

'Don't you think it's a little severe for a wedding?' Kate asked. Her eyes moved up and down the straight skirt and the short-box jacket.

'Not at all; it looks classy, sophisticated. Just try it on and see what you think.'

Kate obediently disappeared back into the fitting room and when the suit was on, she once more emerged for Martin's opinion.

'Ah, now *that* looks lovely.' He eyed her appreciatively.

'I do have to agree,' the assistant gushed, although Kate had already formed the opinion that she would have said the same had she been wearing a paper bag – if it meant getting a sale.

Kate glanced at herself doubtfully in the full-length mirror that took up almost the whole of one wall. It did fit beautifully, she had to admit, but it was so different to the clothes that she normally wore that the long pencil skirt felt strange. Despite what Martin had said when they entered the shop, she glanced at the price ticket and gasped with dismay. This suit cost more than the whole of her wardrobe put together.

'It's rather expensive,' she muttered.

'It's perfect.' Martin took control as he turned back to the woman who was hovering at his side. 'Now – how about a hat, shoes and bag to match? Would you have anything suitable?'

'Oh, *definitely*, sir.' The delighted assistant scurried away, looking as if all her birthdays and Christmases had come at once.

Kate felt a little pang of resentment followed immediately by guilt. After all, Martin was being so generous and it was obvious he did like the outfit.

By the time they left the shop, Kate had the whole of her wedding outfit packed in tissue paper in various bags. The amount at the till left her reeling with shock, but Martin paid it without flinching and ushered her outside with a broad grin on his face.

'You're going to look absolutely stunning,' he assured her. 'Now – let's go and get all that hair chopped off, eh? I've already made you an appointment and explained how you'd like it done.'

Kate bit down on her lip as her hand flew unconsciously to the hair that lay across her shoulders. But then she shrugged inwardly. For as long as she could remember she had worn her hair long, and they did say a change was as good as a rest. The outfit she was carrying was absolutely nothing like anything she had ever worn before, so why not go the whole hog? Nodding her agreement, she followed him back to his car.

'What the . . . ?' Ruby gawped in surprise as Kate stepped into the room, self-consciously touching the short bouncy curls that framed her face.

'Martin thought it might suit me in a shorter style,' she explained. 'But it's not just my hair. Look – I have the whole of my wedding outfit here.' As she spoke she dropped her bags onto a chair and quickly withdrew the suit, holding it up for Ruby's approval.

Jiggling Jenny into a more comfortable position in the crook of her arm, Ruby sniffed.

'Well, I have to admit it is a lovely costume, but ain't it a little bit—'

'A little bit what?' Kate was on the defensive and Ruby was quick to pick up on it.

'*Different* is the word I'm lookin' for,' Ruby said tactfully. 'What I mean is, I'm used to seein' you in more flowing sorts o' things. I just thought it might be a little bit too plain for a weddin', I suppose.'

Despite the fact that Kate had thought exactly the same when she'd first seen the suit, she still looked offended. 'Martin thought it was sophisticated. Perfect, in fact.' Dropping the suit over the back of a chair she lifted Jenny from Ruby's arms and kissed her soft cheek, trying hard to keep the hurt from showing in her eyes.

'How has she been?' she asked, glad of an excuse to change the subject.

'Same as usual.' Ruby rose from her seat and crossed to the sink where she filled the kettle. 'I don't think that little soul has a cry in 'er. Good as the day is long, she is.'

Too good, Kate thought as she stared down into her niece's vacant eyes, and the concerns that she had experienced recently came flooding back. Every week when she took Jenny to be weighed at Riversley Park Clinic she found herself comparing her niece with other babies of the same age; they would sit with help on their mother's lap and coo and gurgle, while Jenny was making no effort to do anything. A kindly Health Visitor had assured her that all babies developed at a different rate when Kate had plucked up the courage to express her worry, but that had been almost a month ago, and Jenny was still showing no signs of making any progress.

Could she have known it, Ruby was concerned about the infant too, although she had kept her worries to herself for fear of frightening Kate unnecessarily.

'Has Nuala helped out with her today?' Kate asked casually as Ruby set the kettle on the black-leaded range.

'Huh! Why ask? I think you already know the answer to that question.' Ruby could not keep the annoyance from her voice and Kate was instantly protective of her sister.

'She doesn't mean to neglect Jenny, you know, Ruby, it's just that she's . . .'

'She's what?'

'Well, she needs someone to look after *her*. You don't need me to tell you that Nuala is . . . slow.'

Seeing Kate's crestfallen face, the older woman's tone softened. 'I've no wish to sound hard, love, but let's bloody face it. Here you are about to be wed an' you're havin' to worry about not only your sister but her baby too. I'll not be a hypocrite an' pretend that Martin would have been me choice for yer, but then, yer have to give him credit where it's due. There ain't many blokes as would take yer on wi' all the problems that come wi' yer.'

'I know that.' Kate hung her head as tears shimmered on her long dark eyelashes and instantly Ruby was at her side, her arm slung across her slight shoulders.

'Eeh, trust me to go upsettin' you on the day you've been shoppin' for your weddin' outfit. Pay me no mind, eh? I reckon I'm just havin' a mardy 'cos I didn't get to come with yer. My Leonard always said I had a gob as big as a parish oven and happen he was right. Things will turn out all right, you'll see. Now come on – let's have a proper look at this outfit. Yer know, the more I look at it the more it grows on me, an' I have to say your hair does suit you that way.'

Swallowing the lump that had formed in her throat, Kate laid Jenny gently into her crib and began to unpack the rest of her outfit.

Lifting the photograph from the bedside table, Martin stared down at the face of his dead wife. Soon another woman would be lying in her place in the bed beside him. Rage began to course through his veins at the injustice of it all. She shouldn't have died so young! Not that Kate wasn't beautiful, she was. But would she ever be able to take the place of Anne? His mind drifted back to the very first time he had ever seen his wife. She had been so beautiful that she'd taken his breath away and he'd known at once that she was the woman he would spend the rest of his life with. But it hadn't worked out that way. Now all he had left of her were memories and a son who could barely bring himself to speak to him on the rare occasions when Martin saw him at all. And the doting grandparents who cared for Adam didn't help the situation, the way they shamelessly spoiled him. Martin thought back to the day they had taken the boy to live with them following Anne's death.

'Of course, you can't possibly bring up a child *and* hold down a job. He'll be so much better with his grandfather and me, and you'll be able to see him whenever you wish,' his mother-in-law had told him, and like a fool he had gone along with it, too locked in grief and anger to care.

He dragged his thoughts back to the present. It was time to put the past behind him. Kate would be his future. *She must be.* Opening the drawer of his beside table, he put the photograph away.

'So – just two weeks till the big day now then, eh?' David smiled at Kate across the rim of the mug of tea Ruby had made him.

Kate nodded as she pressed the big safety pins into the side of the fluffy white Zorbit nappy she was just changing Jenny into. 'Yes, two more weeks and I'll have joined the ball and chain gang.' The remark had been meant as a joke, but as she lifted Jenny and saw David's face darken she glanced across at Ruby who was watching him intently. 'Right, we'd better get you your milk then, little lady, hadn't we?' Hoping to lighten the mood, which

230

had suddenly become solemn, she smiled fondly down into the placid face of the child lying in her arms before dumping her unceremoniously on her uncle's lap. 'There, go to Uncle David while I warm it up, eh?'

Ruby automatically lifted the glass feeding bottle from a jug of hot water and tested it on her wrist before handing it to Kate, who in turn handed it to David. 'There you go, you can do the honours,' she grinned. 'You should be a dab hand at it after having two daughters.'

'Huh, chance would have been a fine thing,' David remarked as he offered the teat to the child. 'Rebecca would never let me near the girls when they were tiny, though I'd have loved to have fed them and bathed them from time to time. She reckoned that was woman's work.'

Once again, Kate realised that she had unwittingly said the wrong thing and glanced across at Ruby for help. However, Ruby kept her eyes fixed on the drink in her hand and stayed well out of it, though her mind was doing overtime. She still sometimes felt angry with David, and could not easily forget the past. After all, it had taken him all his time to be civil to Kate when Beth was alive, and he had all but turned her out on the pavement when his mother died. It was more than obvious that his marriage was in trouble, and frankly, Ruby thought it served him right. Rebecca would have tried the patience of a saint, and now that he'd finally seen her for the snobby, grabbing little bitch that she was, he seemed deeply unhappy. It was his own fault for letting her ride roughshod over everyone, himself included. He was now paying the price.

As for Martin, she just couldn't take to him. He made her flesh creep. Draining her mug, Ruby rose from the table and headed towards the door that led to the stairs. It was too bloody hot for her liking and she was in no mood to sit there and watch the cousins play Happy Families. Perhaps she'd feel better disposed to everyone after a nice lie-down. So thinking, she gave a cursory nod in David's direction and disappeared up the stairs.

Humming softly, Kate tripped up Shepperton Street, smiling at the children who were playing hopscotch on the pavement. She was still smiling when she turned into the entry that divided Ruby's house from her neighbours. She had just visited Dudley's Studio in Queen's Road and booked the photographer for the wedding. Now all she had to do was order the flowers, but that could be done tomorrow. She'd actually quite enjoyed it, seeing as it was the only part of the wedding preparations that Martin hadn't done himself. Glancing at her shiny new wristwatch, which was a present from him, she saw with a little shock that it was well past five o'clock. She had left the house just after eleven in the morning and hoped that Jenny had behaved for Ruby, not that the little lass was ever any trouble.

When she opened the gate, Sally leaped up at her and Kate bent to stroke her. Whyever would Ruby have shut her in the yard? Pushing the back door open, she stepped into the kitchen, blinking as her eyes adjusted to the cool dimness of the room after the blazing sunshine.

Nuala was standing in the middle of the room with Jenny clutched tightly to her chest as she rocked her furiously up and down. She turned startled eyes towards Kate and then flushing guiltily, almost flung the baby at

Kate. 'Here,' she stormed. 'She's done nothin' but cry since Ruby was called away.'

'What do you mean, called away? Where did she go?'

'Some neighbour or other up the street took bad an' Ruby went haring off leavin' me to care for *her*!'

As Kate stared down at the distraught child in her sister's arms, her anger towards Nuala was replaced by concern. Jenny was red in the face and her eyes were rolling; she was also rigid and her breathing was shallow. Sally slunk away under the table with her tail between her legs as she sensed the tense atmosphere, and it was then that Ruby appeared in the kitchen doorway, blocking out the sunshine.

'So what's going on here then?' she demanded as she looked from one sister to the other. When her eyes settled on the child in Kate's arms her face creased with concern. 'What's wrong with the little 'un? I can't have been gone for more than twenty minutes an' she was fast asleep when I left her.'

Nuala frowned. 'Well, it ain't my fault if she woke up the second you set foot out the door, is it? She's been bawling her head off an' I couldn't quieten her. I were just rockin' her to try an' settle her down.'

'Rockin' her! Looks more like she's been shaken to me,' Ruby retorted angrily. 'For God's sake, girl. She is *your* baby, you know. Can't you even be trusted to care for her for a few minutes?'

Nuala glared at her before turning on her heel and flouncing from the room. The two women listened to her banging her way up the steep narrow staircase and when they heard the bedroom door slam behind her they turned their attention back to the baby.

'I think she's all right,' Ruby said reassuringly. 'Here, give her to me an' go an' get her a bottle while I try an' calm her down a bit.'

An hour later Jenny was fast asleep and much more her normal placid self. 'She'll be fine now,' Ruby promised as Kate hung over her crib like a worried mother hen. 'I dare say she got distressed because she's used to you or me looking after her.'

She had no chance to say any more because just then Martin appeared carrying a large box of chocolates.

'For you, madam.' He bowed comically at Kate. When there was no answering smile, he enquired, 'Is something wrong?'

She nodded absently, barely noticing the gift he was offering her. 'Yes, I'm afraid Jenny got really upset earlier and I'm a little worried about her.'

'She looks all right to me,' Martin remarked as he looked down at the sleeping child. 'Don't all babies get upset from time to time?'

'This one doesn't,' Kate declared firmly. 'She's got the temperament of an angel, but something certainly upset her this afternoon.'

'Well, not to worry, she looks fine now, so what say we slope off and get a meal before I go to work?' he suggested persuasively.

Normally Kate would have jumped at the chance but tonight she felt reluctant to leave Jenny. 'I won't if you don't mind, Martin,' she apologised. 'She still feels a little hot and I wouldn't feel right going out and leaving her.'

Martin dropped the chocolates onto the table. 'Fine. Have it your own way.' It was impossible to keep the annoyance from his voice as he turned and headed towards the open door.

Dragging her eyes from the sleeping infant Kate asked, 'Will you be calling back later?'

'I doubt it. It will be late by the time I've done in the churchyard, which is why I was hoping to snatch an hour with you now. But of course – the baby is obviously more important. I have to say I'm disappointed in you, Kate. Nuala will never take responsibility for the child if you keep mammy-pampering her this way.'

Kate opened her mouth to object, but then clamped it shut again. Nuala wasn't capable of caring for the child alone, if only Martin could have known it. Her shoulders slumped as she watched his broad back stride away, but then Jenny stirred and her attention immediately returned to the child whom she adored. He would understand eventually. He would have to.

Martin's fists clenched as he passed beneath the Coton Arches. From the Pingles Fields, the sounds of music from a funfair that was setting up there wafted on the air, but he was so angry that he barely heard it. Just when was Kate going to realise that *he* should be her priority now, *not* Nuala's bloody baby?

Still, once they were married it would be different – he would make sure of it. Nuala would have to muck in whether she liked it or not. There'd be trouble if she didn't!

He paused when he came to College Street and wondered if he should go and get fish and chips, but his appetite seemed to have disappeared, so instead he hurried on to his home to change into his work clothes. He might as well get down to the churchyard and dig the grave for tomorrow before it got dark. The sooner he started, the sooner he'd be finished.

He cursed softly under his breath. 'Bloody women!'

Chapter Twenty

'You should have told me before!' The girl's eyes flashed as the light from the moon sailed from behind the clouds to temporarily shine through the car window.

Gordon Fraser, her boss, slid his arm across the back of her seat and spoke to her coaxingly. 'How was I to know I was going to fall for you? Does it really matter so much? Me and the wife were finished long before you came on the scene. You're just the excuse for me to get out of a loveless marriage.'

'Oh yes? Say that to all your conquests do you, Gordon?'

Hearing the sneer in her voice, his first instinct was to tell her to go to hell, but with the moonlight playing on her long blond hair she did look remarkably pretty. There had been a stream of girls before her, though Linda Ensor couldn't know that. Perhaps as well, because this one was worth hanging on to for a while, if his long-suffering wife Maisie didn't get wind of it, of course. She'd soon put a stop to it if she did, just as she had endless times before. That was the trouble being married to a sour-faced old cow, who just happened to be your boss as well. None of his employees knew it, but his wife saw to it that he didn't forget. The small engineering firm he ran had been left to his wife by her late father – and he made a good job of running it. The perks that came with the job helped, such as the endless stream of pretty young secretaries he got to take on. Most of them were like putty in his hands. After all, there was a certain status to being known as the boss's bit on the side. But this one . . . she'd almost had a fit when she found out he was married, and if he wanted to play her along for a bit longer then he'd have to turn the old charm on big-time!

She was sitting as if she'd been cast in stone staring petulantly across Seeswood Pool. Funny that she hadn't clocked on to the fact that he was married before, being as he usually brought her here to this out of the way lay-by, but she hadn't! It was Jim Bonner in the yard who'd dropped him in it, the big-mouthed sod. Huh! From now on Jim had better watch his step; you'd have thought he was the boss sometimes, the way he stalked about the yard. He'd worked there for years, for Maisie's father when he was still alive, and because of that, Maisie thought the sun shone out of his arse. Well, just let the sly old sod put one foot wrong again and he'd give him his marching orders and bugger the consequences.

Gently taking Linda's chin, he turned her to face him. 'Look, sweetheart, it's not what you think – honest. Like I just told you, me and the wife have led separate lives for years. Just stayed together for the sake of the kids really, but the kids are older now, so—'

'Oh, stop it, Gordon. Do you think I've fallen off a Christmas tree or something? I'm not entirely stupid, you know, and after Jim had spoken to me I made a point of making a few discreet enquiries. Seems to me like I'm not the first little bit you've had on the side. You have absolutely no intention of leaving your wife at all, do you?'

Withdrawing his arm from her shoulders, he said irritatedly, 'In that case then, if you think that, there isn't much point in continuing, is there?'

'No, I don't think there is.' Her temper was rising to meet his now as she fumbled for the door handle. Stumbling from the car she glared at him before kicking his precious car door shut.

Almost immediately, the headlights sliced into the darkness, the engine roared into life, then before she could change her mind, Gordon had reversed out of the lay-by and was roaring away up the lane.

The young woman swiped a tear away as she realised that she'd left her handbag in the back of his car, but then muttered, 'I just hope his poor wife finds it and see how he explains that away.'

Crossing the lane she stood against the railings that divided Seeswood Pool from the road and shuddered. Despite the heat of the day the night air was nippy and the water on the vast pool was choppy. Her summer dress felt thin, and her cardigan was in Gordon's car too, she remembered, too late. To warm herself up, she began to walk tentatively along, trying to avoid tripping in the numerous potholes that skirted the pool. A bat swooped down from a nearby tree and gasping with fear she ducked, sure that it would become entangled in her hair. Eventually she pulled herself together with an effort and set off again, but now every night sound seemed to have become magnified, and tears of fear pricked at the back of her eyes.

She had gone no more than a few steps when she thought she sensed someone behind her. Clutching the cold iron railings, she peered fearfully back over her shoulder, but the moon had disappeared behind the clouds, so it was impossible for her to see for more than a few yards either way.

Gulping deep in her throat, fear lent speed to her feet as she hurried on. She had just begun the uphill climb that would lead her on to Ansley Road when a hand closed across her shoulder, and she almost jumped out of her skin.

'What—' Then another hand settled on her other shoulder and she felt herself being pushed towards the ground. With every ounce of strength she had, she suddenly threw herself backwards, and whoever it was who had hold of her, temporarily released their hold. Without waiting to see the consequences of her actions she scrambled along the ground, then kicking off her shoes she ran, knowing that her very life depended on it. The footsteps were behind her again, and the hand was on her shoulder once more, vicious in its grasp, but this time she knew that she couldn't match his strength; he was forcing her to the ground again and there was absolutely nothing in the world she could do about it. She landed painfully and felt warm blood gush from her nose as it connected with the hard ground. It was then that the moon once again sailed from behind the clouds and her hair was turned to silver in its glow.

'Blonde!' she heard someone gasp and unexpectedly the hold on her loosened and she heard the footsteps pounding away in the opposite direction. She lay there for what seemed an eternity, too terrified to move. Somewhere back along the lane she thought she heard the sound of a car engine start and the sound prompted her to struggle to her knees, then to hide herself, dropping into the deep ditch that ran alongside the road, where she lay trembling and concealed until the first vestige of dawn appeared in the sky.

Chapter Twenty-One

'It's as true as I'm standin' here,' Winnie Trotter declared to her captive audience, hitching her folded arms yet higher beneath her bulbous breasts. 'I had it straight from the horse's mouth this mornin'. Polly Trent called in fer a cuppa on her way home from her cleanin' job at the cop shop, an' she heard all the coppers on about it. The whole place is buzzin' wi' it, accordin' to form.'

'Buzzing with what?' Kate asked indulgently as she approached the little gathering at Winnie's front gate. It was late afternoon and the town was in the grip of a heatwave, but despite that, the women were still dressed in their flowered wraparound aprons and headscarves, which were tied turban-like around their heads to disguise the metal curlers that usually only came out when they set foot beyond the end of the street.

Winnie lived two doors up from Ruby and was known as a bit of a character, but now she was deadly serious.

'There were another poor young woman attacked last night up by Seeswood Pool,' she replied in answer to Kate's question.

Kate wiped the sweat from her brow, all amusement gone now, and asked, 'Has she gone missing?'

'No. Somehow she managed to get away from him, from what Polly could gather, but she's in the Manor Hospital, deep in shock.'

'That's dreadful.' Kate shuddered at the very thought of it. 'But how can they be sure it's the same person who attacked the others?'

'Well, I don't suppose they can be,' Winnie admitted. 'But Polly reckons the cops think it *were* the same bloke. They ain't been allowed to interview her up to now but they think it's him all right. Stands to reason, don't it, when yer come to think of it. All the attacks took place somewhere off the beaten track. It seems to be followin' a pattern an' yer couldn't get much further off the track than down there.'

'But whatever would a young woman be doing, walking there all alone at that time of night?' Kate said thoughtfully.

Winnie's ample shoulders shrugged beneath her flowered apron, setting her great breasts jiggling. 'That I can't say, but it's a place where couples go courtin', in't it? Ech! It make's yer go cold just to think about it, don't it? I mean – helpless women like us ain't safe to go out an' about on us own any more, are we?'

Despite the seriousness of the situation, Kate had a job to refrain from smiling. Winnie was hardly what anyone would class as a 'helpless woman', as her poor downtrodden husband would probably have testified, had he been there. It was common knowledge that Winnie wore the trousers in that particular house which, considering she was a great Amazon of a woman who dwarfed her tiny husband, was hardly surprising.

'Anyway,' Winnie continued, afraid of losing her

audience, 'Polly reckons they're callin' the big boys in from London now to deal wi' it, an' let's face it, it ain't before time, is it? Rumour has it that it'll be someone from Scotland Yard. The local Bobbies ain't seemed to do much good catchin' whoever he is, so they've got to do sommat, ain't they?'

The women's heads bobbed in agreement as Kate hurried on. It was now only one week away from her wedding but this news had driven all thoughts of it away as she thought of the fate that might have befallen the unfortunate victim of the attack.

When she entered the passageway down to Ruby's house, she paused, enjoying the cool air that wafted through it, then shoving open the back gate she beamed when she saw Jenny fast asleep in her pram underneath the kitchen window. Ruby had spread a large mesh net over the hood to keep the cats and flies away, and Kate's heart swelled with love as she looked down on her niece.

The back door was propped open, allowing what little breeze there was to enter the kitchen. Even so it was still stiflingly hot and the first thing Kate saw on entering was Nuala sprawled across the settee.

'Where's Ruby?' Kate threw her bag on to the wing chair that stood to one side of the empty firegrate and looked at Nuala impatiently. Her sister was doing less and less lately. She had even given up her part-time job at the vicarage now, using the excuse that the vicar's wife nagged her.

Having met the woman in question, Kate found this highly unlikely; she was well known in the parish for her kind heart and gentle nature. Even so, Kate had hoped that once Nuala was spending more time at home she might get a little closer to Jenny, but up to now that certainly hadn't been the case. In fact, she was trying Ruby's considerable patience to the limit, which only led Kate to think it was just as well that she was getting married, before Ruby lost her temper with Nuala altogether and chucked her out on her ear. Not that she could have blamed her if she had. Lately, Nuala would have tried the patience of a saint, and she just hoped that she'd try a little harder once they had moved in with Martin.

'She's gone to pick up some salad stuff for tea,' Nuala managed to drag her eyes away from the television set long enough to inform her, and grimaced. 'Can't stand all this rabbit food meself, but Ruby reckons it's too warm for anything hot.'

At that moment, the light was temporarily blocked from the room as Ruby appeared in the doorway with her arms full of lettuce, spring onions and anything else she had been able to find in the corner shop.

Kate immediately noticed that she'd been to the hairdresser's and was wearing a pretty summer dress.

'I was wondering if yer wouldn't mind gettin' the tea tonight,' Ruby asked Kate. 'There's some fresh salad stuff here an' a nice bit o' ham on the thrall in the pantry. And could yer get Jenny ready for bed?'

'Of course I wouldn't mind,' Kate grinned. 'Off somewhere special, are you?'

Glancing at Nuala, Ruby took Kate's elbow and steered her towards the sink out of earshot.

'I don't quite know how to tell you, love, but the thing is, Victor asked me to marry him last night an' he's callin' round in a while to take me out an' get his answer.'

245

'And what's the answer going to be?' Kate's eyes sparkled as she stared at the woman who had come to mean so much to her.

Blushing like a schoolgirl, Ruby fidgeted nervously with the belt on her dress. 'I've laid awake half the bleedin' night thinkin' about it,' she confessed. 'An' in the end I decided I'd say yes. The thing is, nothin' can bring my Leonard back, an' when you've all gone I'll feel the loneliness even more. Victor is a good, kind man an' suddenly I don't want to think o' spendin' the rest of me life all alone. I'm lucky to have found a decent bloke like him. Yer see, as I'm sure people will have broken their necks to tell yer, I was a bit of a gel in me time. What they *don't* know is why I went on the game.' She paused to bite down on her lip before saying softly, 'When I knew my Leonard were dying I didn't know which way to turn. I wanted to make whatever life he had left the best I could, so I . . . Well, you know the path I took an' I don't regret it.' Her chin jutted defiantly as she watched for Kate's reaction. 'None o' them blokes meant a thing to me, they merely put money in my hand that I could spend on my man. Victor knows all about it an' yet he still wants me. That's incredible, ain't it? Do yer think I'm doing the right thing?'

Choking on the lump in her throat, Kate drew her into her arms and kissed her cheek. 'I think you're doing exactly the right thing,' she whispered. 'You so deserve some happiness. I just can't think why you didn't decide to do it before and then we could have had a double wedding.'

'Get away with you,' Ruby chuckled, catching the teasing note in Kate's voice. 'At our ages, we're hardly going to splash out on some big posh do, are we?'

'I hardly think what Martin has organised could be classed as that!' Kate said, but Ruby detected a note of regret in her voice and as she thought of the plain bridal suit hanging on the wardrobe door in the girl's bedroom her blood boiled all over again. The suit had looked plain to say the least on the day that Martin had chosen it, but now that the weather had taken a turn for the better, poor Kate might be in danger of sweating to death before her wedding day was over if she wore that.

Knowing that it would be useless to raise the issue yet again she changed the subject. 'Heard about that young woman who was attacked last night, have yer?' Carrying the salad stuff to the sink she began to wash it under the tap.

Kate nodded. 'Yes, as I was coming back from my shift at the Rose I heard Winnie talking about it to some women in the street.'

Ruby tutted and shook her head. 'Well, at least the poor thing got away from him. If it was the same one as had them other poor souls, she might have been missing altogether now. Don't bear thinkin' about, does it?'

'No, it doesn't,' Kate agreed and then busied herself getting a bottle and a rusk with mashed banana ready for Jenny's next feed.

'The thing is, she doesn't seem to . . .' Kate squirmed in her seat as the young woman doctor across the desk from her smiled at her encouragingly.

'Doesn't seem to what?'

Kate struggled to find the right words to express her fears. 'Well, she doesn't seem to be doing the things other babies her age are doing,' she said finally.

247

Jenny, who was cradled in her arms, stared up at her placidly as the doctor came round the desk and stroked her hand.

'Now that you've raised it, I have to admit that I have found her, shall we say, a little slow?' the woman agreed. When Kate frowned, she immediately went on, 'Now don't get flying into a panic. What you're forgetting is that Jenny was born with a heart defect, and that's probably what's making her have a little less energy than she should have. We'll know more on that score when you've taken her back to see the heart specialist on her next appointment. Then again, some babies are just slower at developing than others. All the same, I suggest we have a few more tests done at the hospital, just to make sure that there's nothing else obvious causing the problem, eh?'

Returning to her seat, she took a sheet of notepaper and began to scribble on it. Eventually she put it into an envelope and turned her attention back to Kate.

'Right, I'll make sure that this goes off to the hospital straight away. You should have an appointment come through within a couple of weeks. In the meantime, try not to worry too much. As I said, babies have a habit of developing at their own pace and I'm sure that Jenny's just fine.'

Kate rose and after thanking the doctor she carried Jenny to her pram, which was standing outside the clinic doors. The day was stiflingly hot and she adjusted the baby's sunshade before turning the coach-built pram about and heading off into Riversley Park.

When she came to the River Anker she sank onto a bench and stared at the weeping willow trees whose branches were trailing into the water. Behind her, children were running and playing, their harassed mothers doing their best to keep up with them. Their gleeful shouts floated on the air, but Kate was oblivious to them as she thought back to what the doctor had said. What if there *was* something else wrong with Jenny? The poor little mite had enough to cope with, with her heart defect, let alone anything else. Kate totally adored her. There was nothing that she wouldn't have done for the child, and already she was worrying about leaving her while she went off on her honeymoon. Then guilt sliced through her as she thought of her handsome husband-to-be. She was so fortunate to have found someone like Martin. After all, how many men would have taken on her sister, her niece *and* a little dog to boot! And yet here she was begrudging him just one week of their married life alone together.

Dragging her eyes away from the slow-moving water, she looked at Jenny again. She'd fallen asleep, and with her eyelashes curled on her tiny pink cheeks she looked like a little angel. For no reason that Kate could explain, a terrible sense of foreboding suddenly threatened to choke her. She stood so quickly that a family of ducks who had been floating on the water nearby flapped their wings and squawking indignantly, hurriedly swam away.

An angel. Try as she might, she couldn't push the thought away. Jenny reminded her of an angel. Was it a sign that she wasn't meant to remain on earth?

Grabbing the handles of the pram, Kate turned and headed for the bandstand as if she could somehow leave the disturbing thoughts behind her. The doctor had told her that there might be nothing wrong with Jenny and she had to hold on to that. The alternative was just too terrible to contemplate.

On the day of the wedding Kate was woken by Ruby who was standing at the side of the bed with a tray in her hands.

'Come on, sleepy-head! Ain't no more time for lying about today.' Plonking the tray of tea and toast precariously on the end of the bed, Ruby crossed to the window and swept the curtains aside, allowing the early morning sunshine to flood into the room. She beamed with satisfaction. 'There you are, yer see. They reckon the sun always shines on the righteous and it's certainly shinin' fer you today.'

Struggling up onto the pillows, Kate's eyes went to the empty cot at the side of her bed.

'No need lookin' for Her Ladyship. She's downstairs all fed and foddered,' Ruby informed her with a twinkle in her eye. 'I crept in an' took her over an hour ago, an' I kicked Nuala out o' bed an' all, not that she were too pleased about it. I figured yer deserved a bit o' quiet time an' a lie-in before yer started to get ready, so get some of this food down yer, eh?'

A million butterflies suddenly fluttered to life in Kate's stomach and she felt sick. This was her wedding day. In just a few short hours, she would be Mrs Martin Denby.

'Come on now,' Ruby coaxed as she spread a liberal amount of homemade marmalade on to a slice of toast for her. 'You should always start the day with somethin' inside yer, especially on a big day like today.'

As Kate reluctantly took the toast from her, Ruby began to potter about the room.

250

'Suitcase all packed, is it?' she asked.

When Kate nodded through a mouthful of toast, Ruby fingered the silk stockings that lay across the back of the chair all ready for the bride to slip into. 'Right then, I'll be off an' let yer enjoy yer last breakfast as a single woman in peace. The copper's been on the boil so as soon as yer ready yer can have your bath an' then we'll get yer hair done.' Giving Kate a cheeky wink she slipped from the room, leaving the bride alone with her thoughts.

Kate's eyes settled on the suit that Ruby had gone to great pains to press, hanging ready on the wardrobe door. This was it, her wedding day. The day she had dreamed of. Slipping from the bed, she crossed to the window and inched it open and was just in time to see a florist's van turn into Shepperton Street and pull up outside. This must be the bouquets arriving. Glancing at the small clock on the bedside table, she was shocked to see that it was almost half-past nine. The night before, she had lain awake, sure that she wouldn't sleep a single wink and yet here she was, overlaying. Grabbing her dressing-gown, she hurried downstairs to inspect the flowers.

'Aw love. You look absolutely gorgeous.' Ruby noisily blew her nose as Kate emerged from the stairs door.

'I'll second that,' David agreed.

Kate blushed becomingly as Ruby placed a small bouquet of freesias in her gloved hand. The suit showed off her slim figure to perfection as she peeked from beneath the tiny veil on her hat. Her hair had already begun to grow again and framed her face in soft dark curls, but more than that, there was a glow about her.

The glow that all brides seem to possess on their wedding day.

Even Nuala had managed to look smart today and Jenny looked divine in a tiny little dress that Ruby had spent hours painstakingly smocking.

'I'll just take your case out to the car,' David tactfully offered, and lifting it he ushered Nuala, with Jenny in her arms before him, and hurried away leaving Kate to have a moment alone with Ruby.

'Now, you are quite sure about this, ain't yer?' Ruby couldn't keep the concern from her voice as she draped her arm affectionately across Kate's shoulders. 'What I mean is, it ain't too late to change yer mind.'

Kate giggled. 'Oh Ruby, why would I want to do that? I must be the luckiest woman alive to get Martin, and we're going to live happily ever after.'

'Of course you are.' Forcing a smile back to her face, Ruby propelled her towards the door then suddenly stopped. 'Oh, I almost forgot. There's something I want yer to have.' Plunging her hand into the pocket of her dress she drew out a small heart-shaped sapphire dangling from a delicate gold chain. 'This was me mam's,' she told Kate softly. 'She gave it to me on my wedding day an' I always hoped that one day I'd give it to me daughter on hers, but it weren't meant to be, so seein' as you're the nearest I've ever had to a daughter I want you to have it. It should go with yer suit a treat.'

Kate had to swallow hard to stop the tears from flowing as Ruby removed the necklace that Martin had bought her, and replaced it with hers. 'Oh, Ruby. Thank you . . . for everything. If it hadn't been for you . . .'

Ruby pecked her on the cheek. 'Come on now. Enough said, else you'll have me blartin' all over the place.' She tucked a clean hankie in Kate's handbag. 'Now you're fully equipped: something old, something new, something borrowed, something blue. Right – best not keep the groom waiting, eh?'

At the door, Kate paused just once to glance back over her shoulder. She had been happy living here with Ruby, but when she returned from her honeymoon she would be moving straight into Martin's house. In fact, almost all of her clothes were already there.

Taking a deep breath she stepped outside where the neighbours were gathered about the gate to wish her well.

As David helped her into the car she waved at them and then they were on their way.

When they arrived at the register office, Kate's heart did a little somersault as she saw Martin patiently waiting for them. He looked breathtakingly handsome, standing there in his smart suit and tie with his hair all neatly Brylcreemed into place. Her heart filled with love, and there and then she silently vowed that she would make him a good wife.

'I now pronounce you man and wife. You may kiss the bride.' The registrar beamed as Ruby clutched Jenny tightly to her with one arm while she blew noisily into her handkerchief with the other. As Kate looked adoringly up into the eyes of her new husband, Ruby thought that the girl was positively glowing with happiness. And yet . . .

Then Ruby mentally shook herself. What was done was done.

After the register had been signed the small congregation made their way outside into the bright sunshine where Ruby took some photographs on her old Brownie camera.

Nuala scowled and shuffled uncomfortably from foot to foot but Kate was so taken up with her new husband that she didn't notice anything but him.

The town was teeming with people and many of them stopped to offer their good wishes to the happy couple before hurrying on their way.

'Right,' Ruby told them, 'I know you didn't want any fuss but there's still nearly an hour to go before your train leaves so I've got you a cake an' some drinks ready in the George Eliot Hotel.'

When Kate went to protest, Ruby held up her hand. 'Now then, no arguments. This is *my* treat an' I'll be offended if you don't come along.'

She thought that she detected a hint of annoyance in Martin's eyes but when he took Kate's elbow his voice was light. 'Come along, darling. As Ruby says, we've got plenty of time before we need to be at the station and we wouldn't want to throw kindness back in Ruby's face, would we?'

By then Kate was so happy that she would have followed him to the ends of the earth, so she allowed herself to be led through the marketplace until they reached the hotel.

Ruby had done them proud. A small room had been set aside for them with a wedding cake and a bottle of champagne ready to toast them. Kate laughed as the bubbles went up her nose, and when they left half an hour later to make their way to the train station she knew without doubt that she would remember this as the happiest day of her life.

As David lifted her case aboard, Kate turned to hug Nuala, who was shuffling from foot to foot, a habit that she always adopted when she was troubled about something. Her eyes were vacant as Kate drew her into an embrace and Kate knew that her sister had retreated back into the silent world she always escaped to when she felt out of her depth about anything. Guilt flooded through Kate, sharp as a knife, shaving the edge off her happiness. They'd never spent a day apart in the whole of their lives apart from the time Nuala had been in hospital following Jenny's birth, and Kate knew that she was finding the situation difficult to deal with. She turned to kiss Jenny, who was sitting placidly on Ruby's hip, and then clung to Ruby as if she might never see her again as Martin waited impatiently to usher her aboard.

'Now are you *quite* sure that you'll be all right with Jenny?' Kate asked for the tenth time in as many minutes, as tears pricked at the back of her eyes.

Sensing her distress, Ruby forced a chuckle as she pushed her towards the carriage door. 'I'll be absolutely right as ninepence, thank you, madam. Now will you *please* get aboard before the bloody train goes wi'out yer? It ain't goin' to be much of a honeymoon fer the groom if he ain't got a bride now, is it?'

Kate hopped aboard and pulled down the window as the guard began to walk the length of the train slamming all the doors. Martin had his arm around her and she felt as if she were being torn in two. Half of her felt as if she might burst with happiness. The other half of her felt as if she was leaving her family behind for ever. From this day forward, life would never be the same again for any of them. But she owed it to her husband at least for the duration of their honeymoon to give him her undivided attention and so she smiled up at him.

Suddenly remembering her bouquet, she flung it high into the air and giggled when it landed in Ruby's arms. 'Your turn next,' she shouted above the sound of the engine chugging into life, and laughed when Ruby blushed to the roots of her hair. Then amidst a cloud of smoke they were off and she hung out of the window and waved until Ruby, Nuala and Jenny became specks in the distance.

At last she turned and sank down onto the seat beside Martin. He smiled at her, but the smile didn't quite reach his eyes and she had the impression that he was annoyed at her reaction to leaving Nuala and Jenny.

'Sorry about that.' She felt that she owed him some sort of an explanation. 'Nuala and I have never been apart before and I'm worried about how she'll cope. My sister isn't very good at handling changes in her life.'

'Understandable,' he remarked. 'But it would be nice if you could at least try to forget about those at home for a while. After all, it is our honeymoon.'

'You're quite right. Now – shall we start again?'

His arm slid across the back of the seat and settled about her shoulders. 'Hello there, Mrs Denby,' he whispered, and suddenly Kate thought she would explode with joy.

'Will you tell me *now* where we're going?' She was as excited as a child as he smiled at her indulgently.

'We're going to Cornwall. But now . . . how about giving your husband a kiss?'

Only too happy to oblige, Kate nestled into his strong arms. Suddenly the future was bright.

Chapter Twenty-Two

'Wake up, Kate. We're there.'

Kate started awake and knuckled the sleep from her eyes as she struggled to sit up. She had a crick in her neck and her mouth was dry, but as she realised where she was, she instantly forgot her discomforts. Glancing at the windows of the carriage she saw that it was dark outside and guessed that she must have been sleeping for some time. Martin was wrestling the cases down from the overhead luggage rack, so she quickly tried to straighten her skirt and fasten her hat back on as he manhandled them to the carriage door. Once he had them safely on the platform he turned to help Kate down from the train and she looked about her with interest. They seemed to be the only two passengers to alight from the train. A guard was hovering nearby, ready to blow his whistle on the deserted platform. Lifting a suitcase in each hand, Martin nodded towards the exit.

'There should be a taxi waiting for us,' he said. 'It's not actually all that far to the hotel but these cases are quite heavy, especially yours. I think you must have packed everything apart from the kitchen sink.'

Kate grinned at him coyly. 'Well, you could hardly

expect a girl to go off on her honeymoon without a good selection of lingerie, could you?'

To her surprise, Martin frowned. 'Kate, do try to remember that you're in a public place, please.'

Embarrassment made her flush and she was glad of the darkness. In truth, her stomach was in knots at the thought of the night ahead. Part of her was terrified about what making love would entail while the other part of her was tingling with anticipation.

'Sorry,' she muttered, and followed him meekly out into the cobbled streets of Newquay.

Gasping with delight, she instantly forgot her embarrassment. The cobbled street swept down to a harbour where boats bobbed gently on the water and everywhere she looked were quaint picture-box cottages.

'Oh Martin, it's absolutely *beautiful*.' She was so taken with the breathtaking view that she didn't even notice the taxi that was waiting for them, until Martin had loaded the cases into the boot.

'Come along. If we hurry we might be in time to get an evening meal at the hotel. You can admire the view later.'

Ignoring the irritability in his voice, she scrambled into the taxi and gazed enraptured from the window as it pulled away from the kerb. It took them down the steeply sloping hill before following a road that wound up around another, equally steep cliff. Kate was totally enchanted with the place and momentarily was reminded of the beaches back in Durham where she had spent so many happy hours with Matthew.

Forcing the memories away, she turned to smile at her husband. Within minutes they reached the clifftop and the taxi drew to a halt outside an impressive hotel that had magnificent sea views.

It was all Kate could do to stop herself from clapping her hands in sheer delight as she waited for Martin to pay the driver and retrieve their cases from the boot.

'Right,' he said, after giving the driver a generous tip. 'Let's go and see if we're in time to get something to eat, eh? It's a long time till morning.'

Kate followed him into the hotel. They entered a huge foyer where a great crystal chandelier sparkled down on them. Kate felt her feet sink into a luxurious wall-to-wall carpet and she stared around her in awe. It was like something she had only ever seen in magazines and she felt slightly out of her depth. Martin on the other hand might have spent every day of his life in such a place as he marched up to an impressive mahogany desk and rang the bell. Almost instantly a small bespectacled man in a smart suit appeared from a door concealed by a heavy velvet curtain.

'Ah, Mr Denby,' he gushed. 'How nice to see you. We have your room all ready for you, sir. Will you be requiring an evening meal?'

'Yes, please,' Martin replied as the man looked curiously past him at Kate. She felt colour sting her cheeks and for no reason that she could explain, suddenly felt uncomfortable. She had the distinct impression that Martin had been here before, but surely he would have told her. There was no time to ponder on it, for almost immediately the man rang a brass bell on the desk and a porter appeared as if out of thin air.

'Would you take Mr and Mrs Denby's bags up to the

260

honeymoon suite,' the man instructed him, then turning his attention back to Martin, he asked, 'Perhaps you would like to go to your room and freshen up after your journey before dinner?'

'That would be most pleasant.' Taking Kate's elbow, Martin ushered her towards a lift that stood in one corner of the impressive entrance hall, and once again she had the impression that he knew his way about. The lift was mirrored, with carpets as thick as those in the foyer, and she felt as if she had stepped into another world. Once it stopped and the doors slid open, Martin led her along a landing past huge windows that overlooked the sea. She would have liked to stop and drink in the view but his hand was firmly on her elbow and so she meekly allowed him to steer her on.

He finally stopped in front of an elaborately panelled door and after fiddling with the key he unlocked it and drew her inside.

She was shocked to see their cases already standing there, but was so taken with the room that she didn't even comment on it. Instead she crossed to the window and sighed with contentment.

'This must be what it's like in heaven,' she sighed dreamily, but Martin had already crossed to a door that led to a full en-suite bathroom.

'Perhaps we could enjoy the view later?' he suggested dryly.

Kate could hear him running water into the sink and as she took the hatpin from her hat and fluffed up her hair, she gazed around her. The bedroom was stunningly beautiful and she could well understand why it was used as the honeymoon suite. A huge, intricately carved four-poster bed surrounded by chintz curtains that matched those hanging at the window, took up almost the whole of one wall. An enormous dressing-table on which stood a fancy gilt mirror, took up another. On the third wall was a matching wardrobe and chest of drawers. The fourth wall gave entrance to the bathroom and housed the full-length window, which she soon discovered led onto a wrought-iron balcony. Stepping outside, she gasped with delight at the panoramic view spread before her. A great silver moon was suspended in the sky, surrounded by stars. The sea was as calm as a millpond and looked as if it had been sprinkled with stardust as the stars reflected on it. Below her, the lights of the houses twinkled in the darkness and she felt peace slowly seep into her soul. She could have stood there enjoying her opulent surroundings and the view from the balcony for ever, but as Martin emerged from the bathroom it was obvious that he had other ideas.

'Come along then. They won't keep the restaurant open indefinitely and it's been a long time since lunchtime.'

'But what about the unpacking? Shouldn't we—'

'No,' he said firmly. 'The unpacking can wait. Now come on, I'm starving.'

Straightening her jacket, Kate followed him from the room. It had been a long day and she guessed that he was tired. Not that he would be doing much sleeping tonight, if what the customers at the Rose had teased her about wedding nights was true. She blushed at the thought as they took the lift to the ground floor.

The restaurant impressed her, with its crisp white table-cloths and sparkling silver cutlery. As the waiter led them to their table, people glanced at her buttonhole, which was beginning to wilt now and smiled at her, bringing warm colour to her cheeks yet again.

Martin ordered the meal without even looking at the elaborate *cordon bleu* menu, and as Kate relaxed in her seat she was happy to leave the choice to him. It was nice to be waited on and pampered, and she determined to make the most of every second. Fleetingly she wondered if Jenny and Nuala were all right, but pushed the thought away. This was her wedding night and she mustn't allow anything to spoil it.

They dined on homemade chicken soup and crusty bread rolls followed by fresh salmon and a delicious chocolate soufflé that melted in her mouth. Martin ordered a bottle of wine and by the time the meal was finished, Kate was in a fine good humour and more than a little tiddly.

Martin took her elbow and escorted her to the bar and there they sat and drank a glass of brandy as Kate enjoyed the view of the sea from the window. At last Martin glanced at the clock and drained his glass.

'Would you like to go up and get ready for bed?' he suggested. 'It's almost half-ten. I hadn't realised how late it was getting.' When he grinned at her, Kate felt her heart start to beat faster.

'Er . . . yes, I'll g-go up,' she stuttered, suddenly deeply embarrassed. 'Will you be long?'

'Not at all. I'll just have another drink and give you time to get changed then I'll be up. Would you like me to show you to our room?'

'Oh no,' Kate blurted, feeling like a silly gangly

schoolgirl. 'You just stay here and enjoy your drink and I'll see you in a minute.'

As she went to rise, he noticed the heart-shaped sapphire dangling around her neck for the first time and his face hardened. 'I thought I'd bought you a necklace to wear today? That isn't it, is it?'

Fingering the necklace, Kate shook her head. 'No. I hope you don't mind, but as we were leaving for the register office, Ruby gave this to me. It was her mother's. She wore it on her wedding day and wanted me to have it. Seeing as you'd bought everything else I was wearing I didn't think you'd mind . . . You don't – do you?'

He forced a smile to his face but his eyes were cold. 'It's a bit late to worry about it now even if I did, isn't it? Now off you go. I'll be up shortly.'

Kate threaded her way through the tables in the bar, conscious of the appreciative eyes of the men as they followed her progress. As she took the lift to their room she tried to block out the look she had seen in his eyes when he noticed Ruby's necklace. But then she tried to see it from his point of view. He had gone to the trouble of buying her a necklace to wear, so no wonder he was hurt. As the lift stopped and she emerged onto the landing that led to their room, she determined to make it up to him and hurried on.

Once inside their room she snapped open her case and as her eyes rested on the beautiful nightdress that Ruby had forced her into buying she blushed a deep brick red. It was a virginal white see-through affair that left little to the imagination, and she could almost hear Ruby laughing as she had looked at it in the shop.

'*Go on, girl, treat yourself,*' she had said as Kate flinched at the price tag. '*He might have got to choose yer bloody weddin' outfit but at least yer can choose what to wear on yer weddin' night!*'

'But, Ruby, it's so expensive,' Kate had pointed out and Ruby had fallen about laughing.

'*So what? Go on – push the boat out. He'll be putty in yer hands when he sees yer in that.*'

And so Kate had bought it, though now she was wondering if she would ever dare to wear it. It was certainly far removed from the prim up-to-the-neck cotton affair that she usually wore. But still, this *was* a special night. It would never come again and she did want to look her best.

After laying it across the foot of the bed along with her dressing-gown which was much more sedate, she hastily unpacked the rest of her case, then crossing to the bathroom she quickly bathed and dried herself on the fluffy white towels that the hotel had provided.

Bath-time for Kate was usually a rushed affair; she usually had Jenny to see to, and tonight was no different but for other reasons. She was terrified that Martin would come back and find her naked so she rushed into the bedroom and pulled the flimsy nightgown across her head, then crossing to the dressing-table she hastily tugged a brush through her springing dark curls and sprayed herself liberally with her favourite perfume, by Bourjois, Evening in Paris. As a finishing touch, she put on the necklace that Martin had bought her. Ignoring the urge to hop into bed she then crossed to the long French windows and slipped out onto the balcony to enjoy the view one last time. After the heat of the day, the cool sea breeze was like a kiss on her bare skin and

265

she breathed in the salt air with a smile on her face. One side of the balcony looked down across the town and the other side looked down onto a winding path that led to a small private beach belonging to the hotel. As her eyes adjusted to the moonlight she became aware of a figure on the path. With a little start she realised that it was Martin. She would have recognised those broad shoulders and that walk anywhere . . . but what was he doing, making his way down to the beach?

Hastily retreating into the bedroom in case he should turn around and see her watching him, she began to pace up and down the room, her arms locked around herself. Slowly the smile returned. He was probably just getting a breath of fresh air to give her a little more time to get ready before he returned to their room, and if that was the case he could walk through the door at any moment. As panic gripped her she dived into the enormous bed and pulled the sheets up to her chin. Glancing at the clock she saw that it was just after eleven-thirty. Settling herself back against the pillows, she waited.

An hour later, she got out of bed and crossed to the balcony but there was no sign of Martin whichever way she looked. The night had turned cold now and she shivered and pulled the doors shut as she went back into their room. Clicking on the light she briefly considered getting dressed and going to look for him, but then dismissed the idea almost immediately. Where could he be? As her eyes moved around the room they settled on Martin's suitcase and she decided to unpack it for him. At least it would give her something to do. Snapping open the lock she took out his shirts and hung them on hangers in the wardrobe, then she took out his underwear and placed it neatly in a drawer next to hers. Methodically she worked her way though his things until she came to a photograph frame in the bottom of the case. Lifting it, she stared into the faces of a smiling couple – a younger Martin with his arms wrapped tight about a pretty woman. Her heart skipped a beat. She might have been looking into a mirror, for the young woman bore a close resemblance to herself. She had the same slim build, the same dark hair, cut in an almost identical style to hers. Even the suit she was wearing bore an uncanny resemblance to the one Martin had chosen for her to wear for their wedding. But why?

Tears stung at the back of her eyes as her hand fingered the short curls surrounding her face. It was Martin who had suggested she had her hair cut into this style. The woman in the photograph was obviously his late wife . . . but was he trying to turn her into a copy of Anne? She shuddered at the thought as tears slid down her cheeks. Suddenly all the anticipation of the night ahead was gone, to be replaced by a sick feeling in the pit of her stomach. Gently standing the photo on the end of the dressing-table she clambered into bed and cried into her pillow as she waited for him. Her wedding night was certainly not turning out to be anything like she had expected it to.

'Room service.'

Kate started awake, blinking in the bright sunshine that was flooding through the French doors. For a moment she was disorientated but then as she remembered where she was and the events of the night before came flooding back, she struggled up onto her elbow.

With a little start she saw that Martin was fast asleep at the side of her. Climbing gently from the bed so as not to disturb him, she wiped the sleep from her eyes before slipping on her robe and crossing to the door to admit the waitress who was laden down with a breakfast tray.

'Where shall I put it, madam?' the young woman asked, grinning knowingly as she looked across at the shape of Martin in the bed.

Kate flushed, suddenly all fingers and thumbs. 'Er . . . just put it on the table over there would you, please?'

'Of course, madam. Will there be anything else?'

'No, that will be fine. Thank you.'

She kept her eyes on the view from the windows until she heard the door close, then breathing a sigh of relief she crossed to the tray and poured herself a strong cup of tea, keeping a tentative eye on Martin all the time. At some point in the early hours she must have fallen asleep from sheer exhaustion, so she had no idea what time he had finally come in. Not that it mattered now; their wedding night had been ruined and it would never come again. Once more the urge was on her to cry as she looked at the photo that had made her sob herself to sleep. She'd always sympathised with Martin for being widowed, but why had he brought a photo of his late wife on their honeymoon, and why had he tried to change her into a carbon copy of Anne?

She was on her second cup of tea when Martin suddenly yawned and stretched. Pulling himself up onto his pillows, he smiled at her.

'Morning, darling. Sleep well, did you?'

Kate blinked in confusion before quickly averting her

eyes as he slid from the bed and padded across the carpet towards her stark naked.

'Be a love and pour me a cup of tea, would you?' he asked as if nothing untoward had happened at all.

She poured the tea into a china cup with shaking fingers then looked down into her own as he sat next to her and proceeded to butter some toast.

'Not having any breakfast?' he enquired.

Kate shook her head. 'No. I . . . er . . . I'm not all that hungry.'

Martin tucked in as if he hadn't eaten for a month before telling her, 'We're going to do a bit of sight-seeing today. There's a bus that you can get in the town that takes you all along the coastal road. I think you'll enjoy it.'

Kate's confusion and disappointment was now being swallowed up with anger. 'Martin,' she barked, unable to stop herself any longer, 'have you been here before? To this hotel, I mean?'

'Of *course* I have.' Swallowing a mouthful of toast, he stared at her as if she had taken leave of her senses. 'Anne and I came here for our honeymoon to this very suite. I thought I'd mentioned it? We enjoyed it so much I thought you'd like it here too. I've been here a number of times on my own as well since . . .' He looked around as if remembering would conjure his late wife up from thin air. 'We got married on the same day in June as you and I did too. I remember the weather was much as it was yesterday, and after supper we strolled along the beach hand-in-hand. It was so romantic . . .' He stared off into the distance, seemingly oblivious to Kate's presence as the memories flooded back.

269

Standing up abruptly, Kate swept past him to the bathroom, unable to listen for another single minute. Once inside she locked the door and leaned heavily against the sink as shock washed over her like waves. Whatever had possessed him to bring her to the same place as he had taken his first wife? Surely she was worthy of a new beginning? What sort of a start to married life was this going to be if they were forever treading in his first wife's footsteps? A tap at the door brought her thoughts sharply back to the present.

'Are you going to be long, darling? It's a beautiful day and we don't want to waste it, do we? There's so much I want you to see.'

Hastily mopping her tears, Kate unlocked the door and strode silently past him. No wonder the proprietor had recognised him. The hotel had become a shrine to his dead wife.

The next three days of their honeymoon fell into a pattern. By day, Martin would take her sightseeing before returning to the hotel for their evening meal. Once the meal was over he would then escort her to their room and disappear off on one of his long walks. Their marriage had still not been consummated although he still showed her affection and each night Kate cried herself to sleep and longed for the end of the week when she could go home.

Sometimes she yearned for Ruby to talk to, but at other times she shuddered at the thought of having to admit what a disaster their honeymoon had been.

The young maid who brought their breakfast to their room each morning soon noticed the sad look in Kate's eyes and she was gossiping about it one morning to the chambermaid when the hotel proprietor came across them.

'I'm tellin' you, there's something not quite right there, as sure as eggs is eggs,' she was heard to say in her broad Cornish dialect. 'Every mornin' when I go in, the poor bird's eyes are red raw from cryin'. Do you think he's perhaps bein' a bit rough with her? It's weird, if you ask me. Word has it that the mister brought his first wife here to this very hotel for their honeymoon. Died, so they say – the first one, that is. Don't you find it strange?'

Before the chambermaid could reply, the proprietor bore down on them like an avenging angel.

'Haven't you got anything better to do than gossip?' he demanded.

The young maid, who knew his bark was far worse than his bite, smiled at him saucily. 'Sorry sir. But you must admit it's a bit of a rum do. I mean, *did* he bring his first wife here, or is that just hearsay?'

'He did, as a matter of fact,' the balding man admitted. 'But that doesn't give the staff the excuse to go gossiping about him. Now get about your work, the pair of you, before I decide to dock your wages.'

The young chambermaid clutched the pile of sheets she was holding to her chest and scurried away like a frightened rabbit, while the other maid set off for the kitchen in a more leisurely fashion, intent on pumping the cook, who had worked there for years, for even more information.

'Come on, Kate. You must be hungry with all this lovely fresh sea air?' Martin offered her a slice of toast but Kate

271

shook her head. They were now four days into their honeymoon, but as yet, Martin had done no more than give her a chaste kiss on the cheek.

Shrugging, he bit into the toast himself while he eyed her curiously. 'Not feeling unwell, are you?'

Kate glared at him before turning her eyes back to the view from the window. If only they could move to another hotel. Another room even. She felt uncomfortable in this one now, but how could she suggest it? Martin seemed to think that it was perfectly all right to bring her to the same room as he had shared with his late wife. She imagined him making love to *her*, here in this very room – and shuddered.

Mistaking the shudder for a shiver, Martin's face creased with concern. 'You *are* unwell, aren't you? Would you like me to call a doctor?'

The hurt she was feeling was slowly bubbling into anger and before she could stop herself, she rounded on him. 'Of course I'm not ill, I'm just . . .' She struggled for the right words as he stared at her in amazement and all the time Anne's photograph seemed to mock her from the end of the dressing-table. 'I'm just sick of walking in Anne's footsteps,' she suddenly blurted out. 'Martin – I'm *me*, not Anne. Couldn't we have gone somewhere different? I mean, you haven't even offered to . . . Well, you know.'

'Haven't even offered to what?' As it suddenly dawned on him what she meant, he slammed away from the table, almost overturning it.

'Oh, you mean . . . *that*. Huh! Is that all that marriage means to you women – *sex*? Well, fine. If that's what you want, you can have it.'

Grabbing her arm he thrust her roughly towards the bed and before she knew what his intentions were, he had ripped the nightgown she so treasured from top to bottom.

'*Martin, please don't!*' Tears of humiliation stung her eyes as he threw his robe aside and advanced on her, but her pleas fell on deaf ears. Roughly parting her legs, he flung himself across her and suddenly she had the sensation of being ripped apart as he thrust himself into her. He took her with no love, no feeling whatsoever, as an animal would have done, and Kate felt as if she could have died with shame and hurt. So this was married life? This was making love? This would be her life from now on. She had imagined their coming together as whispered endearments and tenderness, but instead it had been as she had imagined rape would be. Cold and humiliating.

As she turned her head, her eyes fell on the photograph of Anne, which was still on the dressing-table. The woman seemed to be laughing at her, and as his thrusts increased, her tears wet the pillow. Thankfully it was over in minutes and he rolled to one side panting while she lay, too humiliated to even try to cover herself. She was sure that she would die of shame, but Martin suddenly rose and disappeared into the bathroom as if nothing untoward had happened. She crawled under the blankets and seconds later his voice carried to her.

'Hurry up then, darling. I thought we'd go to Land's End today.'

'I'm not feeling so well after all. Could you go on your own?'

He appeared in the bathroom doorway looking none

too pleased. 'I suppose I shall have to. Let's hope you're feeling better for tonight, eh?'

Her frightened eyes followed him as he dressed and made for the door.

'I'll see you later then. Have a good rest. You've probably picked up a bug.' With a cheerful wink he disappeared through the door and Kate heaved a sigh of relief.

Much later that morning, Kate ventured from the hotel and headed for the town where she purchased a new nightgown. It was a modest white cotton affair, and as she thought of the beautiful one that Martin had destroyed earlier in the day, she could have cried. It had been chosen so carefully and now it was ruined. No needle and thread would ever be able to repair it, but she was too embarrassed to dispose of it in the small bin in the bedroom. She would have to throw it away when they got home. *Home.* Her home now would be with Martin. The thought made her shudder with apprehension.

'I trust you have enjoyed your stay, sir?' The hotel proprietor flashed a false smile as he stamped a receipt for their room.

'Most enjoyable, thank you.'

Glancing at the bride, whose eyes had dark circles beneath them from lack of sleep, the small man wondered if she would have said the same, but years in the hotel trade had taught him discretion.

'Then may I congratulate you again on your marriage? I hope you will come to see us again some time.'

Martin inclined his head before taking a case in each hand and ushering Kate towards the taxi that was waiting outside for them. She left the hotel without so much as a backwards glance. It held no happy memories for her and personally, she hoped that she would never set eyes on it again. It had become little more than a luxurious prison. But now at last they were going home, to Nuala and Jenny, to Ruby and Sally and all that was beloved and familiar. Things would be better there. They had to be – otherwise she didn't know how she would bear it.

Chapter Twenty-Three

Glancing in the mirror that hung above the fireplace, Ruby settled her hat at a jaunty angle on her newly permed hair. She looked at the clock before turning her attention to Nuala who was lounging on the settee as usual.

'Are you coming out for a bit of fresh air? Kate and Martin will be back late this afternoon and I thought I'd pop out and get a bit of shopping in so they've a nice meal to come back to.'

Nuala shook her head and lumbered clumsily from her seat as Ruby grabbed the handles of the pram and manoeuvred it towards the kitchen door.

A wealth of emotions were coursing through Ruby; before this day was out, Kate, Jenny, Nuala and even little Sally the dog would be gone from her house for good, as the packed cases standing at the side of the door testified.

She'd missed Kate and as her eyes settled on Jenny who was sleeping peacefully, she wondered how she would manage without them. Nuala, however, was a different kettle of fish entirely and Ruby had to admit that she would be relieved to see her go. Nuala had barely said a word since the second they'd seen Kate and Martin off on their honeymoon. She had simply moped about the house with a face like a wet weekend, content to leave Jenny in Ruby's care.

There had been times during the week when Ruby had felt almost sorry for her. It was as if Nuala couldn't function properly without her older sister there to guide her. But what a burden for poor Kate to have to take to a brand new marriage. Now more than ever she understood Nuala's difficult personality, which led her back to her dilemma. There were things that Kate should know, things that Ruby longed to tell her, but she had promised Beth and Kate's mother that she would keep the secret for ever. She wondered if Martin was aware of just what he was taking on. Still, he'd known that Kate came with dependants, so she could only hope that it would work out for them, though she had grave doubts on that score.

Nuala was just disappearing through the stairs door as Ruby bundled the pram through the back door into the bright sunshine. Positioning the pretty broderie-anglaise sunshade over the baby she set off down the narrow entry, cursing beneath her breath as the pram wheels scraped against the whitewashed walls.

In no time at all she was back, with the tray beneath the pram laden down with fresh vegetables and four nice pork chops that she'd collected from the butcher's. Smiling, she left the sleeping baby beneath the kitchen window and hurried away to prepare the meal.

As Kate stared from the train window and recognised the rolling Warwickshire countryside a bubble of excitement formed in the pit of her stomach. Soon she would be home and she would see Jenny, Nuala and Ruby, not to mention Sally, who would probably be all over her like a rash. She had missed them all so much that it had been almost painful. She'd spent the last part of the week in her hotel room while Martin went off on day trips here and there, revisiting the places he'd taken Anne on their honeymoon.

Strangely, he had been as attentive as ever and never once mentioned the incident when he had abused her. And to Kate it *had* been abuse, not at all as she had imagined it would be.

Still, there was no point in dwelling on that now. They would soon be home and then things were bound to improve. Glancing across at him she saw he'd fallen into a doze and with his hair hanging across his forehead he looked breathtakingly handsome. She determined there and then to try harder. Perhaps she had over-reacted to Anne's photograph and the fact that he'd chosen the same place for their honeymoon. And what had happened the other morning – perhaps she had brought it about? From now on she promised herself she'd definitely try to be more patient with him.

By the time the train chugged into Trent Valley she was smiling again for the first time in days. David was on the platform waiting for them as he'd promised he would be and he helped Kate down from the train as Martin struggled with the heavy cases.

'Had a good time, have you?' he asked.

'Yes, we have, thanks.' Kate managed to keep her voice light as she studiously avoided his eyes.

The men took a case each and soon they were inside

David's car and on their way back to Ruby's. When they pulled up outside the little terraced house in Shepperton Street it was all Kate could do to stop herself from leaping out of the car and running inside, but she forced herself to wait patiently while the men unloaded the cases before walking sedately up the entry.

The smell of the meal Ruby had cooked for them met them the second they opened the gate and for the first time in days Kate realised that she was starving, but her hunger was forgotten as her eyes fastened on Jenny who was still fast asleep in her pram underneath the kitchen window.

Scooping her into her arms, Kate buried her face in the soft downy hair and breathed in the clean baby smell of her niece. She vowed there and then that she would never leave her again.

Ruby had heard them come through the gate and rushed out to clasp Kate to her as Martin stood back and watched with a disapproving expression on his face.

Ruby looked at the dark circles beneath Kate's eyes and commented, 'What's this then? Yer look as if yer could do with a holiday instead of just comin' back from one.'

'Kate was unwell for the last couple of days. She picked up a bit of a bug that was going around,' Martin informed her coldly.

'Well, I'll be blowed. How's that fer bad luck then, eh?' Ruby ushered them all into the kitchen. 'Never mind, I dare say all your tongues are hangin' out for a good strong brew, eh? I've got the kettle on and I've cooked you a nice dinner so as Kate won't have to bother tonight.'

Martin's lips tightened into a straight line. He had

hoped to pick the rest of the cases up and get straight home, but if he said anything it would only make him look churlish, so reluctantly he followed them inside.

Turning to David he shook his hand. 'Thanks for the lift from the station.'

David inclined his head. 'No trouble at all. I could hold on and help you get all the rest of the stuff up to your house if you like.'

'That won't be necessary, but thanks for the offer. I left my car here so it won't matter if I have to make two or three journeys. Looking at that lot, I probably shall.' As he nodded towards the mountain of cases at the side of the door, David shrugged.

'Just as you like. I shall get off then.' Turning to Kate he smiled. 'Right, don't be a stranger just because you're an old married woman. You know where I am if you should need me.'

'She won't need you, she has *me* to look after her now,' Martin informed him as he slid a possessive arm about Kate's waist.

David turned on his heel and headed for the door.

'Ain't you stopping for a cup of tea?' Ruby asked him.

David shook his head. 'No, I won't, thanks. I may as well get back to Hinckley. Lucy has a piano lesson in a while and if I go now I can take her. Goodbye.'

Kate bent to stroke Sally, who was throwing herself at her legs as if she hadn't seen her for a year rather than a week and smiled up at him. 'Thanks, David. Do come and see us, won't you?'

'Of course.' David had every intention of doing just that, though judging by the look on Martin's face there was one there who wouldn't be too pleased to see him.

Well, he'd just have to lump it. As far as David was concerned, he had a lot of making up to do to Kate for the way he'd treated her when she first came to live with his mother.

The meal was delicious and when it was over Kate helped Ruby to clear the dirty pots into the sink while Martin started to load the luggage into his car. After three trips down the entry with both hands full he appeared at the back door mopping his brow.

'I'll just take the first load,' he told her. 'I'm afraid I shall have to come back for you all. There's no way you'll get in the car it's so full of cases, and I still have to fetch Jenny's cot yet.'

Kate nodded. 'That will be fine. I'll dismantle the cot while you're gone and have a natter to Ruby.'

He turned and disappeared back the way he'd come, leaving the two women alone at last. Ruby hurried away to fetch a screwdriver and side-by-side they made their way up the steep narrow staircase to the bedroom and began to dismantle the cot.

'So, how was the honeymoon then?' Ruby asked nonchalantly.

Kate could feel the older woman's eyes boring into the back of her head. 'It was fine.' She bent to undo another screw so that Ruby wouldn't see the stain that had crept into her cheeks.

'Mmm, well, don't worry if it wasn't everything that honeymoons are cracked up to be – they rarely are,' Ruby said wisely. 'I remember my honeymoon night. Huh! By the time we got to the hotel we were both so knackered we didn't know if we were on our heads or us heels.' She chuckled as the memories flooded back.

'Did it get better?' Kate dared to ask.

Ruby's head bobbed up and down. 'Course it did. Once we were back in us own little house we were at it like bloody rabbits for months.'

The gentle flush in Kate's cheeks now turned a deep crimson and she giggled.

Sitting back on her heels Ruby suddenly became serious. 'You know, if there's ever anythin' you're worried about, yer can always come an' talk to me. One of my deepest regrets is that me an' my Leonard never managed to have any children. Somewhere along the line you lot have become my family. Your mam would have been so proud of yer, God bless her soul.'

Dragging a crumpled handkerchief from the pocket of her dress she blew her nose noisily as Kate enfolded her in her arms.

'And you've become *our* family too,' she whispered softly. 'I really don't know what we would have done without you these last months, Ruby, and that's a fact.'

'Ah, get off wi' you, yer daft ha'porth.' Ruby grinned through her tears. 'It's been my pleasure. I wouldn't have missed that little 'un down there comin' into the world fer nothin'. An' talkin' of the little 'un, I've just remembered, this came for you while yer were away.' Hurrying across to a chest of drawers she lifted an envelope and pressed it into Kate's hand.

Kate turned it over. It was from the hospital, probably the appointment that the doctor at the clinic had requested for Jenny. Slitting it open she was shocked to see that the appointment was with a paediatrician for the very next week. She handed it to Ruby who quickly read it and nodded.

'Ah well, better to find out sooner than later if there is somethin' wrong. Chances are that she's just a little slow as the doctor told yer, due to her heart problem, but better to be safe than sorry, eh?'

Kate nodded in agreement but her stomach had formed into knots and the terrible sense of foreboding was back again, but this time stronger than ever.

For the next hour she had little time to dwell on it as she and Ruby manhandled the cot down the stairs and piled all the rest of their possessions ready at the side of the door for Martin to take.

He'd done four journeys in the car before he finally had room for the passengers, but at last it was time to say their goodbyes and Kate and Ruby clung to each other at the door.

'Now you make sure as yer come and see me regularly,' Ruby told her. 'And I want to know how yer get on at the hospital next week with Jenny.'

Bending into the back of the car she kissed the sleeping infant, who was curled up on her mother's lap. Then she passed Sally's lead to Kate and bent down to stroke the little dog's head one last time.

'By, I'm going to rattle round in this house like a pea in a bleedin' pod now you lot are going,' she complained. 'Just as well Victor's going to make an honest woman of me come December, ain't it?'

Kate clambered into the car and lifted Sally onto her lap before tilting her head to give Ruby one last kiss. Then at last they were off and Ruby stood and waved until they turned the corner at the bottom of the street.

Only then did the smile slide from Ruby's face as she turned to look at the house that now suddenly seemed so empty again. She'd grown to love Kate just as she had loved Kate's mother before her. It was that love that had stopped her from telling Kate things that she thought she should know, but a promise was a promise and there was nothing to be gained but pain from Kate discovering the truth, so she had remained silent. It was a heavy weight to bear and she prayed that she had done the right thing. With dragging steps she entered the house to be greeted by silence.

'Here we are then, Mrs Denby, you're home. If you put that damned dog down I'll carry you over the threshold.'

Kate giggled as she handed Sally's lead to Nuala, who was scowling behind her. Then suddenly Martin lifted her off her feet as if she weighed no more than a feather and she was carried into the neat and orderly front room.

Nuala followed, dragging Sally along behind her. It was posh here, she had to admit. Perhaps Kate marrying Martin wouldn't be such a bad thing, after all.

Martin deposited Kate on her feet and grinned down into her sparkling eyes. 'Right, Nuala, I think you'll find all your things in your own room. Give me a shout if I've mixed any of the cases up. We can unpack tomorrow, though I'll just have to get Jenny's cot set up.'

Entering the middle room, Nuala dumped Jenny none too gently on the settee before following Martin up the stairs. She gasped with delight when she saw her room. It was much bigger than the one she had shared with Kate at Ruby's and very tastefully decorated. Her delight soon vanished, however, when Martin reappeared with the side of Jenny's cot.

'What you bringin' that in here for?' she scowled. 'Jenny always sleeps at the side of Kate.'

'Not any more she doesn't,' Martin replied firmly. 'Jenny is *your* baby and from now on she'll be sleeping in *your* room.'

'But what if she wakes an' wants anythin' durin' the night?' Nuala protested feebly.

'Then you'll have to see to her, won't you? Now, pass me that screwdriver and make yourself useful.'

Glaring at him, she did as she was told.

Kate seemed little happier than her sister when she found out about the sleeping arrangements but something about the set of Martin's face held her silent. After all, the child would only be just along the landing, she reasoned, and she could always get up and go to her in the night if she was needed.

Sally was the next one to be organised. Martin placed her basket and bowls in the kitchen and looked at Kate sternly. 'From now on, *this* is where she will sleep,' he told her in a voice that brooked no argument. 'She is a dog after all, and as far as I'm concerned, dogs *do not* sleep on the end of their owner's bed.'

Kate nodded meekly though Sally's soulful dark eyes were tearing at her heart. 'What you have to remember is that these carpets are best quality Axminster,' Martin continued, as if the poor dog being banished to the kitchen to sleep wasn't enough. 'I really can't see why she should be allowed out of the kitchen at all. She can have free rein of that room and the garden, but I don't want to see dog hairs all over the carpets. It's just so unhygienic.'

Again Kate reluctantly nodded, though secretly she

was already thinking that while Martin was at work what he didn't see wouldn't hurt him.

'Now, I think it's about time you saw our room, don't you? I've put the rest of your things in there and you can unpack them whenever you like. Come along.'

When Kate followed him upstairs he led her to the room at the front of the house. She had never actually been into what she had thought of as Martin's room before, and was curious to see if it would be as she had imagined it. The first thing she saw when she entered was a wedding photograph of Martin and Anne hanging in pride of place above the bed. Her heart dropped but wisely she said nothing; instead she averted her eyes to look around. Like all the other rooms in the house it was tastefully decorated, though once again not entirely to Kate's taste. Anne had obviously been very fond of chintz and everywhere she looked, flowers seemed to jump out at her. The curtains were brightly flowered, the carpet was flowered, and even the bedspread was covered in pretty pink roses. Kate felt as if she was standing in a florist's but realising that Martin was waiting for a re-action she smiled brightly.

'Why, it's lovely,' she declared and was relieved when she saw him visibly relax.

'Right then, I'll leave you to unpack what you need for tonight while I go and put the kettle on, shall I? All this lugging cases about has given me a thirst. You can hang the rest of your things in that wardrobe over there. I put most of the stuff we brought up before we went away in there but you should have enough room.'

Kate smiled at him gratefully and as soon as she heard him clump away down the stairs she turned her attention back to the room. Once more her eyes settled on the photograph of him and Anne.

That will have to go, she thought to herself. But not just yet.

Heaving her case up onto the bed she quickly undid the catch and started to unpack it. Glancing around, she saw a large mahogany chest of drawers standing in the bay window, so lifting her underwear she carried it across.

The first drawer she opened was full of Martin's underwear and she grinned as she saw how meticulously tidy it all was. The second drawer was equally as tidy and full of his socks, each pair laid out neatly side-by-side. When she opened the third drawer her stomach turned over as she saw women's underwear laid inside in orderly piles. Bras to one side, knickers in the middle and an assortment of underskirts to the other. She backed away from it as if it had bitten her. This was Anne's underwear; it had to be. But why had he kept it for all this time? And why, when he was perfectly aware that he was bringing *her* home, hadn't he taken the trouble to clear it all away? As she sank heavily onto the edge of the bed a wave of nausea swept through her. Surely he didn't expect her to live with Anne's personal possessions in what was now to be *their* bedroom?

She knew that she was going to have to put her foot down, but as she thought back to the incident on their honeymoon she decided not to do it just yet. She would wait until they'd all settled in together and then she would start to make the house her own. Surely he would accept that different women had different tastes? As lovely as the house was, it was definitely too fussy for Kate's liking and she could hardly wait to tone it down a little.

'The tea's mashed, darling. Are you about ready for it?'

Martin's voice floating up the stairs startled her and she had to compose herself before she replied, 'Yes, I'll only be a second. You can pour it if you like.' Standing up on legs that seemed to have developed a life of their own she hastily shut the drawers, leaving them exactly as she had found them before hurrying downstairs to her husband.

When she joined him in the kitchen she was shocked to see Sally cowering in her basket. Sally had never been the most obedient of dogs, yet she made no move to run and greet her as she normally would have.

Following her eyes, Martin smiled. 'She's probably feeling a bit nervous being in a strange place. She'll settle down eventually, but now come and have this tea before it gets cold.'

Kate nodded, but felt very ill-at-ease.

'There you are then.' Kate smiled at Nuala as she tucked the blankets around Jenny, who was fast asleep before her tiny head even hit the pillow. 'I doubt very much that she'll wake you. She usually goes all through the night without so much as a whimper.'

'But what shall I do if she *does* wake?' Nuala was far from happy at the new sleeping arrangements, as her face showed.

'I've just told you, it's highly unlikely that she will. But if she does and she doesn't go off to sleep when you give her her dummy, then come and fetch me. But do try not to wake Martin, won't you?'

Nuala turned heavily over and pulled the blankets above her head. Kate was just as unhappy about the new arrangement as her sister was, although she could understand Martin wanting some time to themselves. They were just back off honeymoon, after all – if she could call it a honeymoon.

Tiptoeing to the door she clicked off the light after checking once more that Jenny was comfortable. 'Good night, love,' she whispered, but only silence greeted her as she pulled the door to.

Pausing, she stood on the landing for some seconds before hurrying to the bathroom to get washed and change into her nightclothes. Downstairs she could faintly hear Martin locking the doors and shutting the windows. She hoped that she would be in bed before he came up as she thought of the photograph hanging over the bed.

Once the door had closed on Kate, Nuala pulled the blankets down and gazed at the strip of silver moonlight shining in through a slight gap in the curtains. Her cheeks were wet with tears as she listened to Martin's footsteps on the stairs. Life, she had decided, was totally unfair. Take Jenny for a start-off. She'd never wanted her, yet here she was fast asleep at the side of her. Why couldn't it have been Kate who had given birth to Jenny instead of her? And why was it Kate who had just got married instead of her? The answer came to her loud and clear. *Because Kate is beautiful and you are plain*, it said. *No man will ever want to marry you, particularly a lovely handsome man like Martin.*

The tears fell faster. For as long as she could remember, Kate had always been the favourite with everyone. Her father, Aunt Beth, Ruby, David – even Jenny, her own child, preferred her aunt to her . . . the list was endless.

And yet without Kate she was nothing. Until Martin had come along she had always demanded Kate's undivided attention, and Kate had always been there for her. Nuala had an awful premonition that from now on, life as she had known it was about to change. Kate's new husband would demand that *he* be her main priority and she herself would have to be more involved with Jenny, whereas up to now, Kate or Ruby had cared for the child between them.

As she turned her head, her eyes settled on Jenny and hatred rose in her. She wished that the child had never been born. She wished that Kate had never met Martin. She wished that Martin had fallen in love with *her* instead . . . Nuala Cleary wished for many things, but as she'd found out long ago, her wishes never seemed to come true.

Chapter Twenty-Four

The following Wednesday morning found Kate in the waiting room of the baby clinic at the George Eliot Hospital with Jenny clutched to her chest.

She'd pleaded with Nuala to come with her, but her sister had refused and gone off into a sulk as she was more and more prone to do of late. There were lots of other mums in the room, some with babies even younger than Jenny and some with toddlers, who appeared intent on wreaking havoc as they tottered about and got into all sorts of mischief on their sturdy little legs. Kate was so engrossed in watching them that when a nurse appeared from the doctor's room and called out 'Jennifer Cleary,' she started.

Rising hastily she shifted the baby into a more comfortable position on her hip and followed the nurse into a bright, sunlit room. The doctor immediately noticed the way Jenny's head lolled on what he presumed was her mother's shoulder, but he wisely didn't comment. Instead he ushered Kate to a chair in front of his desk and smiled at her kindly.

'So, Mrs Cleary. I believe from the doctor at the clinic that you have some concerns about your daughter?'

'Oh, I'm not Mrs Cleary and, um . . . Jenny isn't my daughter,' Kate explained quickly. 'Jenny is my sister's child. I'm her aunt.'

'I see, so do you mind me asking – why didn't her mother bring her today? Is she at work?' The doctor was well aware that a lot of women were taking jobs lately. Personally, he didn't approve of it at all. He was of the old school and believed that a woman should be at home tending to the needs of her husband and family. Still, they were now almost halfway through the fifties, and he supposed that this was progress and nothing was going to stop it.

'No.' Kate shifted uncomfortably in her seat. 'Nuala, that's Jenny's mother, is . . .' She struggled to find the right words as the doctor waited patiently. 'Nuala is what you might call . . . a little slow.'

'I see, and are you concerned that Jenny might be the same?'

Kate had never dared admit it to herself but now that the doctor had actually voiced her fears, she nodded miserably.

'Well, then, let's have a look at her, shall we? You can get her undressed on that couch over there.'

Twenty minutes later, with Jenny once again dressed and on her knee, Kate sat back down in front of the doctor, her eyes mirroring the fear she felt inside.

'Mm.' Leaning his elbows on the desk the doctor smiled at her. 'As you've just seen, I've checked her out thoroughly and I have to say that physically I can't find anything wrong with her, apart from her heart condition, which we already know about, but . . .'

It was the *but* that made Kate's heart start to race.

'I am a little concerned about her reactions,' he told her as gently as he could. 'Now tell me, when you say her mother is a little slow . . . what exactly do you mean?'

Kate took a deep breath. 'She's not very good at looking after herself and she was always very slow in her development. At school she lagged behind the others in her class and I remember my father telling me she was late in walking and talking.'

'How late?'

Kate tried to remember. 'I believe my father said she was almost three before she walked and it was difficult to understand what she said right up until she was about five. She's always been very slow at learning too.'

The doctor tapped his chin with his forefinger as he studied Jenny closely and a silence settled between them that seemed to stretch for ever until eventually he said, 'I'm afraid that there's really nothing much I can do at this stage. Of course, from now on we'll watch her development closely. Thankfully, she seems to be doing as well as can be expected – but I have to warn you, it could be that she *will* be the same as her mother. On the other hand, it could just be as the doctor at Riversley Park Clinic pointed out, that's she's a little slow to develop. Anyway, make an appointment for six months' time at the desk as you go out and I'll look at her again then. And please . . . try not to worry too much.'

Kate managed to raise a smile as she staggered towards the door with Jenny clutched to her, but inside she was crying. Half of her was relieved that physically the doctor had found nothing else wrong with the child, but the other half of her looked towards the future with dread. What if Jenny *did* turn out to be like her mother? It would mean that Kate would always have two of them to look after then, and how would Martin react to that?

Instantly ashamed, she shrugged the thought away. Jenny was a beautiful child, the apple of her eye, and Kate was determined she would be there for her as long as the child needed her. She would tell Martin that they had found nothing wrong with her apart from what they already knew, which was not really lying. As the doctor had pointed out, physically the little girl was fine. Kate would cross any other bridge when she came to it.

By the time she had made another appointment and strapped Jenny into her pram it was almost lunchtime. Stepping out into the late June sunshine she decided to go and pay Ruby a visit. There was one person she could talk to at least.

'Isn't this awful,' Kate commented as she looked up from the newspaper at Martin, who was lounging in the chair at the side of the empty fire-grate.

'What's that then?' They'd just finished their evening meal and he was comfortably full, although he was also aware that he would have to shape himself up soon because there was a grave waiting to be dug that evening.

'This poor woman, Ruth Ellis, was hanged today.'

His face darkened. 'Yes, I know, and I have to say, I think it's disgusting. The bastard she killed had two-timed her, so from where I'm standing he deserved all he got.'

The words were spoken with such venom that Kate was shocked. Seeing her face, he struggled out of the chair joking, 'You're going to have to stop cooking me such lovely dinners or I'm going to end up the size of a house.

I didn't realise you were such a good cook or I would have married you long before I did.'

The fate of Ruth Ellis was instantly forgotten as Kate returned her husband's smile. It was now mid-July and their life had slipped into some sort of a pattern. Now that they were home, Martin had reverted to being the thoughtful, tender man she had fallen in love with. He would kiss and caress her, although as yet, he had made no further attempt to make love to her. Kate was not altogether disappointed at this for a number of reasons. Firstly because of the experience on their honeymoon, and secondly because, try as she might, she found it very difficult to settle in their bedroom with a picture of his late wife hanging above their bed.

'Do you *really* have to go tonight?' she asked as she saw him collecting his work clothes. It was the first grave he had been asked to dig since their marriage and the thought of it still brought her out in goosebumps.

''Fraid so, otherwise the family of the dear departed won't be too pleased tomorrow when they turn up and there's no grave, will they?'

Kate sighed as she followed him to the door. Sally was lying in the doorway but she scuttled away to her basket as he approached. Martin stopped on the doorstep to give his wife a long lingering kiss, much to the disgust of Nuala, who was sitting in the backyard looking at the pictures in a magazine.

'Will you be late?' Kate asked, disentangling herself from his arms.

He shook his head. 'It's highly unlikely. Though the ground's going to be baked solid with all the sun we've had, so that might take me a while longer. I should think I'll be back for half-ten at the latest.'

'All right.' Kate offered her lips for one last kiss and when the gate closed behind him she hurried away to clear the table. After that she bathed and fed Jenny and tucked her into her cot. By then the sun was sinking on the horizon and Nuala was yawning loudly.

'I reckon I'll have an early night,' she declared. 'I've got a bit of a headache.'

'It's probably the heat that's brought it on. Why don't you slip into the bath first then I'll bring you a nice cup of cocoa up,' Kate suggested tactfully. Nuala had never been much of a one for personal hygiene and Kate often had to tempt her into the bath, much as she would have done a child. Nuala scowled but stomped off to the bathroom all the same, at last leaving Kate to her own devices for a while. She sank onto the chair, grateful of the cooling evening breeze that was lifting the net curtains from the window. Sally immediately leaped onto her lap, almost as if she knew that she had to make the best of any fuss that was going while Martin wasn't about. Kate absently fondled her silky ears as she looked about the room. Somehow it still didn't feel like home and she longed to put a few of her touches about the place. She let the peace and quiet wash over her for a few minutes then with Sally tucked under her arm she stood up and climbed the stairs to their bedroom.

The photograph of Anne and Martin seemed to leap off the wall at her just as it always did each time she entered the room. Placing Sally gently on the floor, she advanced on the photo, studying it closely. And it was then that her breath caught in her throat as she looked at the ring on Anne's left hand. It was identical to the one that Martin had given her when they got engaged. She decided he must have had it polished and hoped that she would think he had bought it especially for her. Her eyes dropped to the sparkling diamonds and she shuddered. She was wearing a dead woman's ring. Her first instinct was to snatch it off her finger and fling it as far away as she could but then common sense took over and she turned back to the photograph instead.

'Sorry,' she muttered. 'No offence meant but enough is enough.' Lifting the picture from the wall she crossed to the chest of drawers and slid it in out of sight.

'What are you doing?'

The voice almost made Kate jump out of her skin; spinning around she found Nuala staring at her curiously from the doorway. She'd undressed ready for her bath and was swaddled in a huge fluffy bath towel.

'We've been here for over a month now,' Kate said with some of her former spirit, 'and I think it's about time we started to make this place into *our* home, don't you?'

Nuala shuffled uncomfortably from foot to foot. 'Martin won't like it,' she muttered flatly.

'Then he'll just have to lump it, won't he?' Kate declared with a toss of her head. 'This is our home too now and I'm ready to make some changes to it.'

'Rather you than me,' Nuala mumbled and turning on her heel she shuffled away to the bathroom leaving Kate to stare at the blank space on the wall.

After a time she made a decision and before she could change her mind she hurried downstairs and came back to the bedroom with a large empty cardboard box. As she opened the drawer containing Anne's underwear her heart began to hammer in her chest. Once more she glanced at the blank space on the wall then carefully she began to pack all the underwear in the drawer away into the box. This was *her* bedroom now, and as far as she was concerned it was time Anne was laid to rest.

Kate was just preparing to go up to bed at ten o'clock when Martin appeared.

'I didn't expect you so early,' she remarked as she hurried to peck him on the cheek. He grinned as he swiped a grubby hand across his weary eyes.

'I didn't think I'd be done this soon,' he admitted, 'not with the earth as baked as it is, but it went better than I'd thought.'

'Shall I make you a nightcap?' Kate suggested.

He nodded as he headed towards the stairs. 'Right you are. Just give me ten minutes or so to have a quick bath.'

Kate's stomach did a funny little flip as she heard his footsteps clatter away up the stairs and into their bedroom. She wondered what his reaction would be when he saw that the photograph of him and Anne was missing, or if he would even notice for that matter. She didn't have to wait long to find out; seconds later she heard him thump down the stairs again.

Hand on hips, he glared at her. 'Just what the bloody hell is going on? What have you done with Anne's photograph? And where has all her underwear that was in the drawers gone?'

Drawing herself up to her full height, Kate took a deep breath as she confronted him. She'd half expected this but she was so sick of living with a ghost that she was prepared to make a stand, especially after her discovery about the ring.

'Martin, I know the last few years haven't been easy for you and I sympathise. But the thing is . . . Anne is gone now. You're married to me. I know I can never take her place and I have no wish to. You're quite entitled to your memories. But should I really have to live with her things in what is now *our* bedroom? Can you try to imagine what it's like for me? It's like . . . well, it's like living with a ghost.'

When he took a step towards her his face was so livid with rage that for a moment she almost expected him to lash out at her.

'You had no right to—'

'I had *every* right.' Kate glared back at him and now her temper matched his. She waved a hand towards another photograph that hung on the wall in the living room. 'I wouldn't dream of taking that down, or any of the others that are scattered about the house for that matter, but as I said, I will *not* and I repeat, *will not* live with a photo of her hanging above my bed.' She decided it might not be wise to incense him further by mentioning the ring.

Martin took a step back as shock registered on his face. He had never seen Kate in a temper before and until now had been unaware that she even had one. He could see that she was going to stand firm on this point and so, snatching his jacket from the hook, he swung about and headed for the door.

'*Where are you going?*'

Turning to look back at her he saw that tears were coursing down her cheeks.

'I think for both our sakes it might be better if I went out to get a bit of fresh air. Perhaps by the time I get back you'll be ready to be more reasonable.'

Kate slowly shook her head. 'If by reasonable you mean I'll be ready to put the photo back . . . then you're wrong.'

He turned on his heel and strode away without a backwards glance.

Chapter Twenty-Five

Glancing at the cheap watch on her wrist, Caroline Codey shifted her weight from one stiletto heel to another. It was almost eleven o'clock and every single limb ached. It had been a long day and an even longer evening. The last customers were now straggling out of the Cock and Bear pub, but as yet not one had given her so much as a glance despite all her best efforts. She'd had one client earlier in the night but that had consisted of little more than a quick fumble and a hand job behind the pub. Fingering the ten-shilling note in her pocket she sighed. Ten measly bob to show for a whole night's work. It would hardly pay her tick at the corner shop, let alone put any food on the table for her kids. As she thought of them she frowned into the soft night. Becky, her ten year old, should have put the little two to bed by now. She'd better have done, otherwise she'd get a clout round the ear when she got in!

Her thoughts were interrupted when the bar door opened and a middle-aged man emerged. He had a bit of a sway on and was certainly not the handsomest creature she had ever seen. All the same, she thought, a punter is a punter so it's worth a try.

'Fancy a good time, do yer, love?'

'Piss off, yer ugly little whore,' the man replied as he staggered past her.

'Well really! There ain't no need fer that!' Caroline retorted indignantly, hitching up her sagging bosoms and clutching her leopardskin handbag more closely to her.

She watched the man walk unsteadily away up the Cock and Bear Hill, and then she heard the landlord of the pub slide home the bolts on the door.

'That's it then, gel,' she muttered aloud to herself. 'Might as well get me arse home an' make the best of a bad job.'

She began to trip away on her high stiletto heels, setting her heavy breasts jiggling. 'It's all that no-good bastard's fault,' she murmured to herself as she climbed the hill. If that swine of a husband hadn't left her for that tart she would never have been reduced to this. She'd been a good-looking woman once, but now the only thing she had left to be proud of was the crown of tight dark curls that framed her face, and even they were showing streaks of grey if she dared to look closely enough.

When her husband had first left her she had managed to get a shop job to keep the wolf from the door, but the school bobby had soon put a stop to that when he found out that she was keeping Becky off school to look after the two little 'uns. Once threatened with the Welfare, her job options were narrowed considerably, and she had to do something to put food on the table for the kids, didn't she? And so she'd resorted to walking the streets. She remembered how the neighbours had reacted when they first discovered she'd become a lady of the night. Most of them had cut her dead, the stuck-up silly cows.

Little did they know that most of their husbands had already trodden the path to her door *and* gone away with big smiles on their faces.

She was so lost in thought that for a moment she wasn't aware of a car pulling up at the side of her. When the driver wound his window down she found herself staring into the face of a handsome stranger. Struggling to get her breath, which was laboured from climbing the hill, she asked, 'Lookin' fer a good time, are yer, love?'

When he nodded she tripped round to the other side of the car and opened the passenger door, instantly filling the car with the scent of the cheap perfume she was wearing. Clambering into the car, she settled herself into the seat and stared at him as he pulled away from the kerb. No doubt about it, he was nice looking. She might actually enjoy this one.

At the top of the Cock and Bear Hill he turned into Tomkinson Road.

'Yer don't say much, do yer? Are yer allus this quiet?' she asked provocatively.

He continued to drive in silence so shrugging her shoulders she settled further back into the seat. They continued along Haunchwood Road and then up Buckshill.

'Where we goin' anyway?'

'Hartshill,' he informed her shortly, and with that she had to be content. Despite the fact that she had lived in Nuneaton all her life, she had never been to Hartshill, which was a small village on the outskirts of the town, so she looked around her with interest as they drove along Victoria Road. They passed a small school with the name *Nathaniel Newton* on large wrought-iron gates before turning a sharp right into Church Road. Almost

303

immediately he then took a left turn into Oldbury Road, and as the houses gave way to dark country lanes, she felt the first shiver of apprehension.

'Ere, how much further were yer thinkin' of goin', mate? I do 'ave kids to get home to yer know!'

He suddenly turned into a wooded copse and as he switched off the engine the silence settled around them like a cloak.

'Get out,' he ordered abruptly as he climbed from the car.

She frowned. 'But there ain't no bleedin' lights. I can't see me hand in front of me face.'

The passenger door was suddenly yanked open and she felt his hand close around her upper arm in a vice-like grip. Perhaps this ain't goin' to be as much fun as I hoped, she thought, but she clambered from the car just the same. He wouldn't be the first punter who liked it rough. She just hoped he wouldn't mark her too much. It was no good for trade standing outside pubs with a black eye.

Once outside on the hillocky grass she squinted as her eyes tried to adjust to the light. He pulled at her arm and as she tried to follow him she twisted her ankle and yelped with pain. 'Slow down, will yer, mister? I've got heels on an' they weren't meant fer walkin' on this sort o' ground.'

She wished that he would answer her; his silence was beginning to seriously unnerve her now. When he suddenly released her she rubbed at her arm. They'd come to a small opening in the woods and as the moon sailed from behind the clouds she was shocked to see the look on his handsome face. It was twisted with hatred.

'What's up?' she faltered. 'Yer know, if you've changed yer mind it ain't a problem. Just take me back an' we'll say no more about it, eh?'

He began to rummage inside the jacket he was wearing, but at that moment the moon disappeared behind a cloud and she could only stare into the pitch-black night as her heart began to hammer in her ribcage.

Seconds later the moon reappeared and she saw the man was holding a knife. The moonlight was making it glint like liquid silver as she hastily took a step back. She didn't say a word; somehow she knew that there would be no point. There was no one to hear her – no one to help.

'I . . . look, mate. I've got kids at home waitin' fer me. Just take me back to where yer found me an' we'll forget this ever happened, eh?'

He was advancing on her with a strange look in his eyes and as his hand lunged forward, a sharp pain seared through her chest. She felt something warm and sticky dribble from the side of her mouth and raised her hand to swipe it away. It was blood. Her legs had gone all wobbly but she had no chance to sink to the ground, for at that moment she felt his hands around her neck. As he increased the pressure on her windpipe she stared dully up at the moon; it seemed to be smiling at her.

Chapter Twenty-Six

At the sound of the latch on the back gate lifting, Sally hurtled off Kate's lap and fled to her basket in the kitchen.

Seconds later the back door opened and Martin appeared looking tired and weary. The first thing he saw was Kate sitting in the chair at the side of the fireplace, her eyes swollen and red-rimmed from crying.

'Kate . . .' He spread his hands helplessly. 'I'm so sorry.'

'No, it's me that should be sorry,' Kate said flatly. 'I'm not going to apologise for moving the photo or Anne's clothes, but I am sorry about the way I did it. I should have talked to you about how I felt first.'

'No. I shouldn't have been so thoughtless.' He sank down in the chair opposite her. All the rage he had felt earlier in the night had gone and now he felt desperately tired.

Tentatively placing her hand over his, Kate leaned forward. 'Look, Martin, I won't ever expect you to forget Anne. She was part of your life and you're entitled to your memories. I know you will always love her, and that's just as it should be. But, the thing is – *we're* married now. We've both got to try if we're going to make it work. I know it isn't easy with Nuala and Jenny and even Sally in tow, but I'm beginning to think that . . . Well, to be honest, I don't feel married. Apart from that one night on honeymoon when you . . .' She squirmed with embarrassment beneath his steady gaze but forced herself to go on, 'How do you think it made me feel, going to the same hotel as you took your first wife to? Seeing you go off on the same walks that you took with her.' Tears started to her eyes and brimmed over to spill down her cheeks.

Martin hung his head in shame. 'You're quite right, it was unforgivable of me, but things will be different from now on, you'll see.'

'Then let's go to bed, shall we?'

He looked up into her adoring eyes and without a word took her hand and led her up the stairs.

The early-morning dew on the grass glistened like diamonds as the man strode through the woods with his dog playfully leaping and running ahead. As far as Ernie Mayer was concerned, this was the very best part of the day. In an hour's time he would be deep beneath the earth in the bowels of the pit, but for now he could enjoy the beautiful countryside that surrounded his home. He'd lived in the Woodlands in Hartshill all his married life and every morning at the same time for as long as he cared to remember, he'd taken this same walk come rain or shine. Many dogs had shared his walk over the years. There had been Bessie, a little Jack Russell who he had bought shortly after his marriage. She had been a loyal little thing and had grown up with his three children as they arrived at yearly intervals one after the other. It was many years now since she had died of old age, and there had been many dogs in between, but Bessie still held a special place in his heart.

Bending, he lifted a stick and flung it into the bushes for Ben, his one-year-old cocker spaniel. Ernie was determined that Ben would be the last dog he would own. He was due to retire from the pit in a year's time and hoped that he and Ben would grow old together.

Lost in thought, he wandered on and then suddenly realising that Ben wasn't following him he stopped to look back the way he had come. The sun was struggling to cast its light through the branches overhead but there was no sign of Ben.

He began to retrace his steps, cursing softly as he went. Damn the little mutt. If he'd decided to go walkabout it meant that Ernie was going to be late for work and he'd always prided himself on being a good time-keeper.

'Ben!' His shout startled a little rabbit sitting amongst the bushes and it scurried away, its bright bobtail dancing behind it. He'd gone some way when he heard Ben in the bushes.

'Ben, come here, yer bad lad. I ain't got time fer yer antics this mornin'.'

He peered into the thick bushes and when Ben wasn't forthcoming he muttered another curse and began to fight his way through them. Within minutes he found himself in a clearing, and there was Ben noisily scratching and sniffing at the ground.

'You bad dog,' he scolded. 'What is it that's so interestin', eh?'

As he approached the dog he saw a hint of scarlet on the grass. Bending closer, he grasped the dog's collar and sighed as he saw that it was blood. 'Looks like some poor rabbit come to a sticky end 'ere last night – eh, boy?' Fastening the lead to the dog's collar as he spoke, he turned and began to make his way back through the bushes. It was then that his eyes fell on a leopardskin-patterned high-heeled shoe. A broad grin creased his face.

'Someone must have lost that in a moment o' passion – eh, lad!' He chuckled and kicking the shoe further into the bushes he hurried on his way, yanking the dog behind him.

'But *why* can't you have her in your room?' Nuala whined.

Kate sighed as she cradled Jenny in her arms and began to feed her. 'You know why not.' She was trying to keep her patience but finding it increasingly difficult. 'Martin wants us to have some time to ourselves. We are newlyweds, after all.' She blushed as she thought back to the night before. Martin had finally made love to her and although it still wasn't quite what she had expected it to be, it had been very nice all the same.

'But she's kept me awake half the night again,' Nuala complained.

'That's because she's teething. I'll get some gel we can rub on her gums today and she might feel a little more comfortable then. I really don't know what you're moaning about, Nuala. I take over from the second she gets up. You only have to have her sleep next to you. And she is *your* baby, as Martin quite rightly pointed out.'

'Huh, not from choice,' Nuala grunted and turning her back on Kate she tucked into the bowl of cereal in front of her without another word.

Kate looked down at the infant in her arms. Jenny

had always been a model baby until recently when she had started to teethe. Now Kate would lie awake at night and listen to her crying as she lay next to Martin. Sometimes, once he was asleep she would creep out of their bed and hurry to Nuala's room, then she would lift the baby from her cot and walk up and down the long landing with her until she had managed to rock her back to sleep. It was no good expecting Nuala to do it. When Jenny cried, the girl just put the pillow over her head and snuggled further down in the blankets so that she wouldn't hear her.

Martin was becoming increasingly annoyed about it. 'Can't you just shut her up? Give her a dummy or something. That's what Anne used to do when Adam was teething.' He then looked guilty but Kate had been quick to reassure him.

'It's all right, Martin. You are allowed to talk about Anne – and Adam, for that matter. Speaking of which, isn't it about time I got to meet him?'

Martin had nodded slowly. 'I suppose it is. What about if I bring him to dinner this Sunday?'

Kate had beamed from ear to ear. 'I'd like that.'

Sunday was now only two days away and the nerves were beginning to set in. What if Adam didn't like her? She shrugged. It was too late to worry about it now one way or the other. Martin had arranged with Adam's grandparents to have him for the whole day. She thought it was strange that he hadn't invited them too, but then decided that perhaps he wanted to take it just one step at a time. A whimper from Jenny brought her thoughts sharply back to the present. There would be plenty of time to worry about Adam's visit a little later. For now she had a very unhappy baby to placate.

By the time Sunday arrived, Kate felt fit to drop. Jenny had kept the whole house awake for two solid nights and no one was in a very good humour. The day before, Kate had taken her to the doctor at Red Roofs surgery, but as she'd suspected there was little that could be done for teething babies apart from the various gels and powders that she had already tried. Jenny was hot and fretful and Kate became more and more anxious as she noticed the disapproving looks Martin bestowed on her as she walked her endlessly up and down the small sitting room. Even so on Sunday morning she was determined to make an effort for Adam and so got up early and made the base of a strawberry trifle, which she placed on the thrall of the walk-in pantry to set.

By the time Martin put in an appearance with his hair hanging across his forehead, she was just taking the first batch of cakes from the oven. He rubbed the sleep from his eyes and sniffed the air appreciatively. 'Mm, something smells good,' he remarked.

'Well, they say the way to a man's heart is through his stomach, so I'm hoping that Adam will take after his father,' Kate teased.

Martin became serious. 'Kate, I ought to warn you, Adam is . . . Well, we're not that close any more, to be honest. He misses his mum and since he's lived with his grandparents he's become a little spoiled.'

'That's understandable. But don't worry. I'm sure once we get to know each other we'll get along just fine. It would be lovely if he could come to live with us one

311

day. He might feel that he's part of a proper family again then. Not that I could ever take the place of his mum, of course,' she added hastily.

'I'd better get ready to go and get him.' Martin quietly turned about and hurried away to get changed.

Half an hour later Martin returned with a lanky boy who stared at her sullenly. Adam was tall for his age and had obviously inherited his mother's dark good looks.

'Hello, Adam,' Kate greeted him brightly as she nervously smoothed her skirt over her hips. 'I've been so looking forward to meeting you.' She held out her hand and after some hesitation he shook it reluctantly. He was obviously feeling deeply uncomfortable and Kate felt sorry for him as she saw him looking around the room. Everything was probably just as he remembered it in here, though Kate soon intended to change that. The flowered theme had started to get her down and she'd been looking at wallpaper and curtain material, although she hadn't mentioned it to Martin yet. Perhaps it would be easier for Adam when things *were* changed a little, she decided. It must be hard for him to come back to the home that he remembered living in with his mother – especially as Kate was now there. She decided that she'd try extra hard to make him feel at ease but soon discovered that it was going to be hard work.

'This is Nuala, my sister, and Jenny, her baby. And this is Sally, our dog.'

Adam gave each of them a cursory glance before sinking into a fireside chair and staring into the empty grate.

'Would you like some lemonade?' Kate asked pleasantly, determined not to be beaten.

'Grandma says fizzy drinks rot your teeth.'

'Oh, in that case, perhaps you'd like a homemade cake then? I got up early to make them especially for you.'

'Grandma doesn't like me eating before a meal. She says it will spoil my dinner.'

Kate looked at Martin for help but he was studiously reading the paper. Kate tried again.

'So, what do you normally do on a Sunday then, Adam?'

For the first time he smiled. 'We usually go to the service at our local church, then if the weather is good, Grandad takes me into the park and we have a game of football while Grandma cooks the dinner.'

'That's nice,' Kate muttered, feeling totally out of her depth. 'Would you excuse me while I just go and check on our dinner? I'm sure Nuala will keep you entertained for a moment.' Escaping to the kitchen she sighed with relief. It looked like it was going to be a very long day.

'Goodbye, Adam. It was lovely to meet you. I hope you'll come again very soon.' Kate once more extended her hand to the surly child standing at the side of the door. The day had seemed to go on for ever but now Martin was about to return Adam to his grandparents. She couldn't pretend to be sorry to see him go. The whole day had amounted to one disaster after another from where she was standing. Adam had played with his dinner, refused all offers of her cakes and trifle and basically made it more than obvious that he would much rather have been at home with his grandparents. Still, she consoled herself, things could only get better. When the door closed on him she turned to see Nuala grinning.

'What's so funny then?'

Nuala shrugged. 'He ain't exactly the most cheerful of kids, is he?'

Kate thought that was rich coming from her sister, but tactfully refrained from saying so. Now that she came to think about it, she couldn't remember hearing Adam or Nuala say so much as one word to each other for the whole day.

Lifting Jenny, she started to get her ready for bed and prayed that tonight she would let them all get some sleep. She wondered briefly if Martin was right to suggest she pack in her job at the Rose and Crown. She'd cut her hours down to two dinnertimes a week since they'd been married and while she was at work, Ruby looked after Jenny. The arrangement had worked well up to now. Ruby loved to have Jenny, and Kate liked being with Vera and the friends she had made at the pub, especially Lindsay, the new barmaid Vera had employed. Lindsay was like a ray of sunshine on a dark day and never failed to lift Kate's spirits. She made no secret of the fact that she was having an affair with a married man. Half of the time she was deliriously happy and convinced that he would eventually leave his wife for her. The other half of the time she was in the depths of depression and threatening to clear off back to London where she had originated from. All the staff had got used to taking her moods with a pinch of salt and Kate had grown more than a little fond of her, possibly because she was the nearest to a friend that Kate had ever had of a similar age to herself. Martin, on the other hand, was not happy with it. He considered Lindsay to be a bad influence on Kate and insisted that she was what he termed, much to Kate's amusement, 'a loose woman'.

Kate had stood her ground up to now, but if Jenny didn't start sleeping through the night again soon, she knew that she'd have to hand in her notice from sheer exhaustion. When Jenny was washed and changed she hurried to the kitchen and made her a bottle for her last feed.

'For God's sake! Isn't that child *ever* going to shut up?' Martin groaned as he pulled the pillow over his head some hours later.

Kate frowned into the darkness. It was the early hours of the morning and Jenny had been crying almost nonstop since she had tucked her into her cot.

'She can't help it. She has two more teeth coming through and the poor little mite is in pain,' she defended her. 'Should I go and see if I can quieten her down?'

A grunt answered her from beneath the blankets so she slithered from the bed and felt her way to the door in the darkness.

When she opened Nuala's bedroom door it would have been hard to say at first glance who was the most upset of the two occupants. Nuala was sitting up in bed with her hands pressed across her ears while Jenny had cried herself into a frenzy.

'There, there then,' Kate soothed as she lifted the sobbing infant from her cot. 'Let's see if we can't make you feel better, eh?'

Nuala glared at her. 'I ain't had a wink of sleep yet with her screamin' her head off.'

'Well, get tucked down then. I'll see to her now.'

Nuala instantly disappeared beneath the bedclothes as Kate began to rock Jenny to and fro. Half an hour later she tucked the sleeping child back into her cot and tiptoed away.

An hour later, Jenny's thin wail again floated along the landing. Sighing, Kate staggered out of bed, rubbing the sleep from her eyes as she groped for her dressing-gown, which she had flung across the back of a chair. She crept along the landing, fearful of waking Martin yet again and quietly entered Nuala's room. She found her sister standing at the side of the cot with her fists clenched.

'I'm telling yer, Kate, I can't take much more of this.'

Ignoring her, Kate leaned across the baby's cot and as she did so Jenny instantly stopped crying. As she bent towards her, the child's tiny face suddenly creased into a smile that seemed to lighten up the dim room. Kate's heart skipped a beat with pure joy. For months she'd sat in the baby clinic week after week watching babies much younger than Jenny gurgle and smile up at their mothers, but until this minute Jenny had never smiled, never even shown any recognition. The long sleepless nights were forgiven as love washed through Kate.

'*She smiled,*' she gasped incredulously.

Climbing back into bed, Nuala shrugged. 'Halleluiah! Makes a change from yarking all the while, don't it?'

Ignoring the sarcasm in her sister's voice, Kate expertly pinned a fresh nappy onto her niece and placing her back in her cot she stared down at her for a while. She looked like a little angel lying there, so beautiful and innocent. The child's eyelashes slowly drooped onto her cheeks as she drifted back to sleep and Kate quietly slipped away with a big grin on her face. Jenny had given her her very first smile.

An hour later the baby woke again and her cries bounced off the flowered walls. Kate was just about to go to her when Martin groaned and stumbled out of bed. She lay where she was and listened to him potter across the landing and enter the bathroom. It was while she was waiting for him to come back that the crying stopped. Uttering a sigh of relief, Kate pulled the blankets more tightly about her and by the time Martin returned she was already fast asleep.

Chapter Twenty-Seven

Handing Martin his lunchbox, Kate yawned as she followed him to the door. He looked less than happy but she kept her voice light as she pecked him on the cheek.

'Have a good day.'

'Huh! If I manage to keep my eyes open I might,' he grumbled. 'I'd forgotten what noisy little beggars babies could be.'

'It'll get better once this tooth she's cutting comes through,' Kate promised, still basking in the pleasure of the first smile Jenny had bestowed on her the night before.

'That's as maybe; it's the rest of them still to come through that worries me.'

Kate giggled. 'Oh, stop moaning. She can't help it and she *is* sleeping in for a change. I'm usually up with her before you even set foot out of bed.'

'More fool you then, that's all I can say. If you didn't trip along the landing every single time she murmured, that mother of hers might pull her finger out and care for her own child for once.'

Hoping to avoid an argument, Kate pressed him through the door. 'Go on, get off with you or you'll be late for work. I need you to keep me in the manner to which I've become accustomed.'

At last a smile cracked his face as he kissed her for one last time. 'I'll see you at teatime then. Are you at the pub today?'

'Yes, I am. I thought I might drop Jenny off to Ruby a few minutes early and get a bit of shopping in before I do my shift.'

'You'd have a lot more time for shopping if you'd just quit work and stay at home as I asked,' he told her.

'Martin, will you *please* just go? You seem intent on causing an argument this morning, and I warn you, I'm not going to bite.'

He shrugged and she held her breath until she heard the entry gate close behind him.

When she was finally alone she put the kettle back on and lifted the morning paper. It wasn't often she had the luxury of a few minutes to herself and she decided that she was going to make the most of it. With the coming of September the weather had changed and there was a nip in the air that made her pull her dressing-gown more tightly about her as she settled down to read the newspaper. The headlines jumped out at her: James Dean had been killed in a car crash. Nuala wouldn't be happy about that. James Dean was one of her idols. Glancing up at the ceiling she assured herself that all was still quiet then, shrugging, she settled back in the chair and turned the page.

At eight-thirty, Kate went upstairs to get washed and changed into her day clothes. As she tugged a brush through her dark curls she frowned at her reflection in the mirror. Her hair had grown since the wedding and only the other day Martin had suggested she should have it cut short again. Kate was reluctant to do as he asked now. She was determined to keep her own identity. With it cut short she bore a strong resemblance to Anne and so had decided that she would let it grow again.

After hastily making the bed and tidying the room she crept along the landing to listen at Nuala's door. It was unheard of for Jenny to sleep in this long, and a little niggle of unease was beginning to wriggle its way around her stomach.

She tapped on the door. 'Nuala?'

No answer. She tapped again, a little harder this time before easing the door open a fraction. Nuala was sitting on the edge of the bed staring off down the garden through the window, her expression blank.

Entering the room, Kate smiled at her brightly. 'It's all right for some,' she teased. 'I've been up for ages. I'm amazed that Jenny's slept for so long.'

'She won't wake up,' Nuala said bluntly.

'What do you mean, she won't wake up?' The smile slid from Kate's face as she hastily crossed to the cot and looked inside. Instantly she knew that something was wrong. Jenny's lips had taken on a bluish tinge and she was ghastly pale. Reaching into the cot she found that the child was cold, and it was then that panic gripped her.

'Nuala, run next door and ask Mrs Howells to phone for an ambulance . . . *and hurry*!'

Still in her nightgown, Nuala sauntered away as if she had all the time in the world as Kate lifted Jenny from her cot. Sinking onto the edge of the bed, she cuddled the baby to her as a feeling of dread turned her insides to ice.

She was still there when two ambulancemen pounded up the stairs almost fifteen minutes later.

She clutched the child to her and wouldn't let her go as one of the men tried to take Jenny from her arms, and he saw at once that Kate was in shock.

'Look, love. We need to get your baby to the hospital as quickly as we can – there's not a minute to lose. Will you bring her downstairs for us?'

Kate nodded numbly as he took her elbow and led her down the steep staircase. Within minutes she was seated in the back of the ambulance and the sound of the bells pierced the air as it raced towards the hospital. Recovering her voice, Kate explained about Jenny's heart problems, her voice thick with fear.

The second the ambulance drew to a halt, the doors were thrown open and a waiting nurse prised the child from Kate's arms and raced away with her as if the hounds of hell were at her heels. Kate was led to a small room where another nurse was waiting for her.

'Look, you sit down here and I'll go and get you a nice cup of tea while the doctor has a look at your baby, eh?' The nurse looked at the ambulanceman who had escorted her there and he shrugged sadly. His job was done now, but what a way to start a morning.

Kate perched on the edge of the uncomfortable chair as nausea washed over her. Where had they taken Jenny, and why was the doctor taking so long?

The nurse returned with a cup of tea, which Kate left to go cold on the table. Outside the room she could hear the sounds of the hospital coming to life. Tea trolleys and porters trundled past the door but the sounds were lost on Kate. All she wanted was Jenny, or at least for

321

someone to come and tell her that she was going to be all right. The minutes ticked away as Kate gazed dully from a little window that overlooked a small garden at the back of the hospital. It was a poor apology for a garden really, with a few straggly late flowers here and there and an area of grass that was in desperate need of a cut, but even so Kate fixed her attention on it and tried not to think about what was happening.

After what seemed an eternity the door opened and a nurse and a doctor in a crisp white coat with a stethoscope slung around his neck stepped into the room, closing the door quietly behind them.

'Mrs Cleary?' The doctor smiled at her; a sad smile that made her blood run cold.

'Actually, I'm Mrs Denby, Jenny's aunt.' The words seemed to lodge in her throat but somehow she managed to force them out as she searched his face for a flicker of hope.

Taking a seat at the side of her, he took her small hand in his two large ones.

'Mrs Denby, I'm afraid I have very bad news for you. Jenny was already dead when you arrived at the hospital with her. We did try to revive her, I assure you, but I fear she had been dead for some time.'

'No!' Snatching her hand away, Kate jumped to her feet, her hands balled into fists at her sides. 'You must be mistaken – she *can't* be dead. She hasn't even been poorly, apart from teething.'

'I know it must have come as an enormous shock to you, my dear, but these things sometimes happen. We will be doing a post-mortem, of course, but it appears that her heart might have just stopped. She *did* have a very serious heart condition, as you informed us. Failing that, it could be that she died from cot death. Many healthy babies do unfortunately, for no apparent reason at all.'

'Please God, no.' Kate began to pace the floor, her face as pale as chalk, muttering to herself.

The doctor and the nurse exchanged a glance and then the young nurse stepped forward and placed her hand on Kate's arm.

'Would you like to see her?' she whispered.

Kate nodded. That smile, that wonderful smile that Jenny had given her, she thought in a panic. Surely it couldn't be the one and only one she would ever see?

At the children's ward she was taken to a corner where curtains were closed.

'She's in here.' The young nurse's eyes were brimming with tears as she drew the curtains aside, leaving Kate to stare down at the still child lying in the cot. 'Take as long as you like,' she whispered, and then Kate found herself alone.

Scooping the baby into her arms she sank onto a chair that had been placed at the side of the cot and buried her face in Jenny's sweet-smelling hair. It should be Nuala that's here now, she found herself thinking, but Nuala *wasn't* there, nor had she shown the least inclination to come.

As Kate gazed down into the perfect little face she felt as if her heart would snap in two. Jenny had been such a lovely baby. She'd never known her mother's love, but she had known Kate's right from the first moment that her aunt had set eyes on her. Sometimes Kate had felt as if Jenny *was* her child – and so it was right that she should be here with her now.

Cuddling the tiny body to her, she drank in every feature of her sweet face, locking them away into her heart and her memory. She whispered words of endearment and sang lullabies and told her how very, very much she loved her, over and over again until eventually the young nurse and doctor reappeared and, with infinite tenderness, took the child from her arms. Only then did the tears start to fall as emptiness settled around her like a cloud.

'Is there anyone we can call to take you home?' The nurse's voice seemed to be coming from a long way away. Kate shook her head, her eyes fixed on Jenny, and when the nurse laid the little body back in the cot and drew a tiny blanket across her face, Kate knew, in that moment, that Jenny was gone from her for ever. Snatching the curtain aside, she raced out of the ward. Suddenly she knew that she must get as far away as possible before the grief that was like a physical pain made her scream. Kindly hands reached out to her, but she slapped them away and headed for the doors. It was hard to breathe and she needed to be outside in the fresh air. Panic gripped her as she stumbled along the corridors. They all looked the same and she began to think that she would be trapped in this nightmare for ever, staggering along one after the other, but then there was a door and she urged herself on until at last she felt the cold September air on her face. She drank it in greedily, willing her heart to stop its wild beating. People looked at her strangely before hurrying by her, sure that they were in the presence of a madwoman. And she *was* mad – she knew it. She must be, otherwise why would this be happening?

Of their own volition her feet carried her homeward.

In her haste she had come out without a coat but she didn't feel the cold or even notice the glances she was attracting. As she hurried along Heath End Road, two snotty-nosed little boys who had decided to play truant from school stared at her curiously. They were sitting on the edge of the pavement nonchalantly rolling marbles along the gutter as she lurched past them.

'Blimey. Do yer reckon she's escaped from the loony bin?' the smaller of the two sniggered, as he wiped his nose on the sleeve of his threadbare blazer. His words carried to Kate on the cold air and she stifled the urge to laugh. Perhaps he was right. Perhaps she *was* a loony. After all, her mother before her had been – so perhaps it was she who had inherited the seed of madness rather than Nuala. She certainly felt as if she were going mad at that moment. In fact, if madness could have helped her escape the pain she was feeling, then she would have welcomed it with open arms.

Martin's kindly neighbour was waiting for her with Nuala when she entered the house and one look at her ashen face sent the woman into floods of tears.

Making the sign of the cross on her chest she hurried away to put the kettle on as Nuala gazed at her sister blankly.

Swaying slightly, Kate gulped deep in her throat and forced herself to croak out the words. 'Nuala . . . I'm afraid Jenny is dead. They think it might have been her heart or a cot death.'

Without a word, Nuala rose from her seat and disappeared away up the stairs, leaving Kate to the kindly ministrations of the elderly neighbour.

Mrs Howells was a gentle-natured soul, and once she had Kate seated at the table with a steaming mug of tea in front of her she went immediately home to phone Martin at work and tell him what had happened.

The woman had lived next door to Martin Denby for many years and as she hobbled down the narrow entry she wondered if perhaps this house wasn't cursed. First Martin's late wife Anne and now this. She clucked and shook her head sadly. It just didn't bear thinking about, the poor little love.

Martin arrived home to find Kate staring off into space. She was so lost in thought that for some moments she didn't even realise that he was there until he coughed softly.

'Mrs Howells phoned through to the works and told me what happened.' He twisted his cap in his hands as he stared helplessly at his wife.

Raising her head to look at him, Kate smirked. 'Oh, and I bet you're going to say now how *very* sorry you are, aren't you?'

'Of course I'm sorry. What a wicked thing to say, Kate.'

Kate glared at him. 'Well, at least you won't have to worry about her keeping you up night after night now, will you?'

Turning on his heel, Martin slammed away into the kitchen and she heard him filling the kettle at the sink. Tea, he was making yet more tea. Mrs Howells had made her tea as if it were the answer to every problem in the world. Now Martin was making some more. Kate felt as if she might drown in the bloody stuff soon. But she didn't want *tea*. She wanted *Jenny*. The urge to laugh

326

came on her as a vision of herself floating in a great ocean of tea swam before her eyes. She began to titter as Martin appeared in the kitchen doorway and stared at her in bewilderment. The titter turned to a laugh as she noted his bemused expression. Huh! Anyone would believe that he'd cared for the child as he stood there, but she knew better. Oh yes, she knew all right; from the time they'd all moved in with him he'd done nothing but complain about Jenny. And now here he was, pretending that he was sorry she was gone. It was only a matter of time before the laughter turned to hysterical sobbing, and she was still sobbing as Mrs Howells, who had heard the commotion through the adjoining wall, appeared over Martin's shoulder.

Hurrying to Kate, she grabbed her into her arms and began to rock her to and fro as Martin wrung his hands and looked on.

'Get round to my house and phone the doctor, lad,' she told him gravely. Glad of an excuse to escape, Martin shot away.

Jenny was buried on a cold autumnal day in September. The skies were leaden and overcast, and as the hearse bearing the tiny white coffin on its final journey arrived at Shepperton Church churchyard the heavens opened as if they were dropping tears to join those that were swelling in Kate's heart.

The service was brief and then Kate found herself being guided in and out of the tombstones until they came to the side of a small open grave. Martin had dug the grave himself the night before and Kate found herself examining it almost as if it had been some sort of a test for him.

The rain was lashing down on them and their feet sank into the mud as they listened to the vicar solemnly intoning the final words of the funeral service.

'Suffer the little children to come unto me . . .'

The words went on and on as the yew trees that surrounded the churchyard swayed towards them in the driving wind. There were only eight other mourners besides Kate and they all stared at her anxiously rather than at Nuala who stood dispassionately examining her nails.

There was David and Rebecca, Ruby and Victor, Mrs Howells, Nuala, Martin, and Vera from the Rose and Crown. Rebecca, Ruby noticed, seemed more worried about the effect the weather was having on her hair than on the child who was being interred.

At last it was over and the vicar offered his condolences, slammed his Bible shut and bade them a hasty goodbye, before hurrying away to the tender ministrations of his wife, Nuala's ex-employer, who would have tea in his favourite bone-china cup waiting for him back at the vicarage.

Normally, Martin would have been hovering on the sidelines ready to fill in the grave that he had dug the night before, but today the vicar had arranged for a gravedigger from another parish to come and finish the job.

The bedraggled mourners filed silently away, leaving Kate to stare down for the last time at the coffin, which appeared even smaller now that it was in the ground.

'Come on, darling. Let's get you out of the cold, eh? Otherwise you'll be ill next.' Kate allowed Martin to lead her away although she longed to throw herself into the grave with the child that she'd loved as her own.

'Why don't yer all come back to the pub to dry off an' have a drink?' Vera offered thoughtfully when they caught up with her at the lychgate. It was breaking her heart, seeing Kate looking so lost.

Rubbing his hands together, David nodded gratefully and ushered Rebecca towards the car. 'Sounds good to me,' he remarked, and the rest of the mourners nodded in agreement.

'We won't bother, though it was kind of you to offer.' Martin was shepherding Kate into the passenger seat of his car as he spoke. 'Kate isn't really up to it so I think I'll just get her home.'

Vera looked more than a little miffed. 'Suit yerself then, but the offer's there if yer should change yer mind.'

Martin smiled politely as he held the rear door open for Nuala.

'But I want to go the pub with the rest of them,' she protested.

'*Get in!*'

Something in the tone of his voice made her hastily scramble into the back of the car, where she wrapped her arms across her sodden coat and slipped into a sulk.

'Shame on you,' Martin growled once he had started the engine. 'Jenny was *your* baby, though no one would ever have thought it.'

'Not from choice she weren't!' Nuala retorted and glared at him in the mirror as he swung the car away from the kerb.

329

Kate had no energy left to care; she let their bickering go over her head. She was going home, but she would leave part of her heart behind her in the tiny grave.

Chapter Twenty-Eight

'So you're not planning on coming back just yet then?' As Vera stared into Kate's gaunt face she tried to hide her concern. Kate had lost a great deal of weight, and the sparkle that had made her so popular with the regulars at the Rose and Crown had disappeared.

'No, not just yet.' Kate pulled her cardigan more closely about her as she stared into the blazing fire.

An uncomfortable silence settled on the room until Martin suddenly stood up and took his coat from the cupboard under the stairs.

'I'm going down to the churchyard, Vera. I could give you a lift if you'd like.'

Suppressing a shudder, Vera nodded. There didn't seem to be much point in staying, if she were to be honest with herself. Kate had barely uttered more than a dozen words to her since she'd arrived and she felt in the way.

Standing up, she pulled her gloves on and leaning towards Kate she pecked her affectionately on the cheek. 'You just shout when yer feel ready to come back then, eh, love? We all miss yer – especially Lindsay. Eeh, she's a card that one. How's about I get her to come an' see yer? She's been sayin' how she'd love to.'

'I miss her too, and I'd love to see—' Kate had no time to say any more when Martin cut in abruptly with: 'I can't see Kate returning to work in the foreseeable future, Vera. And I don't think it's wise for Lindsay to call just yet. Kate needs peace and quiet. It might be wise to employ someone else in my wife's place rather than go on being short-staffed.'

'I'll decide when an' if to do that!' Vera retorted as she glared back into his cold eyes. 'Seems to me comin' back to work might be the best thing for her. She's just told yer she misses Lindsay an' it would take her mind off things. I mean – look at her! She's goin' out of her head just sittin' there. She needs somethin' to distract her.'

'Thank you for your concern but I think *I'm* the best judge of what's right for my wife, and *I* think she needs some time to grieve. So now, if you wouldn't mind, I really ought to be off. This damn grave won't dig itself.'

Vera sniffed as she drew herself up to her full height. Arrogant, pompous bastard, she thought. He never had liked Kate working in the pub. From where she was standing it looked like he was just using the baby's death as an excuse to keep the poor girl housebound. But then at the end of the day it wasn't her place to come between husband and wife, so with a final sympathetic smile at Kate she followed him out of the door.

The October night was bitterly cold and the fallen leaves underfoot were treacherously slippy as she crossed the pavement to Martin's car. A light drizzle had begun to fall and it was dark and damp.

Fancy havin' to go off an' dig a grave on a night like this.
She kept the thought to herself as she slid into the car
beside him. The journey to the pub was made in silence
and when he drew into the car park she smiled at him
politely before climbing out of the car without a word.
She watched him drive away and then turning, fixed a
smile to her face and hurried inside. It wouldn't do to
be all doom and gloom in front of the customers,
although after seeing Kate she was more than a little
uneasy. It had been over a month now since the child's
death and Vera felt that her young friend should have
been over the first bitter feelings of grief by now. Then
again, everyone handled bereavement differently. Either
way, there wasn't much she could do about it.

Back at the house, Nuala stared at Kate resentfully. Her
sister just hadn't been herself since Jenny's funeral and
the girl was sick of her always being depressed. After
all, Jenny had been *her* baby, so why should Kate miss
her so? She herself certainly didn't. In fact, things had
been a whole lot better to her mind with that snivelling
brat out of the way and not keeping her awake night
after night. She felt sorry for Martin, having to come
home to Kate's long face every day though. He'd been
quite nice to her lately – he'd even talked her into going
back to her little job at the vicarage and she quite enjoyed
being out and about again, even though the idea hadn't
appealed to her to start off with. From where she was
standing, Kate was being really selfish to him and didn't
deserve to have such a handsome, caring husband. She'd
just sit there day after day feeling sorry for herself and
not even bothering to cook him a meal to come home

to half the time. That was why Nuala herself had begun to cook for him and he was always grateful. In fact, Nuala had an idea that he was getting to really like her, which suited her down to the ground. She could take much better care of him than Kate ever could and he deserved to be pampered. Smiling smugly, she wondered what to cook him for supper. He'd be cold when he got in and would probably be grateful for something hot.

Martin carried the pick and shovel from the tiny shed tucked in the corner of the churchyard and flung them down beside the space where the grave was to be dug. His hands were shaking with rage and he cursed as the drizzle turned into a downpour. A mist hovered over the ground and the tombstones surrounding him rose drunkenly out of it like rotting teeth.

'Interfering old cow,' he cursed aloud as he thought back to Vera's visit. Why couldn't everyone just leave them alone? At least now he had Kate all to himself – apart from Nuala and that damn dog. As far as he was concerned, the house was better without Jenny. No more crying in the night, no more having to watch Kate flap over her like a mother hen day and night. It wasn't even as if Jenny had been *her* baby, damn it, though she'd acted as if she were.

The pick rose and fell in the dull light of the lantern at the side of the grave. Somehow he had to think of a way to keep Kate at home now, but how? The options most certainly did not include getting her pregnant. He had had more than enough of babies.

It came to him almost an hour later, by which time the grave was half dug and his boots were heavy with mud. Adam – that was it! He would bring his son back home to live with them. That would mean that she had to stay at home, to care for the boy. He'd always intended to do it at some stage, so why wait any longer?

The more he thought of it, the better the idea seemed, but still the rage coursed though his veins. Ruby was the next one to sort out. She was another interfering old so-and-so that he needed to get out of Kate's life. Since the day of Jenny's funeral she'd visited almost daily and Martin was sick of coming home to find her planted there. Well, it wouldn't go on. He'd go and see her tomorrow and tell her in no uncertain terms to give them some privacy. If she took offence, it would be all to the good; at least it would ensure she kept away.

With his mind made up, he renewed his efforts and an hour later the grave was finished. He kicked his steel-capped boot into the muddy earth at the side of the grave and climbed up out of it to stand breathless from his exertion on the grass. Most normal folk, as Martin well knew, would avoid a deserted churchyard at night, but for him it was a sanctuary where he felt completely at home.

Chapter Twenty-Nine

'God above, would you look at that then? It's raining cats an' dogs out there.' Lindsay Bennet shrugged her arms into her coat and looked across at her friend, Beryl, who had called into the Rose to have a drink with her. Lindsay had just finished her shift and felt dead on her feet.

As they put up their umbrellas, Vera shouted, 'Night, love. Mind 'ow yer go now an' don't get loiterin' about.'

Raising her eyebrows, Lindsay stared out into the rain. 'Night, Vera.'

'Hope my Frank's got the pot on,' Beryl remarked as side by side they lurched out onto the street.

'Huh, yer should think yerself lucky that you've got someone to make a fuss of you,' Lindsay remarked peevishly. 'That no-good louse I've just wasted the last six months o' me life on wouldn't know what a kettle was if it jumped off the cooker an' hit him in the bloody face. He's too used to bein' waited on by that stuck-up wife of his.'

Beryl frowned as she clung on to Lindsay's arm. 'Is it definitely over this time, then?' she dared to ask.

'Too bloody right it is,' Lindsay replied. 'I've wasted

all that time on the bastard – an' what 'ave I got to show fer it, eh? I'll tell yer what – piss all. Fer two pins I'd pack up an' bugger off back to Bermondsey where I belong.'

Beryl had heard the same comment so many times that she didn't even bother to answer, and for a time the two women splashed along in silence. When they reached the end of Coton Road they turned as one into Queen's Road, bending their heads against the driving rain.

'Stone the crows,' Beryl wailed as the icy water trickled down the back of her neck. 'We should 'ave ordered a taxi – we'll catch us death bein' out in this.'

'Huh, good for you if yer could afford one 'cos I certainly couldn't.'

By the time they reached the overhanging canopy of the Palace cinema they were breathless and paused to shelter from the downpour.

Beryl lit a Woodbine and inhaled deeply as she stared dismally up and down the street while Lindsay looked enviously at the films advertised in the brightly lit foyer window.

'Don't know what I'm botherin' to look at these for,' she sighed. 'I can't remember the last time a bloke took me to the flicks.'

'Yes, well, you were the one who decided to 'ave an affair wi' a married man,' Beryl pointed out.

'It wasn't quite like that,' Lindsay rejoined hotly. 'I never planned it. It just sort of happened.'

Beryl tossed her cigarette end into the gutter and pulled her coat collar up. 'I bet all the women in your position say that,' she giggled. 'But never mind that now. Come on, I don't know about you but I can't wait to

337

get 'ome. I'm going' to 'ave a lovely long soak in the bath then I'm goin' to bed wi' a nice hot-water bottle tucked at me feet.'

They moved on past the gasworks and turned into Pool Bank Street. As they splashed past the Co-op Hall the strains of a waltz floated to them on the air and Lindsay grinned.

'Must be the old-timers having a knees-up,' she laughed as they hurried past. By now her coat was so saturated that great drops of rain were dripping from its hem and running down her seamed stockings before puddling into her shoes. She cursed softly. 'If the rain don't give up soon the half-a-crown I paid fer this coat at the rummage sale will 'ave bin wasted.'

Beryl nodded sympathetically as she paused to say her goodbyes, and the two friends smiled at each other before going their separate ways.

When Lindsay came to Mount Street Passage, a dark cobbled alley that was a shortcut to her home in Duke Street, she hesitated. Common sense told her that it would be wise to stick to the road, but she was shivering with cold now and if she went that way it would take a few minutes off her journey.

'Sod it,' she muttered, and before she could change her mind she plunged into the darkness, wrinkling her nose as the smell of stale urine and rotting rubbish met her. She often took this shortcut during the day but soon found out that it was a different kettle of fish altogether in the darkness. When her shoe sank into something soft she cursed as the foul smell of dog muck wafted up to her. She had taken no more than two dozen steps, but already the light from the street lamps had disappeared and she was in total blackness. Leaning heavily against the wall she tried to wipe the disgusting mess from her shoe on the cobbles before stumbling blindly on.

The wind was whistling along the alley, snatching at the raindrops and flinging them into her face like sharp little needles. Nearby, a randy tomcat was wailing and it sounded so like the cry of a new baby that it made the hairs on the back of her neck stand to attention. Someone had dumped an old settee in the alley, and as her leg connected with it, she almost went her length and cried out in pain. Perhaps it was her cry and the lashing of the rain that masked the sound of the footsteps behind her, for when someone suddenly placed their hand on her arm she almost jumped out of her skin.

''Ere – what's yer game then?' she said shakily to the dark shadow that was towering over her. The dark shadow said nothing, and with a bravado that she was far from feeling, Lindsay tried to shake his hand off her arm. 'Leave off, yer perverted bastard, or my bloke'll knock yer block off. He—'

The words were cut short when she was suddenly rammed so hard against the fence that the air was forced from her lungs. In that instant she knew that she was about to be raped, and she began to babble.

'Look . . . don't hurt me, eh? Let's get to the end o' the alley an' . . . an' we'll talk.'

A large callused hand closing painfully around her breast was the only answer, while the other hand loosed her arm and with lightning speed clamped across her mouth. Her handbag clattered to the ground, spewing its contents all across the cobbles as she was wrestled to

339

the ground. Tears slid sideways down her cheeks to mingle with the falling rain as she thrashed beneath him, but her strength was no match for his. And then came the pain as he tore mercilessly into her.

Squeezing her eyes tight shut, she held her breath and prayed for it to be over. If only he would talk. Say something – anything. She wanted to remember his voice so that she could identify him when it was all over. Her buttocks danced painfully across the rough cobbles as he ceaselessly pushed into her and the sound of his deep animal gasps echoed along the deserted alley. Strangely, he smelled nice and she tried to concentrate on that. Perhaps she would be able to identify him by his smell?

Never in her whole life had she felt so degraded and she swore in that moment that somehow she would have her revenge. But then at last, just as she was thinking that it would go on for ever, he suddenly shuddered and she felt him climax inside her.

She lay perfectly still, hardly daring to breathe, willing her ordeal to be over. Surely now he would make a run for it?

When he finally rolled off her and lay at the side of her she heard his laboured breathing slowly return to some sort of normality. Very carefully she began to inch away from him and pull herself shakily up the wall, gulping air into lungs that felt as if they were bursting. Her legs had turned to jelly and she wanted to be sick, but more than anything she knew that she must put some distance between them. One of her shoes had come off and the sharp wet cobbles were treacherously slippy as she groped her way along the slimy walls. She crept on, and as she turned a bend in the alley she gasped with relief as the lights from the council flats in Coronation Court came into view. Gathering her torn coat over her naked breasts and knuckling the rain from her eyes she prepared to launch herself forward. Just a little way more and she would be safe . . .

It was then that the hand caught her by the nape of the neck and dragged her back into the darkness. Seconds later, she felt something cold and sharp slither between her ribs. She briefly welcomed the warmth of the fluid that was now flowing down over her flat stomach, but she didn't have long to think of it before the knife was plunged into her again and then again. The attack was frenzied, but she had gone beyond pain now. It would be nice to sit down and rest, she found herself thinking, but even that was denied her as strong hands closed around her throat and kept her on her feet.

'You filthy stinking fucking whore!'

Somewhere beyond the voice was a darkness even blacker than that of the alley. It was growing closer and closer by the second, and Lindsay Bennet welcomed it.

Chapter Thirty

Nuala was waiting up for Martin when he got home, although it was way past midnight.

'Hello, Martin. I've got you some supper ready an' I've just made meself a cup o' cocoa. Would you like one?' she asked obligingly.

Martin shook his head and yawned. 'No, thanks all the same. The only thing I want right now is my bed. Where's Kate?'

Sally scuttled past him and shot into her basket in the kitchen as he ran a weary hand through his hair.

'Oh, she went up ages ago.' Nuala slurped at her drink as she eyed him curiously. He seemed to be on edge and irritable, but then she supposed it was to be expected. It couldn't be much fun digging a grave on a night like this. She was mildly surprised to see that he looked remarkably clean and dry, considering that it was raining cats and dogs outside.

He must have realised what she was thinking and as he took his overcoat off and hung it neatly away in the cupboard under the stairs he told her, 'I was soaked to the skin so I got changed in the hut at the churchyard. I always keep a clean set of clothes there for emergencies.'

More than a little peeved that he had refused the snack she had ready for him, Nuala had already lost interest as he headed for the stairs.

'Good night.'

'Good night, Martin.'

His legs felt as if they had lead weights in them as he climbed the stairs and quietly entered the bedroom, where he quickly undressed and then crept along the landing to run a bath.

Kate feigned sleep until he returned and slid into bed beside her. Some time later his gentle snores told her that he was fast asleep. She heard Nuala come up the stairs and the clock chime one and then two. By the time she finally fell into an unhappy sleep the first colours of dawn were painting the sky.

'Look at this.' Vera stabbed at her wristwatch. 'We've bin open fer *fifteen* minutes an' there's still not so much as a sniff o' Lindsay! I'm tellin' yer, that girl needs to pull her socks up else she'll be gettin' her marchin' orders.'

Her long-suffering husband watched her swipe a wet cloth along the length of the bar.

'Happen yer won't get the chance to, love,' he grinned. 'I forgot to tell yer – while I was in town earlier today I bumped into Beryl, that friend o' hers. It seems our Lindsay has done a bunk.'

'What do yer mean?' Vera stopped wiping the bar now as she stared at him curiously.

'She ain't seen hide nor hair of her since the other night when she walked home wi' her after her shift. Seems Lindsay were on about clearin' off back to London. Beryl seems to think that she's done just that!'

'Well, I'll bloody well be.' Vera's ample chest swelled with indignation. 'The ungrateful little cow, an' after I took her on wi'out so much as a reference an' all. Yer would have thought she'd at least have had the decency to come an' say ta ra!'

A customer approached the bar and instantly every inch the landlady again, she flashed him a smile. It looked like it was going to be a busy day, with only her and her old man to run the place.

That same night, as soon as Martin had washed his hands at the kitchen sink, Kate hurried into the kitchen and began to dish out the dinner. She'd spent the whole afternoon preparing and cooking it. Outside, the wind was slamming against the windows and it was bitterly cold; cold enough for frost, although it was only October.

Inside, the fire was blazing up the chimney and all was warm and cosy. Today she had pulled herself together with an effort and prepared one of Martin's favourite dinners for the first time since Jenny's death. She had also cleaned the house from top to bottom until everything shone like a new pin.

As she strained the cabbage into the colander in the sink she listened with half an ear to the BBC news. As usual it was full of Princess Margaret and Group Captain Peter Townsend.

'I reckon she'll end up marrying him,' she heard Nuala comment, but the only response from Martin was a grunt as he buried his head in the newspaper.

Within minutes, Kate called them both to the table and placed their food in front of them, then after slipping Sally a tiny bit of steak she carried her own meal to the table to join them.

Martin raised his eyebrows. 'Goodness me, looks like someone's been busy,' he said appreciatively as he eyed the steak and onions on his plate and helped himself to some mashed potato and vegetables.

Kate flushed with guilt. She knew that she'd neglected him shamefully since Jenny's death but determined that from now on she would try harder to be the sort of wife he deserved.

'I thought it was about time we tried to get back to some sort of normality,' she said quietly.

'Well, I'm very glad to hear it. The thing is, there's something I want to talk to you about and . . . ugh!' Martin spat the mouthful of food he'd been eating back onto the plate.

'What's wrong?' Kate asked in dismay.

'*What's wrong?* Taste it and you'll see. I reckon you've put sugar instead of salt in the potatoes and vegetables.'

'No, I'm sure I didn't.' Kate lifted a forkful of food to her mouth and shuddered. Martin was right. It was so sweet that it was uneatable, which meant that all her hard work had been in vain. 'But I . . . I could have sworn . . .' she stammered as tears flooded into her eyes.

Martin pushed his plate away. 'You don't seem to be able to keep your mind on anything lately, Kate,' he snapped. 'You're off with the fairies half the time. Life has to go on, you know!'

'I'm so sorry. But never mind, there's still the pudding. I'll go and get it now. It's your favourite – apple pie and custard.'

Scraping her chair back from the table she hastily

collected the ruined meals and scuttled away to the kitchen. Nuala, who was obviously feeling her sister's embarrassment, kept her eyes studiously fixed on the chenille tablecloth and never said a word.

When Kate returned with steaming bowls full of homemade apple pie and piping hot custard, Nuala eyed hers greedily. 'Never mind,' she remarked cheerfully. 'Kate makes the best apple pie in the world. We can fill up on this.' She'd barely finished speaking before she crammed the first spoonful into her mouth and this time it was she who grimaced.

'Er . . . I reckon you used salt instead of sugar in the pie, Kate. It's vile.'

Without even trying his, Martin rose from the table and stamped away back to his chair by the fire, leaving Kate to look at the ruined meal in misery as she stifled the urge to cry.

'Look, don't get upset. I can always pop down the chippie,' Nuala offered, her willingness to help quite out of character.

Without replying, Kate once again gathered up the dishes and carried them into the kitchen where she scraped the food into the pig bin. Martin meanwhile proffered a ten-shilling note to Nuala and seconds later she appeared in the kitchen with her outdoor clothes on.

'Pop some plates in the oven to warm an' I'll be back in ten minutes with the fish an' chips,' she told Kate brightly.

'You be careful how you go and don't get talking to anyone strange,' Kate warned as she glanced at the dark window. 'You can't be too careful till they find out where all those poor women disappeared to.'

Nuala rolled her eyes at the ceiling. 'Oh Kate, for God's sake. It's only six o'clock at night.'

'I don't care what time it is,' Kate persisted. 'Just don't get talking to anyone you don't know.'

When the door had closed behind her, Kate leaned heavily against the sink and wiped her hand across her eyes. What the hell was happening to her? She seemed to be making lots of silly mistakes lately, and losing things too. Not to mention the fact that she'd started to talk to herself, particularly since Nuala had gone back to her part-time cleaning job at the vicarage.

Only today she'd searched the house from top to bottom for the necklace that Ruby had given her on her wedding day, but it was nowhere to be found. She could have sworn that she'd put it safely away in the bedroom drawer, but although she had tipped every single drawer in the room out onto the bed there wasn't a sign of it. And now this on top. She chewed on her lip. What if she *had* inherited her mother's madness? While he'd been alive, her father had always accused Nuala of being the one that took after their mother, but what if it was *her*?

Plunging her hands into the steaming soapy water in the bowl she began to vigorously scrub the plates as she tried to push the terrifying thoughts away. It was while she was standing there that her eyes suddenly came to rest on a rubber teat in the far corner of the kitchen windowsill. She swallowed the sob that rose in her throat and threatened to choke her. She'd thought that she had cleared the house of everything that had belonged to Jenny and she must have wiped that windowsill dozens of times since the baby's death, so where had the teat

347

come from? Surely she couldn't have cleaned around it all those times and never noticed it?

Unable to control her emotions for another second she fled from the room and sobbing, clattered away up the stairs.

Ruby gazed at Kate who was huddled in the fireside chair. The glow had gone from the girl's cheeks and her hair was lank. Worse than that though was the dejected slump of Kate's shoulders and the empty look in her eyes.

As she strummed her fingers on the chenille tablecloth, Ruby looked around the room. It was immaculate – too immaculate for her liking, with not a single ornament so much as an inch out of place. More like a showplace than a real home – but then an idea occurred to her. The answer to Kate's problems was staring her straight in the face, if she did but know it.

'Look, love, I were thinkin',' she said innocently. 'Now you've got so much time on your hands, why don't you put your mark on this place? You know, make it your own. If I remember rightly, you're a dab hand on the old sewing machine, and nice as this room is . . . well, it's a bit bleedin' *flowery*, ain't it? I reckon some nice plain curtains would tone it all down a treat.'

A flicker of interest flared in Kate's eyes as she followed Ruby's gaze. She was right. In fact, she'd been meaning to change a few things ever since she had moved in, but there had always seemed to be so much to do until recently.

Now though, time was the one thing that she seemed to have plenty of. With Martin at work all day and Nuala off to the vicarage most afternoons, the hours weighed heavy.

Seeing her reaction, Ruby pushed home the point. 'It's market day today, an' if you recall, there's a smashin' material stall comes outside Boffin's cake shop. We'd probably pick up enough material to do this here window for a snip, so what do yer say? Shall we have a measure up and get ourselves down there? Yer look like a bit o' fresh air might do you a power o' good!'

To Ruby's delight, Kate nodded hesitantly. 'I suppose it would give me something to keep me occupied,' she admitted, but then she frowned. What would Martin say if she were to change anything without his consent? Would he be angry? She thought back to his reaction on the day that she'd removed Anne's photo from above their bed and then how sorry he had been for shouting at her. She supposed he'd be glad now to see her showing interest in the house again; it would be a nice surprise for him. A faltering smile replaced the frown and not daring to waste a minute in case Kate had a change of heart, Ruby took the tape measure that Kate had retrieved from one of the ridiculously tidy drawers and began to measure the window.

'Well, go on,' she urged. 'Get yourself away and get ready else the stalls will be shuttin' up afore we bloomin' well get there.'

Twenty minutes later they stepped out of the front door into Heath End Road. A Midland red bus was parked at a stop only yards away, but deciding that a good brisk walk would do Kate good, Ruby took her elbow and steered her past it.

It was a miserable day, but all the same Kate's spirits

lifted as they strode along arm-in-arm; she was glad to be away from the house for a while. They'd taken no more than a few steps when a shrill voice pierced the air.

''Ere, 'old up, you two. If you're goin' into town I'll walk with you.'

Glancing over her shoulder, Kate saw Mrs Howells trundling towards them.

'Phew!' The older woman grinned as she caught up. 'Me head keeps tellin' me as I'm still a young filly but me body tells me I'll soon be drawin' me pension.'

Kate smiled as she and Ruby slowed their steps to match those of her neighbour. 'I'd have thought you'd catch the bus into town,' she remarked.

'Ner, look after the pennies an' the pounds will take care o' themselves, that's my motto. I must say, it's nice to see you out an' about again, love.'

'I thought it was time,' Kate replied. 'Now that I'm not working and I don't have Jenn . . . I tend to get bored. Ruby thought it was about time I put my mark on the house so I'm going to get some new curtain material and make a start. I want to surprise Martin.'

'Oh, dear. I think you'll do that all right.' Concern laced the older woman's voice. 'Does he know you're plannin' these changes?'

'Not yet. Why? Do you think he'll mind?' Kate peeped at Mrs Howells nervously.

'Well, all I can say is, Martin's a bit of a stickler for everything just so. Anne was the same . . . Oh sorry, love, I shouldn't 'ave said that, should I? After all, she's dead an' gone, bless her soul, an' it's *your* house now so you should 'ave a say in 'ow it's decorated an' what not.'

'Well, Martin knows I've been wanting to make a few changes,' Kate replied. 'And I'm hoping he'll be pleased to see me making an effort.'

'Quite right!' Ruby declared indignantly. She and Mrs Howells had met previously at Jenny's funeral and had hit it off immediately.

They walked on in silence for a time until Mrs Howells said, 'I see Nuala is getting herself out an' about a bit more now. Looked quite smart she did, when I saw her settin' off earlier on.'

'She's gone back to her old job at Shepperton vicarage,' Kate informed her. 'And she seems to be really enjoying it, which is quite surprising seeing as she hated the job the last time she did it. I have to say that the vicar's wife seems to think the world of her though. I think they are being extra kind to Nuala since . . . you know. Nuala came home with the most enormous bag full of clothes you ever saw the other day that she'd given her. Hence the new look.'

'Mm, I noticed she'd lost a bit o' weight an' all,' Mrs Howells remarked.

As the two women began to gossip about Princess Margaret's decision not to wed Group Captain Peter Townsend, Kate thought about her sister. Now that she came to think about it, Nuala *did* seem happier lately. She'd lost weight and had taken to washing her hair at least twice a week, and only the day before, Kate had found a lipstick on Nuala's dressing-table when she was dusting her room.

By now the small group were walking past the old workhouse in The Bullring. Ruby and Mrs Howells were still chatting nineteen to the dozen, so Kate could allow her thoughts to continue. What could have caused the sudden change in her sister? She wondered briefly if there might be a boyfriend on the scene, but then dismissed that thought almost instantly. Apart from going to work, Nuala rarely ventured out of the house at night so there wasn't much chance of that.

As they crossed the bridge that ran over the canal and passed the Boot Inn, Mrs Howells asked, 'Heard owt o' that mate o' yours that went missin' from the pub, have yer?'

'She didn't go missing,' Ruby snapped before Kate could answer. 'Everyone knows that Lindsay was unsettled in Nuneaton an' she'd just had a grandaddy of a barney wi' her bloke. I reckon she just upped an' cleared off back to London. She'd certainly threatened to do it enough bleedin' times so don't get readin' anythin' sinister into that one.'

Feeling as if she'd been put firmly in her place, Mrs Howells sniffed and fell silent. Kate felt ridiculously hurt that Lindsay hadn't come to see her before she left – but then she could hardly blame her, if she were to be honest with herself. Since losing Jenny she hadn't much bothered with anyone, Lindsay included, so the girl had probably thought she wouldn't be welcome at Kate's home. It didn't stop Kate from missing her though and she hoped that one day Lindsay would get back in touch.

'Where you off to anyway?' Ruby asked eventually, pulling Kate's thoughts back to the present.

Mrs Howells was instantly all smiles again. 'Off to the library to try an' get a James Bond book. Eeh, now imagine a secret agent tucked in at the side o' yer of a cold night, eh?'

Ruby chuckled; never much of a reader herself, she couldn't understand people who got excited about books, but then it was each to their own. Her idea of a good night was a game of Bingo or to curl up in front of the telly with a bottle of Guinness and a packet of Woodbines.

The trio moved on past Coton Arches and soon the Rose and Crown came into sight. Kate considered paying Vera a flying visit but then decided against it. She hadn't been to the pub since Jenny's death and if there were regulars in they would be sure to commiserate with her. Plus, it wouldn't be the same in there without Lindsay. A pang of regret shot through her as she thought again of the cheerful young woman she had befriended – someone else Kate had cared about to add to the list of people she had lost.

When they reached the fountain outside the Council Offices, Mrs Howells took her leave of them.

'I'm off to the library before I shop for the old man's tea then.' She grinned from ear to ear. 'You two enjoy yourselves now. Don't be too long, though. The weather forecast reckons it's goin' to rain cats an' dogs later on.' With a cheery wink she went on her way. As Kate and Ruby made their way past the cattle market, Kate's kind heart went out to the poor animals that were cramped together in pens as red-faced farmers bid for them or sold them for slaughter. She saw one man prodding a stick into an unfortunate cow's side. Shuddering, she moved Ruby on as she tried not to think of the animal's fate, and soon they came to the gay array of stalls beneath the market clock that sold everything from fruit and veg to household goods.

353

Within no time at all they were standing in front of the material stall outside Boffin's cake shop. The stall was piled high with every type of material imaginable and Kate was glad that Ruby was there to help her make a decision.

'Right then.' Whipping the scrap of paper with the window measurements on out of her pocket, Ruby asked, 'What colour do yer fancy then? If we're goin' plain, how about this nice red cotton here?'

Kate screwed up her nose. 'Too dark – but I like that crushed velvet there, the pink. It's softer than the red.'

Standing back to judge it from a distance, Ruby grudgingly nodded in agreement. 'It *is* nice,' she admitted, 'though red is always warm-lookin' in the winter. Don't decide yet, though. Let's have a rummage an' see what we can find.'

Much to Kate's amusement, Ruby fell on the bales of material like a woman on a mission and began to scrabble through them. One by one she held her finds up for Kate's inspection but each time Kate shook her head. Eventually, Ruby breathlessly stood back to look at her.

'Yer still like the pink, don't yer?'

When Kate nodded, Ruby approached the stallholder who was frantically trying to right the havoc Ruby had caused to her once-tidy stall.

'Right, we want five yards o' this one here. What's yer very best price?'

Kate felt hot colour flood into her cheeks as Ruby began to barter, but eventually the material was cut, the money was exchanged and they walked away from the stall with Ruby grinning like a Cheshire cat.

'Now,' she beamed, 'I reckon we deserve a nice cup

354

o' tea an' a cream cake after that. Come on, we'll go into Boffin's. My treat.'

Knowing it was pointless to argue, Kate meekly followed her.

Just as Mrs Howells had predicted, mid-afternoon it began to thunder, and lightning lit up the sky. Soon after that the heavens opened. Back at home, Kate glanced at the rain-lashed windows before looking at the clock. With a little start she saw that it was after four and so she hastily began to collect the material she'd been sewing into a neat pile. Then, lifting the small Singer sewing-machine, she put it back in its place in the cupboard under the stairs and threw some coal onto the fire before hurrying away to start the dinner. She thought of what Martin would say when he saw the new curtains. She hoped he would like them. They might even be finished tomorrow if she set to as soon as Nuala left for the vicarage at lunchtime. She might even have time to hang them . . .

She was scrubbing King Edward potatoes for baking when the door opened and Nuala almost fell into the kitchen.

'Phew!' Her sister swiped the water from her eyes and shook herself like a dog, sending drops of water flying in all directions. Sally growled deep in her throat and hid under the table as Nuala scowled at her. Her face brightened, however, as she looked at Kate and took off her saturated coat. 'What have we got for dinner tonight then?' she asked brightly.

With a little shock, Kate saw that Mrs Howells had been right. Nuala *had* lost weight – and it suited her.

'Nothing too exciting,' she replied affably. 'I picked some pork chops up on the way back from the market and thought I'd do us jacket potatoes with them.'

'Good. Even *you* can't get that wrong.'

The instant the words had left her lips Nuala looked as if she could have bitten her tongue out. 'Sorry, Kate. I didn't mean that. Anyone could have done what you did the other night. It's easy enough to get salt mixed up with sugar.'

Kate studiously concentrated on the potato she was washing so that Nuala wouldn't see the tears that had sprung to her eyes.

'*Anyone* didn't do it though, did they? *I* did. Along with all the other daft things I seem to be doing lately. I am forever losing something or forgetting something. Speaking of which – you haven't seen the necklace Ruby gave me on my wedding day, have you?'

Nuala shook her head. 'No, I can't say that I have. You haven't lost it, have you?'

Kate shook her head. 'I'd rather think that I'd just mislaid it, though I could have sworn I'd put it away.'

At that moment the door opened again and Martin appeared, so there was no time to say any more. Flinging off his coat, he ran his fingers through his hair as he looked at Kate.

'Had a good day, have you?'

Kate nodded; she would have liked to tell him that she'd gone into town with Ruby but thought better of it in case he asked her what she'd bought. She thought contentedly of the material tucked safely away under the stairs and the surprise he would have when he saw the new curtains.

'Will the dinner be long?'

'Oh, about an hour at most,' Kate replied as she popped the potatoes into the oven.

Discarding his wet boots at the side of the back door, he peeped into the next room and seeing that Nuala had gone up to her bedroom, he sighed with satisfaction. Taking Kate's elbow he led her to the table and pressed her down into a chair.

'Right, while we've got five minutes to ourselves there's something I've been meaning to talk to you about.'

Kate nodded apprehensively.

'The thing is . . .' Martin began to pace up and down the room. 'The thing is, I've always hoped that we could have Adam to live with us, as you know.'

Kate's head bobbed in agreement.

'Well, I got to thinking – what's to stop us having him now?'

Seeing Kate's amazement, he hurried on, 'I know it's a bit soon, but the thing is . . . by your own admission you get bored sitting here all day with nothing to do and I think you and Adam could be good for each other. So . . . what do you say?'

'Well, I suppose I'm a bit surprised, to be honest. I mean – it *is* a bit soon. I've only met him once. And what will his grandparents have to say about it?'

Martin waved her concerns aside with a shake of his hand. 'Oh, don't get worrying about them. At the end of the day, Adam is *my* son so they'll just have to get used to it.'

'And Adam?' she asked anxiously.

'He'll be fine with it when he gets used to the idea.'

The hopeful look in his eyes tugged at her heart but

still she had reservations. Seeing this, he sat in front of her and took her hands in his.

'Look, Kate, there's something I ought to tell you. I should have told you long ago, I know, but I find it hard to talk about. The thing is, you see . . . I was brought up in Henry Street Children's Home. Oh, I didn't have a bad childhood and the staff did their best, but it wasn't like having a home of my own and a *real* mum and dad. When I got married and Adam came along I promised myself that *my* child would have a real home-life, and then of course Anne died and well . . . you know the rest.'

'Oh, Martin.' Kate's soft heart swelled with sympathy. 'Whyever didn't you tell me this before?'

He shrugged. 'As I say, it's not something you really want to remember. But . . . it would mean the world to me if you would have my son back here. I know you can never take the place of his mum, but at least he'd be with me.' In a flash Kate was round the table and had his damp head cradled against her breasts.

'Of course he should be with you,' she whispered soothingly. And so the decision was made, and in that moment she felt closer to Martin than she had in the whole of their married life.

Chapter Thirty-One

'Are you *sure* this is a good idea?' Nuala asked uncertainly as she stared at the curtain material dangling over the side of the Singer sewing-machine.

Kate spat out a mouthful of pins and looked at her. 'Why wouldn't it be?'

Nuala shrugged. 'Well, you know what Martin's like. He likes everything to be just so. I can't see him being too happy with changes.'

'I think he'll be so pleased to see me making an effort again that he'll love them,' Kate replied with a bravado that she was far from feeling. 'Everything round here is going to change at the weekend anyway when Adam moves in with us, and I want this to be a turning-point for all of us.'

Nuala struggled into her coat. 'Can't see why Martin couldn't have just left him where he was,' she grumbled.

'Nuala!' Kate's eyebrows rose into her hairline. 'I would have thought it was more than obvious that his father would want him living back here with him. I hope you're going to try and be nice to him?'

'Won't have much choice if he's under me feet all the time, will I?' Without so much as another word Nuala slammed out of the door, glaring at Sally, who flinched and hid. Kate's shoulders sagged.

In fairness to Nuala, she too thought that Martin was being a little hasty in bringing the child back to his former home so quickly. She'd hoped that it would be done more gradually so that they all had time to get to know one another, but then Adam was Martin's son so she would abide by his wishes. Not that she really had much choice in the matter. Martin could be very domineering, as she'd already learned to her cost.

It was as she was sitting there staring into the fire that a tap came to the back door. Dropping the almost completed curtains into a heap on the floor, she flicked back her hair and hurried to open it then beamed with delight when she found David standing on the doorstep.

'Why, this is a pleasant surprise!' As she held the door wide he stepped past her and rubbed his hands together.

'It's enough to cut you in two out there!' he exclaimed as he hurried towards the welcoming warmth of the fire.

Kate filled the kettle at the deep sink and after she'd put it on the stove to boil she went to join him.

'To what do I owe this unexpected honour then?' she grinned.

Turning his back to the dancing flames he fumbled in his coat pocket and after a moment drew out an envelope with a flourish.

'This was delivered to my mother's old house and got forwarded on to me, but it's actually addressed to you, so I thought I'd pop it up to you in my dinner-hour. It's probably from some friend back home who doesn't know you've got married, because it's addressed to Miss Kate Cleary.'

Kate flushed as she looked at the neat handwriting. It was from Matthew – she would have recognised his writing anywhere.

'Thanks. I'll read it later.' Stuffing it into the pocket of her apron she whisked away to the kitchen to make the tea, glad of an excuse to stop her cousin seeing the colour that had risen into her cheeks. Why would Matthew be writing to her after all this time? It didn't make sense when he'd ignored the letters she'd written to him while she was living at her aunt's.

She warmed the pot with trembling hands and eventually, when she had managed to compose herself, carried the tray back into the small sitting room.

'So, how are things then?' David's voice was heavy with concern as he watched her pouring the tea into two cups.

Fixing a false smile on her face she handed him his and plied him with biscuits.

'Oh, you know? I'm getting there. Some days are better than others.'

David could quite believe it as he noted the way her clothes seemed to hang off her. She'd lost weight, and the old sparkle was absent. Still, Kate had taken a lot of knocks, one after the other over the last couple of years, so it was only natural that it should take some time for her to bounce back to the person she had been.

'How are things with you?' Kate asked to change the subject.

David steepled his fingers as he leaned on the table. 'Better than they were. I'm not afraid to be the man of the house any more. And before you say it – I know it's way overdue!'

'I wasn't going to say anything,' Kate said softly.

He hung his head. 'You know, Kate, sometimes I wonder why you bother with me at all after the way I treated you when you first came to live with my mother.'

'That's all in the past now, and anyway you've certainly made up for it in the last few months. I don't know what I'd have done without you and that's the truth. Particularly when Jenny . . .'

As he saw the raw pain reflected in her eyes, guilt stabbed at him afresh. Kate really was a kind person. It was just a pity that he hadn't seen it while his mother was still alive. Beth would have so loved to see them getting along. Still, as Kate said, that was in the past and from now on he intended to look out for her. They were cousins, after all.

'I passed Nuala as I came in,' he commented. 'I must say, she's looking very well. Quite smart, in fact. Is there a boyfriend on the horizon or something?'

'I did wonder that myself,' Kate admitted. 'But if there is, I can't think when she gets to see him. She sits here in front of the television night after night with Martin until all hours, though I do encourage her to get out and about.'

All the time she was talking she was aware of the letter tucked deep in her pocket and when David eventually glanced at the clock and hastily drained his cup she was almost relieved.

'I shall have to be going, else my boss will have my guts for garters,' he joked as she followed him to the door.

They exchanged a few more pleasantries, but once the door had closed behind him and she heard his footsteps striding away down the entry she crossed to the nearest chair, dropped onto it and withdrew the letter from her pocket. It was definitely Matthew's handwriting; she would have staked her life on it. There was a time when she'd longed to see a letter from him. But what could he be writing to her now for? Deciding that there was only one way to find out, she slit open the envelope and withdrew a single sheet of paper.

With shaking fingers she began to read.

My dear Kate,

I know that you will probably choose to ignore this letter as you have ignored the others I have sent you. Even so, I will keep writing until you ask me to stop. Kate, I bitterly regret ever letting you go. Just as I once told you, you are in every yesterday. I still love you and always will, and cannot understand why you will not write to me. I have recently obtained a position at Birmingham University teaching Art, and wondered if you would allow me to come and see you? I hope you are settled with your aunt and look forward to your reply. Perhaps we could take up where we left off? If not, I hope that we can remain friends.

Forever yours,
Matthew xxxxxx

As the letter floated from Kate's hand tears welled in her eyes and ran in rivers down her thin cheeks. How *dare*

Matthew have the audacity to write to her after what he'd done to Nuala? And what did he mean – all the letters *she'd* ignored? Could Aunt Beth have kept them from her? The idea rankled, but if it wasn't her there was only Nuala who could have intercepted them, and Kate knew that her sister would never do that.

Matt obviously wasn't aware that he'd become a father to Nuala's child, nor that Kate herself was now a married woman. But then how could he know? Only she herself could have told him – and she had certainly not done so. Not that it mattered. She wouldn't touch him with a bargepole now, even if she were still single, after the way he had taken advantage of her sister all the while protesting his love for her!

So why then, did her heart ache as a picture of his face swam before her eyes? He had betrayed her in the worst possible way and she would never forgive him for that. With a muttered oath she flung the letter into the heart of the fire and returned to the job of finishing the curtains.

'*What the . . . ?*' Martin's mouth gaped open as he stared about the room. Not only had Kate hung the new curtains but she'd also replaced the hearthrug and some of the pictures on the walls with ones of her own choice.

Both sisters watched intently for his reaction as Kate told him nervously, 'I wanted to surprise you. It looks nice, doesn't it? I got the material for the curtains when I went into town with Ruby. She thought it might perk me up a bit if I made a few changes.'

'*Did* she now? Well, perhaps the interfering old cow

should mind her own bloody business for a change,' he stormed. 'There was absolutely nothing wrong with the room as it was. This just looks . . . *tacky and cheap*!'

Kate glanced at Nuala, who she thought for a brief instant looked smug, and then her lip trembled as she stared back at him in astonishment. 'I thought you'd be pleased,' she whispered.

'Then you thought wrong and I'd appreciate it if you'd kindly put everything back the way it was. This is *my* house and when I want anything changing I'll tell you.'

As he turned on his heel and began to stride towards the back door, Kate caught at his arm desperately. 'Where are you going?' she cried. 'You've only just come in – I have your dinner ready,'

Shrugging her arm off he glared at her. 'I'm going for a drink. Damn the dinner . . . and when I get back I shall expect to find everything as it was.'

'But Martin, please be reasonable. I live here too now. Surely it's only natural I want to put my own mark on the place?'

His lips set in a grim line as he loomed over her. 'You liked the house well enough when I brought you here, didn't you? Oh yes, I was a good catch, wasn't I? There weren't many that would have taken you, along with your sister, a brat *and* a bloody scrap of a dog, were there?'

Kate was openly sobbing now and could hardly believe her own ears. 'How could you say such a thing? And Jenny wasn't a brat, she was my—'

'*No*, Kate! If you were about to say she was *your* baby, you're wrong. She was *her* baby.' An accusing

365

finger stabbed towards Nuala, who slithered down in the chair behind the newspaper. 'Though no one would ever have known it, the way you put the kid before everyone else.'

'That's not true. Please, *please* don't go like this. Stay and have your meal.'

'Huh, and what culinary delight did you have in mind for me tonight then, eh? Another burned offering, is it? No, thanks – I'll get something from the chippie. At least that will be edible. You're in a world of your own half the time lately. Why don't you do us all a favour and make an appointment with a psychiatrist?'

He shoved his feet into his boots without even bothering to tie the laces and snatching up his coat, slammed the back door so loudly as he left that it danced on its hinges.

Nuala crept from behind the paper and crossing to her sister she placed a comforting arm about her shaking shoulders.

'Don't mind him,' she whispered soothingly. 'He's probably just had a bad day at work.'

'Nuala, *am* I going mad?' Kate sobbed, suddenly remembering the look on her sister's face a few moments ago. For the briefest of instants she'd thought that Nuala had looked smug, but she must have been mistaken. The girl had probably just been nervous as she was.

'Of course you're not. Now come on, sit yourself down an' I'll make you a nice cup of tea. Then we'll set to and get this room back to how it was.'

Kate looked around the room at all her hard work. She had hoped that Martin would be pleased but she had been dreadfully wrong. Slowly she began to unhook all the new pictures and roll up the hearthrug.

Ruby was engrossed in the newspaper report she was reading. A full list of all the women who had gone missing from the town had been printed and it was reported that the police were stepping up their investigation. They had finally brought in someone from Scotland Yard to help out, which to Ruby's mind was long overdue. The dates and times when the women had gone missing were supplied, with a request for anyone who had seen anything at all to come forward. Ruby was so interested in the report that when the rap came on the back door, she almost jumped out of her skin. She was even more rattled when she hurried to answer it and a red-faced Martin barged past her into the room.

'*What the—*' she began, but he cut her short with a threatening gesture.

'So what do *you* want then?' she asked, her chin in the air. How dare he march into her home as if he owned it! Outwardly calm, Ruby was shaking inside, though she would have died rather than let him see it.

'What *I* want is for you to keep away from my wife! You are no longer welcome in my house, do you hear me, woman?'

Colour burned into her cheeks as she stood up to him. 'Oh, I hear you all right, but may I ask just what it is I'm supposed to have done to bring this about?'

'What you've done,' he ground out, 'is interfere in our lives once too often. Neither Kate nor I need you coming in and telling us how our house should look. Perhaps it's time you took a look around *this* dump and practised what you preach.'

Ignoring the last remark, Ruby drew herself up to her full height.

'I was *not* interfering,' she spat at him. 'I was simply trying to give Kate something to occupy herself. A blind man on a gallopin' horse could see that the poor girl is about at the end of her bloody tether. She's had so many losses over the last couple o' years – even her mate Lindsay has gone an' done a bunk wi'out so much as a by yer leave now. Yer do want her to get well, don't yer?'

'There's nothing wrong with her, and once Adam has moved back in with us she won't have time to wallow in self-pity. She certainly won't have time to go gallivanting off with you spending time and money on things that don't need changing, on your say so. And as for Lindsay . . . well, all I can say is goodbye to bad rubbish. She was never the sort of person that Kate should be mixing with anyway.'

The atmosphere was charged as they glared at each other across the table, but eventually Ruby crossed her arms and turned her back on him as she stared into the roaring fire.

'If you've said everything you've come to say, I think yer should leave now, don't you?'

She heard his shoes clicking on the lino as he headed for the back door but avoided looking at him so that he wouldn't see the tears that had sprung to her eyes. She'd grown to love Kate as she had loved her mother before her, and now more than ever she was regretting not telling her the secret that haunted her day and night.

Martin turned at the door.

'I meant what I said,' he repeated ominously. 'I don't want you near Kate or my house *ever again*. Do I make myself quite clear?'

'*Perfectly* – now will yer please just piss off?' she managed to say.

The slamming of the door was her only answer. She listened to the sound of his heavy footsteps echoing down the narrow entry then burying her face in her hands, she cried as if her heart would break.

'Adam, it's lovely to see you. But please don't stand there – this is your home, come on in.' Kate would have given her stepson a hug, but one look at his surly expression stopped her in her tracks.

'This isn't my home,' he said sullenly. 'My home is with my Nanny and Grandy.'

'You won't feel like that once you've settled back in,' Martin told him cheerily as he deposited his son's suitcase on the lounge floor. 'Come on through to the back room. Kate's been baking all day and if my sense of smell is anything to go by, she's cooked you a few treats.'

'Don't want any treats. I want to go home.' Adam crossed his arms and stayed where he was.

Taking his wife's elbow, Martin led her away. Once they were in the privacy of the kitchen, he told her, 'Don't worry about that little outburst. It's bound to feel strange for him. It didn't help when he heard me arguing with his grandparents.'

'They're still against him coming back here then?'

Nodding, he sampled a jam tart that was cooling on

369

a rack. 'Always were too full of their own opinions, those two. They were quick enough to whip Adam away from me when his mother died. Back then I didn't have much choice but to go along with it, but it's a different kettle of fish now, so they'll just have to get used to it.'

'Let's just hope that Adam will too,' Kate said quietly. 'Couldn't you persuade him to come through for something to eat?'

'He'll come through when he's hungry enough,' Martin informed her in a voice that brooked no argument. 'Just put the dinner out and pop his in the oven to keep warm.'

Lifting the newspaper, he retired to his chair at the side of the fire as Kate did as she was told.

Leaning across his shoulder, Nuala pointed at the headlines. 'Look, it's all about them women that went missing,' she said unnecessarily. It seemed that there was something about them in the papers almost daily now.

'I can read. And I would like to read in peace,' Martin retorted coldly.

Taking the hint, Nuala joined Kate in the kitchen. 'He certainly got out o' bed the wrong side this mornin',' she stated sulkily. 'An' why is he leavin' the little 'un all alone in the front room?'

'He won't come through,' Kate whispered back. 'Couldn't you go in and get him to come for some dinner?'

Nuala shuddered at the thought. 'No, I can't! Adam is his kid an' if he wants him to eat with us then he can damn well fetch him himself.'

Kate rubbed her brow to relieve the beginnings of a headache. Adam's homecoming wasn't turning out to be what she had hoped for at all, and she wondered if this was a taste of things to come.

Standing at the gates of Middlemarch School, Kate watched Adam cross the playground. His shoulders were stooped as he dragged his satchel dejectedly across the ground. Despite the fact that he seemed to despise her, she found herself feeling sorry for him. After all, he was only a child at the end of the day and it couldn't be easy for him having to adjust to a new family and a new routine.

'Why do you have to take me to school? I'm not a cissy, you know. I could go to school by myself,' he had declared earlier in the morning.

'I don't *have* to take you,' Kate had replied pleasantly. 'I *want* to take you. It will be nice to have some time together – just you and me. Give us a chance to get to know one another.'

He had looked at her scornfully, as if she had taken leave of her senses, and not said so much as another word since. Now she slowly turned and retraced her steps. Adam had been with them for almost a week now and during that time the house had become like a war zone. Nuala and he did nothing but argue as two children might and Kate was forever having to get in between them. Added to that was the fact that Martin was barely civil to his own son, to the point that Kate was beginning to wonder why he had ever wanted Adam to come home in the first place.

She briefly thought of paying Ruby a visit but then decided against it. It was strange though, now she came to think of it, that Ruby hadn't been to see her this week.

Probably too busy with her wedding plans, Kate decided as she hurried past the Griff and Coton Sports Club. The trees surrounding it looked strangely appealing. The odd few leaves that clung desperately to the branches were every shade of russet and gold and sparkled like jewels in the early morning dew. A damp mist hovered over the ground and Kate drew her coat collar more tightly together.

She hurried on along Heath End Road intent on getting home to a nice hot cup of tea before she began her daily chores. It was as she was passing the hospital that she suddenly thought of Matthew again. She'd thought of him often over the days since David had delivered his letter and sometimes bitterly regretted burning it. She'd even considered questioning Nuala about the missing letters but couldn't face the argument that would surely follow. Not that she thought Nuala was capable of being so sly.

Thinking of Matthew automatically brought thoughts of what he had done to Nuala and she hardened her heart. No, she'd done the right thing – Matthew was in the past now. How could she ever forgive him for what he'd done to her sister and the child he had never known he had? As always, memories of Jenny brought tears pricking at the back of her eyes. The pain was still there, as raw as on the day she had lost her, but Kate knew she must somehow come to terms with it. She had a new husband and a stepson to worry about now, and they must come first. Why then, she wondered, did the thought bring her no joy?

'Cor! An' to think he comes from Nuneaton, eh?' Nuala swivelled her head to glance at Kate who was laying the table for tea. She had just read the appeal by the husband whose young wife had been the first victim to go missing in the newspaper. He was begging anyone who might have any news of where his wife had gone to come forward, and there was a picture of him with his two little daughters.

'Let's hope it does some good and jogs someone's memory,' Kate replied. She smiled at Adam, who was curled up in a chair with a copy of the *Beano*. He scowled at her and turned his head. Kate sighed and went back to preparing the dinner.

'Martin's late, ain't he?' Nuala commented, losing interest in the story as she strolled into the kitchen to join her.

'Yes, he's got a grave to dig tonight and being as the weather's so bad he decided to go straight to the church from work. I shall have to put his dinner in the oven and warm it back up later on.'

Glancing towards the window, Nuala shuddered. It was the worst November they'd had for years and although it was still early evening it was pitch black and the pavements were already white over with frost.

'Rather him than me,' she commented, but then as a thought suddenly occurred to her she hurried away and reappeared seconds later dressed in her outdoor clothes.

'Where are you going?' Kate asked. 'Tea will be ready in an hour.'

Nuala shrugged. 'I just remembered I said I'd help the vicar's wife sort some stuff out for the rummage sale on Saturday.

'Well, don't be too late,' Kate told her anxiously.

Nodding curtly at her sister, Nuala ignored Adam and stomped away. As Kate heard the back door slam, she sighed at the prospect of being alone with her hostile stepson. You could cut the atmosphere in this house with a knife!

Chapter Thirty-Two

The grieving widow, supported on either side by her two sons, stood at the side of the open grave as the coffin was slowly lowered in. For now there were no tears. The pain she was feeling went beyond tears to a tearing emptiness that squeezed at her heart.

The words that the shivering vicar was reciting were snatched away by the cutting wind that sliced across the churchyard. But then at last it was over and the woman's older son began to lead her past the mountain of earth that would soon cover her beloved husband for all time. The young man paused as something amongst the towering mound of dirt caught his eye. Bending, he picked up a slim gold chain from which dangled a pretty heart-shaped sapphire that reflected the light from the cold winter sun.

Nodding at his brother to continue, he raced away to catch up with the vicar who was already striding towards the vicarage. He would give it to him. The vicar would know what to do with it. Better that than have to waste precious time down at the police station handing it into Lost Property.

*   *   *

Ruby wrung her hands as she stared into Victor's concerned eyes. 'What do you think I should do? I can't just abandon the poor girl, can I?'

Placing a comforting arm around her, he drew her head onto his shoulder. Following the death of his first wife, Victor Skinner had thought he would never love again. But he *did* love Ruby, with a fierceness that took his breath away. He would have walked through fire for her if she'd asked him to, and it pained him to see her so distressed.

'The way I see it, love, there ain't that much you *can* do. I know you care for the girl, an' it's harsh. But the thing is, you can't come between husband and wife,' he said wisely. 'He's told you to back off an' from where I'm standing you don't have much choice. If you go round there again after he's told you you're not welcome, you might just make it worse for her.'

'But he's a bad 'un, Vic. I bloody know it. There's just somethin' about him that makes me skin crawl.'

Victor shrugged. 'Happen he is, but he were her choice, an' as my mother was always fond of sayin', she's made her bed an' now she's got to lie on it. I shouldn't worry too much though. Kate's got spirit. She'll only take so much an' then she'll give him what-for an' she'll bounce back.'

'Huh! She might have done at one time, but losin' her aunt an' then the baby so soon after has knocked the stuffin' out of her.'

Kissing the top of her head he hugged her gently. 'Try not to worry,' he encouraged. 'Things have a habit of coming right in the end, you'll see.'

Tears trembled on Ruby's lashes as she stared up at

him. She wanted to believe him with all her heart, but somehow found that she couldn't.

'You know gel, I've been thinking,' Victor mused. 'Why don't we just go ahead and get married? The only reason we decided to wait till Christmas was so that Kate could come to the wedding. But if truth be told there don't seem much chance of Martin allowing that now, does there, so what's to stop us?'

Ruby blinked in surprise. 'When were you thinkin' of?'

'Today, tomorrow, as soon as it can be arranged.' He grinned. 'Think about it, Ruby. Neither of us is spring chickens an' the way I see it, we're bein' given a second chance at happiness. Every day apart is a day wasted to my mind. So – what do you say?'

Ruby smiled through her tears. 'What I say is, it ain't the most romantic proposal I ever heard, but it'll do, an' happen you're right. Go ahead an' plan it fer as soon as you've a mind to. This house is empty now an' the sooner I can get away from it the better.'

Victor beamed with satisfaction as he held his bride-to-be tenderly in his arms.

'Are you trying to poison me or what?' Martin demanded as he slammed his snap box down in front of her.

'What do you mean?' Kate asked. 'I made those sandwiches fresh for you this morning.'

'This is your idea of fresh then, is it?' Angrily he upended the box and as the sandwiches inside spilled out onto the tablecloth, Kate gasped in horror.

The bread was green with mould and a musty smell crept into the room.

'But I . . . I don't understand,' she faltered. 'I threw

the stale bread out last night and made those with the fresh loaf.'

'Huh! If that's what you call fresh then I wouldn't like to sample what you call stale,' he ground out.

As Kate ran a hand distractedly though her limp hair his lip curled with contempt. Grabbing her by the elbow, he dragged her towards the mirror that hung above the fireplace and shook her roughly.

'*Look* at you! You're a disgrace. And when are you going to get this mess chopped off.' Snatching a handful of hair that was now almost shoulder-length again, he grimaced at her reflection in the mirror over her shoulder.

As a strangled sob escaped her, Sally, who had been cowering beneath the table, suddenly lunged forward and snapped at his ankles in defence of her mistress.

'You useless bloody mutt,' Martin growled, and bringing his foot back, he kicked out at the little dog with all his might. Sally seemed to sail across the room before connecting with the leg of a chair with sickening force. She howled in pain as Kate struggled free of his grasp and hurried to help her.

'*You bastard!*' The words broke from her lips before she had time to stop them. At that second, Nuala, who had been reading in her bedroom appeared at the stairs door, just in time to see Martin raise his hand to her sister.

'*Don't you dare!*' In seconds she had placed herself between them as she glared at him, hands on hips.

Martin slowly lowered his fist.

'Two women in the house and the pair of you put together couldn't make *one* of my Anne.' His eyes were no more than slits of rage in his red face as Nuala gathered her sister into her arms. He was stopped from going any further when Adam appeared from the front room where he had been playing with his Corgi cars.

The child looked solemnly from one to the other as his father stabbed a finger towards the stairs.

'Get yourself up to bed. *Now!*'

'Don't want to go to bed,' Adam told him defiantly. 'I hate you – and her – and I want to go back to my Nanny and Grandy. I hate livin' here.'

He suddenly fled past his father with tears streaming down his cheeks and clattered away up the stairs.

A deafening silence settled on the room until Martin snatched up his coat and headed towards the back door.

'Talk about Happy bloody Families,' he fumed and then the door slammed and he was gone.

Kate was shaking like a leaf as Nuala walked towards the highly polished sideboard and opened it. Producing a bottle of sherry with a flourish she poured some into a glass.

'You need a drink,' she stated. 'The vicar's wife gave me this to put away for Christmas but you look like you could do with a drop now.'

'But I . . . I don't drink,' Kate stuttered.

'You do tonight.' Nuala pressed the glass into her sister's hand. 'Here, get that down you.'

Kate obediently swallowed and almost choked.

'Where do you think Martin's gone?' she asked miserably.

'Don't know an' don't much care,' Nuala growled. 'With a bit of luck, to hell. Whatever happened to bring that lot on?'

As Kate told her about the mouldy sandwiches, Nuala

dropped her eyes. 'Well, you have been a bit . . .' She spread her hands as she tried to find the right words and the colour in Kate's cheeks rose with her indignation.

'I *did not* use mouldy bread!' she defended herself.

'Are you quite sure?'

Kate almost laughed at the irony of it all. Here was Nuala questioning her as if *she* were the backward one.

'The thing is,' Nuala pointed out, 'you have been a bit forgetful lately, to say the very least. I mean, you're forever forgetting something, or losing something.' Seeing Kate's enraged expression, she held up her hand and hurried on, 'I'm not saying that that excuses Martin's behaviour. I'm just saying well . . .'

'You think I'm going mad like he does, don't you?' Kate's voice was heavy with pain as Nuala squirmed and avoided her eyes.

'I don't think you're going mad exactly,' she replied slowly. 'I just think . . . perhaps you need some help.'

'Are you quite sure you'll be all right on your own?' Nuala asked yet again as she fastened her scarf around her neck.

From the depths of the armchair, Kate peeped at her above the newspaper she was reading. Nuala had been befriended by a young married woman who did the laundry for the vicarage, and tonight they were going to the Palace cinema to watch a film. Kate was glad that her sister was beginning to make friends. She'd talked about nothing but the trip to the cinema for days and was positively glowing with excitement. The only minus side to it was the fact that Kate was worried about her being out on the streets alone at night. She would have asked Martin to pick Nuala up in the car when the film finished, but for the last two days she had hardly seen him. Adam was confined to bed with a bad dose of the flu and had just about worn her out running up and down the stairs after him, so now she was looking forward to a peaceful night with the dog in front of the fire – and her nightly glass or two of sherry, of course.

Nuala shouted out, 'Goodbye!' before disappearing into the freezing night air. Kate waited until her footsteps had died away down the entry then crossing to the stairs, she listened. Not a sound from above. Sighing with contentment she went to the cupboard beneath the stairs and feeling over the shoes, she took out the bottle of sherry she had fetched from the off-licence earlier in the day.

Nervously, she glanced at the clock. It was still early evening, yet here she was about to start drinking already. Shrugging, she poured a generous measure into a glass and gulped at it greedily.

What did it matter? A few glasses of sherry eased the loneliness and the pain, and nothing seemed to hurt quite so much after that. Not Aunt Beth's or Jenny's deaths. Not Nuala's newfound independence. Not the fact that her stepson despised her. Not even the fact that she felt as if she was trapped in a loveless marriage; in fact, these days, Martin seemed to despise her.

She shuddered involuntarily as she pictured his cold eyes staring at her with disgust. At the same instant she caught sight of herself in the mirror: her hair hung limply around her face and her eyes seemed to have sunk into their sockets. The dress she was wearing swung from her shoulders and she realised with a little shock that she'd lost a tremendous amount of weight.

No wonder Martin had lost interest in her. Shame coursed through her. How could she have let herself go so badly? She had always prided herself on being neat and tidy and making the best of herself, but for months now she'd been locked in so much self-pity that she hadn't cared about anything or anyone. If she were to be *really* honest with herself, she couldn't blame Martin for his lack of interest in her. But was it too late to do something about it?

Hurrying into the kitchen, she tipped the contents of the glass down the sink, then quickly making her way upstairs to the bathroom she began to run herself a hot bath. She sprinkled a liberal amount of the lavender crystals that Ruby had bought her for her birthday into the water. Then quickly peeling off her clothes she crossed to the sink and washed her hair and wrapped it in a soft fluffy towel before climbing into the sweet-smelling water. It was then that she heard someone on the landing and Nuala shouted, 'It's only me, Kate. I had to come back because I'd forgotten my purse.' She heard the girl go into her bedroom then a few minutes later she shouted, 'I'm off again then, bye.' She listened to her clatter away down the stairs again, making enough racket to waken the dead, but then that was Nuala for you. Shortly after, the sound of the back door slamming echoed up the stairs and then there was silence again.

Lying back, Kate stared up at the ceiling and allowed her mind to go over the events of the last months. The pain as she thought of her aunt and Jenny was still there, raw and stinging. But now she found that she could smile as she thought of them, which she hoped was a step in the right direction.

Her thoughts moved on to Martin. They had never really had any private time together, apart from the few days following their wedding in Cornwall, and that hardly brought back happy memories as she remembered how he'd raped and ignored her. There had always been someone else beside themselves to worry about. Nuala, Jenny, Sally the dog, and now there was Adam. Kate had hoped that his arrival at the house would be the start of happier times for all of them, but up to now it had been quite the opposite. In fact, Martin himself seemed to dislike the child, despite the fact that Adam was his own flesh and blood and the only living memory he had left of his first wife.

As she clambered out of the bath, she cursed as she realised that she had forgotten her dressing-gown. Grabbing another dry towel from the airing cupboard she wrapped it around her and inching the door open, peeped along the landing. Adam's bedroom door was closed tight with a faint light shining from beneath it. Satisfied that he wasn't roaming about, she sprinted the length of the narrow passage to the door that led to her room. As she slipped inside, an overpowering smell took her breath away. Fumbling for the light switch, she gasped in horror at the sight that met her eyes. Every single cosmetic that she possessed was plastered about the room. Perfume dripped from the end of the dressing-table into puddles on the carpet. Panstick foundation cream, lipstick and mascara were smeared across the beautifully papered walls. Talcum powder had been sprinkled across the bed along with shampoo, and lay in a congealed mess on the intricately embroidered bedspread. The fumes from the cocktail of cosmetics floated in the air and made her cough. But it was the dressing-table mirror that her eyes were drawn to, and as she saw what was written across it her hand flew to her mouth. It read – I AM MAD!

She knew at a glance that no amount of cleaning would ever put the room back to rights. The whole place would have to be totally redecorated and she trembled to think of what Martin would say when he saw it. Leaning heavily on the edge of the dressing-table, she lowered her head and wept, and as if her thoughts had conjured him from thin air, her husband's harsh voice suddenly demanded, 'Just *what* the bloody hell is going on here?'

Turning on her heel she clutched the towel to her with one hand as she held the other out to him beseechingly.

'I . . . I don't know, I—'

'You don't know! You mean to tell me you're going to stand there and tell me you didn't do this?'

Shock registered on her face as she looked back at him. 'Of course I didn't. I went for a bath and I'd just come back to get—'

'SHUT UP!' His voice rocketed across the room and stopped her mid-sentence. Suddenly the anger seemed to drain out of him and he ran a hand distractedly through his hair. 'Oh Kate,' his voice seemed to hold the weight of the world. 'What's happening to you? I came back to apologise for being short with you earlier, to find *this* . . .' He spread his hands to encompass the wreckage that had once been his bedroom.

'Martin, *please*. Why would I do this?'

She watched helplessly as he strode to the door, where

he paused to look back at her. 'Have you been drinking again?'

Shame made colour flame into her cheeks. 'What do you mean, drinking?'

'Do you really think I'm such a fool that I haven't noticed? It's been going on for weeks, Kate, don't bother to deny it. You might have put your glass in the sink earlier on but you forgot to hide the bottle again.'

Kate gulped deep in her throat and words momentarily failed her as she stared back at him.

He tore his eyes away from her stricken face to look at the mirror behind her. 'You got that bit right at least, didn't you?'

As her eyes followed his to the words emblazoned there, she began to cry again – harsh sobs that shook her slight frame.

'I didn't write it. I swear it.'

'No? Well, who else could have done this?' he demanded. Then he sighed. 'I shall be sleeping on the settee tonight. And tomorrow . . . well, I think it's about time you got some help, don't you? Because I'll tell you now – I don't know how much more of this I can take.'

He left the room, closing the door softly behind him as she stared back in horror at the words scrawled on the mirror.

Of course I didn't do it, she told herself. *Did I?*

It was then that another thought occurred to her. *Adam!* He was the only one who could have done it – or Nuala – but she dismissed that thought immediately. Adam was the only one who'd been on his own upstairs for some time. Dear God! Surely he couldn't hate her enough to do something like this? All right, he had never pretended to like her. He had even shouted abuse at her, but she had thought that this had been caused by the fact that he was missing his grandparents.

Sinking onto the end of the bed she let her thoughts run riot. It *must* have been Adam, she decided finally. There was no other explanation.

Slowly, a little of her former spirit struggled to the surface. If it was him, then this was no more than a cry for help – and she *would* help him. From now on she'd try even harder.

Chapter Thirty-Three

'So that's about the long and the short of it.' Ruby blushed prettily as the vicar smiled with delight. 'Victor and I would be honoured if you'd bless our marriage after the register office ceremony. There's nothing I'd have liked more than to get wed in the church – but the thing is, Leonard and I were married there and it wouldn't feel right somehow to . . .'

'I quite understand, Ruby.' Paul Brown, the vicar of Shepperton Church, was a kindly man and thought highly of Ruby, whom he had known for more years than he cared to remember. 'It would be my pleasure to bless your marriage and I'd just like to say I'm thrilled for you. I hope you and Victor will enjoy many years of happy married life.'

Ruby beamed as she rose from the chair in the rectory and extended her hand. It was then that her eyes came to rest on a small sapphire necklace on the vicar's desk.

As the smile slid from her face she frowned and asked, 'May I?'

His eyes followed hers and he flushed guiltily. 'Yes – yes, of course.'

Lifting the necklace, Ruby recognised it as the one

she had given to Kate on her wedding day. 'May I ask where yer got this?' she asked, bemused.

Looking slightly embarrassed, the vicar replied, 'Actually, it was found at the side of a new grave by one of the mourners some days ago. I feel quite awful now. I've been meaning to hand it over to the police but I've been so busy that I haven't got around to it.'

'I'm glad you didn't,' Ruby told him solemnly. 'I can save you the trouble because I know who it belongs to.'

Relief washed over his features. 'All's well that ends well then. May I call upon you to return it to its rightful owner?'

Slipping it into her handbag, Ruby nodded. 'Of course. And now I shall have to be on my way. I have a million things to do before the wedding and I've taken up quite enough of your valuable time.'

'Rubbish.' All smiles again, Reverend Brown took her elbow and walked her to the door. 'Goodbye, Ruby. I'll see you on Saturday afternoon following the register office ceremony. Will you be having a reception?'

'No.' Ruby shook her head. 'Victor and I don't want any fuss and palaver at our ages. He's taking me to a hotel in Bournemouth for a couple o' days and then we'll be busy moving the rest of me stuff into his house.'

'Then good luck. Actually, I'll walk down the path with you. I need to see Martin, if he's arrived. He's digging a grave for me tonight and I need to show him where it's to be.'

Ruby bristled at the sound of the detested man's name but even so she walked quietly along at the side of the vicar until they parted at the end of the path, he to disappear into the churchyard and she to proceed to the gate.

As she continued on her way she pouted thoughtfully. What could Kate's necklace have been doing at the side of a newly dug grave? She had the urge to go and see Kate there and then, but by the time she'd reached the gates had decided against it. Martin had made it more than clear that she was no longer welcome at their home and she did have a great many things to do. Perhaps it could wait until after the wedding. With her mind made up she quickened her steps and hurried away to the florist's to order their buttonholes.

Kate started awake, blinking the sleep from her eyes as they adjusted to the light. It was mid-afternoon – she could tell. The sounds of children returning from school floated up to her from the pavement outside.

Her mouth felt dry, and as her eyes fell on the empty bottle of cheap sherry on the bedside table, a wave of shame washed over her. She could vaguely remember staggering upstairs at lunchtime, but after that everything was a blank. Sighing, she dragged herself painfully up onto her elbow.

A chink in the curtains was allowing a thin shaft of light to spill into the room, highlighting the dressing-table, and it was as she looked towards it that her breath caught in her throat. There was a message smeared across the mirror. Another one. Zombie-like, she dragged herself from the bed and went to stand in front of it. *INSANE*, it read.

Her heart began to hammer in her chest, and the lump that was growing in her throat threatened to choke her. The message was again written in lipstick – *her* lipstick – and as she lifted her hand to swipe away a lock of

389

limp dark hair that had straggled across her face, she saw that her hands were covered in it.

A loud hollow laugh echoed eerily around the bedroom and she realised with a start that the sound was coming from her. She could deny it no longer. Everything that Martin had told her was true. She *was* going mad, just as her mother had before her.

Lowering her head, she wept.

Straightening her back, Ruby glanced at the piles of orange boxes stacked neatly against one wall. She'd begged, borrowed and stolen them from the market for weeks, and now each one was packed full of things that would soon be moved to Victor's house. It was just two days to go to the wedding now and nerves were beginning to set in.

She dithered for a second wondering if she should allow herself a tea-break, and it was as she was standing there that a knock came at the back door. Quickly running her dusty hands down her pinny front she hurried to open it and smiled with delight when she saw David standing there.

'Why, this is an unexpected pleasure,' she gushed, grabbing his elbow and hauling him into the room out of the cold. 'Come on in, lad. I was just debatin' whether or not to put the kettle on, but you've made me mind up fer me now.'

As David sat down at the kitchen table she struck a match beneath the kettle and noticed that he looked concerned.

'So what's up then?' she asked bluntly as she crossed to join him.

'It's Kate,' he said. 'I just popped in to see her, and I don't mind telling you, Ruby, I'm worried sick about her.'

Ruby frowned. This time last year she had harboured a strong dislike for David, yet now she looked forward to his visits.

'What's wrong with her then?'

He shrugged. 'Just about everything, from what I could see. She's a mess, and I'd swear she's been drinking. She jumps at her own shadow and you get the feeling that she could burst into tears at the drop of a hat. And she told me that she thinks she's going mad as her mother did before her. What are we going to do about her, Ruby?'

Concern flashed across Ruby's face as she wrung her hands. 'I don't rightly know what we *can* do, lad,' she admitted. 'Martin's banned me from the house as yer know, an' I don't mind admittin' I miss her somethin' terrible. It's as plain as the nose on yer face that she's unhappy – but what can we do about it?'

Just then the kettle began to sing and rising from the table she hurried away to make the tea as David took an unopened letter from his pocket.

'I called around to give her this,' he told Ruby. 'It came for Kate to my mother's old address but she wouldn't even open it. She told me to take it away else it would go in the back of the fire like the last one.'

Taking it from him, Ruby glanced at the Birmingham postmark on the stamp. 'Who would Kate know in Brum?' she mused.

David pursed his lips. 'I have no idea. What do you think I should do with it?'

Ruby thought for a minute before saying, 'I'd open it, lad. Whoever it's from, it's obviously someone she knows, an' from where I'm standin' Kate needs all the friends she can get right now.'

Suddenly the secret she had kept from Kate was burning her and she leaned across the table to him. 'David, there's somethin' as I need to get off me chest. As far as I know, I'm the only person left alive as knows what I'm about to tell yer, but if I don't share it wi' someone soon, I reckon I'll burst.'

Taking a deep breath, she told him the secret she had kept for so long, and as she spoke David's eyes stretched wide with amazement.

When she had done he leaned back in his chair and whistled through his teeth. 'But why didn't my mother ever tell her this?' he asked.

Ruby sniffed. 'Happen Beth didn't think any good could come of it. But now I ask yer, what should I do? I can't bear to see her torture herself like this.'

'I think you should shame the devil and tell her,' David decided. 'It might get that cruel bastard she married off her back. I tell you, Ruby, he rules her with a rod of iron from what I can see of it, which is why I think she's taken to the bottle. Seems to me he should never have married her. He's still in love with his first wife and Kate has to live in her shadow. That would get any woman down, even a caring woman like Kate.'

'Yer right, lad,' Ruby conceded. 'I never wanted her to have him in the first bloody place, there's somethin' about him as sends shivers down me spine. But I reckon Kate thought that by marryin' him she could secure a good future fer Nuala an' Jenny. Huh! As things have turned out they'd have been happier stayin' here wi' me.'

He nodded in agreement just as Ruby suddenly

thought of something and hurried away to get her handbag.

'What do yer think o' this then?' Extracting the sapphire necklace from her purse, she dangled it in front of his face. 'The vicar were goin' to hand it over to the police but I spotted it an' recognised it straight away. It were my mam's – she gave it to me on my weddin' day, and I gave it to Kate, who's like me own flesh an' blood, on hers.'

'Where did the vicar get it?'

'Ah, well – that's what's so strange. The vicar reckons as it were found at the side of a newly dug grave. An' who digs the graves at Coton, eh?'

'Martin! But why would he have had Kate's necklace on him?' David gasped.

Ruby sighed. 'Your guess is as good as mine, but I happen to know that Kate thinks she's losing things. What if it's *him* takin' 'em an' tryin' to drive her mad?'

'Oh, now steady on, Ruby, that's taking things a bit far,' David protested.

'Is it?' Ruby stared at him. 'Then *you* explain what he'd be doin' wi' her necklace.'

He scratched his head as he tried to think of some plausible reason and when he couldn't Ruby nodded smugly.

'See what I mean now? You just mark me words, there's somethin' dodgy afoot here.' She thought of the film *Gaslight*, in which a woman is made to feel she is going insane by a scheming husband. Ruby had seen it at the pictures, and never forgotten the menace of it.

The clock on the mantelshelf suddenly chimed one, and David rose reluctantly.

'Look, Ruby, I shall have to go. I'm late back to work as it is, but I'll come and see you tonight and we'll decide what's to be done. Meantime, you get on with preparing for your wedding.'

'No, don't come tonight,' she told him. 'I reckon yer right. It's time Kate knew the truth so I think I'll go an' get it over with once an' for all.'

'Good for you,' he told her approvingly. 'And good luck.'

She saw him to the door but long after he'd gone she paced the floor in a state of high agitation. Every sense she had screamed at her that something was terribly wrong, but what could she do about it?

It came to her in a flash. She would go and see Martin before visiting Kate. Perhaps if she confronted him and let him know that she wasn't going to give up on Kate, he might go a little easier on her. If she *was* going to see Martin, then she needed to see him alone – and where better than the churchyard? The vicar had told her that Martin was digging a grave that night so she'd go there and give him a piece of her mind. Never one to put off till tomorrow what could be done today, Ruby instantly felt better now that she'd decided on her plan of action. Luckily, she had agreed not to see Victor again until the day of their wedding, so no one need be any the wiser. With her mind made up, she continued with her packing.

'Kate, where are you?' Nuala's voice rang through the house and seconds later she heard her sister shuffling down the stairs. Nuala stifled her shock as Kate appeared. Her eyes were sunk deep into her face and her hair was wild and dishevelled.

'Don't you think you ought to tidy yerself up a bit,' the younger girl suggested softly. 'Martin will be back from work soon an' he'll be none too pleased if he sees you lookin' like that. What's more, there's no dinner on the table . . . An' where's Adam?'

'His grandma picked him up from school and took him to have tea at her house,' Kate answered dully.

Nuala chewed on her lip. 'Martin won't be none too pleased when he hears that neither,' she warned.

Kate shrugged her thin shoulders as she hugged her crumpled cardigan about her then shuffled away into the kitchen.

'Have you seen Sally?' she asked as she saw that the dog wasn't in her basket.

Throwing her coat across the back of a chair, Nuala shook her head. 'Can't say as I have. But then I've only just come in from work, ain't I? Where was she the last time you saw her?'

Kate tried to think. 'She was curled up in front of the fire when I went up for a lie-down a couple of hours ago. I know she was because David called in to see me in his lunch-hour and I remember him fussing her.'

'Hope he didn't let her out when he left,' Nuala remarked. Seeing the panic appear in her sister's eyes she tried to calm her. 'Look, you check upstairs an' I'll check the garden an' down here.'

Five minutes later Kate was back in the small lounge. Nuala had disappeared off up the garden and the draught from the open back door was making the fire flicker and spit. Kate stood as if she was cast in stone as a cold finger of fear crept up her spine. She could hear Nuala calling Sally's name and then suddenly there was silence and for no reason that she could explain, Kate had the urge to cry.

Nuala appeared straight-faced seconds later with Sally hanging limply in her arms. Kate knew that she was dead.

Nuala hovered in the doorway, uncertain of what to say until Kate crossed to her and took the dog from her.

'She were lyin' by a saucer full o' food. It must have been rat poison. One o' the neighbours must have put it out,' Nuala said helplessly.

Sally was stiff and cold and froth had matted the fur around her mouth. Her eyes were open and staring and as Kate hugged her beloved pet to her she felt yet again as if her heart were about to break.

Nuala wrung her hands and looked on until Martin suddenly appeared across her shoulder.

'Just what the hell do you think you're doing, standing here with the door wide open?' he barked. 'You wouldn't be so damn keen if you had to pay the gas bill . . .' His voice trailed away as he caught sight of Kate and Sally.

'Oh for God's sake. What *now*?' There was no compassion in his voice, and Kate's eyes when she raised them to his were full of hatred.

'*You did this, didn't you?*'

Martin's mouth gaped open but before he could reply she hurried on, 'Don't think I didn't know you couldn't stand her. It showed every time you so much as looked at her. You would do anything to hurt me, wouldn't you?'

'Don't be so bloody melodramatic,' he cried. 'Why would I do this?'

'*Because you hate me.* Because I can never hold a candle to Anne in your eyes. Don't bother to deny it. I knew the very first week I married you that I'd made the biggest mistake of my life. You're trying to break me – drive me mad – but I'll tell you this. *You won't succeed.'*

Crossing to Nuala, she placed Sally's lifeless body in her arms then without another word she headed to the stairs door and ran up to her room. Only then did the tears come.

Ruby shuddered as she drew her coat around her and marched down Shepperton Street. The pavements were like glass even though it was only eight o'clock at night. All day she had waited for this chance to confront Martin, and now she was eager to get it over and done with. The streets were almost deserted but that didn't surprise her. Most people had more sense than to wander about in this weather unless it was absolutely necessary.

In no time at all she had reached the gate to the church-yard and as she pushed it open, it squeaked in protest. The church was in darkness and she had to pick her way through the gravestones. When a bat suddenly swooped from a nearby tree, Ruby jumped. She paused to allow her heart to steady and it was as she was standing there, with her breath floating in front of her on the chilly air, that she saw a faint light glowing in the darkness. Guessing that this would be the light that Martin placed on the side of the grave while he was digging, she started towards it. Sure enough, as she approached she heard the sound of a pick slamming into the frozen ground and the sound of his laboured breathing.

When she was almost within the circle of light she paused to draw herself up to her full height. Although she was nervous she knew that she mustn't show it to Martin. She must be strong for Kate's sake.

'Martin – I'd like a word.' When her voice sliced through the eerie silence she had the satisfaction of seeing the man almost jump out of his skin.

His pick stopped in mid-air as his head snapped around to see who it was. He peered into the darkness and when he saw Ruby standing there, he visibly relaxed.

'What do you want?' His voice was as cold as the earth he was digging.

'I just told you what I want,' Ruby answered, equally as coldly. 'I need to talk to you – about Kate.'

He laughed; a bitter sound that echoed around the deserted churchyard. 'Well, you certainly choose your time and place, I'll give you that. Did it *have* to be here?'

'Where else could I have bloody caught yer?' she retaliated. 'I'm banned from your home and I hardly think you'd appreciate me turning up at your other place of work, would yer?'

Sighing heavily he slung his pick up onto the side of the grave and heaved himself out of the gaping hole.

'Say what you've come to say and then clear off,' he growled. 'I've better things to do than stand here talking to a silly interfering old woman.'

Now Ruby bristled and any nervousness she had felt was swallowed up by anger. 'Like bein' at home an' tryin' to drive yer poor wife mad, eh?' she spat.

'Have you been on the cheap sherry?' Martin quipped as a flicker of amusement played across his handsome face.

'No, lad. I leave that to Kate. After all, it's the only way she can escape from your bloody cruelty, ain't it?'

'What's *that* supposed to mean?' Martin's colour was rising with his temper.

'It means that I know what yer up to, yer lousy bugger. It were as plain as the nose on yer face that yer regretted marryin' Kate from the word go, so happen you're tryin' to drive the poor girl away. Or drive her mad . . .'

'It's *you* that's mad.' Martin's voice was dangerously low and he took a threatening step towards her, but Ruby would not be intimidated, not now that she had come this far.

'How do yer explain this then?' Snatching Kate's necklace from her pocket she dangled it in front of his face, and as the dim light from the lamp caught the sapphire it sparkled as black as midnight. 'How come it were found at the side of a newly dug grave, eh? Does Kate think she's mislaid this an' all, like all the other daft things she thinks she's doin'? Well, let me tell yer now, I'm on to yer an' I know there's somethin' fishy afoot. I'll tell yer somethin' else as well, so listen good. I'll not stop houndin' yer till I find out what it is.'

Martin's hands clenched into fists of rage as fear coursed through him. The silly old cow was getting a little too nosy for comfort and he was going to have to shut her up.

Quick as a flash he bent, and the next second the evil-looking pick was tight in his hand. Realising his intention, Ruby gasped and stepped back, dropping the necklace, which lodged against a clod of earth halfway down the grave and lay winking there. The next second she was falling and she landed painfully in a heap at the bottom of the grave. Struggling, she tried to heave herself up onto her elbow. She longed to cry out but the fall had badly winded her and all that escaped from her mouth was a whimper.

She raised terrified eyes to the moon, which had just sailed from behind the black clouds, but then the comforting light was gone as Martin leaped into the grave at the side of her. As he landed lightly on both feet his voice cut through the silence.

'You would have done well to mind your own business.'

She watched helplessly as the pick was raised high above his head before it hurtled towards her, and then she knew no more.

Dropping the pick, Martin stared down at Ruby's lifeless body as fear turned his blood to ice. Wiping his bloody hands down the front of his trousers, fear lent speed to his limbs as he sprang nimbly from the grave and grabbed up his shovel. In no time at all, the dead woman was covered in a blanket of cold earth – hidden for ever as all his other victims had been.

Breathless now, he glanced around to make sure that all was as it should be. It was then that his glance fell on Ruby's bag at the side of the grave. She must have dropped it when she fell in. Cursing softly he collected it, together with his tools, before hurrying away to his tiny shed in the corner of the churchyard. It was only when he got there and fumbled with the padlock that he realised he was covered in blood. There were no more clean clothes stored in the shed – just a pile of discarded garments, each bearing the life blood of the whores he had despatched to the next world. A growl rose in his throat. His mouth set in a grim line, as he threw the tools and the bag into a far corner. All he could do was hope that Kate and Nuala would be in bed when he got home, then he could clean himself in peace.

His hopes were dashed when he entered his back yard to see a light shining through the back room curtains. Damn! It would probably be Nuala waiting up for him again. She'd taken to doing that of late though he had tried to tactfully tell her that it was unnecessary. Standing there in the darkness, he wondered what he should do. Had it been warmer, he would have cleared off until she was forced to go to bed, but as it was he was frozen to the bone and dog weary. Deciding to brazen it out, he pushed the back door open, stormed through the small kitchen and the back room past Nuala who was curled up in a ball on the settee.

'Martin, is that you?' she asked sleepily. 'Would you like me to make you a cup of tea? You must be—'

'No, I *don't* want you to make me a cup of tea. Why don't you just get yourself off to bed,' he snarled.

Jolted awake by his nasty tone, she stared at his retreating figure. Was that blood she had seen smeared down the front of his trousers? Had he hurt himself, digging the grave? She had no way to be sure, for at that second the stairs door clicked shut behind him and she was left with a thoughtful frown on her face.

401

Chapter Thirty-Four

Smart as a new pin, Victor nervously paced up and down the corridor of the register office as he waited for his bride to arrive. He had no doubt that when she did, she would take his breath away. His Ruby was a smart-looking woman for her age, and he considered himself to be a very lucky man.

David and Rebecca, who were going to be his witnesses, were trying their hardest to stop their two little girls from fratching, but every now and again David would flash Victor a reassuring smile.

The groom's eyes flew to the door every time someone entered but up to now he had been disappointed each time.

'She's going to be late at this rate,' he fretted as he glanced at his wristwatch.

David grinned. 'It's a bride's prerogative to be late on her wedding day,' he pointed out. 'And anyway, at your age you should know that anything worth having is worth waiting for, Victor.'

David smiled at his wife, who returned his smile. He'd been pleasantly surprised when Rebecca had agreed to attend the wedding with him, which just went to show

how much she had changed in the last few months. They were getting on a lot better since he'd decided that from now on *he* would wear the trousers, and he just wished that he had done it years ago while his mother was still alive. Still, he thought, better late than never.

At that moment a door in the corridor opened and a starry-eyed young couple spilled from the room where the marriages took place, followed by their guests who were all in high good spirits. The registrar appeared moments later and approached Victor with a smile on his face.

'Are we all ready then, Mr Skinner?' he enquired.

Victor tugged at his starched white collar and flushed. 'I am, but the bride seems to be draggin' her feet, son. She ain't put in an appearance yet.'

'I see.' Now it was the registrar's turn to glance at his wristwatch. 'Well, we've no need to panic just yet. I'm sure she'll be here any second. The next marriage isn't for half an hour or so. I'll be in that room there. Just give me a knock when she arrives and we'll proceed.'

With a friendly nod he disappeared back the way he had come as Victor hurried to the window and peered worriedly up and down the street outside. It was bustling with shoppers but there was no sign of Ruby.

'It ain't like Ruby to be late,' he muttered, unable to keep the concern from his voice. 'You don't reckon as summat's happened to her, do yer?'

'Of course it hasn't.' David patted him on the shoulder. 'Look – you keep your eye on my girls, Victor, and I'll go and have a look for her, eh? I've no doubt she'll be tearing along the street in a right old lather because she's late.'

403

Some minutes later he reappeared with a frown on his face. Ruby was almost fifteen minutes late for her own wedding and now even he was beginning to get concerned.

'Any sign of her?' Victor asked hopefully. When David shook his head, Victor seemed to shrink. 'She's bloody gone an' stood me up at the altar, ain't she?'

'What a load of rubbish.' Rebecca addressed him for the first time. 'For a start-off, Ruby worships the ground you walk on, Victor. There is *no* way she would miss today. It's all she's talked of for months. And I hate to remind you, but there isn't an altar here. We're in the register office.'

'Same difference,' Victor sniffed.

Five agonisingly long minutes later, the registrar stuck his head round the door. 'Any luck?'

When the wedding party shook their heads in unison he sighed. 'Then I'm very sorry, but I'm afraid I shall have to prepare for the next wedding. I'm sure that there's some perfectly good reason why the bride didn't arrive. Perhaps you could re-schedule the wedding for another time?'

Tight-lipped, David nodded and taking Victor's elbow he led him towards the door, closely followed by Rebecca and the children.

He herded them all towards the car, which was parked only yards away. 'Let's get ourselves round to Ruby's and find out what's gone wrong, eh?'

Victor had gone a ghastly shade of grey and was almost unrecognisable as the happy smiling man he had been less than an hour ago.

As they were speeding towards Shepperton Street,

David asked, 'Was Ruby in good spirits when you last saw her, Victor?'

'Aye, she was, though that were three days ago. She refused to see me after that till today, said it were bad luck for the bride to see the groom afore the weddin'. I tried to tell her that only counted fer the night before, but she reckoned as she had too much to do an' she said I'd soon be seein' her every day so I let her have her way.'

'Well, I saw her on Thursday and she was bright as ninepence then,' David told him. By then they were passing beneath the Coton Arches and seconds later had turned into Shepperton Street. The minute the car drew to a halt, Victor almost tumbled out of it in his haste to get to the front door. He hammered on it loudly but there was no reply. Scowling, he then strode up the narrow white-washed entry with David and his family close on his heels. The first thing they saw when they opened the back gate were the tightly drawn curtains.

'Tain't like Ruby to leave the curtains shut,' Victor fretted. 'Yer don't think as she's took bad, do yer?'

'There's only one way to find out,' David told him solemnly and elbowing past him he began to bang on the door. When there was no reply he tried the handle and gasped when the door swung open.

Stepping tentatively inside, he looked around the room. An empty teacup and plate were on the table. There was curdled milk in the pressed glass milk jug and the fire had burned out, spilling ash all across the tiled hearth, but there was no sign of Ruby.

'Ruby, where are yer?' Victor's voice from right behind

him made him jump. They all listened for the sound of Ruby clattering across the landing or down the stairs but heard only silence.

'Tain't like Ruby either, not to make the fire up first thing,' Victor said fearfully.

'Seeing as she wasn't going to be here she probably didn't bother,' David sensibly replied.

Victor shook his head. 'Naw, there's more to it than that. Neat as a new pin, my Ruby is. Even if she didn't set another fire she'd have cleaned the grate out.'

Rebecca pushed past them to check the upstairs but when she came back down she shook her head. 'The bed's not been slept in, by the looks of it. Her wedding suit is hanging on the wardrobe door and her hat and everything is all laid out on the chair ready for her to get into them. I can't understand it.'

David swivelled round and headed for the back door. 'I'm going to have a word with the neighbour. Find out when she last saw her. Ruby would never go out and leave the door unlocked unless she was just popping out for a few minutes.'

Dropping heavily onto a chair, Victor waited anxiously until David reappeared some minutes later.

'It seems that no one's seen hide nor hair of her for a couple of days. I don't know what to make of it, Victor. What do you think we should do?'

'There's only one thing we *can* do,' Victor told him heavily. 'Happen we'd best phone the coppers an' report her missin'. Somethin's badly amiss – I can feel it in me bones. I'd stake me life that Ruby wouldn't have stood me up wi'out good reason.'

David once more hurried from the room to do what

Victor suggested. When he had gone, Rebecca crossed to Victor and placed a reassuring hand on his arm.

'Try not to worry too much,' she murmured. 'I'm sure there'll be some plausible explanation for all this.'

Victor's head wagged from side to side and in that moment he looked like an old, old man. 'This should have been one o' the happiest days o' me life. It's funny when yer come to think of it, ain't it? What I mean is, when I met Ruby I thought me luck had changed. I should have known that it were too good to be true. She were such a lovely woman an' I'd have made her so happy.'

'Stop talking like that,' Rebecca scolded. 'You're behaving as if Ruby's dead. Why, she'll probably walk in that door bright as a button any minute.'

'She won't.' Victor's voice was laden with sorrow. 'Don't ask me how I know but I just feel as I'll never see her again.' So saying, he dropped his face into his wrinkled hands and cried as if his heart would break.

'David, would you *please* stop pacing up and down. You're making me dizzy. You'll wear a hole in the carpet at this rate.'

Pausing in front of his wife, David shook his head. It was the day after Ruby's disappearance and he was worn out. The police had scoured Ruby's house from top to bottom but found nothing amiss. There was no sign of a struggle or a forced entrance. It appeared that Ruby had just walked out and vanished into thin air.

'I just keep thinking there must be *something* I missed when I visited her. Something that she might have said that would give us a clue as to where she could be,' he said for at least the hundredth time.

'Whipping yourself won't make you remember,' his wife sensibly pointed out. 'While you're so wound up, you won't be able to think straight. Why don't you let me pour you a whisky? It might calm you down a bit.'

David forced a weak smile. Rebecca had been surprisingly supportive throughout the whole sorry episode, but then she had changed a lot over the last months and thankfully for the better.

While she hurried away to get his drink he resumed his pacing as his mind worked overtime. Rebecca had just re-entered the room when he suddenly exclaimed, '*Kate!* Ruby was unhappy with the way Martin's been treating her and she mentioned she was going to see her that evening. That's what we mainly talked about. I wonder if she did go there?'

Rebecca shrugged. 'What if she did? I can't see what that could have to do with Ruby's disappearance.'

He shrugged. 'You're probably right. But if she *did* go to see her, Kate might have been the last person she talked to. Perhaps she said something to her that might give us an inkling as to where she's gone?'

Rebecca looked dubious, but now that the idea had occurred to him, David had to chase it up. 'Sorry, love, I shall have to go and see her. I shan't rest now until I do. *You do* understand, don't you?'

Placing his untouched drink on the coffee-table she nodded. 'I doubt they'll be that pleased to see you at this time on a Sunday night, but if you feel you must, then go. Knowing you, you'll not get a wink of sleep unless you do.'

He pecked her gratefully on the cheek before turning away to get his coat. The roads were like a skating rink and he shuddered as he drove along, a picture of Victor's heartbroken face flashing before his eyes. The journey from Hinckley to Nuneaton took twice as long as it should have as the car swerved dangerously across the road on the black ice, but at last he pulled up outside of Martin's home in Heath End Road.

It was then that a terrible thought occurred to him. Would Kate even be aware that Ruby was missing? Because her disappearance had not been reported until Saturday it would not be in the papers until Monday, which meant he would have the unenviable task of telling her. He took a few moments to compose himself, then with his mouth set in a tight line he climbed from the car and rapped on the front door.

'Keep your hair on,' someone shouted rudely, then a light shone through the curtains and he heard the bolts on the door being drawn back.

Nuala peered into the darkness and when she saw him standing there she scowled as she tightened the belt on her dressing-gown.

'What do *you* want at this time o' night?' she demanded. 'We was just about to go to bed. No doubt you've woken the whole street wi' yer bangin'.'

'Sorry, Nuala. I'm afraid it's important.' Competely forgetting his manners, David elbowed by her and rushed through the front room into the back parlour. Kate and Martin both looked up from their seats on the settee as he entered, and Kate paled as if she somehow sensed he had brought her yet more bad news.

Ignoring the frown on Martin's face, David hunkered

down and took Kate's warm hands in his own cold ones. Gently he told her of Ruby's disappearance and as the story unfolded, Kate's face crumpled.

'So why have you come here at this time of night to tell *us* about it?' Martin snapped. 'Couldn't it have waited until a more godly hour?'

Ignoring him, David centred his attention on Kate as he asked softly, 'Did Ruby come to see you on the night she went missing, love?'

She shook her head miserably.

'Are you quite sure?'

'Of course I'm sure,' Kate sniffed through her tears.

It was then that an idea occurred to David and he rose and faced Martin again. Unable to keep the dislike he felt for him from showing on his face, David left Kate to Nuala's ministrations and asked, 'Could I have a word? In there.' Thumbing towards the front room he cast one last worried glace at Kate and then turned on his heel and retraced his steps with Martin close behind him.

Once the door was closed behind them, David looked Martin in the eye. 'Did Ruby come to see you on Thursday?' he asked without preamble.

Martin glowered at him. 'No, she didn't. Why should she? We haven't seen her for weeks and if you want to know the truth, we didn't want to. Ruby is too fond of interfering in other people's business and I told her to keep away.'

When David stared him out he looked slightly uncomfortable and dropped his eyes.

'She was coming to see Kate because she wasn't happy about the way you're treating her.' David's voice was ice cold. There was no pretence any more as he stared at

Martin with detestation. 'I happen to know that the vicar had told her you were digging a grave that night so I wondered if she wouldn't have come to see you first. You must be blind if you can't see that Kate appears to be on the edge of a nervous breakdown. Ruby wasn't happy about it, and I may as well tell you – neither am I!'

'I've already told you, haven't I? She didn't come anywhere near me and now I'll tell you the same as I told that interfering old cow. *Get out and stay out!* What goes on between my own four walls with my own wife is nobody else's business.'

Striding to the front door, Martin threw it open, letting in an icy gust of wind. *'Now get out and don't darken my door again!'*

Drawing himself up to his full height, David walked calmly to the door where he paused to stare into Martin's livid face. 'You haven't seen the last of me. Be warned – I shall be watching you. There's something funny going on here and I intend to find out what it is.'

He had barely stepped across the threshold when the door banged shut resoundingly behind him.

Once in the car again he peered blindly ahead. Every instinct he had screamed at him that Martin knew more about Ruby's disappearance than he was letting on. There was nothing he could do about it for now, but just as he had warned – he would be watching.

'Kate, will you *please* eat this sandwich I've made for you?' Concern lent an edge to Nuala's voice as she pressed the plate into her sister's hands. 'You're thin as a rake,' she groaned. 'If you don't eat something soon you'll slip through a gap in the pavement. Starving

411

yourself to death ain't going to make Ruby turn up again, is it?'

'I'm fine,' Kate told her dully, but Nuala knew that she was lying. Since the death of Sally and Ruby's untimely disappearance, Kate seemed to have put up a shutter that no one could penetrate – even Martin. Not that he tried. He no longer even attempted to be a loving husband but ignored her completely. Sometimes she felt that she was living in a battleground. Martin was barely civil to anyone any more, even Adam, who was growing more and more resentful of them all.

Nuala shrugged her arms into her coat, keeping an eye on her sister all the time. 'Are you quite sure that you'll be all right on your own if I go to work? I could always phone Angela and tell her that you need me here.'

Kate smiled at Nuala's use of the vicar's wife's first name. Nuala was becoming more and more confident as time passed, which gave Kate one less thing to worry about at least.

'I shall be perfectly all right. Now go on. Get off or else you'll be late.'

Nuala hovered by the door. 'You er . . . you won't get doin' nothin' daft, like hittin' the bottle again, will you?'

Kate stared into the fire. 'I haven't had a drink for weeks,' she said. She didn't add that the urge was there all the time. At least a drink had made her forget her heartbreak, if only for short spells at a time.

Satisfied, Nuala gave her a cheery wave and stepped out into the bitter early December afternoon.

Loneliness closed around Kate like a cloak and suddenly the ticking of the clock was the only sound to be heard. Martin was at work. Adam was at school and now there was no visit from Ruby to look forward to, and no Sally to curl up on her lap and lick away her tears. Ruby had been missing for over a week now and Kate was terrified that she might never see her again. The police had questioned both herself and Martin, and anyone else who had known Ruby, but so far their enquiries had drawn a blank.

The only bright spot on the horizon was the change in Nuala. It was as if they had undergone a role reversal, for now it was Nuala who looked after *her*. She had taken to doing almost all the cooking. She would painstakingly prepare all Martin's favourite food and Kate knew that she did it so that he wouldn't have a reason to take his frustrations out on her. Nuala also now did most of the washing and ironing too, going to great trouble to make sure that every single item of Martin's was ironed just so. She would send Kate off to bed, fussing over her like a mother hen, then sit up and wait for Martin so that she could make him some supper or a last hot drink. Kate was more grateful than Nuala could know, yet didn't have the strength to say so. It was as if all the stuffing had been knocked out of her and now all she could do was lurch unsteadily from one tragedy to another.

More and more she found herself thinking of Matthew and wishing with all her heart that she had taken him up on his offer when he'd asked her to marry him. But then she would think of Jenny and what he had done to Nuala, and her heart would harden against him all over again. It all seemed such a long time ago. Matthew was probably married by now. He would never know that he'd briefly been the father of

413

a beautiful baby girl. Thoughts of Jenny brought fresh tears burning into her eyes and in no time at all she was sobbing uncontrollably.

Glancing around the churchyard to make sure that she was alone, Nuala went straight to the little shed in the corner that housed all of Martin's tools. Fumbling in her handbag she produced the spare key that would unlock it and grinned with satisfaction as she thought how pleased he would be when he knew what she was doing. She could only imagine that there must be many dirty outfits inside, for lately he'd taken to coming home in clean clothes after he had dug a grave, leaving the dirty ones here. Imagining his pleasure when he saw that she had washed and ironed them all, she hurriedly unlocked the door and stepped into the tiny enclosed space.

A pick and shovel leaned drunkenly against one wall, and just as she had thought, a pile of muddy clothes were stacked in an untidy heap in another. Producing a big brown carrier bag she started to lift the dirty clothes and fold them inside it. A lot of them had dried brown stains on them, which she took for mud. She had packed no more than three items when she noticed a darker patch on a pair of trousers. Carrying them to the doorway, she peered at them in the misty daylight and frowned. It looked like a bloodstain. Her stomach did a somersault but then she grinned with relief. Martin had probably just cut himself while digging the grave. Funny, he must be doing that quite often, since he had had blood on him last week, she could have sworn it. Stuffing the trousers into the bag along with the other clothing, she once again bent to the pile on the floor. It was then that her eyes settled on the handbag, which she instantly recognised as Ruby's. But what would Martin be doing with Ruby's bag, and why would it be in his shed?

As her heart started to race she stood there with the bag clutched in her cold hand. Then instantly making a decision, she emptied the carrier bag and placed all the clothes and the handbag back exactly where she had found them. She had to get away, quickly, before Martin could know that she'd been there.

Her hand was shaking so much that she could barely pull the shed door to and close the padlock, but at last she managed it and then she scuttled away across the churchyard like a thief in the night. Once in the shelter of the church doorway she allowed her heart to settle into a steadier rhythm. *Martin* had Ruby's handbag. As the implications of this sank in she made a calculated decision. She must keep this secret to herself. No one must know. Not yet.

Fingers steepled beneath his chin, David stared down at the unopened envelope on his desk. All around him people were tapping away on typewriters but he was oblivious to the sound as he concentrated on the letter. It was almost the middle of December now and there was still no sign of Ruby. The town was teeming with police though there seemed little point in them being there. Most women knew better than to venture out at night alone now unless it was absolutely necessary.

No matter how he tried, David couldn't rid himself of the feeling that Martin was somehow responsible for Ruby's disappearance. And then there was this letter. It had been burning a hole in his pocket. Who could be writing to Kate unless it was some friend from her past? But that made no sense. Kate had originated from Durham and the postmark on the letter was Birmingham.

Unable to contain his curiosity for a second longer, he slit the envelope open and as his eyes scanned the letter inside his face broke into the first smile for weeks. So Kate *did* have a friend. Suddenly, he didn't feel guilty any more about opening her mail. From where he was standing, Kate had never needed a friend more than she did right now. Lifting the phone he quickly dialled the number at the bottom of the page.

'You've done *what*?'

The girls were kicking each other underneath the table and after glaring at them sternly, David looked guiltily at his wife.

'I opened Kate's letter,' he repeated. 'The way I see it, desperate times call for desperate measures. It was from a chap in Birmingham who used to live by Kate back in Durham. Between you and me, it sounded like he's head over heels in love with her. It's just a pity she didn't marry him instead of that bastard she's hooked up with now.'

When Rebecca glared at him he flushed and looked towards the girls apologetically. 'Sorry, girls. I didn't mean to swear.'

They both giggled and turned their attention back to their food as David leaned towards Rebecca.

'I rang him,' he told her. 'The bloke's name is Matthew and he sounded really nice. He was very concerned about Kate when I told him how she was.'

His wife's fork stopped in mid-air halfway to her mouth as she asked, 'Is he going to come and see her?'

'Yes, I think so,' David replied through a mouthful of roast beef.

Rebecca looked unsure. 'Then all I can say is, "on your own head be it". It's pretty obvious that if Kate had wanted to see him she would have got in touch with him herself. I just hope you haven't opened up a can of worms. She is married now, after all, for better or worse.'

For worse, David thought to himself, but he did not say the words.

Chapter Thirty-Five

Kate blinked awake to find Martin standing beside her chair, a look of pure hatred plastered across his handsome face.

'Oh, sorry, I must have fallen asleep. What time is it?' she asked groggily as she tried to focus on him.

'It's time you pulled yourself together, if you ask me,' he spat. 'Just *look* at the state of you. It's five o'clock in the afternoon and here you are, still in your dressing-gown. You haven't even bothered to brush your hair. You're a disgrace, Kate, I don't mind telling you. I'm beginning to wonder what I ever saw in you in the first place. When Anne was alive I came home to a cooked dinner and a clean house every evening.'

'The house *is* clean, and there *is* some dinner. Nuala's cooking it now,' she defended herself.

His lip curled back from his teeth. 'Shouldn't it be *you* doing it? You are supposed to be my wife.'

At that moment, Nuala appeared in the kitchen doorway looking neat and tidy. 'Don't get on at her, Martin,' she pleaded. 'Kate isn't well; she's tired all the time. I keep telling her to get herself to the doctor's but she won't.'

'Huh! It's not a doctor she needs but a good swift kick up the backside. And where's Adam?' he demanded, and Nuala lowered her head and shuffled uncomfortably from foot to foot.

'His grandma came round earlier to collect him so that he could go and stay with them for a few days. Just until Kate's feeling better,' she explained nervously.

His hands balled into fists of frustration. 'That's *all* I needed to hear, with Christmas just around the corner.' His angry eyes settled back on Kate. 'This is all your fault. No wonder the child doesn't want to stay here. No one would ever know it's almost Christmas, looking round this place. You haven't even put up a tree. Anne would have had the house looking like Santa's grotto by now. There would have been pretty paper chains hanging from the ceiling, fairy lights on the tree, and the Christmas pudding would have been soaking in brandy for weeks.'

'I'll put the tree up tonight after I've washed up if you tell me where the trimmings are.' Nuala tried to placate him, but he was having none of it.

'You shouldn't have to do it,' he roared. '*She's* supposed to be the lady of the house, but if it weren't for you, this whole place would have gone to pot by now.'

Suddenly unable to bear any more, Kate rose unsteadily to her feet and began to stagger towards the stairs door, sobbing uncontrollably.

'I'll bring you a nice hot drink up in a minute.' Nuala's voice carried across the room to her as Kate hauled herself up the steep, narrow staircase. She could understand why Martin was so angry, but she was just so tired all the time. And yet no matter how long she slept, she still got up each morning heavy-headed and feeling as if she hadn't been to bed.

Dropping onto the mattress she listened to Nuala and Martin talking downstairs. They sounded like an old married couple. Turning on her side she closed her eyes, and in no time at all she was fast asleep again.

It was the day before Christmas Eve and it had just started to snow, much to the delight of the children who were playing on the pavement in Heath End Road. They paused in their play to watch a car cruise slowly along, the driver obviously looking for a door number. When it came to a halt in front of Kate's house the children quickly lost interest and resumed their game of tig.

The man who climbed from the car checked the house number on the scrap of paper he held in his hand then strode purposefully to the door and knocked.

Seconds later the front door inched open and Nuala peered out at him. Her mouth dropped open as she glanced fearfully up at the bedroom window above them.

'What do *you* want?' The words came out on a hiss.

Slightly taken aback, Matthew told her, 'I've come to see Kate – and you too, of course.'

'Well, we don't want see *you*, so clear off an' don't come back!'

Matthew blinked, scarcely able to believe he had heard aright. 'Look,' he said gently, 'I know it must be a shock, me just turning up out of the blue like this, so let's start again, eh?'

Nuala's colour had risen, giving her a blotchy appearance that was far from flattering, and she seemed nervous

420

and on edge. 'How did yer find us?' she demanded, none too politely.

'That's rather irrelevant, don't you think?' Matthew retorted. 'The thing is I did find you and now if you don't mind – I'd like to see Kate.'

'She ain't in,' Nuala lied glibly.

Matthew frowned. 'Then when will she be in?'

'Not till late tonight.' Nuala's heart was beating like a drum as panic washed over her like a tide. If Kate and Matthew should get together, then all hell might break loose. Somehow she *had* to stop it happening – and she was prepared to lie through her teeth to make sure that it didn't.

Disappointment was evident on Matthew's face as he stared back at her. He had the distinct impression that she was lying, but what could he do? He could hardly barge his way in and refuse to budge until Kate put in an appearance.

'Would it more convenient if I called back at some other time?' he suggested.

Nuala's head snapped from side to side. 'Kate doesn't want to see you so you'd have a wasted journey,' she said harshly.

'But why? What have I done? I've written to her time and time again but she's chosen to ignore all my letters.'

'So take the hint then,' Nuala snapped peevishly. 'Kate is a happily married woman now an' she don't need no reminders of her past. Just think yourself lucky as Martin ain't home right now else yer might be goin' away wi' more than a flea in yer ear.'

Realising that she wasn't going to budge, Matthew took yet another scrap of paper from his pocket and

421

offered it to her. 'In that case, perhaps you wouldn't mind giving her this then. It's the phone number of where I'm staying in Birmingham. She can reach me on that most any time.'

Snatching it from his hand, Nuala began to back into the room and the next moment the door was shut firmly in his face.

Matthew's shoulders sagged. Truthfully he hadn't expected them to roll out the red carpet for him, not after all the ignored letters, but he *had* hoped for a civil welcome at least.

Brushing away the snow that had settled on his broad shoulders, he wearily plodded back to the car and climbed in.

Nuala watched him through the crisp, white net curtain, scarcely daring to breathe until she saw his shiny red car pull away from the kerb. Then she began to tremble in reaction as she wondered what the outcome of his visit might have been, if Kate hadn't been upstairs in bed fast asleep. It hardly bore thinking about and she had to struggle very hard to compose herself. After some minutes when she was sure that he had really gone, she hurried into the middle room and paused at the stairs door to listen. When only silence greeted her she crossed to the fire and, screwing the scrap of paper into a tiny ball, she tossed it into the heart of the fire, smiling with satisfaction when the hungry flames devoured it. Then she went slowly into the kitchen and put the kettle on to boil. It was time for Kate's afternoon tea.

Christmas was a sorry affair. Adam stayed at his grandparents' and Nuala spent most of her time down at the vicarage with the vicar and his wife. Angela had been unwell and Nuala was taking care of her, which meant that Martin and Kate were left pretty much to entertain themselves for the majority of the time.

Kate chose to stay in the bedroom as much as she could while Martin curled up in front of the fire and watched the Christmas films on the black and white television set.

The only visitors they had were David and Rebecca who called on Christmas morning with their girls to deliver their presents.

Kate cringed with embarrassment, deeply aware of how drab she looked in comparison to Rebecca, who as usual looked as if she had just stepped from the pages of a magazine.

'I . . . I'm so sorry,' she stuttered. 'What with worrying about Ruby and one thing and another, I'm afraid I never got round to Christmas-present shopping.'

'You've had a very difficult year,' Rebecca told her kindly. 'Let's hope that in the New Year, things will look brighter for you.'

At Rebecca's unaccustomed kindness, Kate's eyes welled with fresh tears and she hung her head, too overwhelmed with emotion to speak.

When David and Rebecca had left and she opened the gift they had bought for her she was again reduced to tears. It was a beautiful silver photo frame with a picture of her Aunt Beth holding Sally in her arms inside it.

The sight of them made Kate's heart ache afresh and she wondered if the pain of all the losses she had suffered would ever ease. For Martin, they had bought a lovely warm woollen scarf, which he unwrapped and threw disdainfully to one side.

Determined to make an effort because it was Christmas Day, Kate went upstairs and washed her hair and bathed. Then she sat at her dressing-table and applied a little make-up for the first time in months before brushing her hair to a shine as she dried it. Strangely, she didn't feel quite so lethargic today, possibly because it was such a special day. Or could it be that with Nuala being so busy for the past few days down at the vicarage, she'd *had* to make an effort? Whatever the reason, she decided to make the best of it and hurried downstairs to start the dinner before Nuala returned from the vicarage.

On Christmas Day, Victor went over to Ruby's house as usual. He stood in the middle of the room and gazed around him. With no fire in the grate it was cold. But worse than that, with Ruby missing, the heart was gone from the place. He had called round to her house every single day since the day they should have married, just to make sure that she hadn't somehow miraculously returned. Each day he had been sorely disappointed, and now as the long lonely days turned one into another, his depression increased. Today was the bleakest Christmas Day of his life. The police had been honest with him and told him that each day she was missing, the chance of finding her alive and well was more and more remote.

Climbing the stairs, Vic entered her room to gaze at the suit she had lovingly chosen for their wedding. It was still hanging on the wardrobe door, where she had put it, all pressed and ready for her to step into.

It seemed to mock him as he looked at it and he hung his head and openly wept for what might have been.

'Would you like me to make you a last drink, Martin?' Nuala asked from her seat at the side of the fire.

'No,' he told her shortly as he rose from the settee. 'I think I might go up and get an early night.'

'But it's New Year's Eve,' she protested. 'I thought we might stay up and see it in together.'

He looked at her as if she'd taken leave of her senses. 'What would I want to do that for? If my own wife can't even be bothered to stay up and see it in with me, then I'm hardly likely to want to stay up with *you*, am I?'

Swallowing her hurt, Nuala flashed him a smile. 'Just as you like. It was only a thought.'

When he disappeared through the stairs door without another word, the smile slid from her face and she scowled. How *dare* he talk to her like that after all she did for him? If it wasn't for her he'd soon find out what it was like to have no clean shirts or dinners on the table. After all, Kate was little more than useless nowadays. She just slept for most of the time. The smile returned. Aw well, it couldn't be too much longer before he realised her worth. She would have made him a much better wife than Kate ever had. Lifting the cushion he had been leaning against, she sniffed the masculine scent of him. Why was it that Kate always got the men she wanted, she wondered, as she gazed forlornly into the fire.

Eventually she rose and began to lock up and switch off the lights before retiring to her lonely room. There she thought back to the night she had visited Martin's shed in the churchyard. He'd probably be a lot nicer to her if he knew that she'd discovered he had Ruby's handbag, but she wouldn't tell him. Not yet, at least. A little smile played about her lips as she began to get ready for bed.

The insistent ringing of the phone on his desk as he entered his office at the Council in Nuneaton had David scurrying across the room. It was his first day back at work following the Christmas break and it looked set to be busy.

'Hello,' he said breathlessly as he snatched up the phone.

'Hello, David. It's Matthew, Kate's friend.'

Relief swept across David's face. Perhaps Matthew was ringing to tell him that he'd managed to see Kate. He'd thought a lot about Kate since last seeing her on Christmas morning, and that, added to the worry of Ruby's disappearance, had somewhat taken the edge from his family's Christmas.

'Did you manage to talk to her?' David asked without preamble. The answer when it came had his heart sinking into his shoes.

'No, I'm afraid I didn't, though I did call at the house. Nuala answered the door and I can tell you that the welcome she gave me was cool to say the least. To be honest she kept me on the step and couldn't get rid of me quickly enough.'

David frowned, puzzled. 'Why wouldn't she let you see Kate?'

'She said that she wasn't in and wouldn't be back until late that night.'

'Rubbish! Kate has turned into a virtual recluse.

She hardly ever steps out of the door any more, let alone for a whole day at a time. I tell you, Matthew – those two are almost keeping her a prisoner. I went to see her on Christmas Day and I don't mind telling you, she looked bloody awful. She's a shadow of the girl she was but I don't know what to do about it. She just looks so unhappy. I have a horrible feeling that she's on the verge of some sort of a breakdown.'

A silence settled on the line for some moments until eventually Matthew asked, 'Look – do you think you and I could perhaps meet up somewhere? I really need to see her.'

'Good idea,' David declared, though he really couldn't see what good it would do. 'Name the time and place and I'll be there.'

Some minutes later he replaced the phone in its cradle. Matthew might be just the tonic Kate needed – someone who she had known and hopefully trusted in her past. But first he had to get him past Martin and Nuala.

'Here, drink this up for me before I get off to work. At least I'll know you've had something inside you then.' Nuala pressed a cup of tea into Kate's trembling hand as she emerged bleary-eyed from the bedclothes.

'What time is it?' Kate asked as Nuala crossed to the window. As she twitched aside the curtains an eerie grey light flooded the room.

'It's gone ten o'clock, an' the snow's still comin' down thick an' fast. It'll take me twice as long to walk to work at this rate,' Nuala grumbled.

Standing at the side of the bed, she watched patiently as Kate drained the cup. Eventually she took it from her sister's shaking hand and tucked the covers more closely about her.

'That's it. You get back to sleep now an' rest,' she urged. At the bedroom door she paused to look back. Kate's eyelashes were already drooping onto her pale cheeks. Smiling with satisfaction, Nuala softly closed the bedroom door behind her.

Chapter Thirty-Six

David and Matthew had agreed to meet in the George Eliot Hotel in the marketplace. Once they had both been served with pints of bitter they found themselves an empty table in a far corner where they could talk undisturbed.

After taking a great gulp of his drink David said, 'To be perfectly honest with you, now that you're here I don't quite know where to begin.'

Matthew smiled at him pleasantly and tried to put him at ease. 'Why don't you start at the beginning, eh?'

And so David did. He left nothing out, even going so far as to telling him how he had suspected Kate when she had first appeared on his mother's doorstep. 'I thought she was out for my mother's money, you see,' he muttered apologetically, as shame washed over him. 'But that was soon proven to be wrong. When my mother took ill, Kate visited her every single day in hospital and even offered to give up her job to look after her. It was then that I realised I'd misjudged her and I've been trying to make it up to her ever since. We got quite close – but then she married Martin and everything started to change. I'm telling you, that man isn't human. He's like some sort of a dictator. I fear she's on the edge of a breakdown, though when you come to think about it, it's hardly surprising, is it? First she loses her father then she ups roots and travels here to live with my mother. Next thing, my mother is ill and she and Nuala go to live with Ruby. On top of all this she's trying to hold down a job and care for her pregnant sister—'

'*You what?*' Matthew's eyes almost popped out of his head. 'You're telling me that Nuala has a child?'

David's eyes were sad as he shook his head. 'No. She *did* have a child but she died last year. She was a beautiful little girl. Jenny they called her, after Kate's mum. I don't mind telling you I thought it would kill Kate when she died. She's never been quite the same since, then she lost Sally, she was my mother's little dog. Kate adopted her when my mother moved in with me. Then Lindsay, her friend, cleared off back to London without so much as a by-your-leave and then the final straw – Ruby went missing. I ask you, is it any wonder the poor girl's in a bad way?'

Matthew's forehead creased into a deep frown as he tried to imagine the heartache that Kate must have gone through.

'That's not the worst of it though,' David continued sombrely. 'The day that Ruby disappeared I went round to see her. Martin had ordered her to keep away from Kate and Ruby was worried sick about her. On the day that Kate got married, Ruby gave her a necklace, which Kate thought she'd lost. Purely by chance Ruby discovered it in the vicarage. It seems someone had found it amongst the earth at the side of a freshly dug grave.

Now bearing in mind that Martin is the gravedigger for Shepperton Church, it doesn't take much adding up, does it? He obviously had the necklace but chose to let Kate believe she'd misplaced it. Ruby was convinced that Martin was trying to drive her mad. And there's more . . . Ruby told me a secret that my mother and she had kept from Kate and Nuala. It was like this . . .'

When he had finished his story, Matthew's eyebrows had disappeared into his hairline and he let out a long breath.

'Kate needs to know this,' he said.

'I'm in full agreement, but how do we tell her? She never sets foot out of the house any more and if you try and visit her, either Nuala or Martin will tell you she's in bed.'

Matthew scratched his chin. 'There's more to this than meets the eye,' he muttered. 'What are those two up to? You don't reckon Kate's in danger, do you?'

David suddenly paled. 'My God! There's been something troubling me for weeks and I've just realised what it is. On the night that Ruby disappeared, Martin had a grave to dig. You don't think she went to see him there do you, and he . . .'

Matthew looked horrified. It just didn't bear thinking about.

'I've *got* to see Kate.' It was said more to himself than David, and there was a note of panic in his voice.

'As I told you, that might prove to be easier said than done. What do you think we should do?'

'Nothing just yet; I need time to think about all that you've told me. In the meantime, I think that you and I should keep in close touch.'

431

The two men drained their glasses and made their way back into the bitterly cold marketplace where they shook hands.

'Just out of curiosity – and I hope you won't mind me asking this – was there anything ever between you and Kate?' David asked softly.

Matthew coloured. 'Not officially. Kate was always too busy looking after Nuala and her father. I did ask her to marry me, but I left it too late. By then she'd agreed to come to the Midlands to live with your mother.'

'But you *do* love her, don't you?'

Misery washed across Matthew's face as he hung his head. 'Yes, I do. I always have. I should never have left it so long before I made my feelings known to her. It was always sort of an unspoken thing between us. Letting her go is the biggest regret of my life.'

David patted his arm sympathetically. Although they'd only just met, he'd taken a liking to Matthew.

'I'll be in touch very soon,' Matthew told him, and David watched the young man stride away with hunched shoulders and a heavy tread.

'How are you *ever* goin' to get better if you don't get no goodness inside you?'

Kate stared at the steaming mug of cocoa in Nuala's hand. She knew that Nuala was doing her best to take care of her, but sometimes she felt as if she was swimming in tea and cocoa.

'Come on now. Drink it up,' Nuala commanded.

Kate struggled out of the blankets and took the drink from her sister's hand. 'Is Martin home yet?' she asked.

Nuala shook her head. 'No. He had a grave to dig tonight. I don't envy him, I don't mind tellin' you. It's cold as clouts out there.'

'He hardly seems to spend any time at home since Adam went back to live with his grandma and grandad,' Kate commented sadly. The child had never settled with them and ever since he had gone, Kate felt as if she'd failed him.

Nuala sniffed. Personally she'd been glad to see the back of the spoiled little brat, but she couldn't tell Kate that, of course. 'He'll probably come back when you're feelin' better,' she said instead, and slightly placated, Kate sipped at her drink.

'I might get up in a while and cook Martin some supper,' she mused. 'It's about time I started to make an effort.'

Nuala stood at the side of the bed until Kate had finished her drink, then taking the mug from her thin hand she headed back to the door. 'Just as you like – that is, if you don't drop back off again.'

Pausing on the landing she listened, and sure enough within minutes the sounds of Kate's gentle snores reached her. Sighing, she hurried downstairs to check on the liver and onions that was cooking in the oven for Martin's supper. No doubt he'd be glad of something warm in his stomach when he came in tonight.

Once she'd basted the food, which was spreading a delicious aroma around the whole house, she threw some coal onto the fire and tidied her hair in the mirror above the mantelpiece. Then settling into the chair she waited for her brother-in-law to come home.

* * *

From his position behind a tall yew tree, Matthew watched as Martin struck the frozen earth with his pick. It was almost nine o'clock at night and he was so cold that he'd lost the feeling in his hands and feet. Even so he was determined to continue with his vigil. If the suspicions he had were correct, his discomfort would be worth it.

Slowly, Martin disappeared as if into the bowels of the earth as the grave grew ever deeper and it was only then that Matthew crept from his hiding-place and slunk across the churchyard keeping to the shadows. In no time at all he reached the gravedigger's shed that housed Martin's tools. Casting a last wary glance across his shoulder to make sure that Martin was still digging, he slipped inside. Martin had left it open. Fumbling in his pocket he produced a torch and swept its beam across the contents of the shed. At first glance there appeared to be nothing but a pile of dirty clothes in one corner, but then the thin ray of light played on what appeared to be a black leather handle peeping from beneath them.

Stealthily he bent and moved the clothes aside, then gasped when a woman's handbag was revealed. His breath caught in his thoat and he strained his ears into the night. When the melancholy sound of the pick striking the hardpacked earth reached his ears, he carefully opened the catch and looked inside. There was a purse with some loose change, but nothing to determine who the bag had belonged to. His fingers were shaking so much that they felt as if they weren't a part of him, but then they closed around something flat and shiny. A photograph. Shining the torch on it, he found himself looking down on a snapshot of Kate holding a baby on her lap. She was staring adoringly down at the child. Gulping deep in his throat, he pushed the photo back and continued with his delving. A piece of paper rustled: it was a receipt for some flowers ordered for a *Mrs Ruby Bannister*. It was Ruby's bag! Perhaps David had been right to be suspicious of Martin?

At that moment, Matthew suddenly became aware that the rhythmic sound of the pick had ceased. Panicking, he shoved the receipt back into the bag and pushed it beneath the clothes, then quickly turning off the torch he crept to the door in the pitch darkness and peered out into the black night. He could just make out the shape of a figure working its way towards the shed amongst the tombstones. Bending low, he scuttled away to the shelter of a tall yew tree, hardly daring to breathe as Martin moved towards the shed. Within minutes he heard the sound of the pick and shovel being flung into a far corner, followed by the metallic sound of the key in the padlock. At that moment the churchyard was washed in moonlight and he saw Martin rub his hand wearily across his eyes and stretch.

Leaning further back into the shadows, Matthew waited until moments later, Martin turned and walked away to be swallowed up by the night. Eventually, the lych gate squeaked and Matthew knew he had gone. Resting his head against the cold bark of the tree, he finally relaxed as he let out a deep breath.

But now what should he do?

* * *

'Come on, get yourself here by the fire,' Nuala urged. 'I've got you a nice bit o' liver an' onions all ready an' your slippers waitin' by the grate.'

Martin did as he was told. 'I suppose Kate's in bed?' he said wearily.

Keeping her voice light, Nuala nodded. 'Right first time. But never mind. You don't need Kate if I'm around, do you?'

Martin would have liked to tell her that it would be a cold day in hell before he needed *her*, but was just too tired to argue.

Nuala bustled away and returned minutes later with his steaming food all laid out appetisingly on a tray. 'There you go,' she said brightly as she placed it on his lap. 'That should warm you up a treat. You might as well sit there an' eat it by the fire.'

Martin hated eating off a tray. Anne would never have allowed it. Everything had to be just so for her. The table laid with candles and crisp white napkins. The cutlery polished to a shine. But then Nuala wasn't Anne. Neither was Kate, as he'd discovered soon after their marriage.

As his appetite suddenly fled he pushed the tray back at Nuala. 'I'm not hungry,' he told her shortly.

'But . . . I stayed up all evening making you that!' Nuala declared indignantly.

'Well, that's your bloody fault then! I didn't ask you to, did I? And while we're on the subject I wish you wouldn't wait up for me. When I've done a hard day's work, the last thing I need is to come home to *you* harping on in my ear.'

Nuala's lip trembled at his harsh words and she had to blink to hold back the tears. Even so, she wasn't prepared for him to see the hurt he had caused, so turning silently she hurried towards the door and fled up the stairs. Once in the privacy of her room she began to pace up and down the confined area. The hurt slowly turned to anger and her teeth clenched with rage. How *dare* Martin talk to her like that, after all she did for him? Washing, ironing, cooking, cleaning – the list was endless. Well sod him! From now on he could paddle his own canoe. A few days of coming home to no clean clothes and no dinner on the table and he'd soon change his tune. Angrily she began to tear off her clothes and threw them on to a chair before clambering into bed.

In a small room in Birmingham, Matthew was also pacing the floor as he thought back over the night's events. There could be no doubt at all that it was Ruby's bag he'd found hidden in Martin's shed – and that could only mean one thing: Martin must somehow be connected to Ruby's disappearance. Kate could be living with a killer. The thought made his blood run cold and he knew in that moment that he couldn't ignore it.

Snatching some coins from his bedside table, he raced down the threadbare stair carpet of the boarding house where he was staying and along to the kiosk at the end of the road. After rummaging in his pocket for the scrap of paper with David's phone number on it, he dialled with shaking fingers, ready to press Button A when someone picked up.

A woman's voice answered on the third ring. She sounded tired and after hastily apologising for ringing so late, Matthew asked to speak to David, explaining that it was urgent. Within seconds David's voice floated down the line.

'Whatever are you ringing so late for?' he asked groggily. 'Has something happened to Kate?'

'No, but I fear it could, if what I found tonight is anything to go by,' Matthew said grimly.

Hearing the panic in the other man's voice, David tried to calm him. 'Right, now take it easy and try to tell me what's gone on.'

Taking a deep breath, Matthew launched into an explanation of the night's happenings as David listened in shocked silence.

'Look,' Matthew suddenly told him, 'I think we need to move now. Can you meet me in an hour? Shall we say outside Ruby's house?'

'I'll be there.' David slammed the phone down and rushed away to get dressed.

When Matthew's car screeched to a halt on the icy road in Shepperton Street some time later, David ventured from the warmth of his own car and hurried to meet him.

'What are we going to do?' he asked without preamble.

'I don't think we have much choice. We're going to the police.' Matthew's mouth was set in a grim line. For every second that they hesitated, Kate could be in danger, if his suspicions were proved to be correct.

David solemnly nodded in agreement and as one they both piled into Matthew's car. In seconds he'd turned it around and they were heading to the town centre and the police station.

Chapter Thirty-Seven

'Now remember, lads, I want this done as quietly and quickly as possible,' the Inspector told his men before the silent posse moved amongst the gravestones. Once they came to the shed, a young policeman stepped forward and expertly opened the padlock. The door creaked in protest as it swung open and tension settled on the party gathered outside.

Detective Taberner was the first to enter the shed, and just as Matthew had said, within minutes he had found Ruby Bannister's handbag. He emerged holding it in a gloved hand. Slipping it into a waiting plastic bag, he asked, 'What now, gov?'

'Get some of those clothes as well. We can check them to see if there's any blood on them, then just leave the door open as it is. I want it to look like it was just kids that broke in. He might think he hadn't closed the padlock securely. We don't want this bloke to know we're on to him just yet, though you can be sure I'll have him watched like a hawk.'

The silent party made its way back to the gates and in no time at all, no one would ever have known they had been there.

*   *   *

The next morning, Martin rose to find no fire in the grate. True to her word, Nuala had chosen to go on strike. He shrugged – what did he care? He would be leaving for work within minutes. When he drew his car away from the kerb, he didn't notice another car slowly pull out and follow him.

'Kate, *please* try and listen to me,' David pleaded as he stared into her dull eyes. 'There's something I have to tell you. Something you should have known about years ago.'

As Kate's chin sank to her chest and he saw that she was struggling to stay awake, a wave of compassion swept over him. She'd changed so much from the girl she had been when she first came to live with his mother, but he hoped that what he was about to tell her would lift her from this deep depression.

'It's something Ruby confided to me the day she went missing,' he went on, and for the first time there was a spark of interest in Kate's eyes.

'The thing is . . .' He struggled to find the right words. 'The thing is, you believe that your mother died in a mental asylum, don't you?'

Tears smarted at the back of her eyes as she slowly nodded. 'I know she did. Da took us to see her grave. And now *I'm* going mad too.'

'No, Kate. You're not going mad. You see, the woman who died in a mental asylum was Nuala's mother . . . not yours.'

She stared at him in disbelief. 'What do you mean?'

He gently took her hand in his. 'It was like this. Your mother was a great friend of Ruby's, as you know, when they were younger. Ruby was heartbroken when your mother moved away after marrying your father. For a while your mother kept in touch but then suddenly the letters stopped coming. My mother didn't hear from her either, so she went on a visit and apparently when she came home she was worried sick. She said that Jenny had changed almost beyond belief. Your dad was knocking her from pillar to post and my mother had begged her to leave him and come home.'

Kate's eyes were full of pain but David knew that he must finish his story.

'Things got no better when you were born; apparently his bullying got worse. She tried to leave him once by all accounts when you were little more than a baby, but he caught up with her and took you home. Of course, she followed for your sake. It seems from then on, things went from bad to worse. You were only about a year old when your mother discovered your father was having an affair. The woman he was seeing was from a good family and he was besotted with her. What he *didn't* know at the time was that she was mentally unstable. Anyway, the long and the short of it is – he kicked your mother out and moved this other woman in with him. She was Nuala's mother, Kate – not yours. So you see, you're *not* going mad.'

'So, what happened to my mother?' Kate asked tremulously.

David looked down at the floor. 'Apparently by the time she got back here she was really ill and half out of her mind with worry about you. She tried to get you back through the courts but your father was a good liar and convinced them that she was an unfit mother. Not long after she came home, she developed pneumonia and died. She isn't buried in Ireland as you thought, but just up the road, in Shepperton churchyard. She died round about the same time as Nuala's mother had to be admitted to the asylum. When she died, your father took you both off to Durham to live, and the rest you know.'

'So Nuala and I are only half-sisters then?' Kate was reeling from the shock of what he'd just told her. She could scarcely believe that her mother was buried in the same place as little Jenny.

'Yes, you are. But that doesn't mean that you have to feel any differently about each other than you always have. I'm only telling you this now so that you'll know there is no trace of insanity in our family. What you're going through is a deep depression but you're *not* going mad. Do you hear me?'

'So why am I so tired all the time?' she demanded. 'And why have I been doing all these strange things. I lose things . . .'

'If it's the necklace that Ruby gave to you on your wedding day you're talking about, I can shed some light on that too,' David assured her. 'It was found at the side of a newly dug grave at Coton churchyard. It must have fallen out of Martin's pocket.'

Kate began to tremble. 'But why didn't he tell me he had it? All the times he saw me searching for it,' she cried, then as an afterthought. 'You don't think it's *him* trying to drive me mad, do you?'

David swallowed. He longed to tell her of the handbag and what was going on even as he sat there, but he'd been sworn to secrecy. Tonight, under cover of darkness, the police would be exhuming the body from the grave that Martin had dug on the day of Ruby's disappearance. Until that was done he must bite his tongue.

Dragging her eyes away from her cousin's, Kate stared into the flames that were licking up the chimney. She could scarcely take it all in. But why hadn't her aunt told her all this? When she asked David the selfsame question, he shrugged. 'I can only imagine that Mum didn't want to upset you any more than you already were when you came to live with her by telling you that you and Nuala were only half-sisters. I know she used to write to you regularly when you were little, but then when your father moved you to Durham she had no way of getting in touch.'

Now Kate understood why all the cards and letters she'd found following her father's death had been addressed to her and not Nuala.

'So I'm really *not* going mad then?'

'No, you most definitely are not.' David glanced at the clock ticking away on the mantelpiece and rose. Nuala and Martin would be home from work soon and the last thing he wanted at the minute was for Martin to find him there.

'I have to go now, but listen. I want you to think on what I've told you, and I also want you to do something for me too. Will you promise not to tell Martin? Not just yet at least.'

When her head slowly nodded he sighed with relief and quickly headed for the door. 'I'll be back to see you as soon as I can,' he promised, and then paused with his hand on the doorknob.

'There's just one more thing I think I should tell you,' he said a little awkwardly. 'I met a friend of yours – someone who used to live near you in Durham.'

When Kate looked at him curiously he went on, 'His name is Matthew Williams. He's very keen to see you again. In actual fact, he's already called round here once, but you were sleeping and Nuala wouldn't let him in.'

'Nuala did quite right,' Kate snapped with some of her former spirit. 'If I never set eyes on Matthew Williams again it will still be a day too soon.'

Now it was David's turn to be confused. 'But he seems like such a nice chap. And he obviously thinks the world of you.'

'Huh! That just goes to show how much you know then, doesn't it, David?'

Casting a worried look at the clock again, he sighed. 'Look, I can't talk to you about it now. As I said, I'll get back as soon as I can.'

The door closed behind him and she was left to try and digest what he'd just told her. Her heart was heavy as she thought of the pain her mother must have suffered at the hands of her father, but then it hadn't come as a complete surprise after seeing how cruel he had been to Nuala. She was also vaguely aware of a feeling of relief growing inside her. If what David had told her was true then she wasn't going mad after all. And what about Matthew turning up out of the blue like that? However had he managed to find her? And why hadn't Nuala told her about his visit? It must have been dreadful for her poor sister, him turning up on the doorstep like that.

Suddenly cold, she wrapped her arms tightly about herself. If only she wasn't so tired. Then she might be able to get her head around all that David had told her.

* * *

The group assembled at the entrance to Coton church-yard held their breath as a young officer tumbled out of a police car and raced towards them. Leaning into the window he told Inspector Harry breathlessly, 'Denby's just gone into his house, sir!'

'Right.' This was the moment the Inspector had been waiting for. 'We've got the exhumation order, so let's get this show on the road before we freeze us balls off.'

Instantly a stream of people all loaded down with various pieces of equipment swept past him. Casting a glance at the pathologist's unmarked van parked at the kerb in case his suspicions should be proved right, the Inspector, pulling up his coat collar against the bitterly cold night, quickly followed them

Taberner was at the graveside barking orders. 'Come on, you lot, jump to it, let's get those lights fixed up. We can get cracking with what we came to do then.'

His orders were carried out in a remarkably short time and a silence settled on the group as they stared at the illuminated grave. It was Inspector Harry who broke the spell.

'So come on then. Let's get on with it, eh?'

Two young policemen, each bearing picks that glinted evilly in the harsh lights, stepped forward. Another hastily removed the frozen wreaths from the grave and the first pick was raised.

The sound of the tools striking the frozen earth echoed hollowly around the graveyard as the assembled party looked on solemn-faced.

Soon the two policemen who were digging were sweating despite the harshness of the night, as the pile of earth at the side of the grave grew steadily bigger. Thankfully, once they were past the surface, the ground

445

was softer and they made good time. An eerie mist floated around their feet as the vicar stood, silently praying that what the Inspector suspected might prove to be incorrect.

Matthew and David had been allowed to be present but stood well back, each locked in their own thoughts. The sound of the picks rising and falling was almost rhythmic, so it was a shock to everyone when the sound of metal striking the coffin lid suddenly bounced off the surrounding gravestones.

'This is it, sir.' Sweat stood out on the constable's face as he gazed up out of the grave at his superior.

'Good, now go steady, lads. That's someone's loved one in there. I want them treated with respect.'

'*Sir!*' The two young men nodded in unison as spades were lowered into the grave to them and the picks were handed out. They worked on, more carefully now and soon the brass nameplate on the coffin glowed dully in the light.

'Right, pass them the ropes,' Taberner ordered when the lid was cleared.

Gingerly, the sombre-faced policemen slid the ropes beneath the wooden casket and ready hands reached in to pull them up out of the pit.

'Go gently now,' Inspector Harry ordered as it was raised from its resting-place. After what seemed an eternity the coffin was finally lowered onto the frozen earth at the side of the yawning hole.

Following a nod, another officer armed with a lethal-looking screwdriver stepped forward and began to unscrew the nails on the coffin lid. By now the atmosphere was so charged that they were all holding their breath. Once the screws were removed the man stepped away.

Another nod from the Inspector and four men took a corner of the coffin each and lifted it as the vicar began to pray.

'Our Father, who art in heaven, Hallowed be thy name. Thy kingdom come, thy . . .'

His voice trailed away as the occupant of the coffin was revealed. Two of the younger officers gagged and stumbled back as a frown creased the Inspector's forehead.

'Damn and blast!' he cursed softly. It seemed that all their efforts had been in vain. 'Get the lid back on.' His voice cracked like ice. 'No need to disturb the poor soul any more than we need to. I would have sworn that Denby had got rid of his victims in the coffins before he filled the graves in. I'm still going to arrest him on suspicion of murder though. I want him to explain the blood on his clothes and why he had one of the missing women's handbags in his possession.'

He glared across at David and Matthew whose faces appeared to be almost as white as the corpse they had unearthed as the lid was gently lowered back onto the coffin.

Depression settled like a cloud over the group as the screws were then hastily put back into place. The Inspector strode up and down, his hands balled into fists of frustration behind his back. It was as he was doing so that something shiny caught his eye in the bottom of the grave.

'Bring that light over here!' he commanded. Instantly the light was wheeled closer as he strained his eyes into the pit. 'Down there. *Look*. What's that?'

One of the policemen who'd dug the grave instantly leaped back into the hole. Following the Inspector's pointing finger, he began to rake his cold fingers across the earth until they connected with what appeared to be a thin chain. Holding it aloft, he gasped as the light caught a heart-shaped sapphire suspended on a golden chain.

'It's a necklace, gov,' he said unnecessarily as the sapphire winked in the artificial light.

David felt a great weight in his chest. 'It's Kate's necklace,' he muttered. 'The one that Ruby gave to her on her wedding day.'

A shocked silence, more deafening than any noise, surrounded them as they each thought of what this could mean.

Lowering a spade back into the grave the Inspector ordered, 'Dig a little deeper . . . and go gently.'

They all held their breath as once again the digging began. The policeman had dug down no more than a few inches when a woman's hand was revealed, then an arm concealed in a coat sleeve.

'Dear God above.' Tears began to roll unchecked down David's cheeks. 'I think we've just found Ruby. May God bless her soul – what a terrible way to die.'

Jerking his head at one of the assembled officers the Inspector said brusquely, 'Go and get the police photographer, and we'll need a stretcher and a body bag. This is one for the coroner.'

The man slipped away as the gruesome task of revealing Ruby's body continued.

'Is that Ruby Bannister?' the Inspector asked when her poor body was eventually in full view.

David could only nod as he stared down at the terrible

wounds on Ruby's body. It needed no expert to see that the woman had been subjected to a frenzied attack. Those present reverently bowed their heads as the pathologist's team laid down a body bag in readiness while the police photographer did his job. It was then that the Inspector's temper exploded.

'You lot – follow me!' he snapped. 'Denby's game is up. We're going to fetch the bastard in *right now*.'

Turning to the vicar, he told him, 'I want a list of every funeral that's taken place here since the disappearance of the first woman on our list – Diane Dorkin. I've got a horrible feeling that Ruby won't be the only victim to have been unofficially buried here.'

The vicar made the sign of the cross and scuttled away in the direction of the vicarage, and in that moment he questioned God. 'Dear Lord – how could You allow such atrocities to happen?'

Chapter Thirty-Eight

'Is everyone in position?'

'Yes, gov. The back is covered as well.'

'Good – then let's get on with it.' The Inspector stepped forward with a small army of officers close on his heels. Striding to the door, he rapped sharply and was rewarded when a light clicked on and shone through a chink in the curtains in the room beyond.

He heard the bolts being drawn back and seconds later a mousy-haired girl peered out at him through a small gap in the door. 'Yes, what do you want?'

'Is this the home of Martin Denby?'

Nuala frowned. 'Yes, it is. Who wants to know?'

Flashing his identity card, he pushed past her all in one smooth movement.

'Where is Mr Denby?' he asked, as his officers stormed past him. Nuala's mouth dropped open. Trembling, she motioned towards the middle door. He followed his officers to find Martin just rising from the fireside chair.

'*What the—*'

A policeman grabbed him and slipped some handcuffs onto his wrists before Martin even had the chance to realise what was happening.

'Martin Denby, I am arresting you for the murder of Ruby Bannister.' The Inspector's voice droned on as he read Martin his rights.

Nuala was leaning heavily against the wall with tears streaming down her cheeks as she looked on in distress.

At that moment, Kate, who had been woken by all the noise, appeared in the stairs doorway. 'What's going on?' she asked groggily as she tied the belt on her dressing-gown.

Nuala ran to her and flung herself into her arms. 'They're saying that Martin killed Ruby,' she sobbed.

Kate's startled eyes flew to her husband who was watching the whole thing with a hint of amusement playing about his mouth.

'What's wrong, *beloved*?' As his eyes found hers he laughed. 'Didn't you think I was capable of such dastardly actions? Just think yourself lucky that *you're* still here.'

'*But . . . but why?*' Kate hugged Nuala to her as she stared at him aghast. She felt as if she was caught up in some dreadful nightmare.

'Why? Because she was a silly interfering old bitch, that's why.' His eyes had taken on an insane gleam now and in that moment Kate wondered if she had ever really known him at all.

'She wasn't the first,' he boasted, as his smile gave way to a look of fury and he strained towards her. Two officers had a firm hold on each of his arms as he tried to get closer to Kate.

'An' I reckon they've cottoned on to the fact where all the rest are buried as well,' he mocked. Spittle flew from his mouth as he threw back his head and laughed

451

aloud. 'Serves them all right, *that's* what I say. Woman are whores, every last one of them!'

'But . . . what about Anne?' Kate gasped. 'I've lived in her shadow ever since the moment we got married. You adored her!'

'Oh yes, I *adored* her all right. Problem was – *she* didn't adore *me*.' As he struggled to be free, pain showed on his face for the first time. 'I didn't tell you that she was off with every Tom, Dick and Harry she could get her hands on, did I? Huh! There was me, keeping her in the manner she demanded, while she was out flying her kite every chance she got. *That was why I had to kill her!*'

'You did what?' Her voice was no more than a strangled whisper.

'Everyone was heartbroken when she had such a massive heart-attack so young – but then it wasn't totally unexpected. Anne had always had a weak heart.' He suddenly became still and stopped fighting against his captors as his eyes narrowed to slits and he remembered.

'Not many people know that some plants can bring about what appears to be a heart-attack. Wolfsbane is one of them – not so easy to find nowadays unless you know where to look. It contains poisons that are almost undetectable if they're administered in the right dose. *But I knew – and I got away with it!*'

'B . . . but why did you kill the other women?' Kate stuttered.

His lips curled back from his teeth in terrifying contempt as he spat, 'Because I thought the hurt would go away then . . . but it didn't. The years went by and it was still there, and I knew that I had to have even more revenge. So one year, on our wedding anniversary, I hunted for a woman who looked like Anne – and I killed her to save her husband being hurt as I was. That satisfied me for a long while, until recently – and then *you* came into my life. It's all *your* fault, looking like her . . .'

Kate felt the hairs on the back of her neck stand to attention as shock coursed through her. All this time she had felt second-best. All this time she had tried to be the woman that Anne had been, while in reality, Martin had not only hated her for what she had done to him, but had killed her! She could hardly believe it.

'Take him away,' Inspector Harry ground out and suddenly Martin seemed to come to himself and struggle again as he cried, 'I didn't mean what I said! I just made it up! I didn't really—'

'I said, get him *out* of here.'

As the policemen began to drag him, kicking and shouting towards the door, Kate looked on as if cast in stone. Somehow, she knew that she would never see him again. She supposed that she should be distraught, yet instead she felt nothing but a profound shock, and disgust at what he'd done to Ruby and all those other poor women. How could she have been so blind?

'Is there anyone you'd like us to get for you?' The Inspector's eyes were kindly as he looked into her pale face. Kate tried to ignore Martin's cries as she shook her head and cradled her sister's trembling body against her.

He patted her arm before leaving the room – and suddenly there was nothing but the sound of Nuala's sobs and the police cars clanging away into the night.

It came to her then. She was back where she had started. There truly was just her and Nuala again.

* * *

453

A week passed – seven days of unrelenting horror, as Martin's past crimes were, literally, uncovered. How Kate got through it, she would never know. David was a great comfort.

This afternoon, he had come to see how the sisters were coping. Kate looked ghastly, he thought. There were dark purple circles under her eyes and every movement she made was obviously an effort. All around the room, bags and boxes were packed with the sister's belongings.

'Where will you be going?' David asked.

Kate shrugged. 'I don't know. I just know we can't stay here. We won't be leaving for a while though. I thought we'd hang around until the court cases are over then start somewhere afresh.'

'You could always come to us,' David offered.

She shook her head. 'I appreciate that, David, but it wouldn't be fair on Rebecca to have two more people in the house.'

'Actually it was Rebecca who told me to ask you,' he admitted.

Still Kate declined his offer. 'It's very kind of you both, but to be honest, looking back it's been like one long nightmare ever since we arrived in Nuneaton. We need to go somewhere new where no one knows us. I've already seen a solicitor about a divorce, and given what's happened, he doesn't see why it shouldn't be granted fairly quickly.'

Nuala was curled up in a chair, her eyes red-rimmed from crying.

Kate thought back over the last few days and of all the poor women whose bodies had been found buried beneath coffins in the churchyard. To think that Martin had been capable of such wickedness turned her stomach every time she so much as thought of it. As for the victims' families – it almost broke her heart to think of all the motherless children and the horror and heartache they'd been forced to endure. At least now though, they would be able to give their loved ones a decent, proper burial.

David fidgeted nervously before suddenly blurting out, 'Look, Kate – there's someone outside who really needs to see you.'

She guessed immediately who it was. 'If it's Matthew, you can tell him I have no wish to *ever* see him again after what he did to Nuala,' she said bitterly.

'Is that right? And just what is it that I'm supposed to have done?'

Startled, Kate's eyes flew across Martin's shoulder and there was Matthew, just as handsome as ever.

'I don't remember inviting you in.' Her eyes flashed as she tried to calm herself.

'No, she didn't, so sling yer hook.' Leaping out of the chair, Nuala planted her hands on her hips and glared at him.

Completely ignoring Nuala, Matthew continued to gaze at Kate. 'I ask again – *what* am I supposed to have done? It should be *me* that's angry with *you*. All those letters I sent that you never replied to, and all the time it's taken to track you down, only to discover that you'd married someone else. *Why*, Kate? You knew I loved you.'

'All those letters – huh! That's a joke. A couple when I first arrived at my aunt's and then nothing. But then it's hardly surprising is it, with the state Nuala was in? I suppose you were too ashamed to carry it on.'

Nuala was highly agitated now and ran to stand between them. 'Get out!' she screeched, and her trembling finger stabbed towards the door. Matthew ignored her, brushed her aside as he answered Kate.

'And just *what* is that supposed to mean – the state Nuala was in? Nuala was bound to be upset; she'd just lost her father, which was hardly my fault!' Matthew's temper had grown to match hers now and they faced each other like opponents in a boxing ring.

'Didn't you even stop to think of what the consequences might be when you were seeing her?' Kate cried.

'Seeing her?' Now Matthew looked genuinely confused.

'It's a pity you never got to meet your daughter. She was so beautiful.' Kate's eyes welled with tears as she thought of the darling little girl she had adored.

'My daughter!' The colour drained from Matthew's face as he reeled with shock. 'How the hell could Nuala and I ever have had a child without lying together? You know it was always *you* I loved, not your sister. Who in God's name told you that I'd fathered a child? And as if I would ever even behave like that in the first place.'

His words brought a deafening silence crashing down on the room as all eyes turned to Nuala.

Kate looked in confusion from Nuala to Matthew. Which one of them was telling the truth? It must be Nuala. After all, they were sisters – or half-sisters at least.

'Nuala, promise me that Matthew is lying,' she said. 'You wouldn't tell me such a terrible lie, would you?'

Suddenly, Nuala stopped trembling, and she reared up. 'Wouldn't I? Why not? After all, it was always *you* in everything, wasn't it? *You* were the favourite at school. *You* were the one that had friends. *You* were the one that all the boys wanted to go out with. *You* were the pretty, clever one. I didn't mind so much when I was young, but then I got older and met Matthew and I knew that I was in love. Huh! Fat lot of good it did me as usual. He only had eyes for you. It was different with Da though.' Her eyes took on a look of cunning. 'He beat me when you were there, but when we were alone, he loved me. I mean – *really* loved me as he *never* did you.'

When Kate dropped heavily into a chair, Nuala laughed. 'Jenny was Da's child. Why do you think she was so slow? But you never guessed, did you? When I told you she was Matthew's, you fell for it hook, line and sinker. Then we came to live with Aunt Beth and it started all over again. *You* were the favourite once more. One night when you were working at the pub we had a blazing row and she called me a selfish little madam. I soon shut her up when I sent her hurtling down the stairs though. Ha ha! That was what caused the stroke. Pity it didn't kill her outright, silly old cow.'

As David gave a cry of anguish, Kate clutched his hand and looked speechlessly on in horrified disbelief. Nuala was still ranting on. It was if now she had started, she couldn't stop.

'Then you met Martin – and once again I couldn't stand *you* always being the happy one.'

'But I *wasn't* happy – you know that, Nuala,' Kate faltered. 'Martin was cruel. He tried to drive me mad, and he almost succeeded.'

Nuala threw back her head and let out an insane cackle. 'That wasn't Martin, it was me,' she boasted. 'And do you know what? I *almost* did it. It was so easy to sneak in at lunchtime and swap salt for sugar. Martin

457

wasn't too keen on that dinner, was he? Then there was Jenny, the screaming little brat. You made me keep her in my room so you could stay in your little love-nest with your new husband, didn't you? But I soon shut her up too, didn't I? I thought she might struggle, but she didn't even blink when I put the pillow over her head – she just looked up at me from those trusting blue eyes.'

Kate nearly collapsed, and her hand flew to her mouth as a strangled sob escaped her, but there was no stopping Nuala now. 'What did you think of the little lipstick messages I left on your mirror, eh? And Sally?' She chuckled. 'Now she *did* struggle when I forced the rat poison down her throat. You'd be amazed how quickly it worked; within minutes she was writhing in agony and foaming at the mouth . . . But the best bit of all was watching you sleeping.' She giggled as if she had just told a huge joke. 'All the time you thought I was taking care of you I was keeping you drugged up with sleeping tablets I took from Angela's bathroom cabinet. It was just too easy. Then one night I went to collect Martin's dirty clothes from his shed. I was going to wash and iron them as a surprise for him. But I found Ruby's handbag in there and I knew then that he was somehow connected with her disappearance. I was waiting until you'd gone completely mad and he'd had you carted off in a strait-jacket, then I was going to tell him. He would have loved me then, I know he would, but once again everything was spoiled.' Her shoulders suddenly sagged and in that terrible moment Kate realised that Nuala was insane, just as her mother had been before her.

There was a pain in her chest the like of which she had never known, and a deep sense of sadness. Despite her sister's crimes, she couldn't stop loving her. 'Nuala, you're not well, but we can help you.' As she started towards her sister, the girl backed towards the door, her face twisted in a grimace of hatred.

'I don't *want* your help, do you hear me? I *hate* you!'

Kate, Matthew and David all suddenly lunged towards the deranged girl as they realised that she was about to run away. But Nuala was quick and had the front door open as they jostled to follow her. Then suddenly she was running as Kate's terrified voice echoed across the road, '*Nuala, watch out for the bus—*'

A Midland red bus was trundling towards them and when the driver saw the girl run out in front of him, he slammed on his brakes and swore, but the road was slippery and he could only watch in horror as it swerved towards her. The girl paused to raise terrified eyes to his then there was a sickening bump and Nuala was tossed into the air, landing with an ominous thud some yards away. Her neck was at an unnatural angle and her staring eyes looked to the heavens as blood slowly began to seep from the side of her mouth.

Sobbing, Kate threw herself onto the road to take the limp body of her sister into her arms. Through a haze of pain she heard Matthew screaming, 'Someone get an ambulance!'

David dropped to his knees beside her and searched for a pulse. After a time he looked at Kate fearfully, but he had no need of words. She already knew that Nuala had gone from her for ever.

By the time the ambulance arrived a small crowd had gathered. Kate's tears had stopped now; she watched silently as the ambulancemen gently lifted Nuala's broken body onto a stretcher and covered her with a blanket. Then the vehicle was pulling away with its bells clanging and the crowd began to disperse. A warm, strong arm came around her shaking shoulders.

'Come on, darling. Let's get you in out of the cold, eh?'

Looking up into Matthew's eyes, she nodded and allowed herself to be led away from the blood on the road that was all she had left of her sister.

Much later that evening, when everyone was finally gone, Kate sat and stared into the dying fire. She was alone now. More alone than she had ever realised she could be. Her mind played back over the last tragic couple of years and all the faces of the ones she had loved and lost flashed before her eyes as if in slow motion.

There was Aunt Beth, happy and well. Jenny, bestowing on her the only precious smile she had ever given. Sally, running to meet her, her tail wagging furiously at the sight of her. Lindsay, with her quick wit and lively sense of humour. Ruby, who had become like a mother, and Martin. *Oh, Martin.* The thought of him brought fresh tears stinging to her eyes. Once, what seemed a lifetime ago, she had married him full of hopes for the future, but all her dreams had turned to ashes. She'd realised long ago that he had never loved her. She had only ever been a substitute for the wife who had let him down.

And lastly, and somehow worst of all, was Nuala – the sister she had loved and protected for as far back as she could remember. But Nuala hadn't returned her love. She had hated her and envied her, to the point that she had tried to drive her insane.

Dragging herself out of the chair, Kate wearily climbed the stairs to the bathroom as the silence wrapped itself around her like a cloak. She was so very tired, tired to the limits of her soul. There was nothing and no one to live for any more.

The bathroom filled with steam as she turned the geyser on and ran the water into the bath. Opening the cabinet, she took out Martin's razor. The blade glinted evilly as she placed it within reach and climbed fully clothed into the steaming water.

Gripping the razor tightly in her hand she leaned back, willing herself to find the courage to end the heartache. And it was as she was lying there that she suddenly had the sensation of no longer being alone. Peering through the steam she thought she saw the outline of a figure standing at the end of the tub.

'Who . . . who is it?'

She closed her eyes tightly and thought of her Aunt Beth.

'Oh Auntie,' she whimpered. 'I feel so alone.'

'You're not alone, my love, and you mustn't even think of ending your life. It's only just beginning, and there are people who need you and love you.'

Shock coursed through her veins as Aunt Beth's dear face swam in front of her eyes. She looked just as she had before the crippling stroke that had deprived her of her life after Nuala had pushed her down the stairs. Around her throat were the pearls that had been her trademark and even her lipstick was in place, for all the world as if she was just about to pop into town to do some shopping.

'I have no one now. Everyone I ever loved is gone. *You* should hate me too. After all, it was *my* sister who ended your life.' Kate's voice was dull and without hope as tears spilled down her cheeks.

Aunt Beth laughed softly. '*That wasn't your fault, or Nuala's if it comes to that. She couldn't help herself; the poor girl was insane. You must try to put all this behind you now and remember the good times. I wouldn't have missed a single minute of the time we spent together. But you have to go on now. Matthew adores you and you're going to have a good life together. Please, my love . . . think on what I've said. There has been so much heartache already. It isn't time for you to join me yet . . . I have to go now, but remember, Kate: I shall never be very far away from you . . .*'

At that moment Kate's eyes snapped open and she heard footsteps clattering along the landing. The bathroom door suddenly burst open to reveal Matthew who was breathless and sweating.

'Oh, Kate.' As his eyes rested on the blade in her hand he leaped across the room and dragged her shivering body from the water, sending the wicked-looking razor clattering to the floor.

'I suddenly got a terrible feeling that you might do something like this, and I had to come back.' His voice held such anguish that guilt flooded through her as he clutched her to his chest.

'Don't you know that if anything happened to you, I would want to die too?' he implored her. 'I'd have nothing to live for any more. Please, Kate, promise me that you'll never think of doing anything like this again? I couldn't bear it if I lost you now. We're going to get through this . . . I promise.'

As she nestled against him she suddenly knew that she did have someone to live for again and that somehow they *would* come through it together.

Epilogue

July, 1960

'I really don't know how you cope with these two,' Rebecca laughed as she chased one of the twins around the table leg. 'Now that they're crawling you need eyes in the back of your head.'

Kate looked away from the stack of terry towelling nappies she was folding into neat piles to grin at Beth, who was now happily chewing on a wooden clothes peg. Her sister, Ruby, was sitting only inches away from her as usual.

The girls were as alike as two peas in a pod to look at. Even Matthew got them mixed up from time to time, but in natures they were as different as could be.

Beth was placid, whereas Ruby was more demanding and more mischievous.

Adam, a fine young man now, bent down and scooped the two wriggling infants, one into each arm, and headed for the small sandpit in the garden. 'I'll keep this pair occupied for a time while you two get the birthday cake iced,' he volunteered good-naturedly.

'Thanks, Adam. Give me a shout if they get too much for you.' Kate smiled.

At that moment, Matthew and David strolled into the

kitchen. 'Mmm, something smells good.' Matthew sniffed at the air appreciatively.

'It's the cakes we're cooking for the twins' party,' Kate informed him. 'I shouldn't get thinking about pinching any before tomorrow though. When your mum and your aunt arrive from Bournemouth they'll probably eat us out of house and home if their last visit is anything to go by.'

'You know you love them to come really,' he teased as he patted Kate's bottom affectionately.

'Matthew, please,' Kate blushed. 'Not in front of the guests.'

'Huh! Since when have we been guests?' David snorted, helping himself to a cake despite her warning. 'My wife seems to spend more time round here with those girls of yours than she does at home. Mind you, that may have to change a little soon . . .' Grinning at Rebecca, he asked, 'Have you told them yet?'

'Er . . . no, I haven't got round to it.' Rebecca flushed prettily as David slid his arm around her waist.

'The thing is, we'll be having a new addition of our own in about six months' time,' he went on. 'Becky only found out yesterday. I don't mind telling you it was a bit of a shock at first, particularly since our girls are growing up. Still, now that we've got used to the idea we're thrilled, aren't we, darling?'

Rebecca nodded happily as Kate flung her arms around her. 'Why, congratulations! That's *wonderful* news. The twins will have a new cousin to play with.'

As she gazed into Rebecca's eyes it was hard to imagine that they had ever been anything but the best of friends. Since the birth of the twins the two women had grown very close.

'I reckon this calls for a drink,' Matthew declared as he strode to the cupboard in the corner of their neat little home in Greenmoor Road and returned with a bottle of dry sherry, which he poured into glasses and passed around. The house in Heath End Road had long since been sold and the money from the sale placed in a trust for Adam for when he was twenty-one. This was how Kate had wanted it to be and Matthew had gone along with it wholeheartedly. That house had seen far too much tragedy, and he had wanted them to start afresh in somewhere of their own choosing, which they had.

Matthew raised his glass. 'To the new addition to the family!' The glasses were duly chinked together and they all took a swallow of the sherry.

'Hear, hear!' The cheer went up as Kate gazed out into the garden and thought how blessed she was. The lush green lawn swept down to the canal, framed by weeping willow trees that trailed their delicate branches into the water. Matthew had erected a high fence along the perimeter of the canal to prevent accidents until the twins were older, and a bench was placed in front of it. Kate and Matthew never tired of sitting there beneath the canopy of trees and watching the girls as they crawled around getting into all sorts of mischief.

Their life together had not always been so idyllic. It had taken Kate a long time to get over the horror of the tragedies she'd endured, and she knew that the light-hearted girl she had once been was gone for ever. But time was a great healer and now, the shock and hurt she had felt at Nuala's attempts to destroy her had been forgiven. After all, the way she saw it, the poor girl had been deranged and more to be pitied than blamed. Martin had been given three life sentences to run concurrently for the lives he had taken and would never walk free again; a fact that gave Kate considerable satisfaction. After what she had suffered at his hands she knew she would never find it in her heart to feel an ounce of compassion for him.

On the other hand, Adam, his son, was now a regular visitor to the house, and although he still lived with his doting grandparents, Matthew often teased him saying that he might as well move in and become a nanny to the twins as he never tired of playing with them.

Matthew had secured a job at the local technical college, teaching Art, which he loved, and all in all, Kate was happy. Except – she still missed her Aunt Beth dreadfully and the other people she'd lost. She knew that David missed his mother too, and she suffered all sorts of guilt when she thought of how Nuala had brought about the gentle-natured soul's untimely death. Had it not been for her aunt opening her door and her heart to them, she might still be alive.

However, she had no time to brood on sad thoughts today. News of Rebecca's pregnancy had induced a party atmosphere.

'Come on, everyone,' Matthew encouraged. 'You can ice the twins' birthday cake later. It's too nice to be indoors. Let's go out into the garden.'

Needing no encouragment, David happily followed him as the women trailed behind. Soon they were all seated on the bench at the bottom of the garden watching the twins' antics.

'Where's Beth off to?' Kate sighed as the tiny girl crawled away to disappear behind one of the weeping willow trees. Trotting off after her, she found Beth sitting on her sturdy little backside smiling into the shadows.

'What are you laughing at?' Grinning, she bent to scoop the child into her arms. Beth started to gurgle and point excitedly. Kate stroked her daughter's soft cheek and peered into the shadows as the child's attention turned to the string of pearls around her mother's neck. There was nothing there. At least nothing *she* could see.

A feeling of peace swept through her as she cuddled her aunt's namesake to her chest.

'I have a feeling you just saw an angel,' she whispered into the child's soft curls. Then turning, she made her way back to her husband and her family.

Author's Note

As I'm sure many authors would tell you, the inspiration for a novel can come from the strangest of places and *Yesterday's Shadows* was no exception. It was an evening in late spring when a friend of mine called in to see me on her way home from work, and so we sat out in the garden, having a cup of tea and a chat. My friend was in an awful mood as she had had a row with her manager that day at work.

At the time, we were having a downstairs extension added to our house and because of its location the builders had to dig ten feet down and underpin the wall that the room would lean against. No sooner had this enormous hole been dug than the heavens opened, and the hole now resembled a rather muddy swimming pool.

'Mm,' my friend fumed as she looked towards it. 'I know who I'd like to throw in there right now!'

I burst into laughter but then suddenly I became serious as an idea occurred to me. We've all read in the newspapers of bodies buried under patios etc. but what if . . .

'Excuse me,' I shouted across my shoulder as I headed for my study. 'I've just got to go and write something down.'

From that second on *Yesterday's Shadows* began to grow in my mind. A couple of days later I was talking to a neighbour, Wilf, who happened to mention that in the 1950s he was a gravedigger for a local church. He also originated from Durham, so I reasoned that this would be a good place to begin the story.

Wilf told me some intriguing tales of the time he had spent gravedigging. Back then, of course, there were no mechanical diggers used in churchyards and the men had to dig the graves the old-fashioned way with a pick and a shovel the night before a burial, be it rain, hail or shine. They always worked at night by the light of a lamp that they stood on the side of the ever-deepening hole. When the grave was finally deep enough they would then kick their way out of it by pushing their steel-toe-capped boots into the sides and hauling themselves out. On one particularly cold night, Wilf was doing just that and, as he heaved himself up from the grave, a young woman, who was walking her dog, happened to be passing close by. It's hard to imagine who must have been the more alarmed out of the two of them. She screamed loudly enough to waken the dead as she hared off in one direction whilst her terrified dog went in the other and Wilf was so unnerved that he fell back into the grave to land in an undignified heap at the bottom! I have no doubt that to this day the girl must have thought she had seen a spectre rising from the grave, poor thing! But, I must admit, the thought of it had us all roaring with laughter.

Part of the pleasure for me is researching the places I am going to write about and Durham was no exception, especially as I had made two trips to neighbouring Newcastle upon Tyne last year.

And so I now had the basic idea for the story and it was time to create the main characters. I also had to think of a good twist for the end as I do love a few twists and turns.

I decided that this book would centre around two sisters who were as different as chalk from cheese and so Kate and Nuala were born and in no time at all their personalities began to grow in my mind. As always, once I had written the beginning, the characters became real to me and I was on my way. I absolutely loved writing this book and I hope you have enjoyed it too.